Falling for Fury

Brittany Rianne

Cover: Leevi Crawford

Editing and Formatting: Indie Proofreading

Contents

To all my angry girls.
Who never felt delicate and were always told they were too loud or too much.
This one is for you. Embrace your superpower and never let anyone bury your strength.
Your fury is yours; it does not control you.

playlist

1 - An Onslaught of Pity and Sadness - **Quarter Life Crisis - Taylor Bickett**

2 - Love only Kills You - **Fear and Friday's - Zach Bryan**

3 - Try not to Spiral - **Ferris Bueller - Emei**

4 - Pint-sized Godzilla - **Stunnin' - Curtis Waters, Harm Franklin**

5 - Denial, meet Addison - **Anti-Hero - Taylor Swift**

6 - The Strawberry Devil Herself - **I Think - Tyler, The Creator**

7 - Basketball, Beers and Trauma Dumping - **Ceilings - Lizzy McAlpine**

8 - The One and Only - **I wanna be your slave - Maneskin**

9 - The Most trivial of all triggers, a man - **Chronically Cautious - Braden Bales**

10 - A Drop of Sunshine - **Heavy - Elli Ingram**

11 - One Tall Drink of Water Please - **Scatterbrain - Emei**

12 - Contagious Rage - **Sloppy - KiNG MALA**

13 - A Challenge of Idiocy - **Be - Hozier**

✔ 14 - Sweeter than I Imagined - **Earned It - The Weekend**

15 - Sappy Words & Insanity - **Bad Liar - Imagine Dragons**

16 - Professor Genius Reporting for Duty - **Vampire - Olivia Rodrigo**

17 - Denial is a River in Maplewood - **Reason to Stay - Olivia Dean**

18 - Noah and Addison, sitting in a Tree - **Lost on you - LP**

19 - Men, who needs them? - **Don't Blame Me - Taylor Swift**

20 - You are my problem - **Jealous - Nick Jonas**

21 - No longer interested? Unlikely. - **Oh My God - Adele**

22 - Entering How Era - **IDGAF - Dua Lipa**

꙳ 23 - Just Another territorial 5 year old - **Bad Idea right? - Olivia Rodrigo**

꙳ 24 - Promises, promises - **Dangerous Woman - Arianna Grande**

25 - Be a Peach and Play Along - **I know it won't work - Gracie Abrams**

26 - Third time's a charm? - **Mastermind - Taylor Swift**

27 - The Elephant in the Rage Cage - **What falling in love is for - Emmit Fenn**

28 - Is Rage-Crying the New Foreplay? - **You are the Reason - Calum Scott**

꙳ 29 - Little Demon, You've Ruined Me - **Mount Everest - Labrinth**

30 - The Return of James/Jack - **I.F.L.Y - Bazzi**

31 - My Nemesis, The Dark Place - **We Go Down Together - Dove Cameron, Khalid**

32 - You Put Me Back Together - **Put me back together - Caitlyn Smith**

33 - Thank You Karma Gods - **Stand and Deliver - Patrick Droney**

꙳ 34 - I Do-You Too - **Till forever falls apart - Ashe, FINNEAS**

35 - Broken Bits and All - **Still - Seinabo Sey**

꙳ 36 - Let Me Show You the Stars - **Crazy in love - Beyonce (from 50 shades soundtrack)**

꙳ 37 - There are those Stars Again - **I ain't ever loved no one - Donovan Woods**

38 - It's All Very Romeo - **Tattoos - Renee Rapp**

39 - Big-Big Love - **Cardigan - Taylor Swift**

content warning

Book contains adult themes and is not suitable for readers under 18 years.

Included are explicit sex scenes, suicidal thoughts, on-page panic attacks, struggles with rage and anxiety, and some physical altercations between characters.

Reader discretion is advised.

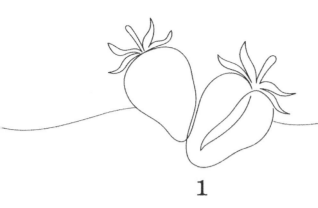

1

an onslaught of pity and sadness

Addison

"Fuck you, too, Geoff!" I shout at the back of my apartment door as I finally managed to storm my 25-year-old tantrum having ass inside my apartment. This day couldn't get worse. I never thought I would see the day when coming home to my beautiful apartment in the Upper West Side of New York City would make me sick with rage. I turn to the living room, taking a moment to settle my fury, admiring the afternoon sun streaming in from the living room windows, sunning my beautiful Areca and Ficus babies.

"Woah, firecracker, what has your titties in a twirl?" Of course, Rosie can't say knickers in a twist or something remotely common and normal.

Geoff, that's who has my titties in a twist. That pompous pettifogger fucking fired me. After months of working up the courage to ask that dick if I could take on more responsibility before my brain dries up and falls out of my eye sockets from lack of stimulation, he decided he didn't "have the capacity" to keep me on. The fifth casual job in twelve months that has let me go, only weeks or days after asking for more. The cost of living is killing my savings account, and I have been trying to land a permanent position that not only will allow me to stay part-time, while not boring my brain to death, but will pay me enough that I can cook an actual meal instead of living off ramen noodles.

"Addy... are you ok?" Casey asks with concern in her voice.

Rosie, Casey, and I have been best friends since kinder, and we moved into this apartment right after Casey graduated college and Rosie returned from Madrid. Rosie's parents might own the building, and sure, they rent this apartment to us below market value, but I allowed myself to overlook this when I could still make some sort of rental contribution. I know they wouldn't kick me out on my ass; doesn't mean I plan to mooch off them while I'm unemployed.

"Geoff let me go this morning. Told me they '*don't have the capacity*' to keep me on anymore," I reply while mocking Geoff's patronizing tone. I can feel my rage boiling under my skin, like little prickles making me feel sweaty.

"That motherfucker!" Rosie shouts, echoing my previous rage.

Although I know this is more out of anger for me, rather than just joining in. Both Rosie and Casey have listened to me complain on repeat about how much he demanded of me—the meetings I helped him prepare for, extra shifts I pulled, including overtime and working on scheduled holidays—all because he is a haughty shyster and refuses to do any work that is beneath him. He employed me as a casual admin assistant, giving me the workload of a full-time paralegal, and refused to pay me for it.

"We should create fake Google accounts and leave him a string of bad reviews. Maybe we should prank call his wife about suspecting an affair?" Rosie plots. I slump on the couch, huffing a pathetic attempt at a laugh. It's really hard to poke fun when my brain has other plans. Those plans being to send me back to that dark emptiness within my mind. The deep and dark spiral of oblivion and rage.

"Appreciate the offer, Rosie, but I think I'll pass," I grunt, which earns me a scoff and a very dramatic eye roll.

"It's okay, babe, we'll work this out. I'm heading to the studio, but I'll see what job ads I can find online for you. Don't let it get you down; there will be something." Casey, ever the mothering optimist, chirps as she packs her gym bag and heads for the door. Casey has always been a glass-half-full kind of woman. She is your typical rainbows-and-sunshine person who always smells like spring and probably forgot how to frown. The opposite of Rosie, who is Spanish and, somewhat stereotypically, fierce as all heck. She is the person you call to help you bury a body, defeat your bullies, plot revenge plans with, and also has the biggest heart you've ever known. For everything I love about these two, right now, this just adds to my growing frustration.

"Yeah no worries, Case, thanks." She flicks me a sympathetic smile and leaves, but not before I spot her making eyes at Rosie with a look I know all too well, '*oh boy, here we go*'.

The downside to living with your childhood friends is how much of your life they have experienced with you. Albeit they see the surface of the battles I wage internally, but they have still held my hand through plenty of relationship ruining rage and self-sabotage. They are always there for support, a shoulder to cry on, to cheer me up or rage out with me, and never once making me feel like someone who is broken. I just wish I could have a chance to be that for them, too.

"I know just the thing to turn that frown upside down," Rosie chirps as she pulls out her phone.

"If you say se—"

"Sex!" Her eyes bug out of her head. Groaning and throwing my head back to the couch.

"You really have to let this go, Rosie. I am not having sex with a stranger I met on a dating app without knowing them first."

"You need to live a little. You haven't been laid in forever!"

"And how would you know?" She levels me with a deadpan look and, fuck my life, she knows she is right. Don't get me wrong, I have attempted. Downloaded SoulSwipe, the popular dating app among my fellow mid to late twenties peers, but the thought of meeting up with a complete stranger, at the danger rate of women disappearing, being raped and/or murdered? Every time I make a "bonk appointment", as Rosie has elegantly labelled it, my anxiety gets the best of me and I bail. The app was promptly deleted.

Not wanting to feel or see her sympathy for my pathetic plight or risk her trying to set me up on any surprise sex dates—this has occurred many a time—I stand and head for my bedroom. "I think I am going to run a bath and have some wine. Perhaps binge some Vampire Diaries."

"Okay, let me know if you change your mind about Geoff revenge or the bedroom rodeo," she sing-songs as she strolls back to her room with all her Latina spice, dark curls, and olive skin. Sometimes I wish I could have that much light playfulness in me.

I set up my laptop on the edge of the vanity as I light a few balance and calm candles my older sister, Ava, got me for my birthday. It was her way of trying to help, which I guess is more than I can say for my older brother, Jessie. Between him and our younger sister, Riley, I suppose at least Ava tries to connect.

I settle into the scorching hot bath and pour the biggest glass of Chardonnay you've ever seen as I flick to season 5, episode 16. I lay in the bath, quietly sobbing while reciting Damon and Elena's fight about being wrong for each other. Crying is usually the result of the built-up anger inside of me that has no other outlet. A lovely trait I inherited from my father is my inability to manage and display my emotions in a healthy way. In an attempt to control my anger at the world and avoid screaming into oblivion or trashing my room, I just cry. Ten years of therapy, whilst being helpful and probably lifesaving, has yet to teach me how to manage this red hot rage.

How did I end up here? Where did I go so wrong in my life that I have been fired from my fifth job in a year? I didn't even like my job. In fact, organizing meetings, drafting court documents, reviewing contracts, responding to emails... I hated it! The only reason I stuck them out each time was because I was trying to do something that made my parents proud. Something they could rant and rave to their friends about, like they do with my brother and his business, with Ava being a mom and working. I think Riley probably feels the same, too, with the rest of us having moved out. She is with my parents alone and all but forgotten by them.

I guess I wanted to give them a reason to tell me they were proud, tell me that they love me.

I twist further into my thoughts, trying to pinpoint where I went wrong. In my cobwebs of spiralling thoughts, my inability to hold a job is somehow linked to not being able to hold a boyfriend, either. Painfully single now for almost a year, with my last relationship lasting roughly six months, the one before that even shorter.

Guilt at not being able to cover the normal rent rate hits me hard. I could use my Trust, but that gives Dad more leverage over me. I know Rosie's parents would never kick me out—the loss in my portion of the rent probably doesn't even hit their radar—but I don't like the idea of mooching off them, either.

My thoughts continue to spiral out of control, and I topple straight into the never-ending spiral of darkness. The all too familiar feeling creeps in, like a dark monster from the recess of my mind that pools and leaks into every nook and cranny of my brain. I can always feel it there. When you battle depression and rage, it is never truly gone; it just sits there and waits. Waits for a moment exactly like this: when I am tired, exhausted, and truly have lost the battle of a positive outlook. The sticky despair pours itself through my veins like a thick devouring goo, making me feel numb and empty. I can't find the will to physically move my body. *You're worthless, a burden. Unlovable.* The dark and deep heaviness that aches in my bones that weighs me down and hollows out my chest where my heart is—or is meant to be. It doesn't matter how many people I have in my life who I know find me lovable, who don't think of me as a burden or as worthless. That subtle ache of emptiness spreads. I could just allow myself to fall under the water and let it take away the pain.

Slowly, I slip deeper into the bath, feeling the water inch up from my collarbone to my neck, to my chin, until I feel my lips go under, my nose and my eyes, and before I know it, I am completely submerged under water. I can hear nothing but the bubbles and the muffled sounds of Damon and Elena. Keeping my eyes closed, I wonder, *is this the most peaceful way to go?* Feeling that rage, that boiling anger and heavy dark emptiness, I have no idea how to rid myself of. It's exhausting. Like my blood is on fire and has burnt through my body, leaving nothing in its wake but an empty shell.

I don't want to be here anymore. This life—this shitty, pathetic life—this is what we all fight for? For loneliness, failure, and mind-breaking work that still leaves you broke, alone, and exhausted? For me, at least that's how it feels. People like Mom and Dad, Matt and Ava, they seem to have it all worked out. The perfect balance, while I remain perfectly imbalanced. I lay there, feeling my tears merge with the water, and let that deep aching sense of defeat soak into my bones.

I am done.

I just, I can't do this anymore. I don't want to.

What are you doing, Addison!?

I jolt up at the terrifying realisation of where I went in my thoughts, gasping for air.

You defeated this, Addison. This is not you. We are stronger than this. We left that dark emptiness behind.

I give myself a second to gather my thoughts before I slap the laptop closed and drag myself from the bath.

Not today, Addison, today we push on.

I force myself to get up early, pulling on my running shorts, sports bra, and cropped puffer vest, and head for Central Park. It's March in the City, the sun is shining and the blooms of spring show, the breeze carrying happiness with it. This is my favourite place to run. There is usually so much to see and it keeps my mind busy and distracted. I take a huge breath as I step outside the building, hoping some of that happiness finds its way into my soul.

I am unsuccessful.

Instead, it is the same spiky fury rumbling under my skin. The only upside is that the darkness has receded. Enough so that I can at least try to pretend it isn't there. I don't give myself the time to spiral further or analyze my thoughts from last night.

I had booked an appointment with my therapist after I slid into my cold sheets, after my not so settling bath, which I quickly canceled when I remembered that I was fired and officially can no longer afford my therapist. I decided instead I would be active. That's what they say, isn't it? Physical exercise is good for raging depression?

What I know isn't good is the procrastination on my Law School assignments and prepping for May exams, which is probably adding to my growing spiral. Instead of starting college straight after high school, I spent twelve months wallowing in not knowing what to do with my life. I attempted travelling, telling myself I didn't have what it took to finish a degree and just moved from job to job. Until, in a rare moment of one of my highs where I felt invincible, I decided it was such a great idea to grab life by the balls, completed my Bachelor of Economics at NYU, and was accepted into Columbia, picking the most impressive degree on the path to becoming a lawyer. That ought to make Dad proud.

Depression, anger, and anxiety, mixed with Law School though—God, what a recipe for disaster.

Mid run my phone buzzes, and taking the excuse to pause the exercise, I answer Ava's call without hesitation. "Hey!"

"Hey Addy!" Ava says cheerily. "Mia, do you want to say hi to Aunt Dadi?" she calls out to my 4-year-old niece, who I can hear shouting in the background. The name stuck when Mia kept getting confused trying to say, 'Aunty Addison', which turned into 'Aunt Daddison', and thus, Aunt Dadi. It is much cuter when said by a 4-year-old.

"Oh yes, please, I could do with a dose of curly cuteness!" The FaceTime request comes in, and I accept to be met by big brown eyes and a mop of dark curls, a mirror image of her Italian father, Matteo.

"Dadi! Are you coming to my party tomorrow?" Mia screams. A theatrical discussion of Mia's party ensues, descriptions of which friends are coming and who she is most excited to see. She can't wait for all her presents. She informs me she is helping her mom decorate her birthday cake. "I'm adding sprinkles AND marshmal-lows!" Although, I can very much tell the decorating is being handled completely by Ava as I watch her eye roll in the background, which triggers a giggle from me. The conversation is cut short when Mia finds something else interesting and discards the phone on the counter for

Ava to pick up.

Her short mom-cut blonde hair filling my screen with her perfect pale skin, bright blue eyes, and thousand-watt smile.

"Switching to normal call so I can leave the phone alone and chat." I bring the phone to my ear as it switches back from FaceTime.

"How are you Addy? Everything okay?" Her intuition when it comes to me has always been scary accurate. Ava can see deep into my mind without me so much as sighing. I deflect as much as possible, but there is no use denying that my mood today is complete dog shit.

"I was fired yesterday," I say abruptly and prepare for the onslaught of pity, sadness, and *Oh Addison, are you ok?* There is a pointed silence from the other side, and I make a quick glance at the screen to make sure we haven't been disconnected.

"Oh Ads, I am so sorry. I know how much you hated that job, anyway, but it sucks to have to go through this again." My guess was close enough.

"Well, anyway, I am trying not to think about it right now. Casey said she will keep an eye out and Rosie has offered up revenge on Geoff, so there is that," I say matter-of-factly.

Ava scoffs, and I can practically hear her roll her eyes. "I love Rosie, although, I don't know if revenge is the right way to go about this. There will be something else, Ads. Anyway, it's Friday, we have Mia's birthday tomorrow, and the trip to Maplewood Lodge in a week to look forward to. Put the job search on hold, focus on your studies for this coming week, then let yourself enjoy the break. You can't be too hard on yourself; it is okay to put self-care first," she instructs in her usual Mom voice.

I had forgotten about the trip to Maplewood. An annual trip our family has done forever for Spring Break. A huge lodge, surrounded by wilderness and a private lake, with countless bedrooms, a pier, and plenty of trouble for teenagers. It always reminds me of the house from the movie *Grown Ups*. I thought the annual tradition would die out once we all became adults, but it so happens that it is the one time a year you'll get all of us Jenkins' together. Luckily, Mom and Dad still foot the bill for us kids to come, like they assume if they don't, we won't attend—which is probably true—especially for my brother Jessie. He is all broody, 'just leave me alone with my books'; he isn't one for family time. Especially not since his high school sweetheart left to become a Patisserie Chef in Paris and said the whole long-distance thing 'wasn't for her'. From what I hear, they haven't spoken in two years, and Jessie hasn't been the same since.

"What day are you and Matt heading up to the Lodge? Do you mind if I hitch a ride?" I ask Ava.

"Sure, can you meet us here at 9am on Monday? We want to hit the road as early as possible." It is only a two-hour drive from Ava's to the lodge where our family stays every year. Mom, Dad, and our younger sister, Riley, who is freshly twenty-one, will drive up from our childhood home in Great Falls, and will probably just meet us there.

"Sounds great! I'll see you then," I finish, glad to be done with the pity.

"Look after yourself, Ads. I love you."

Forcing through the lump in my throat, "I love you, too."

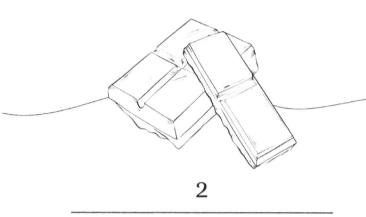

2

love only kills you

Noah

"Adorable. Also insane how you've managed to create a human that is basically your twin while being abundantly cuter."

"Are you calling me cute, Karvelas?" Matt is satisfied with his joke as he sips his beer. I met Matteo De Luca in college. We became roommates, agreeing that a Frat house was the opposite of how we wanted our college experience to go, but we still enjoyed our time like regular students. Or at least I did. Matt had Ava, who is now his wife. They were already dating when we met, and he put a ring on that finger a year after graduating, but he made a fantastic wingman.

"Yeah, at six feet, with unkempt facial hair, you're just a peach." We settle into a comfortable laugh, and a pang of guilt settles in my middle. I couldn't believe how long it had been since I made time for Matt and his family. We used to be so close in college, keeping in regular touch in the years following; phone calls and FaceTime made that easier. Mia loves to kidnap Matt's phone and set me up amongst the tea party; surprisingly making it easy to get a lot of work done because no one else can call me and she just forgets I'm there. It doesn't stop the guilt though. I couldn't believe it had been, I think two years, since I saw them in person. That time really got away from me.

"Why don't you come by this weekend?"

"Hmm?"

"Mia's 5th birthday, it is at the Parks Play House, so probably not your scene, but a few of the other guys will be there, I've sent invites to Ethan and Lucas, Caleb, too, it'd be nice to have some grown ups around to talk to. Although I'm not holding my breath for Caleb and Lucas to show up. I don't know that there will be enough single women for them to harass." I choke on my beer, but it is hard to disagree. Ethan and Caleb also went to college with Matt and I. Lucas, Ethan's younger brother, didn't, but he hung around regardless.

I'm closest to Caleb, and he also works for me. While he is actually a great person, and extremely intelligent, he hides behind an adolescent arrogance; the cliché fuckboy from every bad romance movie.

"It'd be nice to catch up with Ava again and see Mia in person. I wouldn't count on seeing Caleb, though. I've already heard... in detail... what he has planned this weekend." A shudder courses through me as I wash away the TMI conversation with Caleb from earlier with a final chug of my beer. "Send me the details. I'll let you know if I can swing by. I'll probably have a few things to tie up at the office first."

"Dude, it's on a Saturday..."

"I didn't make it this far by taking days off." Matt shakes his head and chuckles as I throw him a wink and a salute, tossing some bills on the table. Enough to cover both our beers and a decent tip for the waitress. Cute, brunette, eye fucking me from the moment I walked in, leaving me to want for nothing.

Perhaps the extra tip is an apology for not reciprocating. Perhaps it is a thank you for the ego stroke. Whatever it is, I hope I work it out soon because this dry spell is driving me fucking nuts.

I leave the bar and head in the direction of my brownstone, deciding on a walk to clear my head.

The New York air has a slight chill to it. Missing the sun from earlier in the day, I stuff my hands into my pockets and pull my coat tighter across my front. Despite it being a weeknight, the bar was relatively busy and the patrons spilling on the street cause a ruckus. As I make my way around the corner and towards the park, I add Mia's birthday party to my calendar, because we all know those ginormous soft brown eyes on the photos Matt just showed me completely did me in, and now I can't wait to see the De Luca clan again. It's hard to reconcile what the feeling of seeing Matt and the pictures of his family do to me. I'm so happy for him, truly warms me to my core to see him gush over his gorgeous wife and kid, to be so confidently in love without a concern in the world. It also fills me with a touch of sadness, or maybe it is jealousy?

Shaking that off, *immediately.*

I won't be jealous, I can't be. I made a promise to myself I wouldn't put myself in that situation.

But it makes me wonder how Matt does it. How he lives each day, with his heart belonging to another person, well a person and a child, who lives outside his body that could be taken, taking his heart with him and killing him. Causing him to live every day while not being alive. Because *that* is exactly what I saw love do. Killing them without taking them to heaven, or hell or the after, or wherever the fuck it is we go, instead it just takes our heart and soul and leaves us as empty shells having to live our days until it is decided it is our time to finally leave, too.

Familiar guilt sits heavy in my chest. Speaking of love, I haven't spoken to my mom or younger sister Evie in a while. I can't bring myself to. Every time I look into my mother's eyes, I just see her grief. I see all the things she won't say. That she wishes I would be home, closer to them, helping them in Chicago and not from another city. My sister pretends she is okay, but really, I know she just holds on to unresolved resentment at my leaving. I didn't know how to explain that I needed to do this. Needed to go to the bigger city, set myself up so that I could be what they needed. So I could support them properly. Get Evie through her college degree and make sure Mom can finally retire. While I feel the guilt, grief is stronger, and until I have something to give them, to show them, I can't bring myself to look them in the eyes.

Jesus Christ.

So much for a walk to clear the head.

Three weeks. That's what it is. Three weeks with no sex. Not that it isn't available, because I guess all I'd need to do is pull out SoulSwipe, or head to a bar, flash my *smoulder,* throw in a few choice compliments and well, the night will really just take care of itself. A wave of nausea rolls through me and I have instant regret over my thoughts, and this is exactly why I am in the middle of a dry spell.

Sex has become a transaction. Constantly torn between wanting—or apparently needing—a connection with someone, but also not wanting them close enough to cause emotional damage. Not wanting more than one night.

Sex turned into something I did to take away the sting of loneliness that, in the end, leaves me empty and hollow, anyway. I don't know when this changed, and it is much to Caleb's dissatisfaction, but the thought of meaningless sex and one-night stands just isn't sitting right. I can't bring myself to want it. And *fuck* do I wish I would snap out of it.

Fine, I will go to this 5th birthday party, because I am a fantastic friend, torture myself over coveting Matt and Ava's happy family, and I will meet Caleb out at Bozzelli's and finally put an end to this hiatus, repairing my brain to its normal settings.

No strings, casual, chill.

I can do that. How hard could it be?

3

try not to spiral

Addison

The morning unfortunately arrives, and I peel myself from bed after a restless night full of skin prickling rage and utter self-loathing. I tossed, turned, shed enough tears to fill the Hudson River, and looped on enough thoughts conjured from deep within the dark spiraling recess of my mind.

How are you ever going to be a successful lawyer or employee when you can't keep anything in your life together?

Do I even want to be a lawyer?

How do I know that this path in life is actually for me and not some attempt at being loved by my parents, showing them I am capable of functioning like an adult?

You're a raging bitch who no one wants to employ or even love. How can you love yourself?

All the therapist-prescribed mantras and determination to master my panic can't hold back the intensity of the pain I feel to my bones. The darkness in my room felt alive, the walls too close. You know when your eyes have adjusted to the dark and you can start to make out shapes and outlines of things around your room, except your mind plays tricks on you? Like the piece of lint on the bedside table becomes a bug crawling, the mirror leaning against the wall becomes a wall caving in, or the robe on the back of the door becomes a giant man-demon stalking towards you to suck out your soul. Yeah, well, that happened.

I drag myself through to my adjoining ensuite—double checking my robe is still there and hasn't been replaced by a stranger—and I force myself into a cold shower in an attempt to reduce the crying-in-duced swelling on my face.

I already take up too much space in my family's lives, with them constantly worried about my mental stability. I don't need Mia's day to be clouded by my burdens, too.

On my way out of my room, I bump into the girls in the kitchen.

"You're up early for a non-work or school day," Rosie says around a mouth full of pancakes. Casey leans against the bench opposite Rosie and looks at me with sympathy in her eyes.

"Coffee?" She gestures to her mug.

"No, thanks, though. I have Mia's party. I am going to head over to Ava's and see if there is anything I can help with before we go."

"Ah. What a great way to spend a Saturday. With five-year-olds." Rosie makes a pretend vomit face and focuses back on her breakfast. The room holds a lingering awkwardness I can't quite put my finger on and Rosie and Casey seem...tense?

"You guys are oddly quiet and... still this morning?" I direct to them both in general.

"I was looking for job ads for you! I haven't quite found anything. A couple of bartending or waitressing jobs, but I assume you prob-ably want something still in the legal industry?" Casey plasters on a half-assed smile that only Rosie and I can detect is fake, and she continues. "We... Rosie and I, well... we... we just—"

"Hate it when you cry," Rosie finishes for her. I roll my eyes and manage to hide the sharp pain in my chest at the comment.

"C'mon guys, you usually aren't this fragile around my phasing. Why suddenly worried?" Because seriously, I have known them long enough. They have seen plenty of my trips to that murky pit of despair and depression. I don't understand the coddling.

Neither of them answers.

"I'm fine! Seriously! I know I'll find another job. As much as I don't like to rely on my parents, I do have access to them and their finances. I am not completely helpless. You don't have to job hunt for me, and you certainly don't have to feel sorry for me," I finish, failing to hold back the sharp anger in my tone. I am not completely wrong. As strained as my relationship is with both my parents, I at least have had the luxury of the trust fund that was accessible at twenty-one, and a dad who thinks money is how you show love. I mean, I would prefer an attentive father, but my broke ass college student life is grateful. I try to only rely on it in emergencies—for tuition, textbooks, and those sorts of things. The less of a leverage I make the trust fund, the better.

I wince at my tone with the girls as I grab my bag, instantly regretting how I handled this. "Ugh, I'm sorry. I didn't mean to snap... I just—"

"It's fine. Don't worry about it," Casey assures. They both meet my eyes with pity, but Casey doesn't miss a beat. She puts her coffee cup down and walks over to wrap me in a hug before I can protest.

"We love you, Ads. Try to just enjoy today, and don't let yourself spiral into that big brain," she says just for me, as I nod a quick thanks and make for the door.

We pull up to the indoor Play House in Oak Ridge, only around the corner from Matt and Ava's place on the outskirts of the city. It's one of those swanky outer suburbs that people with money move to when they still want the "city experience", or in Matt and Ava's case, a safe place to raise kids. The street is already busy and lined with every high end car brand you can think of, the spring sun in full force as I grab Mia from the car seat while Ava and Matt carry in the food.

We enter the door, and I scrunch my nose on instinct as I am immediately hit with the smell of mozzarella sticks, juice, and something that I just *know* is the jumping castle. Mia instantly wriggles from my hold and lets out a gasp in my ear. I quickly place her on the ground.

"SOPHIA!" she screams and runs towards a little girl in blonde pigtails. They hug and hold hands in a way that makes my ovaries twist. They run off towards the playground, and I turn to help Ava and Matt.

"Are we late?" I gesture to the already full room of people. Ava had mentioned Matt's mom and Nonna had come early to set up, but I'm sure we were meant to be here before everyone else? Ava looks over her shoulder at Matt in a forced grumpy-but-I-still-love-my-husband face. Matt and Ava were high school sweethearts, and it is both adorable and sickening seeing how much they love and support each other. He and Ava were surprised at Mia's unplanned arrival almost five years ago, not having planned for a baby but making the best of it, and now they live as a beautiful family of three in a wealthy area with steady jobs—the literal "American Dream".

"Well, we wouldn't be if someone knew how to ever leave on time!"

Matt walks by, catching the conversation, and throws a wink our way. He doesn't antagonize her, instead he grabs the containers from her arms, plants a kiss to her cheek, and stalks into the catering area. I roll my eyes at the gross display of love and playfully shove Ava on the shoulder. "God, could you guys just love each other less in my presence? It is a painful reminder of how very single I am."

She giggles under her breath and then looks at me with narrowed eyes and raised eyebrows. "You know, Matt has a few single, very nice, very handsome friends. I could introduce you?" I scoff and head in Matt's direction, with Ava following on my heels. "Come on Ads, it's been almost twelve months since Jake. You can't swear off men forever!"

"HA! Actually, I think I could. I swear I have '*cheat on me*' written across my forehead at this point. Also, Matt's friends? Wouldn't they all be thirty and... like, boring?" She laughs and rolls her eyes, seeing so clearly through my deflection before directing her attention to her husband.

"Matt, put those in the fridge! I would like to not get food poisoning today," she shouts as she stalks in Matt's direction. I turn on a heel and head to the play area to sit and watch my niece be the cutest child on planet earth. I reach into my pocket to scroll job advertisements when I realize I left my phone in the car.

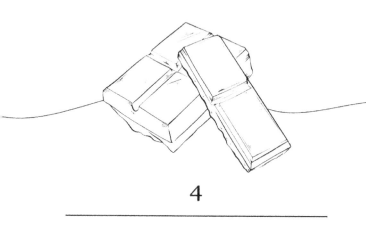

4

pint-sized godzilla

Noah

I pull up out the front of the Parks Play House in Matt and Ava's swanky suburbs, and I sit and stare at the entrance. Why the fuck am I at a kids' 5th birthday party, let alone on a Saturday? "Noah, you are a twenty-nine-year-old bachelor in New York City, and here you are, at a child's party?" I say to myself in the silence of my car, wondering how the hell a catch up with my college roommate brought me here. It has been a while since I saw Mia in person, that I guess, at the thought of her name, I feel a small pang in my chest. I never really let the thought of children affect me; I have no plans to settle down. Love? *God no.* But with Mia's big, brown, I-melt-Noah-into-a-puddle-every-time puppy dog eyes, here I am.

Opening the door to the Play House, I instantly search for Matt and manage to run straight into someone. Recovering my footing, I spin to apologize and lock eyes with a five foot blonde woman with a scowl on her face. A very captivating scowl, so intense I forget the word *sorry.*

"Um hello? Watch where you are going!" She scoffs at me before turning on a heel to walk out the door.

As the door opens, a musky-strawberry soap smell snaps me from my stupor and I jog after her, "Hey, sorry, I didn't see you as I was walking in." Because at six-foot-five she didn't even make it into my eyeline.

"I am a whole ass human, not an ant. You should be more aware of your surroundings." Her retort is laced with rage, and I am almost certain she mumbles the word pig under her breath, but I don't even care. Struck dumb, literally secured in the ground, as she continues to walk away from me. Can confirm she is correct, emphasis on her description of *whole ass. Damn.* I grin to myself and jog after her again. *Goodbye dry spell.*

I catch up and stop in front of her. "Look, I'm sorry, I didn't see you." I try to soften my face and avoid the obvious ogling. *Try,* being the key word here. She doesn't say a word.

"Are you always this amusingly sardonic to strangers? I'm Noah, by the way." I plaster on my best smoulder. Perhaps I can skip the sleazy bar vibes tonight and end the lull in my sex-life.

Holding out my hand in the hopes of shaking hers, but she stares at it, then at the smoulder. No hint of amusement to her face, just disgust.

Huh, my game is not usually this off.

I intensify my grin and try to add a sparkle in my eyes—honestly, I still don't know what Caleb means when he says that—but it clearly earns me some points, as she releases a sigh and rolls her eyes. "Addison. Why are you at a kid's Play House anyway, stranger?" She crosses her arms, and I swear I can see the rage emanating from her. A very sweet strawberry rage because that mouth-watering sweetness is definitely coming from her, and she looks so seriously at me that it feels like she sees through me, causing a shiver to rake down my back.

"I'm a friend of Matt's. Matteo, Mia's dad. We go way back; I hadn't seen Mia in a while, so he invited me along," I say with a wave of the hand, trying to appear casual and not at all like I am flustered by this striking woman.

"Why are you at a kids' party?" I ask with a touch of playfulness and secretly praying it isn't because she is a parent of a child here. Single mom is not my vibe.

It is not lost on me that this tiny blonde—Addison—is drop dead gorgeous. Her tiny figure is complemented by her small curves and, from what I can tell, she has runner's legs but a cyclist's ass.

"Mia is my niece; Matt is my brother-in-law," she replies, annoyance dripping from her, and I cheer internally that she has no minions of her own. I stop myself from reminding her that she ran into *me*. Short people are always so grumpy.

"Ah, you're one of Ava's sisters. Nice to meet you." I attempt another handshake and hope she doesn't notice my eyes snaking down her body and back up to her eyes.

Busted. Head tilted slightly, scowl growing more intense by the second, I did not get away with it. She pushes past me and heads to Matt's car.

"How about a drink? To apologize?" She stops short of opening the car door and spins to pin me dead with the angriest eyes I have ever seen. *Fuck, she is hot.* Why is rage turning me on? I should talk to a therapist about that.

"Buy me a drink?! You run me down like a snowplough and you want to buy me a drink? What kind of horrific 90s rom-com-frat-house-meet-cute do you think this is?!" she shout-whispers at me as her face starts to turn a shade of red. Her tone and her borderline-adorable metaphor-comparison have my guts twisting and brain evacuating. I have no idea what to retort, and I have never been one-upped in a conversational pissing contest.

I open my mouth to respond but she continues, "Also, this is a kid's Play House. They have juice, soda or water, so I am not sure what 'drink' you think you'll be buying me." Her scowl only deepens.

"Okay, that was impressive. '90s rom-com-frat-house-meet-cute' is a new one for me. I think I might use that." Her raging stare grows, but doesn't leave my face. Furious green eyes that feel like a raging forest just daring you to get lost in them. Who is this woman, and why has Matt never mentioned her before? I mean, surely *"my sister-in-law is pint-sized Godzilla"* would have come up in conversation before?

While I think the display of anger and ability to banter is cute, the rage is grating, and I want to cut the tension or just cut the fuck out of here ASAP.

"Look, I just wanted to apologize. We don't have to get a drink. It was by no means anything but a platonic offer from one stranger to another, to apologize for the... snow ploughing." I reference her previous description, try to paste on a polite smile, and count down from five before I spin on a heel and forget this strange interaction. For all her sexy-sass, I can still take a hint.

She huffs a breath and closes her eyes for a beat. I'd almost pay money to know what is going on in that wrathful brain. She heaves another sigh and snaps her eyes back to mine. Scowl in place before she turns to Matt's car, pokes around inside before turning back with a phone in hand. "Suit yourself," she grunts.

"Fantastic. Looks like both our lucks have changed today," I say with as much playfulness as I can get away with.

She scoffs in return and mumbles, "Luck. Right." She shuts the door, turns and heads straight to the playhouse without so much as another look in my direction. I stay quiet as I turn and follow that strawberry musk back into the playhouse.

When we make it back inside, we find a table amongst the other adults in attendance but as far away from the tiny germ-spreading mini-humans as possible. I bring over her raspberry soda and my bottled water, and I place her drink in front of her. "Here you go, sweetheart, a raspberry soda for the luckiest girl on the playground," I say, trying to poke fun at her height but also the fact that she is an adult, a grumpy one at that, and ordered a fucking raspberry soda.

"Don't judge me." Her eyes sweep the area, and she slinks back into her chair mumbling the rest. "The bubbles and the flavor make me feel joy."

I have literally no words.

"Do you typically make it a habit to run people over and tease strangers about what brings them joy?" Her tone is mocking as she uses my previous taunt against me. She stares into my soul with her perma-scowl while playing with the straw of her drink.

"Who knew Satan's helper could feel such a thing?" I throw her a wink, which earns me a scoff and a very dramatic eye roll. But she didn't sneak that almost-smirk past me. "Look, I am actually sorry for not seeing you before," I say, finally accepting that I am probably a dick. I pause but she remains staring at her drink, not saying anything, her eyes appearing vacant. "Well, anyway, I am sorry, and it was nice meetin—"

"You're forgiven." She stops me from getting up. "Thank you for the drink. You can stay. You know… if you want." I sit back down, unsure of what else to say, but unable to move away.

She looks over her shoulder towards Ava and Matt, and I do not miss the eyebrow wag Ava shoots at Addison. Addison rolls her eyes, releases a long sigh, and looks at me with piercing green eyes. "God, I am not going to hear the end of this," she mumbles. Confusion fogs my brain and I make to move on with the conversation when Mia makes her way to me.

"NOAH! Did you bring me a present?" *Shit!* Who comes to a birthday party without a present?

"Sorry, Mia, left it at home. I will drop it off to you over the weekend, I promise." *After I go to the store and buy it,* are the words I leave out.

I hand Mia my pinkie to *swear* she will have her present before the week is up. Her eyes narrow at me as she takes my pinkie in hers and squeezes. Child promises are a big deal apparently.

"Will you come play?" And as if on cue, she levels me with the aforementioned, I-melt-Noah-into-a-puddle-every-time puppy dog eyes. I look up at Addison, who has pressed her lips into a smirk and gestures towards the play area.

"He is all yours, Mia." I don't miss the mischief in her eyes as she grabs her drink and gets comfortable in her chair, but I do ignore the belly flop and prickles that travel up my spine from the way her smirk lights up her face and make her eyes... *sparkle.*

I wonder if that is what Caleb meant.

I grab Mia's hand, shaking my head at Addison, allowing myself to be directed by Mia into the ring of chaos.

I steal glances at Addison every now and then as she sits there sipping on her soda, staring into the distance. It is all I can do to not ask her what she has coursing through that furiously beautiful head of hers.

5

denial, meet addison

Addison

I walk in the door of our apartment and lean my back against it as it closes, letting go of a big sigh. Being around four- and five-year-old's for an afternoon is so exhausting. Add to that, trying to pull myself together enough to socialize with people and put a grand smile on my face for Mia.

I am suddenly distracted by the memory of Noah crawling on the floor, trying to reach under chairs and tables for the soft plastic balls from the ball pit, while having them pegged at him by all of Mia's friends. All that lean muscle rippling under his tight shirt, the goofy smile that was dangerously sexy, the way he melted for the kids and played without complaint, made my ovaries do that twisting thing again. Scientists should explore the link between swooning and men wearing backwards caps because, *yum.*

I shake my head from my stupor and remind myself that Noah, the tall, dark, and handsome stranger I met no less than five hours ago, is just another New York bachelor. He might have had deep brown eyes of whisky and chocolate, a golden-retriever energy, and smelled of spring, and linen, and *man*. But he is that—a man. A boy-man, probably. They all are. He is not worth the wasted brain cells I need focused on other things, like waking up and being a human tomorrow.

I am not sure what possessed me to ask for him to stay and sit with me. I think of the curve of his half-smile and how it made my stomach do a weird swoopy jump as he had apologized and got up to leave. I don't know why, but something told me it would just be nicer to have him... there.

It was also weird that when he left, he looked me dead in the eyes and said, "See you soon, Addison," with that same lopsided grin, adding a wink that sent weird shivers down my spine. I curse myself for letting such a thing have any effect on me. *He ploughed you down like you were an insect and proceeded to ask you out. Men equal pigs, Addison.*

"Um, what is that?" Rosie asks from the couch, finger pointed and twirling, as she gestures to my face. I shake my head, releasing me from my thoughts, and choke on a cough in an attempt to hide my stupid grin.

"What is what?" I move towards the kitchen, dumping my dinner ingredients in the fridge before making my way over to the couch to join Rosie and Casey. They are cozied up with a glass of wine each in hand. I grab a clean glass from the counter on my way down and fill it with the chilled glass of white on the coffee table.

"That little grin you tried to hide from us," Rosie questions as Casey laughs and swats Rosie on the leg as she interjects.

"How was the party?" And I am so grateful for a topic change.

"Good, I guess. The kids are adorably cute but also full of energy. I am exhausted," I reply as I fall to the couch and grab a pillow into my lap. "Actually, had another horrific run in with a member of the male species, reminding me why men are trash." At least I can count on my girls to support my man-hiatus and rage out on their constant and inexplicable need to be such assholes.

"Oooo, and the origin of the grin is exposed. Tea, now, ASAP," Rosie demands. I roll my eyes at her but proceed to give them a run-down of the day's events.

No, no, not good. I can practically see all the dots connecting in Rosie's head as her eyes slowly grow wider and her grin stretches to show a mouth full of white teeth. "YES! This is EXACTLY what you need, Ads! You need good, no strings sex! Wipe the plate clean and get those endorphins spreading!"

"Um, no! You were meant to man-hate with me about everything I just said! You can't be serious. I just met the guy!" Is my friend deaf? "Did you not just hear the horrific display of flirting, not ten seconds after he nearly toppled me to the ground? What about the eye dragging over my body like I am some display available for him to peruse?" *That sent tingles down my spine, causing a familiar ache to spur awake* is what I leave out.

"The man looked like Matt Donovan trying to pull off Damon's smoulder, for Christ's sake!" Well, I mean he didn't *look* like Matt, that wet blanket from Vampire Diaries. "Like a six-foot-five Greek gym-bro version, but still... yuck." I feign ignorance to Noah's obvious good looks, but that is what makes this situation so much more frustrating. He was sexy as *hell,* and he knew it. The girls sit there staring at my rambling denial and Casey, to my absolute horror, looks at me with apologetic eyes.

"Sorry, Ads, I hate to admit this, but Rosie's right."

"I am always right! Did you get his number?"

"No, I didn't get his number. Why would I ask a stranger I spent five minutes talking to for his number?"

"Ugh, missed opportunity. I need to take you out and show you how to do this whole sex in your twenties thing." She throws her head back against the couch in defeat. Casey and I giggle, shaking our heads at her.

"Throwing myself at a stranger is not going to help me right now." I release a sigh and look into my glass.

"Look, I know I am probably nose-diving into another spiral, and I appreciate you both trying so hard to help me, but can you trust me to look after myself and know what is best for me?" They both look at me with sincerity and seriousness that gives me the courage to push on.

"I will give dating another go, I promise," I continue before Rosie has a chance to get too excited and to wipe the look of success off her face. "I am not, however, going to just throw myself at hot strangers who look like Greek gods. I will do it the normal way, okay?"

Casey throws her head into her hands, muffling what I am assuming is a laugh, and I realize Rosie is going to ignore ninety percent of what I just said.

"Soo... Greek god, huh?" Rosie teases. *Oh, for fuck's sake.*

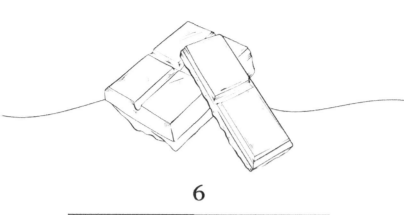

6

the strawberry devil herself

Noah

Monday morning comes quicker than I hoped. Using an early gym session to burn off steam and shake this buzzing under my skin I haven't been able to shake since Saturday. Sunday was unproductive, to say the least. I spent half the day trying to locate Addison on social media, the other half thinking about her to the point of impairment. I went to Target to get Mia that present I promised; I really didn't think that through. Honestly, how many toy selections does a five-year-old need?

I roamed the shelves for all of five minutes before I gave up and decided to ask for help. I spent the next two minutes attempting small talk, which turned into flirting with the hot as fuck brunette retail assistant. Stephanie? Or maybe Tiffany? *God, what was her name again?*

This is where the impairment comes in, with perky tits, fuck-me eyes and legs for days, my dick had never been more limp. Not for a lack of trying. I even pictured fucking her against the storage shelves of the nearest supply closet—uniform and all—and still... nothing. Not even a twitch. It didn't help that Satan's helper took up all my available brain space. Now I was comparing every woman I would normally be interested in against her.

Stephanie/Tiffany's hair was a deep brown, long enough to wrap my wrist in and tug, but it didn't have the golden streaks through it that glowed in the sun like Addison's did. Her eyes were almond and dark, lacking the feisty green fury that strikes you where you stand. The target employee's scent assaulted my nostrils; something like a Walmart brand perfume. Addison's aroma was of sweet strawberries with that addictive musky undertone, like when you find a delicious piece of candy and want another.

Who stole my balls and when can I get them back?

I scold myself for being so incredibly lame and remind myself that I could just as easily pull up a dating app and find any other short blonde—seeing as that is apparently now my type—to end the dry spell. Gave that a whirl Sunday night, then got bored with what was on offer and exited the app, sex-hiatus intact. Of course, I never went to Bozzelli's with Caleb after the birthday party. My brain was riddled with thoughts of one particular woman with emerald eyes that so thoroughly burnt through me. It felt gross to try to hit up some other poor woman. It felt like I'd just be comparing the whole time.

"*90s rom-com-frat-house-meet-cute,*" Caleb repeated back to me. He all but cornered me about missing Saturday night and asked what I did instead. We somehow got onto my meeting Addison.

"That's actually good. I might use that."

"That's what I said. She was barely impressed by it, though. Also, I think you need new tricks. The smolder and *eye sparkling* did not work." I am still yet to meet his eye line as I stare out my office window. The office I secured for my company is decent, high enough that the view over Midtown East is enjoyable, low enough that the rent doesn't kill me.

"I don't think you're doing it properly."

"Mmhmm. Sure. I think she had it down, though."

"What?"

"The eye sparkle. Addison, her eyes were like emeralds. Had a shine to them, like it was reflecting a light, or I guess... *sparkling.*" I hadn't realized I was saying this all out loud, in my office, at my workplace.

"Noah Karvelas, I am going to need you to pull your brain out of your ass. This sex-hiatus has gone on too long and now it is a dire situation." My eyes snapped to him then.

"What the hell are you talking about?"

"Sparkling emeralds? Since when do you use words like that to describe fucking eyeballs? Just get her number, hit her up, one and done, move on." He relaxes into the chair opposite my desk, throwing the basketball stress ball in the air.

"I don't think she is a one and done kind of woman." No, Addison seemed like she was more the murder and bury the body type. But I'd guess that fury could translate into some serious bedroom-fun.

"I also would probably withhold this conversation from Matt. Can't imagine he wants to hear about a booty call with his sister-in-law... or about her fucking eyeballs, you simping weirdo." I scoff at Caleb's sentence and genuinely question how he pulls when he talks about women this way.

"Moving on, have you closed the EcoX Tech deal yet?"

"Closing this afternoon. Their engineers are coming to give some of the specs they're now able to release so we can drip feed some of the minor details into some of the later sales campaigns. I can't wait to get ink on paper with this one." He rubs his hands together, determination and confidence oozes from him. Caleb is a closer—his words, not mine—and there is a reason he manages my sales team of five—he is the best of the best.

"Perfect. Did they say who their engineer was?"

"They've outsourced to AIM Solutions; their lead tech is coming."

"AIM... isn't that De Luca's firm?"

"OH! Matt will be there. They mentioned a Matt; I didn't even put that together." Okay, best of the best and sometimes missing a few brain cells. I roll my eyes and laugh him off.

"Alright, chief, go and do some actual work." Caleb hops up and pegs the stress ball at my head, turning to leave my office, but not before he shouts his list from earlier.

"Addison, number, one-and-done. Out of the system Karvelas."

The reminder of Addison is like a slap in the face. My stomach dips, and I lose any control of my productivity. I thought about asking Matt for her number, but that seemed presumptuous and unlikely, considering I don't actually know Addison, and I probably shouldn't be curious about someone who is more likely to be the exclusive dating type. Also, explaining to Matt that I wanted her number because I thought she'd be great in the sack was unlikely to go down well.

Thoughts of Addison, my sex drought, anticipation about Caleb's luck with getting EcoX to finally sign our engagement contract, flood my brain, ruining my focus. The company isn't doing terribly. In fact, these last six months, we've been experiencing a constant growth. Enough so that I was able to hire a few more designers, including Ava. But we can always be doing better. There is always more that can be done. The revenue that would be produced from the contract with EcoX would set us up. The ongoing branding deal, complete overhaul on all their internet accounts, including their website and the first ever agreement within the company for regular Social Media Management, would enable me to move the company closer to the city center, the business district of NYC, then I could drag more interest from bigger companies, as well as hire myself an operations manager that will let me take a step back, start setting up the work-life balance my dad had mastered in his prime. That's the goal. Get the company set, making money without needing me every day. Then maybe Mom would get off my back about working too hard, and Evie wouldn't give me shit about never visiting. Hell, I could even look at a second location in Chicago, move closer to home.

That would make Dad proud.

The loop continues, my ever-growing brain-dump notes app and emails sending me into an ADHD tailspin. I pack up my laptop and head to JJ's, my favourite non-office space, to get work done in.

JJ's Book & Brew is a bookshop-café located in the heart of Manhattan. Running a marketing and branding agency, with a staff of twenty is hard, but I guess I can't complain too much. With Caleb as our sales manager, and now Ava being a part-time graphic designer, we have a lot of fun. However, I can never seem to get a good amount of work completed when I go into the office, too many distractions and people talking to me. I end up in meetings, advising staff, putting out fires, being distracted by Caleb and whatever stories he has from his weekend triumphs.

I love JJ's though. Their coffee is spectacular and there is something peaceful about the books and coffee scene that makes the short commute worth it.

It is also usually where I attempt to pick up. Much to my own shame, but Caleb's pleasure, it is the *I am cultured with many layers to my personality* card that I play with women. Successful strike rate so far, but today I am ridding my mind of all women—specifically petite angry blondes—so I can finally finish that website I promised to have done by week's end.

Focus doesn't come easy on a good day; I can't risk delaying this work because of a one-time 90s rom-com-frat-house-meet-cute.

Shake that stupid smile from your face, Noah.

Entering the café, I make an effort of scanning the whole shop, and not just at my eyeline, to perhaps avoid a similar event of ploughing over tiny humans.

The café is narrow with high ceilings, a loft type mezzanine where most of the bookshelves are located, with a few couches gathered around a fire that's cozy during the winter. I notice my usual table is taken, so I make to find another table that is secluded enough away that I won't get distracted. Giving the person in my usual seat a simple glance, a quick dip of my stomach, I double take—there is a woman at my usual table.

Small.

With blonde hair.

Oh, get over yourself Noah. You really need to check your head. It can't be Addison, that would be too weird. I shake my head and curse myself for *still* thinking about her. Am I really going to get my stomach in a knot every time I see a woman with blonde hair, for Christ's sake?

I stand awkwardly between my usual table and the doorway, unable to move. I don't usually have this problem. I am the detached guy swatting advances left, right, and center, except here I am, not able to stop thinking about a woman I met once, under weird circumstances. We didn't even exchange contact information. Instead of deciding where to sit, I just stand there... staring at the back of a woman like an idiot.

I startle at a tap on my shoulder and turn to find JJ next to me, looking between the blonde woman and me with a curious, almost angry look on his face. "Hey man, sorry, guess I need that caffeine more than I realized," I say, trying to find anything to distract him from catching me looking like a creep. Caleb was right; I need to sort this out.

"What are you doing?" he asks, raising an eyebrow.

"Uhhh..."

"Do you know Addison?" Oh god, it is Addison. What is she doing here, of all places?

Wait, what the fuck? He knows Addison?

"Ahh..." Because apparently, what are words?

"Noah?!" I hear Addison's question, and I squeeze my eyes shut, trying to teleport myself out of this situation as soon as fucking possible. She stands from her spot—*my spot*—and slowly makes her way over to me. "Ummm... what are you doing here?" She looks curious, and then her face changes to something much angrier.

"Are you following me?"

"Don't flatter yourself, love. This is a public place, and I happen to be a regular." *Nice save.*

"Uh huh, and you just happen to show up on a workday when I am also here?" She throws an accusatory glance my way as she leans on a hip and crosses her arms, happy with her apparent deduction of my motives. I pull out my business card and hand it to her with a satisfied smirk on my face. I got business cards done when I first started, despite the fact no one uses these anymore, stashing them in my laptop bag has certainly come in handy right now.

"Actually, shortcake, JJ is a client, and I come in for content purposes." She takes the business card and glares at it. If superpowers were real, I think she'd have burnt holes straight through it with her laser green eyes.

"I set JJ up with the socials, marketing, and website for this *public* café, and I come here sometimes to get extra work done," I say cheerfully, tapping my laptop bag, smug as all fuck at the look on her face as she eats her words. I look to JJ then, who is staring between us, and for some reason did not leave as we had our back-and-forth. JJ is about my height, his blonde hair its usual mess, dressed in his usual boots, loose jeans, and plain T. Its lucky he makes a killer coffee and keeps excellent book stock, because his personality certainly isn't the winner for his customers, not with that permanent frown.

"Trouble you for a coffee?" I ask with a grin, satisfied to have a bit of my normal brain back. He nods and stalks off as I hear a scoff from Addison. I turn to look at her, just in time to catch her eye roll, before she turns and heads back to my table.

"Pompous dick," I catch the mumble under her breath.

"Sorry, what was that?" I give her a devious grin; she doesn't think I heard her.

"Nothing." She sits and then turns to me with a curled lip, looking me up and down, and for some reason, it just makes me smile wider.

"What are you doing? There are plenty of tables, and you choose one near me?"

"You're sitting at my usual table. But I am a gentleman, after all," I say while ironically making to look her up and down. "So, I think instead, I will just sit over here by the window." I throw her a wink, and her expression melts into one of defeat. She shakes her head and focuses back to her laptop.

"Why are *you* here on a workday?" I challenge as she throws daggers with her eyes. JJ approaches, bringing me my coffee. He stops and stares between Addison and me again with a thoroughly pissed off look. *What is up his ass today?* I give him a curious eyebrow raise.

"How do you two know each other?" he asks, or rather, demands. His voice deep, leaving no room for arguments.

"JJ, don't," Addison scolds, changing the direction of her daggers.

"That wasn't rhetorical, Karvelas. How do you know Addison?"

"Woah, man, what—"

"Jessie, please just go back to the counter. I am fine." Addison levels JJ with a lethal stare that is laced with unspoken words. He grunts and turns to leave, but not before staring into my soul with a message I feel is something akin to *I am watching you,* and a shiver runs down my spine. What is this guy's problem?

"Sorry, he is… uh, protective, I guess," Addison explains, somewhat apologetically.

"You know JJ on a personal level?"

"He is my older brother. He is the eldest, actually." She looks down at her hands. "He wasn't always this broody, but he pulls the brother card when it comes to being a protective ass." She grunts the last part and grabs her coffee to take a sip. I do the same, to allow my brain some time to catch up.

JJ is her brother.

And I am suddenly *painfully* aware of how many dates I have brought to this coffee shop. His angry expression now makes sense.

"JJ never mentioned he had sisters? Actually, Ava and Matt both never mentioned this?" So confused how this has not come up before. She shrugs, also unsure, and I decide it doesn't matter.

"Anyway, I didn't mean to disturb you. I just came here to get some work done." I sit down at a table next to the window, leaving one table between us, and get my laptop set up.

"You never answered my question?" I ask, accepting I will get zero work done with Addison's strawberry scent filling the room.

"What question would that be?" She doesn't look up from her computer, and I don't miss the sigh of annoyance in her voice.

"What are you doing here on a Monday?"

"Studying."

"Oh? What do you study?"

"Law."

"Impressive. Full time?"

"Yep, Columbia. Finish in May."

Our back-and-forth continues, each sentence from her clipped as her eye line doesn't leave her computer.

"Have you decided what area you want to practice in?"

"Why are you so interested in me?" She looks at me then, and something about the look she gives me is pained, something I can't quite nail down but hits me straight in the chest like an arrow.

I shrug, giving her my cheekiest grin. "Humor me." I wonder how far I can push this before she really gets sick of me.

She gives me a concerned side eye as I continue. "What has you so tightly wound that my presence irks you? Is it my charming smile? Maybe it's my fantastic jaw line?" My tone is mocking, going for playful, but it gets me nowhere. "I can usually collect a smile within the first few minutes. Your ability to hold out on me is only making me want one more." I settle into my chair, one arm casually draped over the back, twisting in her direction and resting an ankle on my knee. It is an attempt to get her to lower her walls. Which, of course, is not working. I swallow as she slowly turns her head in my direction, reminding me of a slow-motion scene in a movie when the hero says something to the villain right before the villain unleashes a brutal attack. Her green eyes lock on mine and the angry scowl she delivers has an impact I believe is the opposite of what she is trying to accomplish.

There she is.

I casually readjust my pants as she speaks. "What makes you think you're entitled to my life story? Please, do enlighten me. What have I done to make you think that I will open up to a complete stranger about my woes?" She throws in some patronization in the end there, and her ability to stoke the fire and meet me within the blaze just turns me the fuck on. I have to hold myself back from asking, *where have you been all my life?* Before I can attempt a response, she continues.

"You men can't seem to take a hint. I. Am. Not. Interested." She turns back to her computer. Of course, it just makes me want her more, but I can't blame a woman for being crystal clear. Her response is warranted given my persistence, and I can respect a no. I focus back on my computer when she releases another sigh. "I... I'm sorry for snapping."

"You didn't snap. Don't apologize." I wave my hand at her, she had every right to put me back in my place, semi-in-my-pants or no. She says nothing, and I allow my gaze to fall back in her direction, admiring her profile. Despite her fury, she is effortlessly stunning. Her tight yoga pants and sweater that looks two sizes too big, her hair back in a loose bun, the fly-aways that hang by her face tease me, tempting me to tug them or tuck them behind her petite ears. She slowly hangs her head back, eyes vacant, looking to the ceiling. "I was fired on Friday. I am super stressed about assignments that are due after the break, and I think I might have to find a cheaper apartment, and I am currently... stuck in a spiral of sorts," she says on one breath. She closes her eyes, and a look of pain enters her expression, then those furious eyes finally land on me, her expression reluctantly vulnerable.

"Huh."

"*Huh?* That is your response? What... what does that even mean?!" Her expression is adorably furious.

"Your strength. I just, I guess I didn't expect that." Because I didn't. She is dealing with all of that and can still enter a verbal sparring match. Doesn't take a genius to work out there are some obvious issues; if her fury wasn't a dead giveaway, apologizing for setting boundaries certainly is. Yeah, she has strength. I'd put a solid bet on her wrath powering it. And just like that, I am even more drawn to this woman.

"Oh." She stares at me like I sprung a second head. A smile, or rather a brief smirk, spreads on her face for a second, like a knee jerk reaction to a compliment she has no idea how to handle.

"I don't think that's stren—"

"It is. Clear as day, no point apologizing for it. People should be admiring you for it." And an idea springs to mind.

"Hey, actually, I have a friend who owns a bar. I was speaking to him a few nights ago, and he is desperate for good bar staff. I could give you his details to reach out for a job?" Her eyes narrow in apprehension.

"What do you get out of doing that?" she accuses. I release a laugh and shake my head at her unflinching ability to assume the worst in everyone. Or at least me.

"Look, I am not here to get anything. It was just a friend offering another friend an option." *Is 'friend' presumptuous?* She doesn't say anything about my strange wording.

I dig into my laptop back for Lucas's business card—he saw I had one, he wanted one—it's a whole thing I won't get into. "Here, take this." I place the business card on the table between us. "Call him, don't call him. It is up to you." I can feel her eyes staring into the side of my face as I pretend to do work instead of trying to read her from my peripheral. After a few attempts on her part to ignore me and the business card, she grunts and slaps her hand on the table, taking the card.

"Thanks," she basically whispers. "You didn't have to do that... I... appreciate it."

Is that gratitude from the strawberry devil herself?

I turn my head to look at her, unable to hide my look of triumph. She scoffs and rolls her eyes, and I swear that is a smile she bites down to hide.

"You know... if you ever want to... talk... about the other stuff... I am happy to listen?" What words are these? I am not sure why I offered. I guess I recognize the look on her face and know the demons she probably fights to ignore.

She looks at me, her expression softer, contemplating how much of herself she is going to reveal to me. Before she looks back at her screen.

"Thanks. But I am fine." And I don't believe her for a second.

We settle into a comfortable silence for a good hour, and I actually manage to get a lot of work done. When she stands to leave, I realize I don't want to her to go, immediately shoving down the stomach drop and the sense of urgency that rushes through me I blurt, "Would you like to get some coffee?" She stops and stares at me, then looks around the shop.

"Did you not just have a coffee?" she asks, as though I didn't just ask her out. I huff a nervous laugh and correct myself, standing to face her... tower over her.

"I mean, another time?" I give her my flirtiest smile and tell myself it's because of the dry spell and has nothing to do with just enjoying her company.

She makes to look me up and down, and I don't miss the slight blush that hits her cheeks and the swallow stuck in her throat.

"Umm... why?"

"Do I need a reason?"

"Uhhh... yes?" I blow out a breath. At an utter loss for words, my usual game is out the window, and I decide on exposed honesty.

"Because since Saturday, my brain has short circuited. I think about that smirk you gave me at the Play House that lit up your face, and my skin has been buzzing relentlessly with energy I haven't been able to expel." *Might as well keep going.* "Because I'd like to keep you talking, so I have a chance to see that smirk, to learn more about you and where all that resilient strength came from." My voice lowering as I walk closer to where she stands, so she has to tilt her head to look up at me. Her eyes widen and her blush is now unmistakable. She blinks and shakes her head and chokes on... something.

"Umm, that... okay... what?"

"Look, one coffee. Doesn't have to be today. You have my card. Text me sometime. Or call me, whatever floats your boat." I wink at her then and make my way back to my table and attempt to calm my breathing and my heart rate, which picked up from the proximity to her and those fucking strawberries.

Real smooth, Noah.

She remains standing in place, blinking, before she grabs her stuff and rushes out of the shop without so much as a goodbye. I release a breath I had no idea I was holding as I track her steps across the street, walking away from me.

Reminder: go see the doctor about strange chest pains.

7

basketball, beers, and trauma dumping

Addison

After my attempt at getting out of the house to study and instead having my time *stolen*—yet again—by Noah, I end up at my apartment, exhausted—yet again. I can't work out why his insistent playfulness and stupid sexy grin grate on my nerves so much, but looking at his smug face makes me want to rage out. I slam the apartment door as I enter, cursing under my breath, and quickly realizing I am going to need an outlet before I rage flip the dining table and smash a window. GOD, why does someone like *him* get all the good looks, the successful life thing, confidence of a fucking mad man, AND happiness? I just get unwarranted rage that prickles under my skin for no apparent reason.

I think about that smirk you gave me.

...learn more about you and where all that resilient strength came from.

I ignore the flips my belly does and the butterflies taking flight inside me as I recall the strange way we left things.

"Oookay, we are just going to take a few deep breaths..." I straighten, not realizing that my actions have been witnessed by Rosie, who is leaning on the door frame of her bedroom watching me with a look I compare to a zoo keeper trying to trap a lion. I roll my eyes at her and head for my room, before Case intercepts from the couch.

"Hey, hey hey hey. What happened? I thought today was 'happy-study day'?" she repeats my attempt this morning at having a positive outlook on life.

"Well, of course, *that* didn't go as planned because the stupid... that human... giant just had to pick today to show up at JJ's!" They share a look, probably not missing my stumble on the description of Noah, Casey's being of shock and concern, Rosie's being shock and excitement.

"Is that the guy from the party? Oh my god, did you sleep together on the first date?!" Rosie demands.

"Yes, it is the guy from the party, and NO! First of all, it was not a date. I was there, and he intruded on my study plans. Second of all... NO!" I sound very defensive for someone not lying.

"He seems to have... quite the effect on you," Rosie accuses with wiggly eyebrows.

"What has an effect on me is his stupid permanent smirk, his stupid masculine smell, his stupid... stupid compliments. He doesn't even know me. He has all the arrogance of a man of privilege who has never understood struggle a day in his life. I am just... ugh." I ignore my obvious ignorance at my assumptions because, of course, I too am a child of privilege, but I'd bet my trust fund that the tall ray of sunshine would know jack about living with brain chemistry that would rather you existed in an eternal sleep. I roll my eyes at the girls and push past to go to my room because Rosie and Casey are making eyes again, and it is loud enough to hear the words they don't say. I swear I'm not always such a brat. I miss just coming home and feeling good. Miss walking in the door and relaxing, smiling and laughing with my friends. This is exactly what happens when my routine changes. Being fired has set me off, and my mind has no idea what to do other than panic, cry, rage, and loop me in a never-ending spiral of anxiety.

They both follow me and stop at my doorway as they watch me throw myself face down into my pillow and stifle a scream.

"Ads, c'mon, we're just playing. We... just haven't seen you this tied up over someone since... well, ever. You weren't even this passionate about *Jake's* faces and words," Casey says gently.

"How does hating someone with a passion mean I am lusting all over him?" I ask, not holding back the anger in my question or the look of disgust I throw them as I sit up on my bed. They wander over at that and sit down to join me.

"Maybe it is the constant, 'Greek god' and 'sexy' words you use to try to describe him?" Rosie adds innocently. I roll my eyes and throw my head back against the pillows.

So he is objectively good looking... okay, *fine,* he is the literal description of perfect, look up flawless-sex-on-legs, I'm sure the definition is *Noah Karvelas.* That doesn't mean anything. If my heart has taught me anything, it's that you can't rely on other people to feel loved and worthy. See: Jake, Mom, and Dad.

Even Gods in human form are unreliable.

"Okay. Nope. No more moping and feeling sorry for ourselves. C'mon, you need to freshen up and then we're going out." Casey slaps my knee, grabs Rosie by the arm, and gestures for me to head to the bathroom.

"Where are we going? It's a Monday." *And I'd rather spiral alone,* are the words I don't say.

"Out. Puck & Pint probably." She shrugs. The Sports bar a few blocks down that has become our local. Mainly a hangout for ice hockey fans, but they show all types of sports on various TVs, including NBA, which happens to be a favorite of mine. It helps that athletes *also* sometimes hang out there. "Bulls are playing, and I know tall sexy men are your kryptonite, so we are going to put a smile on that dial." Casey leaves the room, signaling we have no choice in this matter. Rosie claps her hands in excitement and gets up from the bed. "Yay, sweaty athletes!" And she skips out. But I cave, simply because the Bulls are my team and... alright, *fine,* I am a sucker for tall sexy players. I am choosing to ignore the irony of my previous description of *Noah.*

Casey and I stand in the kitchen, waiting on Rosie as we usually do. Casey fiddles in the pantry making a list, I assume for her next baking extravaganza, but I can't really focus on anything except the buzzing fury that sits under my skin. It's not lost on me that I don't have anything to really be angry about, I'm just agitated. Annoyed at Noah's insistence. Frustrated at Jessie having the audacity to insert himself. Angry that my grades have been excellent except I'm on a slippery slope I can't get off of that risks destroying all my hard work.

The rage simmers hot under my skin, and I unzip my jacket and hold it in my arms. "What is taking her so fucking long?" I grumble under my breath, and Casey looks over to me.

"Hey, Addy, why are you crying?"

I angrily swipe at my tears as they betray me and make their way down my cheeks. "I can't help it." Because I can't.

I'm angry for no reason and with no outlet. The furious energy has to leave me one way or another, and this is the only way I know how to get it out.

Casey grabs my arm. "I have an idea." She giggles under her breath as her permanent sunshine tries to warm my icy exterior. She goes to the fridge and pulls out a few chicken breasts.

"I am going to make chicken parmigiana tomorrow night. Want to help me prep?" Her eyes shine as she winks at me, but I just get more frustrated as she gets out a pair of cooking gloves and sets up the chicken with baking paper on a chopping board. "Here." She hands me a mallet and then grabs another out of the drawer. Of course, she has two mallets.

She starts on one chicken breast, slamming it down on the chicken breast before looking up at me. "Give it a go. Pretend it's Geoff. Or Greek sex-god. Even JJ. Whatever helps." She smiles at me, and I can't help it, her sunshine cracks my rain cloud, and I drop my jacket and join her as we mallet the chicken together in silence.

It's dark out by the time we are finally on the way to the bar. Casey didn't bring up the crying or the anger again. She just let me beat the shit out of some chicken breast, and we left as soon as Rosie dragged herself out of the bathroom. My shoulders feel a bit lighter, my chest a bit freer, after getting rid of some of that prickling energy.

As we walk the few blocks to the bar, I play with the two rectangle business cards in my pocket. The corners poke into my palm as I chew on my decision whether to keep my petty dislike for Noah and refuse to take his olive branch of a job offer, or if I swallow my pride and apply for a job because let's face it... I need to get paid. *You also need to get laid.*

Immediately ignoring that inner voice, I release a groan and scold myself for not accepting the kindness for what it is, and I pull out the card Noah gave me and send off a message.

> **Me:** Hi Lucas, my name is Addison. I got your number from Noah Karvelas, who mentioned you were looking for bar staff? I am interested in a position if you have one available. I am super flexible with hours, too.

Is that desperate? I send the text, anyway, and wait for a reply. Rosie and Casey chat amongst themselves, mostly about what we are going to order when we sit down at the bar, reminding each other. "I have work tomorrow, so we are *not* ordering Espresso Towers or Pints. Two drinks, enough to make Ads laugh once... or we settle for a smile and leave before 11pm." I shake my head as I listen to what I have heard plenty of times before, when they inevitably call in sick the next day. Rosie is a junior editor at a major publishing house in the city, whereas Casey co-owns a Pilates & Yoga studio with her sister Grace. They are both qualified physiotherapists, and the studio has so far been successful for about two years.

While Casey and Rosie get lost in conversation together, I take the space and fresh air to breathe, cooling the blood in my veins, willing the bubbling anger to dissipate so I can enjoy this night with the girls; be that happier, calmer version of myself.

When we finally arrive at the bar, Lucas's response comes in.

> **Lucas (Noah's friend):** Hey Addison, Noah has told me a lot about you! Thanks for getting in touch, and I'd love to hook you up with a trial shift. How soon can you start?

Noah mentioned me? No, Noah told Lucas *a lot* about me? The guy doesn't even know me! *Breathe, you are not your anger.*

I type back a few messages asking more about this, but backspace and try again. I type out five different responses before I decide I will just ignore the comment.

> **Me:** I am free any time this week but unavailable from 27th to the 1st for a pre-planned trip. I hope this is ok?

> **Lucas (Noah's friend):** No sweat. How about you pop in tomorrow, around 10am, and we can have a chat before the lunch rush hits. We can schedule your trial shift on Sunday the 2nd?

> **Me:** Both work, thanks! I'll see you tomorrow.

We find a table with an easy enough viewing of the screen, grab a drink each, and get comfortable as Rosie grabs some menus. I don't tell them about my messages with Lucas because, well, I think I'd rather see if I actually get it first. It isn't a job in a law firm. I haven't quite worked out why I'm glad about that, and I'd rather not risk the disappointed looks or judgement that I'm not actively looking for a job at a firm and settling for a hospitality position.

I make to look around the room and realize it isn't as busy as usual. The bar is located in an old corner pub, but renovated into a modern sports bar. TVs line the walls, betting machines and modern décor that seem at odds with the sporty old pub building.

There are only a few guys over near the left bar, cheering at the screen like typical frat boys, slapping each other on the back and spilling their beer. An old couple furthest from the sports screens and a few scattered people sitting at the bar.

Rosie smacks the menus down and stares into my soul. "Were you serious about trying dating again? For real."

"Ugh, yes, Rosie I will, God. Why are you so interested in my sex life?"

"There is a group of appear-to-be-hot, likely-single guys over by the bar. I couldn't see all their faces or ring fingers, but they have hot backs—good asses—quite tall. I think you should go say hi," she says, lowering her head to the table, whispering as though we are discussing a top-secret case. Casey makes her way back from the bathroom and sees us with our heads lowered, Rosie with a look of playfulness on her face, and mine stuck in a face palm.

"Oooo, what are we talking about?" she says in a loud whisper, her smile growing on her face.

"Nothing!"

"I am encouraging Ads to go over and flirt with those dudes." She gestures to the guys by the front bar.

"Ohh... you mean Matt and his friends?" My head snaps to the bar. One of the said frat boys, actually the only one of them dressed in a business suit, is my brother-in-law Matteo.

Huh. "MATT?" I shout.

"Ads! Are you watching this game?" He is excited and very drunk as he makes for our table at a fast pace. He throws his knuckles out that I meet before I look to the screen again, my smile growing with excitement at the display of sexy athleticism on the TV.

"What are you doing on this side of town?" I ask him, confused why he isn't at one of his nice bars near his rich-people village.

"Celebrating, finalized a deal today that is super exciting, that I can't tell you anything about—" he winks, and I roll my eyes, "and the guys wanted to come to Pucks. We decided one beer, but then the game came on, and I guess now it's however many beers until the game is finished." He sips on his beer and continues, eyes remaining on the screen.

"What are you ladies doing out on a Monday night?" he asks the table.

"Just here for din—"

"Trying to get Addison laid," Rosie interrupts me. Matt spits out his beer as he chokes to regain his breath, and I turn my death stare on Rosie, who shrugs her shoulders as if to say, *What, it's true.* "Any of your friends single, Matt?"

"Who are you asking for?" he accuses Rosie with a look laced with meaning. I look over at the group, just out of normal curiosity. It should be illegal for one friend group to have so many tall-ap-pear-to-be-hot-from-behind friends.

"Well... if there is more than one, perhaps we can each have a single Matt-friend?" Rosie says to Matt, wiggling her eyebrows as he chokes down a laugh. Casey just smiles, shaking her head and reading the menu, now thoroughly used to Rosie's antics.

"I only have a few single friends. Noah, Caleb, Ethan, and Lucas." My spine snaps straight at the mention of Noah's name because I am suddenly drawn back to the circle, and I realize the backwards cap wearing tall "friend" to the left of the group, wearing a No. 23 Bulls top, is—

"Oh, you've *got* to be kidding me." I groan as I slam my head to the table and cover my face with my arms.

"What just happened?" Matt asks. Rosie and Casey look at each other, look at the group, and then back at me with questions in their eyes.

"Ads, what's up? What just happened?" I raise my head, look at Matt, and then back to the girls.

"Sexy sunshine God. Ten o'clock." I curse myself at the description in front of Matt and slam my head back to the table, knowing it is the only way the girls will know who I am talking about.

Rosie releases an excited gasp. "The backwards cap one?" she asks with the most excitement I have ever heard.

"Yup."

"Dark curls sticking out of the sides like a fucking romance novel?" Casey mimics Rosie's question style.

"Mmhmm."

"You mean the one wearing your favorite jersey, drinking your favorite drink, watching your favorite sport, with all his tall, tanned, sexy smiliness?" Rosie says as her pitch gets progressively higher. I release a grunt and Matt puts his beer on the table.

"Woah, woah, woah. Hang on a second. What is going on right now?" he asks to any one of us that will answer him.

"Ads has a huge crush on backwards cap guy," Rosie says matter-of-factly.

"I do not!"

"Noah?" Matt raises an eyebrow and curls a lip as if the idea is horrific. He shimmies his body, releasing a cringe, and raises his hand, silencing us all.

"Actually, no. I am leaving this conversation. Please don't tell me."

"What is he even doing here?" I mutter mostly for myself, my annoyance stoking the flames of my fury.

"Celebrating, like I said before. The deal was with Noah's company. Caleb works there, too, hence the bar and beers."

"Noah's company?" I had assumed the company on the card was his dad's or a family business, not *his* company. So he's charming, sexy, nice, *and* successful. *Great.*

"He owns Karvelas Media, who Ava works for. Branding and marketing stuff. AIM signed a pretty big deal with them, thanks to Noah and Caleb's hard work. Should set us both up nicely." AIM was Matt's baby that he and a few of his college engineering buddies set up. The adorable softy named it AIM after his 'greatest creation', Mia.

"Anyway, back to Addison sexing Noah," Rosie chimes in elegantly.

"And that's my cue." Matt gives me a nod and wastes no time vacating the area.

"Oh my god, Ads. I know you described him as sexy, but Christ." Casey looks like she is drooling at this point.

"Go say hi!" Rosie squeals. "This is a sign for sure! You can't have this many run-ins with the same guy and it not be fate," Rosie deadpans.

"No, I came here for happiness and a distraction. Can we please just have our drink, eat our food, and leave? Plus, they are busy... *celebrating*."

Casey releases a sigh and picks up the menu again.

"Bu—" Rosie attempts to protest, but I raise my hand.

"Enough. I am too tired for this. Please, can we just try to have a nice girls' night without you trying to marry me off?" I try to add some amusement to my scolding, letting her have one of my soft smiles. Shoving back the anger that has no business being hurled at my friends.

"Ugh, fine. Be boring then." She picks up her menu then and we pick our food.

We order and eat, finishing two drinks each, and watching the game as it ends. I tell the girls to wait out front while I use the bathroom before we walk back. I turn the corner down the hallway to the toilets and I run straight into a wall. No... not a wall... A six-foot-five body. Christ, that is firm.

"Well, well, well. Now who is following who?" I squeeze my eyes shut. I almost, almost made it out of here without an interaction. I snake my eyes up the solid wall of muscle that is his body, tracing the line of his tanned neck and the little curls flicking out under his cap, over his sharp jawline, to his lips pulled into a lopsided grin, and up to his deep chocolate eyes.

"I could accuse you of the same thing, seeing as I live around here?"

"And how do you know I don't live around here?" he accuses with a playful challenge in his eyes.

"Well, do you?" *Addison, do you hear yourself?*

"Why? Eager to get out of here, are you?" He winks at me then, and his smirk turns into a full watt smile. I scoff at him and roll my eyes as I make to push past him. He steps in front of me with his arm out, reaching across the width of the hall, blocking my path. *Six feet is so much taller in person.* I have to crane my neck to look at his face.

"What are you doing here, shortcake?" His expression remains playful, and I move back a step, putting some much-needed distance between us as I cross my arms. He takes a step forward, closing the space I just opened.

"I was having a drink with friends and watching the game. Why do you care?"

"Magic fan?"

"Bulls."

"Really?" His eyes glitter intensely, and he takes another half step. I take a step back and my back is pressed against the wall. He remains where he is and moves his arm as his eyes make a quick glance to the wall behind me.

"What? Hard to believe a woman could like basketball?" My words are laced with venom, but my efforts fail to dissuade him, and his smile grows.

"Not at all, just hasn't been my luck to find a woman like you who actually roots for my team."

A woman like you.

He has known me for five seconds. What does that even mean?

I am suddenly lost for a retort as he inches ever so slightly closer to me, his scent of spring and whisky flooding my senses. Intertwined with espresso, his glazed eyes probably being his buzz and the relaxed lean a likely effect of the alcohol. Warmth grows toward my lower belly as I rake my eyes over him. God, it should be illegal to have men looking like him just walking around. He really is a Greek god. In all his tanned, tall muscle, his clothes cling to him. It isn't until his eyes darken and he places his hands on the wall above my head that I realize my breathing has quickened and my heart is pounding louder than a drum in my chest. His sudden proximity seems to slap me out of my stupor, and I bring my hands up to my chest in a barricade.

"What are you doing?" I ask with way more fear than I usually allow. He blinks and his smirk is instantly gone. He shakes his head and backs up a step.

"I—"

"Stop following me, Noah." I push him aside and finally go to the bathroom.

"Wait, Addis—"

His sentence is cut off by me going into the bathroom.

What the fuck just happened?

On my way out of the bathroom, I try to shake it off, not letting this ignite me further. I managed to bury the doom and gloom from earlier today with the distraction of a girls' night, and I'm not going to waste all of that hard work on a guy. I will also not analyze any of the feelings that arose out of his proximity. I will go home with Rosie and Casey, and we will watch TV and be friends and I will go to bed happy.

As I leave the bar and turn left to head back up the street, I see Rosie and Casey a few steps up staring at me. Casey with concerned eyes, but a semi-smile, and Rosie with a look that terrifies the crap out of me. I stop dead and look at them, and then check my shoes and clothes for something out of place to explain their faces.

"What are you g—"

"Addison?" My spine snaps straight at the low caramel voice from behind me.

"Oh, God," I grunt. "Noah, what do you want?" At this point, I am so exhausted by this fucking guy.

"I think we got off on the wrong foot. I want to apologize and start fresh." He throws me his biggest smouldering smile that I am *sure* has a 100% panty-melting strike rate. I study his expression, not letting him see my walls dropping as I try to hold them in place.

Damn you, espresso martinis.

I search his eyes. Is that *guilt?* "You apologize a lot." I turn back to walk with Casey and Rosie, whose faces still look the same.

"Addison wait. Can you just put down the pitchfork and talk to me?"

"Pitchfork? I don't know you. I don't owe you anything. What is it that makes you think that because you are..." I stutter on finding the right words and instantly regret the next ones that come out, "...sex personified, that you are entitled to my attention?" I lace my words with venom, and I swear I can hear Rosie hiss uncomfortably from behind me. But I am left disappointed as my blow doesn't land, and in fact, he steps towards me, eyes narrowing with devious challenge, and his grin grows.

"Sex personified?" he repeats. "Not entitled, just... a desire."

"Is that really all you got from what I said?"

"You're right, you don't owe me anything. And perhaps I am being persistent, and it is borderline creepy. But I can't get you out of my head and it is driving me crazy. And then I run into you *again* and it just feels like... well, I just want a chance to talk, to apologize for being weird every time we have run into each other, and to get to know you without the wall of anger you surround yourself in," he deadpans. His face is no longer in a smirk, but his eyes are staring—no—*burning* holes into my face, and the warmth from earlier is back.

"Ads, we'll meet you at home. Text us if you need us," Casey calls back, and I don't miss the Rosie-level cheek in her tone.

"Um guy... Greek sex-god—" Rosie starts.

"It's Noah," Noah shouts back with the biggest grin on his face, but his eyes don't leave mine.

"Right, Greek sex-god Noah. I have a photo of your face, so if Addison goes missing, I will send it to the police. I am also very good at internet stalking so I will find where you live," Rosie shouts as she makes to follow Casey up the street.

He releases a low laugh before responding back in a playful shout. "Last name is Karvelas, happy stalking. I will make sure she is home safe." I am still silent because I have no idea what is happening.

"Wait a second. You bitches are just leaving me with a stranger?"

"Live a little, Ads!" Rosie shouts back with a wink and turns so she and Casey can hightail it out of here. I turn back to Noah.

"I do not need your assistance getting home. I will just order an Uber." I turn to go back inside, pulling out my phone to wait somewhere warm and safe for the ride.

"Addison, I don't bite."

"Well, maybe I do." I practically growl the words at him.

"I can only hope." The fucker winks at me, and I scold myself for walking straight into that. I roll my eyes and fold my arms across my chest as he continues. "Can you lower the barricade and accept a friendly conversation? We can walk in the direction of your place. I will keep five feet between us if you prefer." He says it low and gentle, with a touch of humor, but his eyes are anything but. I stare at him, then stare up the street in the direction of Cas and Rosie up ahead, and then at the time on my phone. *Arghhhhh.*

"Fine!" Turning, I walk up the street, and he jogs two steps to catch up coming up beside me. I can see from the corner of my eye he is staring at me with a stupid smirk of achievement.

"About before, I didn't mean to cage you in near the bathrooms. That was super weird. I just got... well, anyway, I am sorry."

"You just got what?" I give him a boring tone, not letting my eyes leave the sidewalk in front of me.

"Carried away... I guess." My eyes snap to him then.

"And what about our interaction made you get carried away? Were my jeans too tight or my cleavage too visible? Perhaps I should dress like a nun and wear a sign saying, 'I don't like to be touched' so you would get the hint?" I internally grimace at how I've let my anger control me, as I throw probably too much angst into my statement, but it's true. Why is it that us women have to walk around being vigilant with keys between our fingers while men get to just say '*sorry, I got carried away*'?

"Woah, absolutely not. This didn't have anything to do with what you're wearing, Addison." His voice has more pain than I usually get from him, and I let my eyes meet his again and we stop in the middle of the sidewalk. His expression is serious now.

"I am saying what I did wasn't okay. On a separate topic, you smell amazing, and yes, you also look incredible. But I got carried away, probably too many martinis. I was riding a high from a successful day and the game win... I don't really know. I do know I wasn't blaming you. It had nothing to do with something you did or didn't do. I wanted to apologize for making you uncomfortable, and I wanted you to know that I knew what I did wasn't okay." His face remains serious, almost in a frown, like he truly is mad at himself.

I narrow my eyes, trying to pinpoint the lie or the joke that is about to hit me. I don't trust him just admitting all of that, but nothing. He remains silent, holding my gaze like he is trying to communicate telepathically.

I concede.

It is *way* too exhausting to stay this angry at him. He has kept the distance as he promised. He has apologized and appears to take responsibility for the creepy behavior. My shoulders slump forward, and I release a breath. His face relaxes into a peaceful smirk, and he seems to release a breath as well. I drag a hand down my face and turn to walk back up the hill, not wanting to look into his delicious chocolate eyes anymore.

"Ugh, I am sorry, too."

"I am sorry. What's that now?"

"Don't push it, Noah."

"I like the way you say my name with such fury." He releases a low chuckle, catching up to me again in only two steps.

"Is it exhausting being a sunshine person, literally all the time?"

"Is it exhausting hating everyone, *literally* all the time?" he challenges back. I look at him side on before I roll my eyes at his stupid, lopsided smirk.

"When the world and almost everyone in it disappoints you enough, you learn to stop expecting joy, happiness, or really anything good." He is silent at that. "Say it," I scold under my breath. Waiting for the lecture that comes from everyone about how life is only as bad as you let it be, and maybe if I was more positive, positive things would happen, blah blah blah.

"Say what?"

"Whatever positive bullshit you think will cure my permanent raincloud personality." He's quiet for a moment before he finally speaks.

"I don't have any positive bullshit." His smirk is soft, but I detect some sort of sincerity or pain behind his expression, something I can't quite put my finger on. "I think someone who seems to be battling as much as you have has earned a bad day or two," he continues. What? I don't think anyone has ever allowed me to just have a bad day. Rosie and Casey aside, even still, they are constantly attempting to change my mood, coddle me, and protect me from my 'sadness'. I certainly don't expect him to understand, let alone give me a pass for my depressing and rageful moods. "I'm not here to judge." He shrugs. "Perhaps the shitty interactions you get with shitty people mean you've earned the right to assume the worst." I stop in the middle of the sidewalk again. *What is actually happening...?*

I look at him with a raised brow. "And how do you know I am *battling* so much? Or about my shitty interactions?" I accuse, not sure how that was the most important part I picked out of all of that.

"Well..." He looks to the sky, then straight ahead, with his lips pursed and eyes narrowed, he looks back to me.

"I think, and I am making educated guesses here so, feel free to correct me, but perhaps my stupid behavior from earlier has happened before." His eyes search my face, and I try to leave no answers for him, he continues, "But with someone far drunker than me, someone who perhaps didn't pick up on your clear *no* from your body language or even your direct words." *One point to Noah...* name a woman who hasn't had that experience. I'll wait.

He continues, "Definitely someone far less handsome than me." Okay, two points to Noah. He winks and my stomach rolls. "I think that maybe you had a shocking previous relationship ending in betrayal. I think that Law School is stressful for *anyone,* let alone someone who struggles with mental health, has just lost her job, and doesn't feel like they can trust anyone." I actually can't make this shit up—what's that, seven points? I really don't know; my brain is mush. He thinks he is off on that last point by the unknown questioning look in his gaze. I look back to the direction we were walking, and our pace continues, this time more casual, as I try to work out how I have possibly been that easy to read.

"Jake." I mean, he apparently knows my life story. Why not fill in the blanks?

"Hmm?"

"My ex. The horrible relationship you picked up on, his name was Jake." I look to my feet then and release a breath. "We dated for about six months. I have lived with anger issues and some light depression since high school, so he knew going into the relationship. He still stuck his dick elsewhere, and when I found out, he used my *issues* as a reason why he wasn't able to break up with me."

I look up at Noah and his eyebrows are pinched, his face is in a frown. I decide to continue because to have an expression that isn't fucking sunshine is nice for a change.

"I don't think I ever loved him, but he made me feel less lonely." Okay, too honest, Addison.

I clear my throat to move on. "I don't actually know if I want to work in a law firm. I just really need the job for the money, and I typically apply to the firm positions in the hopes that when I graduate, it will be easier to find a job as a lawyer. But with every job, my love for law dies more and more. I actually think the only reason I am still enrolled is to prove I can finish something. Show everyone I am not a complete failure."

"How would dropping out make you a failure?" he asks so seriously, curiosity in his tone. I look into his eyes and decide to answer him, only because he doesn't appear to be judging.

"My parents. I feel like they always just expect the worst from me. They never saw my trouble with mental health as something that needed treatment, but rather a fault in my personality. Dad always met my rage with rage of his own, and anytime it got the best of me, he would be so thoroughly disappointed. Not to mention, women shouldn't be so loud and aggressive. *'It is unbecoming.'* I scoff at the reminder of words I have heard time and time again.

"Ahh..." he says, but with no humor to it. His expression is tight, but he remains silent, quiet permission for me to continue if I wanted to. I take a few breaths and decide this is actually therapeutic.

"My mom, she just always treated me like something made of glass. Too afraid to say or do anything around me for fear of my reaction." He nods then and his eyes turn to me and a ghost of a smile lands on his face. I clear my throat again, look ahead, and continue.

"Anytime I talk about my life, what I am doing or deciding to do, she always meets it with, *'oh, darling, are you sure you're cut out for that?'* or its *'sweetie, I worry about you, do you think perhaps it is a bit much for you?'* I roll my eyes, hearing my mother's words out loud.

"Anyway, I think if I don't finish my degree, it is like proving to them that I was too fragile to finish it, that I wasn't cut out for it, and really, I am just aiming higher than what I have the capacity for. It is why losing the job hurt so much. It was just another reminder that apparently, I am not cut out for this." I look down then. Hearing my fears spoken out loud is scary. Like if I continue to voice them, it will give them room to grow.

He looks up to the sky, his lips pursed as if contemplating whether to turn and escape the absolute emotional shitshow I just laid out. He is silent for another few seconds that feel like years, and I start to scold myself for oversharing. What is wrong with me? I've never even said this out loud to the girls. Now I'm spilling to a stranger?

"I'm sorry, that was a lot. I didn't mean to trauma dump. Honestly, I don't know what got into me. I don't usually spill like that. God, I am such an id—"

"Addison, stop." He grabs my arm and turns me toward him, stopping us in the middle of the street, staring at each other.

"You have nothing to be sorry for, and I'm glad you ...*trauma dumped* on me. Your words, not mine." He raises the left corner of his mouth slightly before it drops and his expression deepens. "You shouldn't know what any of that feels like, and I am sorry that there is no one in your corner." His hand remains wrapped around my shoulder and his other arm comes up to tuck a hair behind my ear. My body tightens at the warmth of his hand against my face, and he pulls back to put both his hands in his pockets. I look down and brush my hands over my shoulders as he takes a step closer to me. He hooks his finger under my chin, forcing me to look into his deep brown eyes. His expression is soft.

"None of what you said to me about your experiences was your fault," he says slowly and seriously, and it steals the breath right from my lungs. Looking deeply into both my eyes, the kernel of warmth in my stomach returns, and tears prick the backs of my eyes. Before I even know what I am doing, I lunge forward, wrap my arms around his waist, and bury my head to his chest in an embrace. He is frozen for a second before his arms wrap around my shoulders, folding me into his chest, and his chin leans on my head as he releases a long breath. The honesty and the seriousness of his words made me feel seen for the first time in a really long time, by a complete stranger no less, and I think I am so shocked to my bones that I feel more of a connection with this man I barely know than anyone else in my life. Between that and the exhaustion of today, all the energy it takes to reinforce the walls around my fury, perhaps it caused my brain to vacate the building. Maybe that's why I launched myself into a hug with this stranger.

He holds me tight, and a sob slips out of me as the dam walls break and the tears pour out. His one hand rests on the back of my head, fingers interlacing my hair, as his other hand rubs warm circles on my upper back. Like we've been doing this forever, like it was natural, an instinct.

"You smell amazing, shortcake," he whispers. My eyes snap open, brain officially back in the building. I am cuddling in the middle of the street! I snap out of it and pull out of his embrace. He doesn't stop me, but he remains close. I take a step back, leaving half an arm's length between us. He reaches his hand to my face, cupping my cheek and wiping a tear away with his thumb, before dropping it back to his side again. I turn to walk back up the street, and he keeps pace next to me without a word.

"I'm sorry. I don't know what came over me. I promise I don't make a habit of... that."

"And you say I apologize a lot, you really are a serial-apologizer. You don't need to say sorry for anything," he says quietly. He clears his throat, and when I look to his face, his eyes have a sheen to them. In a blink, it is gone and his usual smug grin is back.

"In fact, I am going to teach you to stop apologizing to everyone and everything about things you should not be saying sorry for." A small laugh escapes me. "Oh my god. Addison Jenkins. Did you just smile?" His stupid grin and the playful tone work a disgusting magic on me as butterflies take flight, and my smirk grows as I struggle to bite down.

He chuckles under his breath, and I shove him playfully on the shoulder. "Oh, shut up. This never happened." I gesture between the two of us.

"Mmhmm," he says unconvincingly, giving me a devious side eye. "So... Greek sex-god?"

I turn my face to him, absolutely mortified that he ever had to hear that, and I am eternally grateful that it is dark and he cannot see the pink staining my cheeks as we continue to walk in the direction of my apartment.

"No! I am not explaining that one."

"Oh please, no explanation necessary." He gestures to his face and body. I roll my eyes and scoff at him.

"So, you guys were celebrating tonight?"

"Yeah, Caleb closed a huge deal for us today." My shoulders relax as he takes the subject change with ease.

"Matt's engineering firm?"

"No, a different company. Details aren't public knowledge or really anyone's knowledge yet—AIM is just contracted as part of the project. Until they land their patent on a new product, our lips are sealed, but getting their entire company's business is huge for us."

Pride seeps from him, that soft smile showing flashes of his teeth, causing a dimple to form slightly in his cheek. This look on him is of my favorites.

You can't have a favorite look for someone you don't even know, Addison.

I clear my throat and shake my head to stop staring at Noah's gorgeous side profile and avoid making eye contact as we continue to walk. "That's amazing, you must be proud of yourself."

"Caleb did most the legwork." Add modest to his list of traits, and at this point, his perfection is just getting out of hand.

"Well, this is me here," I say awkwardly as we make it to the steps of my apartment building. "Hey. Do you think, uhh, could we start over? Clean slate, no raging-trauma dumping or angry cries?" My face, I hope, is cool amusement. I have a feeling it is more embarrassed pink. A fresh start would be nice. Noah isn't a bad person; I might have jumped the gun a bit with my anger. He might be a typical jock who thinks they broke the mold when he was made, but surprisingly, being around him is... nice. It has been twelve months since I had a boyfriend. Since meeting Noah, I have spent most of my time either yelling at or crying on him. There is no way he is even remotely interested in me. I think friends would be nice, though, refreshing.

"A fresh start." He nods, and a wide smile spreads across his face, almost a bashful smile. *Is he blushing?* "That sounds perfect." His voice is quiet, but his smile doesn't fade. He steps closer, and his eyes are like a simmering chocolate sauce. "I was hoping I would get to see you again, Addison." He closes the remaining space again by placing both his hands on my neck in a loose grip, his thumbs smoothing over my cheeks as his eyes search my face. His expression softens into a grin that, from a distance, looks like his usual arrogance, but from this close, I can see the vulnerability in his eyes.

"Okay," I whisper. His smile grows and his eyes dart to my lips. *Is he going to kiss me right now?!* What happened to a fresh start? I feel like we are skipping steps here.

"Okay," he mimics, then drops his hands and takes a step back. My body grieves the loss of his warmth. "You have my number." He winks at me and turns to walk back down the street. He calls from behind him, not turning to look at me. "See you soon, Addison."

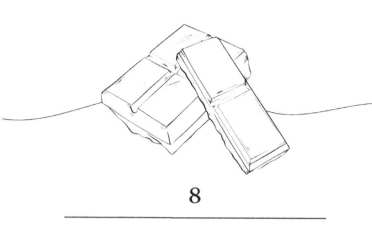

8

the one and only

Noah

After Monday night's run in with Addison at the bar, I was sure she would call me. Text me even. I thought there was something at the end. An understanding. I know for sure there was an electricity between us. When she hugged me, it was like every nerve ending was open to the freezing air. I could feel every part of her body molding to fit mine, like I was made specifically for her small frame to nestle in to. Her strawberry-musk scent wrapped itself around me until my pants tightened, and I was sporting a semi from a fucking hug. I wanted—no—needed a chance to get time alone with her, without all the animosity. *A fresh start.* Ending my hiatus sure has an appeal to it, but there was... something different. I can't put my finger on it.

Tuesday at work was brighter; Caleb, Ava and I buzzing from landing EcoX. I had to secure a small team of very specific staff to include on confidentiality agreements. They were anxious enough about talking to an outside company about their work in general. Even though they mentioned nothing about their recent design, they were still quite anxious about anything being slipped before they had a chance to get their ducks in a row. Ava will be a lead designer along with me, with Caleb being the go-between. His winning charm and ability to sell literally anything will keep all parties happy as this new relationship grows.

My mood is flying high; I feel somewhat lighter for reasons I can't work out, and trying to pinpoint the why is making focusing harder, distractions becoming astronomical as I try to knuckle down on the mountain of work I am trying to get done.

For other unknown reasons, I avoid JJ's, something telling me I'll just be even more distracted in the space that is usually where I'd go to focus. So, I remain sitting in my office, overlooking the city from my window, when a knock at my door startles me.

"You good man?" Caleb says as he lets himself in and drapes his tall frame into one of the chairs opposite my desk. The office was designed to be a sleek and modern space. Not a real 'CEO' office, because it felt like it was putting me at too much of a distance to my staff. So my door is usually always open, and Caleb uses this as an always-open invitation to just come in and sit down.

"Ahh yeah... fine, why?" I focus back on my computer and try to remember the million and one things I need to do today. List, I need a list, or just a pen, so I can stop forgetting shit. I shuffle through my desk looking for post-its. I'm certain I threw a stack of them on here the other day.

Caleb catches my moment of scatterbrain and raises an eyebrow. "Christ, I haven't seen you this distracted in years. Don't lie to me. What is up with you? And if you say fine again, I'll throw you out the window. We just landed the deal of a lifetime. Don't tell me you're fine."

"Just... distracted. I'll be fine. Probably hit the gym at lunch to blow off some steam."

"This have anything to do with the girls at Puck's last night?" he says with a mischievous tone and his grin grows.

I roll my eyes at him. "Please, I am not frazzled by some woman." *Lie.*

"Mmhmm. Sure, buddy. The Latina with the dark curls was hot as fuck. I don't blame you."

"Who?"

"The women... from last night? C'mon man, where is your brain?" Caleb looks almost annoyed at me not recalling last night. Of course, I certainly do remember last night, but it isn't '*the Latina*', who I believe has a name, Rosie, it is the blonde she-devil who has her claws in my chest.

"The woman from last night, the blonde? That was Addison."

"Ohhh, you mean the Addison you met at a Play House... De Luca's sister? That Addison?"

"One and only." I should try to sound less wistful. "Now, unless you have that sales report I asked for, can you leave? You pest." I throw some humor into the last bit, and he rolls his eyes at me.

"Fine. Report was emailed to you yesterday. I am sure, with all that focus you haven't lost, you probably have read it already?" I lift my eyes in a deadpan at him, and he doesn't even try to hide his smirk as he strolls from my office.

By Wednesday night, I have to lock my phone in a kitchen cabinet, forcing myself not to internet stalk her and let her come to me. Then the power is mine, and I can have a bit more wriggle room in encouraging a late-night meet up. By Thursday afternoon, I am calling Matt and asking for her number. So much for retaining the power.

"What the fuck, Karvelas? That is my little sister!"

"Actually, your sister-in-law."

"I have known her for more than half her life; she is practically my sister. Why do you need her number?"

"Okay, I didn't say need..." Although, it does feel that way. "After we ran into each other at Puck's on Monday night, we had a great time. I just wanted to reach out... see if—" See what, exactly Noah? *Where are you going with this because it certainly isn't a relationship?* "Look, I just want to take her out for a drink. Is that so bad?"

"Yes."

"Why?"

"Because I know you, Noah."

"And as my friend, you know what a complete gentleman I am, and Addy would be lucky to have a drink with me?" I don't usually pull the boyish charm on my guy friends, but apparently I'm desperate.

"You go through women like you change your underwear. I am not letting you do that to Addy." He says it like he has practiced this sentence. Ending on a sigh, like it's obvious that she is completely off-limits.

"She is not as fragile as you think. I'm sure if anyone actually listened to her, you'd all probably know that." *Where the fuck did that come from?*

"Oh, and you know her so well after one conversation?" I can't fault him for speaking truth. How do I feel like this after one real conversation? Sure, we had met a couple times before, but Monday night had been the real Addy. I could see it. Hear it and feel it in the way she spoke to me, looked at me, and when her body released into a sob as she embraced me, I could feel her strength.

"You know what? Don't worry about it." I disconnect the call and scold myself for being so desperate. I had already decided she was a relationship girl, and I am not that person.

She hasn't contacted you for a reason. Move on dude. I shake my head, grab my gym bag, and leave the house.

I run back up the stairs to my brownstone, throw open the doors, dump my gym bag in the entry, and stare at my phone.

> **Unknown Number:** Hi. Thank you for Monday night. For listening, I mean. Fresh start?

> **Unknown Number:** It's Addison, by the way.

The message came through as I was benching, my AirPods in my ears reading out the message, and I nearly crushed my chest as the message was read aloud and realized who had finally texted me. I had been too stunned to finish my set. Being near the end of my workout, anyway, I made a fast effort in grabbing my stuff and heading to my car, driving home and racing inside so I could evaluate the situation.

I stand in the space at the bottom of the stairs, my gym bag sprawled out on my oak floorboards. I typically like to keep things clean and tidy, the house generally is a minimalist design with the major furniture pieces and only a touch of décor. I kept the office and my home much the same—sleek sophistication. But the mess spread out on my floors is the least of my worries right now.

I can't work out what this... this *need* is. To be around her, to see her face, to touch soft cheeks, and work for the smiles and hear her snarky comebacks.

I want to get to know her. There is something about her that makes me want to just be around her.

Friends. I think we'd be *great* friends.

I swallow the obvious denial, save her number, and spend about twenty minutes pacing the room typing and backspacing my response before I scold myself. "God, Noah, fucking grow a set and just ask her out."

> **Me:** Hello Addy, fresh start sounds perfect. Want to grab a drink?

I stare at my sent message and decide maybe a drink actually sounds presumptuous? *Shit.* What if she thinks I am just trying to get in her pants? *Well, that'd be nice.*

God, what happened to me? I shake my head and type another message.

> **Me:** Or Dinner? Dinner and then drinks?

> **Me:** I mean, we can have drinks at dinner?

Honestly, I deserve for her to leave me on read at this point. I squeeze my eyes shut, curse myself, and throw my phone on the bench as I head to shower. See if I can locate my balls.

My shower does nothing to clear my head. I still think about Addison. Her strawberry smell seems to be haunting me, along with the sway of her hips when she walks in front of me, the way her blonde waves cascade down and *juuuust* touch her lower back. I picture her bent over, those golden waves wrapped around my forearm as I pull her back against me. The way she fit so well in my arms and how she had immediately relaxed when I wrapped my arms around her. The little sounds she made when she finally gave me a smirk and a giggle. *I wonder what other sounds she would make.*

I slam the water off, wrap a towel around my hips, and make my way back downstairs. I hear the faint vibration of my phone as I reach to grab it on my way to the fridge. I stop in the center of the kitchen and see Addy's message.

Addy ☀: *I think you nervous is my favorite version of you. Raincheck on drinks. I have a lot going on this week, and I am away the following week.*

I try to ignore the sinking feeling in my stomach, the hope that fizzles and dies. She owes me nothing. She reached out, but she doesn't want to see me, that's fine.

Me: *See you soon then, Shortcake.*

I bite down on my lower lip, staring at the phone. The speech bubbles pop up and disappear, then pop up and disappear again. I stare for about a minute and then curse myself. I look up at the ceiling, locking my phone screen. I open the fridge and grab a Gatorade to replenish the fucking sweat storm I am having at texting a woman.

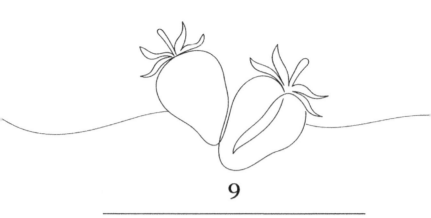

9

the most trivial of all triggers, a man

Addison

The week drags. I realize I am in desperate need of this holiday. Who would have thought a week away with my family would actually be exciting?

My interview with Lucas on Tuesday went well after I recovered from the initial shock at our introduction. Lucas was stupid hot. Very like pretty-boy turned bad-boy, with his straight dark hair that was a mess on top of his head, his tall strapping frame dominating the space. Hazel eyes standing out when framed with dark lashes and olive skin that looked marked with tattoos under the sleeves and neckline of his shirt. Practically had to pick my jaw up off the floor when he threw me a smile. *Damn.*

He asked me the usual job interview questions, and I tried to answer honestly and professionally... maybe some white lies. I haven't worked in hospitality for a while and I have never worked in a nightclub.

"I think you'll pick it up quickly. I mean, you're a law student, so you're obviously smart." I had not actually told him I was in law school, so I am going to assume Noah filled him in on that for the sake of giving my experience for this job.

"I would mostly need you weekends if that's okay. Saturday nights we're open until 3am and things can get... a little bit crazy, so you really need to have a backbone. Noah mentioned you have some fire in you, so I think you'd be perfect for the floor bar." Noah said what now?

"Floor bar?" I had asked, ignoring the other question on my tongue, *What other conversations have you had with Noah about me?*

He walked me through everything—layout and schedule—and introduced me to a couple of other staff, before we transitioned into casual conversation on the way back to the front. He asked me about my degree, and I asked him how long he had the place for. Turns out Lucas and I had more in common than I thought. He is also a 25-year-old, ex-party-boy-trust-fund-kid, well except for the party boy bit. He got into a bit of trouble, which he elected not to elaborate on, and was told to make something of his privilege or he'd be cut off. "Thought I was being clever, party life and all, by actually buying a nightclub. Humor wore off pretty quickly when I realized this is no walk in the park. I think I have aged about five years in the six months I've owned the joint, but surprisingly, I am enjoying it. Helps when you have a great support team. Like Noah."

"Oh?" I choke out. Why on earth did the mention of his name send me in a tailspin?

"Yeah, Noah didn't just do my branding and website, he *runs* my social media accounts. Pretty much controls all my marketing, website material, menu updates, socials—everything. He isn't an employee, obviously, but I keep his company on a permanent retainer, and he just invoices me monthly. He doesn't actually offer this to clients, so I am lucky he decided to help me out. I know nothing about all that shit."

The version of Noah that Lucas described clashes with the version

I had been making up in my head. The arrogant sunshine person who cares about himself and only himself. Or maybe it was easier to think those things and ignore the way he makes my skin heat and prickle by simply being near me, and not the usual kind I'm used to with my fury.

This right here is the problem I keep having. Noah keeps weaseling his way into my brain, giving me feelings he has absolutely no business provoking from me. Except I'm here trying to keep my head above water. New job, the holiday, law school. So much change and so much socializing and meeting new people. Throw in there meeting a new guy and trying to date. It is going to send me off a cliff, and in the end, no one will be there to catch me.

We made it back to the front bar, and he handed me an apron as he dashed out the back in a quick farewell.

I made my way back to the apartment, happy that I now had a job. Added bonus on the eye candy that is Lucas, but also thoroughly overwhelmed. Readjusting to the new job with the cramming I need to do for the final assessments before exams. I got a grade back yesterday for Tax Law that was just over a pass, and I desperately needed to fix that before finals. I managed to score a tutoring session with an alum, but I'm now petrified of failing at this, too. The rest of the week had just been a blur of classes, study hall, panic attacks about starting a new job after the holiday, and, well... trying not to think about Noah.

Despite Lucas being gorgeous, he unfortunately elicited nothing within me that compares to the way Noah seems to have my stomach in knots.

Not thinking about Noah is just another thing I fail at.

"Can I help you?" Thursday, I decide to sit at JJ's to finish my research assignment, taking advantage of the continuous supply of coffee, but Jessie has decided to interrupt my flow.

"Are you talking to Noah?" His questions catch me off guard, and my hackles raise. First of all, *what the fuck,* second of all, the audacity.

"Why is it any of your business?" I bite back my rage and stare back to my computer screen.

"Because I know him, Ads. I know who he brings here and how often. I know his type, also, and it is not something you need."

"Oh, and you're an expert in what I need? You don't even talk to me anymore. Ever since Jen—"

"Don't talk about Jenny," he interrupts me with a deep and low scolding and pins me with an intense stare. Green eyes, like mine, but with a twist of blue, fire back at me, when we match our rage it's like looking in a mirror.

"I am just saying. You lost all right to be a protective brother when you decided to ignore all of us two years ago. You haven't messaged or called. Twelve months ago, when I actually needed you, do you remember what you said?"

I just love it when a productive study session turns into a rehashing of trauma and pain. I have to blink back my rage tears and he just says nothing. His expression softens though, like he is fighting with his heart to not feel anything. Mentally cooling my veins and willing my control not to snap.

"You said, '*that's what you get for being a child and falling in love. Maybe if you grew up and stopped acting like a child, people would stop treating you like one.*' Do you remember that, Jessie?" His brutal attack on me after I ended it with Jake is singed into my memory like a brand, allowing me to recall word for word the way he tore me down.

My question is laced with venom, and my face pinches into a scowl as the memory rises. Skin-prickling rage growing with a vengeance, testing my latch to control. His face drops as he looks to his feet; he looks like he is genuinely in pain. I curse myself for being so harsh with my words, but screw him. He can't have it both ways.

"Ads... I—"

"Save it, Jessie. I don't want to hear an apology until you actually mean it." I dismiss him by turning back to my laptop and putting in my headphones. He stays standing next to me for a few seconds before he slowly turns and walks away. He has lost all right to try the big brother card after how absent he has been. I miss him, and I do love him. It's just... different now. Growing up, he was my biggest supporter. Ava was always there, but she was my soft-cheerleader. Jessie was my fierce defender. Sometimes, I think the reason I have fire in me at all is because of him, outside the obvious rage issues inherited from Dad. But ever since he had his heart broken two years ago, it is like he wants everyone else to hurt just as bad as he does.

I can't help thinking about the words he threw at me, though, *I know him, Ads. I know who he brings here and how often. I know his type.* What on earth is that supposed to mean? Who he brings? What, he has a secret wife? Unlikely. That guy screams one-night-stand.

Not that it matters. *Fresh start.*

He wouldn't even be interested in anything romantic, anyway. I literally cried and slobbered all over him Monday, and before that, spent the few moments we had together scolding him.

Focus, Addison!

I don't have time for this. I can't let a stupid boy ruin my perfect grades. I should be focused on my assignment and my research. This assignment has all but fucked me, and I have never submitted an assignment late. I am not about to start now.

I bring my hands to my face to cover it and take a few deep breaths.

My heart rate has spiked and my hands are shaky, as the telltale signs make their appearance. My thoughts spinning around.

Then why did he want to go to drinks? Why would someone like him be interested in me? I'm just damaged goods. Barely friend material, let alone casual sex material.

Fuck, I need to focus. What if I fail this assignment? What if it is a bad grade again, and then I have to repeat? God, what if I'm just wasting my time completely?

Maybe I should drop this unit and restart it. No use half-assing it, it'll just be another thing for Dad to bully me about.

Also, Noah probably already has someone romantically. I met him like three times; he doesn't already like me enough to date me.

I don't know left from right, and my vision fades at the edges as my body shakes and heart flutters intensify.

Just breathe, Addy.

Heart palpitations.

Short breath.

Panic Attack.

I can feel it growing. After twelve years of these, it gets easier every time to recognize when I will be past the point of no return. I make to pack up my things and head back to the apartment. It doesn't escape me that the topic that caused this is the most trivial of all triggers—a man. Unfortunately for me, panic doesn't discriminate.

The walk up the apartment stairs makes breathing harder. The Uber ride also didn't help and only escalated matters, as I was forced into the silence of my thoughts and the claustrophobia increased my heart rate. Shame at losing my temper with JJ floods my system, the look in his eyes and the way I saw red from the moment he spoke to me.

I run into the apartment. It's empty; Rosie and Casey are both working, thank God. I dump my study bag on the kitchen table and head to the couch. I wrap a blanket around my shoulders and pull it tight around me in an attempt to create a firmness to my body, to feel grounded and collected. *All that therapy and you still can't keep your anger in check.*

I can't... I can't do this.

Noah.

I can't do this again. He will see my broken pieces, and he will just break them more. JJ was right—I don't need this.

I practice my breathing. In for 6, hold for 2, out for 8. *In 2, 3, 4, 5, 6, hold 2, out, 2, 3, 4, 5, 6, 7, 8. Repeat.*

This? What are you talking about, you idiot? There is no this. A rain check is not a "this". You cannot afford to freak out like this. Just stick to your hiatus and everything will be fine. You have exams in two months and final assessment dates looming. You cannot afford to lose sight of everything right now.

I make it two rounds of my breathing before my whole body is shaking, and the crying comes in uncontrollably. For me, this is the peak. This is the point of no return.

I wish I could just stop. Just turn it off. My brain, the thoughts, the what ifs. Why can't I just live a day without thinking about the next or worrying about yesterday?

No. No, I don't want to be here. I don't want to do this. I can't. I CAN'T DO THIS.

My brain screams all the horrific thoughts in my head like it is clambering to get out.

Off, turn off, I just want my brain to stop.

I claw at my chest, trying to alleviate the pressure so I can get air down. The body shakes make it feel like I am convulsing, and my chest tightness makes it feel like someone is sitting on me.

God, all because a boy talked to me? Because of my idiot brother and my uncontrollable rage? All because I just want to make Dad proud of me? I just want Mom to finally see me and finally believe that I am more than my faulty brain.

I can't stop, turn it OFF.

I burst off the couch, a scream-sobbing mess, and head straight for the shower. *Not the bath.* I strip off my clothes and turn the shower head to hot.

Can't... can't breathe.

I climb in and sit on the floor, bringing my knees to my chest.

I can't do this.

Wrapping my arms around my knees to bury my head in them.

I hate this. I hate feeling like this. Off, TURN IT OFF.

I stay like this, heaving tears in a silent, breathless cry, rocking back and forth, for about fifteen minutes when my breathing starts to slow.

My thoughts ease as I focus solely on the feeling of each water droplet hitting my back.

I recognize the feel of my muscles relaxing down my spine and start my breath exercises again.

In for 6, hold for 2, out for 8. Repeat.

I lift my head and let the water pour its way over my face, washing away the salty stains and remaining tears that fall, and let my focus go to the burning of the water on my skin, alleviating the numbness. I give myself another five minutes to calm my breathing, steady my heart rate, and stop the shaking, before I stand and turn off the shower. Too drained, too mentally exhausted to finish my shower. I remain focused only on my breaths and not allowing myself to think of the thoughts that had plagued me.

Each attack is as exhausting as the last. No matter how much I think I have perfected my techniques, it still feels like I have run a marathon after. My stomach muscles are sore, my eyes are red and tender, my brain is completely empty to the point I can't form words, and I feel a deep ache of defeat down to my bones. I decide to make myself a cup of peppermint tea and lay in bed. I end up not even having a sip before sleep finds me the moment I lay down.

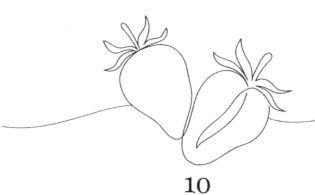

10

a drop of sunshine

Addison

I woke early this morning, groggy, swollen, my head pounding. Remembering, and trying to forget, the awful dark emptiness of last night. I splash my face with cold water, put on my running shorts, and give myself a much-needed pep talk. "Today is your day. Grab it by the balls. Show it who is boss."

Although, I am not sure my subconscious heard that one.

Fresh air and a few laps of the park helped. The spring sun was warm, and I was lucky enough to not run into anyone I knew. Socializing was off the table. Residual anger, sadness, defeat, frustration, and restless energy all powering the run, and I managed to set a new PB for my pace.

Once I make it back into the apartment, it is just past 6am, and both the girls are awake.

"Are you both usually awake this early and I never knew?"

"Yes, little miss night owl. You're never awake this early. What on earth are you doing up? And on your way back from a run, no less?" Rosie chirps, her eyes grazing me from head to toe, red and sweaty from my run. Jeez, I really don't see these girls enough in the morning. I don't think I have ever seen Rosie so happy.

"I ended up crashing super early yesterday and so was able to wake up earlier. Set a new PB, though!" I smile at that and Casey turns with a happy-shocked look on her face as Rosie cheers.

"Yes, bitch! You're amazing. Honestly, a true inspiration," Rosie shouts, hand on heart with mock admiration, and I roll my eyes, hiding my smile. Casey leans over to throw me an enthusiastic high-five. Rosie smacks the stool next to her, signalling for me to come sit. I appease her and plop down next to her.

"Why'd you crash? I thought you'd be holed up in there cramming before the holiday?" Rosie says over her coffee mug as she takes a sip. Rosie loves that most people see her as playful and brainless, but her sharp eye misses nothing. She knows something is up. I shrug. I love these girls and they know I've had previous attacks. It doesn't mean I like to talk about them.

Rosie levels me with a pointed look, and I roll my eyes. "I had a panic attack. Wiped me out. I crashed." I am flippant with my words, hoping they don't harp about it. The last thing I need is to dissect this the day after... with someone who isn't my therapist.

My hopes are lost. Rosie's coffee mug hits the table with force, and Casey has turned the frying pan off the stove and has now turned to face us with a sad look of concern on her face.

"No, no, no, no. We aren't doing this. Don't pity me."

"We don't pity you, babe. We worry about you, it is different." Casey directs stern eyes at me.

"It isn't different, not when you look at me like that and walk on eggshells around me." I gesture between their faces.

"Okay, well, talk to us, tell us about it. Help us understand. We want to be there for you and help. You know that when you hurt, we hurt, too," Casey says softly. I stare at her, her eyes softening, as Rosie reaches a hand to my shoulder and massages firmly before dropping it back to her coffee cup. I look at Casey, and she has a soft smile and nods reassuringly.

"I get it, I do. I love you girls, and thank you. But I don't want to talk about it. There is nothing to talk about." I leave no room for negotiation.

"Well, shall we eat pancakes?" Rosie plasters her usual mischievous smile to her face as Casey turns back to the stove. Rosie gives me a quick once over, squeezing my hand reassuringly. I know they'll be there for me when I need it, but really, I am okay. Totally fine.

I'm going to need some brain food for my lecture in the afternoon, anyway. "Let's." My shoulders release some tension, grateful the girls dropped it.

I spend the rest of the morning with the girls. My lecture isn't until 3pm, Casey says she has no classes today, and Rosie has her RDO, but I'm half of the belief they took the morning off to hang with me. We head out to the bookstore on the corner of our block, do some grocery shopping together, and stop at a new café a few blocks away to try out the coffee. Casey has a thing for trying the weirdest or quirkiest options on a coffee menu just for fun. This time it was a Maple-Bacon infused latte. She wasn't impressed.

By lunch time, my soul feels a little more replenished and my heart feels a little more together, but it doesn't escape me that the girls do their best to never leave me alone and try to cheer me up at every opportunity.

We make it back to the apartment and we fall to the couch, satisfied with our stroll about the city and our latest book purchases.

"We should quit our jobs and do this every day," Rosie declares.

"Don't get ahead of yourself there. We enjoyed today *because* we have jobs." Casey and I chuckle.

"Sooo... how's Noah? Have you heard from him?" Casey says gently from next to me.

God, I was trying not to think about him.

"Uhhhh." I groan and close my eyes. I escaped one emotional conversation today. Might as well placate them with something.

"I texted him. Thanked him for... being nice, I guess. He asked to go for drinks. I asked for a rain check." Rosie scoffs and throws her head to the back of the couch, and Casey remains deep-in-thought as she lets me continue.

"I don't really know what to think. We can't really date. I'm barely holding it together enough to keep my grades respectable. I can't open myself up to all the bullshit that comes with dating, at least not right now. *Especially* after JJ said some things. He might be an ass, but he isn't exactly wrong. I don't think a boyfriend, or dating in general, is something I need right now." And with Noah just oozing sex, I don't think I could really be a friend, at least one that isn't drooling over him.

"What are you talking about?! Why won't you just give it a chance? Leave your mind open and just see what happens?" Rosie slams her hands down on the couch as though she has had enough. I give her a cheeky smile in return.

"Babe, you have been single and untouched for twelve months, just take a chance. What is the worst that could happen, really?" she continues.

"Rosie is right. You were hurt, Jake was a dick, but that doesn't mean every guy you ever meet is going to be the same. JJ also doesn't know what he is talking about; he is emotionally stunted. Give the guy a chance to defend himself against JJ's onslaught. It doesn't mean that if you open yourself up, it will end the same. Didn't you say, 'fresh start'? You can't go into a fresh start with prejudices placed down by people whose opinions you don't even care about anymore," Casey chimes in, and her words sting. They aren't exactly wrong, but because I do care about JJ. Sometimes if I let myself remember how close we used to be, and how much we used to talk about, I think I will start crying all over again.

"Yeah, but what if it does? What happens if he does hurt me? Isn't it my fault if I knew it would happen and I just let it?" I give them my genuine fear, not hiding the anger in my tone.

"Argghh, you hurt my brain! It's a drink, not a fucking marriage proposal!" Rosie screams as she throws her head back and pulls on her face.

My heart sinks a little. Moments like these are stark reminders that I really am alone in my anxiety. They might think they talk sense, but my brain couldn't give two shits. I'm hell bent on overthinking, and there just isn't anything they or I can do to stop it.

Casey rolls her eyes at Rosie but continues. "Ads, your fears are valid and obviously stem from past trauma, but if you shut yourself off from every chance to be happy, you'll never know what it feels like to be alive. Pain, hurt, betrayal, lies—they all come with being alive." I throw my head back in defeat and bite down on the retort that threatens to come out.

Then why even be alive?

She places her hand on my knee, and I reluctantly roll my head in her direction to look into her eyes, which are full of hope and happiness, an expression that screams courage. "But so does love, joy, excitement, fun, new experiences. All of it, the good and the bad, is what makes you alive. The problem is, you can't have one without the other." I shake my head, not understanding what she means. She releases a laugh and shakes her head in return. "How would you ever know what love is if you've never felt the opposite? How do you know what happiness or joy is if you've never felt unhappy? You only know the feeling of excitement because you know what being bored is. You only know peace because you know what stress is. They all go together. You can't avoid love and happiness because of the potential to feel pain and sadness. All of it is inevitable. The question is whether you're going to sacrifice all the possible love and joy for maybe feeling some pain."

I stop, my breath stilling, and my eyes move to stare out the window of our Upper West Side apartment, admiring the way the mid-afternoon sun spills out across the floorboards and drenches the mostly white room in a warm glow. I blink rapidly to hide the tears that threaten to expose my fragility. *She's right.*

"And where in the fuck did that come from?" My eyes snap to Rosie and she has a look of pure astonishment aimed at Casey. We both throw our heads back in a laugh, a full proper belly laugh. I truly can't remember the last time I let myself laugh this deeply. Casey shrugs.

"Guess I have had enough pain and happiness to know what they both are."

"Who needs a therapist when we have you?" I ask with some amusement.

"I'll be sure to send you the invoice." Casey winks at me as she pats me on the knee.

"I'll drink to that." Rosie raises a glass of wine I have no idea where she pulled from, not waiting for Casey or me to inform her we don't have a glass to raise, and she downs the lot. I release a sigh and feel the warmth and love from my best friends filling my soul after this morning with them.

"You know what? You *are* right. I guess I'll... just see what happens." I release a full watt smile, and we all huddle into a giggle in the center of the couch.

The 3pm lecture dragged as usual, my tax assignment was submitted, and I received great feedback. Still a B-, but I'll take it over a C. The rest of the unit had been a B+ average, so I choose to accept this for what it is. "Keep it up Addy, you're doing well. The course average is a C+, so don't beat yourself up. We're having a study group before the final in the library over Spring Break, if you're interested in attending," Professor Reynolds says after seeing my face drop slightly as he handed back my grade.

"Thanks, I will be away, though. I might see if I can schedule a tutor session before the final."

"That will be fine. The break will be good, too. Law School is a lot, you've made it this far, not long to go now." He gives me a sympathetic smile, pushing his glasses up the bridge of his nose as I leave the lecture hall. He's right. I've made it this far coasting on a 3.5 GPA average. My grade improved with only a few tutoring lessons, and this is good news. Whether it is the high I was already riding from my morning with the girls, or the excitement I am letting myself feel when it comes to Noah, but this lecture ended up being a drop of sunshine amongst the gloomy days.

Today really seems to be everything I've been hoping for: a day of just feeling *good*.

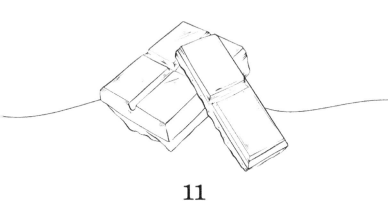

11

one tall drink of water, please

Noah

"Noah relax, I haven't told a soul a thing! There isn't even anything to tell. We have no details from the engineering firm or any of the staff from EcoX—the leak isn't us," Caleb reassures me as I pace the floor of my office.

We were notified this morning that there has been a leak of some of the details pertaining to the latest product for EcoX. Another company, newer on the market, has teased a product that is similar, and now there is apparently some fucking race for a patent. I don't really know the workings, the EcoX contact just dribbled information, and I stopped listening after she said the words, '*pausing the contract.*' Of course, this comes out only a week after they sign with us, and now they have cold feet. Their contract has a cooling-off period, which they are currently sitting on while they investigate the leak of information and work out what went wrong. Until then, the contract is frozen. Which means my goal and my plan are frozen, in the air, potentially at risk. The image of my mom's face when I have to tell her that no, in fact, there will be no Chicago office, I won't be moving back home, and I will probably be working this hard until the day I die or am forced into retirement.

I still haven't seen the doctor about mysterious chest pains.

"I need you and Ava to run a sweep of our systems. I know we have no details on file, but I want everything triple checked. I can't let this jeopardize the deal. We need this deal." *I need this deal.* Caleb pretends to be cool, but he is as concerned about this as I am. He nods and quietly leaves the office as I grab out my phone to dial Matt.

"Karvelas, I assume you heard?"

"They put the contract on hold. Six months of promises and work down the fucking drain." I slump into my chair and run a hand down my face.

"Alright drama queen, nothing is down the drain. They just need to investigate the leak. You guys have nowhere near enough information for it to be you. AIM is also running a sweep, but that is unlikely because again, the only person who has anything is me, and I haven't even told Ava anything, let alone someone in the company. It'll work itself out, I promise." That eternal sunshine Addison complains about shines through, and I wonder if this is what she means. Matt's lackluster explanation of the situation grates on my nerves. He should care more about this. Or perhaps he just doesn't have anywhere near as much riding on this deal going through. I grunt into the phone, which gives me a laugh on the other end.

"Can we organize a meeting next week? I want to go over the details of the contract and perhaps sweep over everything we did to make sure there were no issues on our end, and to also make sure we don't fall behind because of this pause. I can't hire any more staff until we aren't on pause, but I can't make this amount of work happen at the click of my fingers. I'm going to need to make some arrangements." I pull up my laptop to book a time on the calendar.

"We're at Maplewood next week, remember? Didn't Ava put in leave?" Fuck's sake.

"Yes, she did. I forgot." I sit back in my chair and think about my family. My mom and Evie alone in Chicago. I think about my dad, how hard he worked to set both Evie and me up. I can't screw this up, can't let him down. This needs to work out. "You know what De Luca? A vacation is just what I need."

"It's an actual vacation, Karvelas. As in, no work. I get to switch my brain off, vacation."

"It could be fun." I try to convince him.

"C'mon man, it's just a week."

"And we didn't get where we are by cutting corners and taking time off De Luca, you know that." I didn't mean to dad-voice lecture him, but my stress is really gripping me hard right now.

He sighs from the other side and grunts out a, "fine."

"Pack your laptop. We're taking this meeting on the road."

Addison

Two hours in a car with a five-year-old is like an eternity. I love Mia with the entirety of my heart and soul, but my god, can that child talk. Literally, for the entire. Two. Hours.

Monday morning, I met Ava and family as planned to hitch a ride with them to the lodge for the weeklong getaway. Ava spent most of the car ride laughing at my inability to handle the ramblings of her adorable child. It took twenty minutes of me playing along before I asked Mia, "Hey, how about we play the silent game? See who can stay quiet the longest?" I threw her a look of mischief in an attempt to entice her into agreeing. She is unfortunately too smart for her own good.

"Hmmm, that doesn't sound very fun. I want to play I-spy instead." And so, that was the rest of the trip. I make a mental note to find an alternate route next year.

That thought alone... *next year...* still trips me up sometimes. I remember a time where I couldn't imagine a next year. A next week or even the next day. I allow myself to smile softly, a small internal celebration at my growth. As my therapist would say, I need to acknowledge my own strength when it shows, because I worked fucking hard at it.

We arrive at the lodge, a beautiful expanse of nature, a thick blanket of greenery covering the ground with trees surrounding the area, giving us private uninterrupted space around the lake. We head up the porch stairs, me holding Mia's hand and letting her talk at me, while I wrangle the chatter induced migraine throbbing in my head. The lodge is relatively large, with seven bedrooms, a wrap-around porch, and a private jetty.

As we enter the front door, I try to slow down the mini-human from bolting upstairs to get to the playroom—unfortunately, five-year-old's don't understand the need for adult supervision around sixty-year-old stairs—when I hear my name from upstairs

"Addy!" I turn my head as I see my little sister Riley running down the stairs to me. Little in age only, Riley got the rare mix of genes, while JJ, Ava, and I got the fair skin and blonde hair, Riley has the same fierce green eyes but with long dark locks and light olive skin. I think this is the result of some Mediterranean ancestor way, way back through our lineage. JJ and Riley also got the height from Dad's side; Ava and I remain short enough to blend in with toddlers.

"Aunty Ri! We're at the lodge!" Mia yells as Riley reaches down to wrap her in a hug. She stands again as Matt and Ava approach. Matt grabs Mia and offers a quick kiss on the cheek to Riley in greeting, before heading upstairs to set up their room. Riley dramatically wraps her arms around Ava and me in a big and uncomfortable hug. "Thank god you two are here. Please never leave me alone in a car with our parents again," she grunts.

"What's happening now?" Ava asks on a giggle. I trace the room with my eyes and spot Mom and Dad through the kitchen window by the car. Dad is grumbling expletives as Mom is trying to drag the luggage out of the car, not taking his eyes off his phone. His typical behavior of late. The last time we visited for dinner, I don't think I saw his eyeballs once. He even tried to have a normal conversation with me... while checking his phone. I roll my eyes and tune back into the conversation with Riley.

"They just. Won't. Stop. Fighting. It is draining the life out of me. The whole car trip it was, '*You never talk to me anymore, you just stare at your phone*', '*well, maybe if you ever stopped nagging me and said nice things, I'd want to talk to you again*', '*well, if you just did what I asked when I asked, I wouldn't have to nag*'.*"* Riley mimics our parents arguments, alternating between a high pitch and a deep grumble with her face screwed up. She takes a breath and drags her hands down her face in exhaustion.

"Oh, God. Don't worry, you can be our friend for the week. Maybe Jessie will come and distract Mom with his golden-child charm," I say on a giggle at Riley's animated expression.

"Apparently, the golden child will not be gracing us with his presence this week. He has 'business to take care of'. Very ominous," Ava explains with her usual disdain for Jessie being Mom's favourite. After our run in and my not so calm reaction the last time I saw JJ, I'm not sorry he is skipping this week.

I loop my arms around Riley and Ava, and we head back out the front door to get a look at the lake, when I stop dead in the center of the room.

My eyes scrunch close then open wide, like I am trying to make sure I have not fully lost my mind and am now seeing things.

"Woah, what's up, Ads?" Riley asks with concern. She and Ava proceed to look in the direction of my stare and Ava releases a low chuckle.

"I don't get it... wait, who is that?" Riley whines. I slowly turn my head to Ava.

"Is this your doing?"

"Is what her doing? Don't leave me out, tell me!" Riley is practically shouting.

"Shhh, Riley, relax. And I promise this was not me." Ava releases herself from my looped arm, raising her arms in surrender. "But perhaps it is a sign. I saw you guys all chummy at Mia's birthday."

"I knew I should have made Mom and Dad come to that!" Riley interjects. "Now I'm behind on the gossip. Tell me what is going on!" She whacks Ava on the arm.

"Ouch! She can tell you. I don't know anything, and I need to go... help Matt... in the room..." She turns on a heel and bails.

"RILEY!" Dad shouts from outside, holding up her suitcase.

"UGH! You don't get out of telling me what is going on. I am finding you later!" She turns and runs outside to see Dad. Who, might I add, has not even waved to me.

"Addison," the surprise guest greets as he walks through the large front doors of the lodge. The scent of spring fills my nose.

"And what, might I ask, are you doing here, at my family's lodge, Noah?" I give him a semi-scowl while trying to appear confident and not at all like my stomach is flipping the fuck out over the sight of Noah. "Really can't handle the rejection can you, just had to follow me here?" I add with a raised brow. I casually drag my eyes from his warm chocolate ones, past his chiseled jawline, down his very broad torso, to his long legs, and back up to those gorgeous eyes. My memory of him really did not do him justice. The attraction of Lucas just pales in comparison. *Damn.*

He gasps and reaches his hand to his chest, feigning a mock horror at my accusation. "Rejection? Weren't you the one that suggested a raincheck? I was simply moving up the timeline." He ends on a lopsided grin and a wink.

I hate that he is right, and hate the excitement that kicks into gear at him wanting to see me again. I pretend none of these feelings exist. "So you decided to crash a family vacation? A little desperate, aren't we?" I say as I take a few steps to close the gap between us, aiming for snarky, but I think... *was that flirty?*

"I am not crashing anything, shortcake. I am an invited guest. Matt and I had some business that couldn't wait, he suggested I tag along." Again, with the arrogant smile. I scoff and roll my eyes, making to head towards the stairs and attempt to hide my blush. My stomach sinks as I realize that he isn't actually here for me, but I try to quickly shove down those feelings. Again, I have no business feeling *anything* for Noah.

We make it to the end of the stairs when a screech comes from behind me. "Addison! So lovely to see you. God, it feels like forever!" I turn and find our family friends Vicky and George on the front porch, Vicky dropping her bags to run over to me, George remaining unimpressed that he now has to also carry her bags. George and Dad were high school friends, and Mom and Vicky ended up working together in their first jobs after leaving school, so it is fair to say I have known them my whole life. They have kids of their own, mine and Ava's age, but they are constantly traveling and never around for the typical family holidays.

Vicky wraps me in a suffocating hug. "It was only three months ago. We had that dinner at Mom and Dad's remember?"

"I know, but three months is still too long."

I wrap George in a hug as he finally catches up, a guy of few words, but his face is kind as we do our usual greetings. Noah coughs quietly behind me, and I jolt as I remember his presence behind me at the stairs.

"And who is this tall drink of water?" Vicky gestures to Noah and throws some wiggly eyebrows in my direction while poking my side. Noah, to his credit, isn't the least bit phased by her insinuation and throws his firm hand and should-be-illegal forearms out to shake George's hand. "Noah Karvelas, I am a friend of Addy's." Then proceeds to lean down to Vicky and smack a kiss to each of her cheeks. *Damn Greeks and all their charm.*

I do not miss the shady wink he throws my way. Vicky accepts the hello and widens her eyes at me. George shakes his hand, too, throws Noah a, nice to meet you," before he turns to take his and Vicky's bag to their room. I scowl at Noah and roll my eyes. "We are not friends. We met at Mia's party, and then he followed me here—like a stalker." I level an accusatory stare at Noah, who just rolls his eyes at me shakes his head.

"Mmmhmm," Vicky says, unconvinced. "Okay, love birds. I will leave you to it." She throws me a wink and makes to follow George to their room.

"We are not—"

"She can't hear you now, dearest," Noah cuts me off, throwing me a sarcastic grin to match the lovely pet name he has given me.

"Ugh, you're insufferable." I roll my eyes and ignore him as I head upstairs.

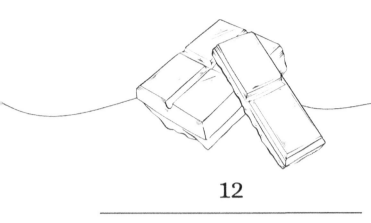

12

contagious rage

Noah

The look on Addison's face when she saw me was worth the surprise. Despite the war of emotions happening inside me, I managed to reel them in enough to appear casual. Seeing her giggling with her sisters, with the breeze flowing in through the front doors blowing her long hair around her face, helped calm me, like all my worries, all my stress, just dissipated. Still there, just less shitty. The reaction to her isn't just mental, it's physical. Like my body knows when she is around. Readjusting a semi this entire week is going to get annoying, borderline creepy, so I really need to sort this fucking thing out. Hopefully, the deal with EcoX keeps me busy, that will be dependent on Matt actually letting me steal his time.

Getting under Addison's skin might be my favorite pastime, though. Maybe I can provoke her instead of flirt with her. Keep it friendly.

Like her fury doesn't turn you on.

It was hard enough trying not to text her, leaving the ball in her court. I nearly lost all self control after a few beers, a warm shower plagued by thoughts of her, and the way she feels pressed up against me. Addison is good. Great, in fact.

Fresh start.

It is better for everyone involved if we don't get into anything serious, though. I won't do serious, can't do it. I just... I don't know how much I can hold back with her. We barely know each other, and I feel myself drawn into her orbit. I am constantly thinking about her, and when I'm not, god, I just want to be in her presence. The few minutes we spent in a verbal sparring match downstairs was enough to get me out of my head, enough to distract me from my worry, only making my need to be around her grow. Like right now, when I feel like every other aspect of my life is holding on by a thread, to be with her and talk to her, like that Monday night walk home from Pucks. Just to make the world feel still for a few moments.

We walked in silence together up the stairs before I realized I have no idea which room is meant to be mine. She must have picked up on my faltering steps, looking around to work out where I would be sleeping, and she explains, "The room next to mine is usually always free. You can take that one." She practically grunts the sentence, clearly unimpressed with being forced to sleep near me. I nod and pull a polite smile on my face as she shows me to the room.

"Here. Bathroom is down the hall on the left. There is also a bathroom downstairs around the corner behind the staircase, but that is the bathroom Vicky and George use... I would advise against using it," she whispers the ending of that, failing to hide her smile.

"Thanks. This place is huge. How many people usually stay here?"

"There are seven bedrooms. Vicky and George always have the guest wing downstairs. Mom and Dad take the master upstairs, which is down the other end to the right. Back when we were kids, Ava and I shared a room, Jessie shared a room with Aiden, Vicky and George's eldest son, and Violet, their daughter, who is my age, would share with Riley. We had two spare rooms for any other friends or guests that came. Ava and Matt now share our old room, this one is the one Riley and Violet used to sleep in, and you're sleeping in Jessie's," she says, almost bored, like she had that whole speech rehearsed. "Oh... he won't mind?"

"Nah, he doesn't come to these things anymore. Or at least, he hasn't in the last two years, and apparently isn't again this year." *Interesting.*

"Well, thanks for showing me."

"No problem." She gives me a tight nod before entering her room and quickly closing the door. I remain staring at the space she vacated, feeling a cramp in my chest that I don't understand. I can tell myself till I'm blue in the face that I don't want anything serious with Addison, but her barely treating me like a friend makes my skin itch. I decide I am not going to over analyze and enter my room.

Everyone heads into town for a picnic lunch, Matt informs me. A ten-minute walk from the lodge around the lake, Matt begged me to join. "The girls spend the whole time gossiping. Can you please give me something else to talk about? Leave work here, we'll talk it over after lunch." An easy enough invitation to accept, which had nothing to do with seeing a certain blonde haired, green-eyed strawberry shortcake again.

On the way out of my room, I hear voices at the bottom of the stairs, and I catch the end of a conversation as I make it to the top. "...he almost kisses me on Monday and then by text, he just left it at, see you soo—" and I lock eyes with Addison at the bottom of the stairs talking to Riley, before she finishes her sentence. Her eyes grow wide as her face goes pink. She stumbles on a cough, lowers her head, and makes quick work of heading for the front door as I leisurely stroll down the stairs. Riley, to my absolute delight, has no idea why Addison hasn't continued her story and is pestering her to continue.

"Hello? Then what?! Did you plan a date?!"

She wanted me to kiss her? Please let me be the 'he' in this story. I don't know if my ego can take it being someone else.

"Shh Riley, shut the fuck up," Addison whisper-shouts while jabbing her sister in the side, and I stroll up behind Riley as they wait on the front porch. Oh yeah, I'm definitely the 'he' in this story. The size of my smile takes up my whole face, and I can't do a thing to hide my smugness.

"No, please, don't stop on my account." Riley spins and her eyes dart up to mine, eyes that are almost as green as Addison's, but seem to lack the sparkle Addison's carry. As she looks between Addison and me, with my devilish grin plastered to my face, I throw a wink in Riley's direction, and I can see the lightbulb flick on.

"Ohhhhhhhh hahahaha." Riley's realization turns into a hysterical laugh, and Addison covers her face with her hands and stifles a grunt.

"Kill me now," she whispers to herself.

We make for the lake and the path around it that apparently leads into town. Riley has darted off, spotting Ava, Matt, and Mia ahead, mumbling something about playing with Mia, leaving Addison and me alone to stroll casually past the lake. The walk is mostly silent, but the energy between us is electric. My body feels like it buzzes with exhilaration at my proximity to her, despite her clearly wishing I was anywhere else.

As we make it into town, the streets are surprisingly quiet, the light breeze rustling the trees, the sun beating down from its full height in the clear, blue sky. We round a corner of a building, Addison leading the way, indicating the picnic area was just around the corner, and I unintentionally ignore the rest of her sentence as I watch the way her hips move as she saunters off in front of me. Very much enjoying the view as I am stopped short in an attempt not to walk right into the back of Addison.

That'll teach you for staring at her ass.

"Oh, this day could not get any worse," Addison grunts. In confusion, I look up over the top of Addison's head to the direction she's glaring and see a relatively skinny guy, who looks to be about twenty-five, staring in the direction of the woman in front of me. His hair is blond and slicked back in a way that reminds me of every rich-kid douche in the movies. His eyes manage to quickly flick to mine and his entire body changes, like a lion who has sensed a threat.

Perhaps a house cat is a better description.

"Addy? What... what are you doing here?" the guy says as he approaches Addison. Reading how uncomfortable Addy gets makes my back straighten, and I take a few steps closer to her... not sure what my plan is here, but surely less damage the closer I am... Right?

"Jake. Hi. Yeah, sorry, it's... well, it's that time of year... the family trip?"

There is that damn word again. '*Sorry.*' She is apologizing for being in the same place with this guy? I think fucking not. Wait, *Jake. The ex Jake?*

"Right, of course. I forgot you'd be in town." There is an awkward pause and a heavy pit sours in my stomach as I recall the little Addy told me of her ex.

He still stuck his dick elsewhere, and when I found out, he used my issues as a reason why he wasn't able to break up with me.

I bite down on the inside of my cheek to stop the rage that begins to climb its way up my spine.

"How have you been?" he asks, sliding his eyes to me quickly then back to Addison.

"Fine. Same old stuff, you know..." She shifts uncomfortably on her feet again, looking down to her fidgeting hands, and damn if it doesn't tighten something in my chest. She is all brawn and bossy with me. I hate that she falls in on herself around him. I step forward and throw my arm around Addison's shoulders to pull her against me, giving myself something to do with my hands that isn't slamming it into the jaw of this prick. I ignore the way she relaxes into my touch and the way her ass presses into my side as I thrust my free hand between me and *Jake* to introduce myself.

"Noah, nice to meet you, James."

"Jake. My name is Jake."

"Ah, easy mistake." I give him my most arrogant grin. I look down at Addison. "We should get going, shortcake. We don't want to be late." I release her from my grip on her shoulders and trail my fingers down her arm to lace my fingers with hers, loving this excuse to touch her. I feel the prickling of her goosebumps and heat of her hand as she slowly turns her head to me.

"Yeah... late," she whispers as her lips part on a sigh. I try, and fail, to stop my eyes from lingering on those full lips. A growl releases from my throat as I force myself to look in *Jake's* direction again, cursing him for ruining this moment with his presence.

"Lovely to catch up, Jack. See you around." And I pull Addison along with me as she remains silent.

Jake's discomfort is visible as his eyebrows crease. A frown forms on his face. "Jake. It's Ja—"

"Of course." I cut him off with a wink as we walk past him. I don't allow a look back, but I can feel his stare burning through my shoulder blades. Addison is still silent but has yet to draw her eyes away from me.

"What?"

Her eyes skim down my arm to our hands that are interlaced and she stares. *Oh right, you're holding hands like you're a couple and you just had a fit of jealousy.* I casually shake our hands free as she looks forward to the park.

"Um… thanks… for that. Whatever that was." She shakes her head, and I can see the look of defeat reach her face again. I stop myself from grabbing her hand or wrapping her in my arms for comfort.

"It was nothing, really. I could see you get all shifty and wanted to leave the awkwardness as quickly as possible. Your ex?" She nods. "You know you have nothing to apologize to him for, right?"

"What?"

"You said sorry, back when you ran into him. You don't need to be sorry for just being here." Her face contorts, and I realize she hadn't even realized she'd said it. It was just a reaction, like an instinct to apologize for taking up space.

The heat rushes me at the realization, anger at the people who have hurt her to the point where she apologizes for existing. God, what is this anger? I need… fuck. I feel like I need to break something right now.

Addison shakes her head and shrugs as we continue to walk towards the picnic area. I can see her locked in her brain, spiraling in her thoughts as she gets lost amongst them. I remind myself to wipe the look of anger from my face. Correcting my emotions in a second to be the picture of calm.

"Things did not end well between us… as you know. I am actually surprised at his audacity to speak to me." Her tone has a touch more rage than I assume she intended to give.

"Do you want to talk about it?"

"Not much else to say that I haven't already told you, I guess. We dated for six months, broke up almost twelve months ago, actually on our last trip here. He couldn't handle my moods," she says in air quotes. "I caught him cheating here the first time, which it turns out he had been doing for almost the entirety of our relationship. When I found out, he tried to justify his actions by saying I apparently wasn't easy to break up with because of how fragile I am all the time." She ends on an eye roll, but I don't miss the rage sitting on her face. I stop in my walk to the park, my mind and body fighting with each other. I really should go back there and slam that fucker's head into the ground.

The *audacity*, as Addison put it, is correct. This fucking guy. Maybe I should throw him off the pier, right into the lake with rocks tied to his ankles. Hike up to the top of the trail in the mountains behind the lodge and throw him off a cliff. *Is Addison's rage contagious?*

"Noah... are you okay?" She pulls me from my descending thoughts. I have no idea if I am okay because I have never felt rage like that before. I shake my head, trying to release some of the smoke blocking my brain.

"Addison, are *you* okay? I can't believe that you had to experience that. That an actual human treated *you* like that. I can't believe I'm going to say this, but how are you not angrier?" I say with more aggression in my tone than I planned, and I instantly regret how I handled this as I watch the walls slam down in her eyes.

"I am angry, Noah. It is my default setting. But I refuse to give him the benefit of seeing how he affects me. He has taken enough from me." She looks over her shoulder in the direction of her family at the picnic.

"Are you coming, or are you just going to stand there and pretend like you have a right to my rage?" She turns on a heel and storms towards them.

I release a breath and curse myself for being a dick. What has gotten into me? This one feisty woman strolled into my world, sunk her talons deep into my chest, and no matter how much I try to pry them out, they remain immovable. Shaking my head at my idiocy, I stroll towards the picnic area following at a distance behind Addy.

Lunch passes in a bit of a blur as I am stuck in my own thoughts about our earlier interaction with Jake. He looked about five-foot-six, maybe -seven, a pale sack of skin and bones with a very, *very* punchable face, and it makes me wonder what Addy saw in him in the first place. She keeps me at arm's length, but dated that guy for six months? I grunt as I work to ignore the way jealousy tightens my chest. Schooling my features into an unbothered placid smile, so as to appear that I am listening to the conversation, but it isn't until Addison's dad addresses her with a flat tone from across the setting that I am suddenly paying attention. "Addison, how is your study going?"

"Fine, Dad. On top of things, but we are technically on break at the moment, so I am letting myself enjoy the vacation." He ignores her tone that suggests she doesn't want to talk about it, and he continues.

"And your grades? Are you ready for exams in May?"

"Yes, Dad. Ready as ever."

"Don't get tone with me, young lady. I asked you a question," he spits between clenched teeth, finally having looked up from his phone.

Addy sighs and drops her fork to her plate. "Fine. I had some issues with one of my units, but the final assessment was good, so my grades are good. I could flunk the exams and I'd still pass with flying colors." Like our interaction with Jake, Addy isn't herself, isn't fiery and determined, she seems... like a shell of who she is. Collapsed on herself and I hate every moment of it.

I attempt to assist in changing the subject and also so I can see those gorgeous green eyes. "Lucas told me about your interview yesterday, said he was super impressed, and is keen for you to start Sunday. That's exciting?" My smile vanishes as she slowly turns her head to me, mouth agape and eyes wide.

Foot, meet mouth.

"What do you mean interview? Are you not at Phoenix Legal anymore?" Henry, her dad, demands from where he sits across the picnic table. We were introduced only twenty minutes ago as we made our way to their spot claimed in the BBQ area. I was presented as Matt's friend, and he barely gave me a sideward glance. I don't know him well but I already don't like him. His tone towards Addison aside.

Addison's eyes close, and a redness inches its way up her neck, spreading across her face. *For fuck's sake, this is probably another thing I'm going to have to apologize for.*

"Geoff fired me about a week ago. I did what you said—I asked for more work, higher pay, and a permanent position—and again, like I told you would happen, he fired me." She stares her dad in the eyes and laces her words with lethal calm. I don't miss the slump of defeat in her body language, though. I go to grab her hand under the table in reassurance and she swats me away.

That is just indigestion.

Henry rolls his eyes and scoffs a humorless laugh. "Christ, Addison. I knew those trusts would be nothing but harm to you children. You'll never learn a work ethic, always entitled and wanting what you don't work for. Did Geoff know about the issues with your grades? Perhaps if you just focused, put in a touch of effort, you'd keep your grades up and would still have a respectable job. Did you at least try to talk him down, you know, using the skills that law degree is meant to be teaching you, and negotiate a different deal?"

Fuck this guy.

Lillian, Addison's mom, who I also have just met, looks at Henry with disgust and then throws a sympathetic look at Addison. Lillian is a small timid thing, kind of reminds me of a chihuahua with the whole shaking, nervous vibe.

"Ignore him, Addy. He is crabby because of his stupid work. Some people don't know how to leave work at work. What is the other job interview for?" Lillian asks with a head tilt and a condescending tone.

"Bozzelli's, Noah's friend owns it, he helped set me up with Lucas," Addison says, poking her fork around the food on her plate.

"A bar?! You leave a secure job at a law firm to sling shots like some hussy at a bar. No child of mine would work at such a venue." Henry's tone drips with disdain and misplaced superiority.

Fury, meet limit.

Whether it's the fact I don't want to have to apologize to Addison for another thing, or just pure shock that this guy is the parent to four children and speaks this way, but fuck. It takes all my self-control to not throw him in the lake with *Jake.*

"Oh, a bar job sounds... nice? Perhaps that is just more your speed." Lillian tilts her head in sympathy and offers a fake smile.

"Mom, stop." Ava glares at Lillian, who appears confused by Ava's interjection. My confusion is the interjection at Lillian and not Henry.

Addison mutters a *'fuck's sake'* under her breath, rests her elbows on the picnic table to run her hands down her face. A mix of confusion and rage builds and fogs my brain. Addy having her claws permanently on display in every social setting, is now starting to make sense. Imagine dealing with these people for twenty-five years and see how well balanced you are.

"You know what? I don't need this right now." She scoffs a fake laugh as she gets up from the table.

"Sit back down, young lady, we are not done here," Henry scolds her like a child, but she ignores him and storms off.

I am stunned into silence and watch as she leaves. I throw her parents a glare from across the table, stopping myself from saying anything that will require me to apologize again, before I get up and go after her.

"Addy, wai—"

"STOP, Noah! God, will you just leave me alone?!" she turns and shout whispers at me through her tears. She turns again and runs, leaving me standing there in stunned silence.

She literally ran from me.

Just indigestion. I need to go see that doctor.

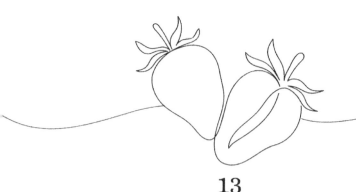

13

a challenge of idiocy

Addison

I run to my room, open the door, and slam it behind me. When I make it to the bed, I sit on the edge and rest my hands on my knees and try to catch my breath. I stand up, pacing the room, trying to wrangle in my thoughts as the words from my parents work their usual damage.

You are not cut out for the adult world. You will never be good enough. Can't you see? They fire you because they know you can't handle it. Have you even tried to show them a work ethic? Do you know what a work ethic is? All the effort in the world and you'd still probably fail. Because you can't do it.

You aren't good enough. Why would you ever think that you'd be good enough, smart enough or strong enough to succeed?

This life isn't for you.

I throw myself onto my bed and scream into a pillow. I scream until my throat burns and the tears fall without control. I sit up and let myself sink off the bed with my back against the edge of the mattress as the gut twisting sobs fall out of me with a violence, and I feel it again. The claws of misery latching on and pulling me back.

The darkness, the thick goo of defeat, slowly traveling my bones and coating every inch of my body in the numbing blackness of noth-ingness.

I don't know what else to do. How to work harder. I feel like I am at my breaking point. Am I not working hard enough? Am I not trying hard enough? Am I really just entitled and stuck in my head, expecting handouts while being lazy and selfish?

As tears fall, I feel my face go numb. My body falls slowly down the side of the bed, and I lie flat to the ground and stare up at the ceiling.

Nothing.

Insignificant.

Worthless.

The words ping-pong in my head until they dissolve into tears. Who was I kidding? My own parents don't think I am cut out for this world. What delusion have I been floating on that I thought I could do this?

Hell, my boss even had a look of sympathy when he fired me, like he knew something I didn't. *This life just isn't for you Addy, the sooner you work that out, the better for everyone.*

The sound of knocking on my door pulls me from my thoughts, but I try and fail to move my body, move my lungs or my mouth to say anything in return.

"Addy?" The soft, deep, caramel voice seeps through the door and into my bones. I manage to reach my hand up to my mouth to cover my sob. *He can't see you like this. You are too much like this.*

"Addy, please. I am so sorry I started that. Will you please let me see you?" Noah pleads from the other side of the door, and I can hear the pain in his voice. Still, I cannot pull myself from my despair. He will be better off without wearing my burdens. I will not pull him down with me.

All you do is cry and talk about your anger like it is a real thing, but honestly, all I hear are complaints, like you don't actually want to fix yourself. How am I meant to break up with someone like that? What if you end up killing yourself and I am left with the guilt of that? I have to be the one to call your parents to say I broke your heart, so you ended it. God, Addy, have you never thought about how your spirals affect the people around you?

Jake's break up speech rushes through my head as a painful reminder of why I should not have let myself become hopeful where Noah is concerned.

No. I will not let my spirals affect the people around me.

"Addy," he sighs in pain. "You don't have to let me in. Please, just know that I am so, so sorry for starting that." He takes a breath. "I just... I—" he takes another breath, probably considering if I am worth the effort of his apology. "You don't deserve to be treated like that, least of all by your parents. I had no idea. I wish I could go back and just keep my mouth shut." He sighs and I can hear him place a hand over the door. "Goodnight, Addy." And as I hear his steps fade and his door next to me close, it is like something in my chest cracks open, and I let the crying take over, being as silent as possible to avoid Noah hearing me through the walls. The body jerking, breathtaking crying that hurts every muscle in my body.

I laid on the floor for what felt like ten years, but was probably close to two hours. By the time I pulled enough strength to stand, it was dark outside. I dragged myself into the bathroom and stared. I knew. Knew the shower was a smarter choice. The lack of control I have on my darkness right now, I do not trust myself to hold it together long enough to make it out of the bath. The rest of the night was a blur of showering, dressing and folding myself into bed. The aching numbness never leaving my bones, like a robot on auto-pilot, moving because I have to, not because I have a choice or control. Sleep, thankfully, found me quickly, although not peacefully.

The next morning, I am woken up by the warm spring sun streaming through the curtains, cursing my robot state of mind for failing to remember to close them. I look up at the ceiling and run my hands over my face, feeling the guilt and embarrassment from my episode soak the numbness out of my bones. "What is wrong with me?" I grunt to myself.

The scent of breakfast cooking downstairs reaches my room, but I refuse to face anyone after yesterday at lunch. I'll just wait until the house is empty before I drag myself downstairs to chug a bucket load of caffeine. I force myself into another cold shower in the meantime, to reduce my disgustingly swollen face and to make myself feel fresh. Or, I suppose, to just, feel.

After pulling on running shorts, a top, hiking appropriate shoes, and sending a prayer that everyone is already on the trail so I can pour coffee into my soul before speaking to a human, I leave my room with brain fog in full force. I turn and run into someone. "Oh sorr—" My apology is cut short as I turn and trail my eyes up the six-foot-five length of muscle to deep brown eyes, as Noah smiles softly down at me.

"Coffee?" he says as he lifts a mug to my eye line, and my stomach drops. I wonder if he heard me crying last night. Or did the higher power hear my prayer for caffeine? I hope it was the latter.

"I promise I was about to knock. I was not just standing out here waiting... like a creep, or anything." He shakes his head. Is he nervous?

I am eager to ignore last night and pretty much ignore every other Noah related feeling, thought, or interaction, just like none of it ever happened. I grab the coffee from Noah's hand and look down the hallway, scrunching my eyes.

"Don't want to talk about it, please. Jus—"

"Talk about what?" I look at Noah then, his lips pulled into a lopsided grin, and he gives me a wink. He is playing along for my benefit. *Or for his, because he also doesn't want to get into all your drama.* I give him a half-assed smile and a slight nod of thanks as we turn and head for the stairs.

Behind the lodge is a set of different hiking tracks, one of which leads to a zipline between two mountain peaks that has an incredible view, or so I am told. I have never myself been brave enough to take the zipline, the usual overthinking and anxiety getting the better of me, and I psych myself out. The short track is the one most of us stick to as it is good for kids in that there is less of an incline and by the time the kids get bored, they are already back at the bottom. This was originally where our family would start the morning before spending the day by the lake, however, Riley, Ava, Matt, and Noah had decided to head for the track that leads to the zip. Of course, this means I can either hang back with my parents, Mia, Vicky, and George, spend time alone in my room, or follow. Time alone holds an appeal until I recall last night.

I follow.

The guys lead the way, leaving Riley and Ava on either side of me as we make our way up.

"I'm sorry, Ads. I should have intervened sooner," Ava says quietly,

I presume to avoid the guys hearing her.

"It's fine Ava, really. You aren't my keeper. I am twenty-five; I can handle myself." I don't hide the snark from my tone. I know my jab has hit home, but I refuse to be sorry. Ava is always making excuses for them, hardly ever takes my side, or Riley's for that matter, when it comes to their belittling or nasty comments. She sits silently and rolls her eyes. If only we all had her ability to let their bullshit roll off our backs.

She purses her lips and nods her head slowly.

"Addy, you're trying the zipline. You need to live a little," Riley declares, which reminds me of the similar words Rosie had said to me. Does it really seem like I'm not living?

"Absolutely not," I assure, but I don't miss the look Ava and Riley share, and I think this means I am going down the zipline.

"I can't do this," I say more to myself, but loud enough for Ava and Riley to hear. Riley is strapping herself in and Ava turns and rests her hands on my shoulders. "Deep breaths, Addy, you got this. I will strap you in myself and go down after you. It is so much fun, and you'll thank me when it is over." I swallow deeply and try to take a deep breath as Riley heads down, her scream swallowed up by the view of the lake. As I take a step closer to the edge, the view is even more spectacular than I remember. The green mountain ranges behind the lodge with a valley in between, the lake nestled perfectly in the middle, the sun shining off and reflecting at us. I take an actual big breath then. *I can do this. I will.* I look at Ava with a smile I hope exudes confidence, and nod. Before I allow her to strap me in, I inch further to the edge and get a good look at the drop to the ground and my throat slowly closes as I try to ignore the fear snaking up my spine. That is a long way down.

"Breathe," a dark whisper, so close to my ear I can feel Noah's warm breath against my neck and the heat of his body against my back. So close that if I only leaned back against him, I'd feel the hardness of his body completely pressed against me.

Hardness? Really, Addison?

I snap my spine straight and look over my shoulder at Noah's deep brown eyes and soft expression.

"You don't have to do this, you know? You have nothing to prove to anyone. It is okay to be scared."

"I am not scared," I retort without hesitation and pull myself from my ridiculous feelings. Who does he think he is, honestly? He has no idea what he is talking about. I am not scared. "Ugh." I scoff at him as I move a step back from the ledge. "How did you get back up here so quickly, anyway?"

"Raced Matt to the top. Obviously, he lost," he responds with the most arrogant smile I have ever seen. Just as I peer around his shoulder I see Matt walking, almost crawling back up the hill, puffing, and trying to find the ground with his hands. Ava is heading over to him trying to suppress her laugh. "You. Cheated. You. Prick," Matt struggles between breaths as he falls to his back and lays flat. Ava bends down to keep him company as she struggles to hold back the laugh. I return my focus to the zip swing and the death drop to the bottom, swallowing my earlier... nausea—*not fear*—as I prepare myself to strap into the seat. Looking at Noah and all his giant tanned muscle, barely tired, hardly a drop of sweat after his run up the hill, that spark of competitiveness fueled by anger inches its way up my spine.

Pfft. Dumb jock. I could run laps around him in my sleep.

Like he is reading my thoughts and feels my energy changing, he throws me one of his arrogant smiles, taking a step back, letting me do this alone. "Okay then, you're not scared. Go for it." And that is a challenge in his eyes. *Oh, you think I won't?* I glare at him as I give

him my own version of his arrogant smile and take a few big steps
back from the zipline, the cauldron of anger inside me builds from his
lack of confidence in my ability, his constant foot-in-mouth syndrome
causing him to apologize every other time we speak, the frustrating
and toe-curling dark chocolate eyes I see every time I try to sleep, it all
builds and, taking advantage of my lapse in control, I sprout the most
stupidest and spontaneous decision I have ever made.

His head tilting look of confusion morphs, and I relish in the look
of death that passes over his face as he realizes what I am doing. He
takes a small step forward as if to stop me. I steel myself, anchoring my
courage in my rage, and letting it fuel my adrenalin. I don't give him
time to say anything as I make the run up, and launch myself on to
the zipline, my hands grabbing firmly to the rope, throwing my legs
around to link as my ass hits the seat, and it takes off down the slope,
with me not strapped in.

It dawns on me then that this was *idiocy*. If my hands let go, I
will—with certainty—fall to my death, because I have decided to
one-up the macho man with my courage and leaped down a fucking
hill without being strapped in. I am now soaring down the line at the
speed of light, the trees and gorgeous view passing by in a blur. The
cold wind hits my eyes, forming tears as they stream past my face. The
fresh air hits me and I take a breath. The breath in feels like the first one
I've taken in years. It smells like spring. Like home. Like fresh grass and
pine. The icy edge to it searing the freshness into my nose and lungs
as I take in another breath, and I realize the air is passing through my
mouth, which is open, *in a smile*. Adrenaline coursing through me,
flooding my veins, I close my eyes and relish in the way it feels, the
fresh air lifting my lungs like I could fly, the joy as my stomach drops
as the line takes a slightly steeper descent, the ground of the landing
approaching rapidly. I never want this to end. *I feel alive for the first*

time in twenty-five years.

I open my eyes just in time to see the landing approaching faster than it is meant to, due to the stupidly fast speed I launched off at, and realize again that I am not strapped in. "SHIT!" I shout as the line hits the rubber tyre stopper at the end post, the line swinging furiously as it swings with momentum against the stopper, throwing me from the seat, flying past the landing strip, landing me in a collection of bushes.

I sit up in a rush and gasp for air, trying to gather my brain enough to work out what the fuck just happened.

"Addison!" Noah is there instantly, probably leaving the tip the moment I left and beating everyone to the bottom with his stupid athleticism. "Fuck! That was so stupid, Addison, are you okay?" His words are pained and laced with fury as his eyes search my body for injury.

"Addison! OH MY GOD! Are you okay?" Ava rushes to her knees in front of me, finally having caught up, and she all but shoves Noah out of the way. With a concerned look on her face, she grabs my cheeks between her hands and scans me for injury.

Riley bursts out into a stomach clenching laugh that has her falling to her knees. I can see Matt attempting to hold his back as he makes his way through the clearing, also, until he receives the no injury report from Ava.

"I... I, uh..." Can't catch my breath enough to speak.

A loud sound jolts everyone, and they stare at me with a mix of shock and amusement. The sound apparently being me, as a burst of laughter leaves my throat. I wipe my eyes of tears as I double over in a laugh, mimicking Riley. Matt finally relents and Ava stands to join him, giving only a small laugh, with concern still written on her face. Noah stares at me in confusion, a soft smile growing on his face.

"Are you sure you're okay?" he whispers. I reach to rest my hand on top of his that is resting on my shoulder.

"Yep. Surprisingly..." I look myself over and take stock of my limbs, checking if there are any aches and pains that shouldn't be there. "Uninjured," I finish. Noah's eyes haven't left mine, and the intensity of the stare heats my skin.

The air feels thicker, his grip on my shoulders tightening, and he looks to my lips for a second before finding my eyes again. His lips move like he is about to say something, but Matt coughs, chilling the charge of energy between us and walks to grab on to Noah's arm.

"Always wondered when we'd see the wild Addy again." Matt winks at me and casually pulls Noah away, putting some distance between us. Ava and Riley make their way back to me and pull me into an embrace before laughing and chatting casually about my spurt of spontaneity. My eyes still haven't left Noah. That charge of electricity lingers over my skin. *What is that?*

I laugh at myself and stand, dusting the dirt and leaves off my pants. Noah hovers nearby and searches my body with his eyes, the look of concern still plastered on his face.

"Addison, why would you do that? You could have slipped. If you had let go... you could have fallen!" Ava's laugh has now turned to a serious face. Noah looks at me and nods in agreement, his face appearing angrier.

"Want to go again?" Riley squeals as she looks at me with evil in her eyes.

"Riley!" Ava chastises.

"Ugh, relax *Mom.* She can be strapped in the second time."

I look up at the top of the hill and I feel a sense of loss in my stomach. The feeling I had, the adrenaline and the sense of being *alive,* is no longer there, and instead, it is just the same as last night, only dormant, like it is just below the surface and ready to show its head as soon as I am alone. In an attempt to harness that feeling, soak it up and hold it hostage to my heart, I mirror Riley's look and plaster the biggest grin I can muster to my face as I respond, "YES!"

Lucky for me, the rest of the day was accident free—I made sure I was strapped in this time, Noah not leaving my side and ensuring he himself had been the one to buckle me in with Ava's final tick of approval, as I chased the alive adrenaline another three times. Towards the end, Noah had the most beautiful and peaceful look on his face. I always knew he was handsome, from the very first moment he ploughed into me, but seeing him there at the bottom of the line with that look to his face, I realized that he wasn't just handsome, he was beautiful. I mean, sure, with all his tall-dark-and-handsome-Greek-sex-appeal on display, it is hard to miss. Ruggedly sexy with a gorgeous smile that sometimes tips up on one side. Briefly teasing a dimple on his left cheek, and it melts something inside me. Something molten and dangerous.

"Okay, I think I am done. Might throw the towel in before my luck runs out and I actually do injure myself." I leave the amusement to my face and direct to no one in particular. "I am going to head back, warm up with a shower before dinner." They each nod their agreement and wave me off, when I hear footsteps behind me.

"I think I might join you." My eyes snap to Noah, and I shove the dip of excitement I get from his proximity and words right down. All the way until they don't exist. He must recognize the look of alarm on my face as he clarifies, "...in my own shower, of course... I need a long shower to ease the ache in my legs from beating Matt twice, before I can consume any food." I look at him from the side of my eyes but focus back to the direction I'm headed in an attempt to avoid the growing flutters in my belly. *Just friends, remember?*

"Thank you."

"What for?"

"For today, just… being here. I think I needed this more than I realized." I admit, to my absolute horror. I shake my head and move to put some distance between us. The rest of the walk back to the lodge is a peaceful silence, and when I make it to the top of the stairs near our rooms, I stop and look at him again.

"See you at dinner?" I ask with a half smile.

"Wouldn't miss it," he practically whispers as he stares at my lips. I nod at him and enter my room, closing the door swiftly.

After lying on my bed for a few minutes scrolling socials, being in denial about the ache in my body from that first tumble, I decide that my hot shower will be my everything shower. I wash my hair, exfoliate my entire face and body, shave my legs, and do a hair mask. After about twenty-five minutes of pampering myself, I step out of the shower with a sigh of contentment. I replay the feeling I had today, closing my eyes and remembering that feeling of the crisp air flowing across my skin, the freshness of the air soaking into my lungs, dark chocolate brown eyes, panty-melting smirk, rugged olive skin, and strong forearms—*pull yourself together.*

I mourn. Mourn for every day that isn't today. For every day that I can't feel this joy.

Why do my lows have to be so low?

I can't remember the last time I had laughed so hard, or smiled so big, or felt such happiness, and so alive. A complete contrast to the feeling I felt only last night, and a picture of Noah's eyes and glowing smile creeps into my mind again. I shake my head. I cannot think about Noah, especially while I am naked.

I towel dry my hair and lather myself in moisturizer and wander back to my room and to my suitcase. I stare at the clothes I prepared to dress myself in, in preparation for dinner in an hour, and I suddenly dread having to leave this room. Having to risk losing this rare flow of joy being crumpled by my parents shitting on me. *Maybe you could grow a back bone and learn to ignore them,* I scoff at myself. Ignoring them would imply that they don't aggressively insert themselves in my business.

You know what, no.

Nope, not doing it.

I am deciding to put my foot down. I grab my pajamas and grab my phone to flick a message off.

> **Me:** Sorry, count me out for dinner. I am feeling exhausted and perhaps a little bit sore after today. I am just going to heat up some noodles and hang out in my room xx

> **Ava:** Ok sweetie, hope you feel ok tomorrow xx

Ugh, *sweetie.* You're not my mother, Ava.

> **Riley:** Nooo, don't be boring pleaseeeee

I leave it at that and decide not to read the next few messages that come in. I dress myself in my Peter Alexander emerald green silky pajama set and busy myself while waiting for everyone to leave for dinner in town to avoid any unwanted conversations. I head downstairs to heat up the kettle and make some mi-goreng, then head back upstairs to set myself up in the bed, propping up the pillows behind me and select a movie from my iPad.

After twenty minutes, the noodles are done, and I am invested in Legally Blonde. Peace. Completely at peace from the day's events and my decision to pamper myself. *This* is what a vacation is.

***

I have no idea at what point I fell asleep, but I only realize I was asleep as I wake up to the sound of knocking on my door. I jolt upright and check the clock next to the bed that reads 11pm. *What the fuck?* I sit still, wondering if perhaps I was dreaming about the knock when it comes again. I stand from the bed and walk to the door, stopping myself just before I open it. *Who is knocking on my door at 11pm?!*

"Ads, are you awake?" Noah's soothing voice makes me release a breath. "Please be awake," he whispers. My heart cracks at his tone, and I open the door, immediately finding his eyes.

His travel a path up my, now soft and smooth, legs. The path of his eyes burn into me as they caress my body, over my torso, and my neck up to my eyes where they lock with mine, and his face relaxes into a soft but pained smile. I notice then that his shirt is creased, his hair is tossed in what looks like a freshly-fucked state, and I wonder where he just came from.

"Is everything okay?" I ask, just shy of a whisper. He starts to speak and then takes a step forward before thinking better of it and looking at me.

"I... can I... uh—"

"Do you want to come in, Noah?" I give a gentle laugh, and gesture for him to enter, saving him the effort of stumbling further, and something warms in my belly at his nervousness around me and the relaxing of his shoulders as I step aside. He steps forward and grabs the door, holding it so that I can continue into the room first. *Ever the chivalrous gentleman.*

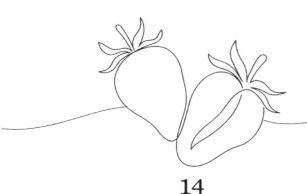

14

sweeter than i imagined

Addison

"You weren't at dinner?" I walk to the room and lean against the wall opposite the bed as he stalks in. "Sorry, it was just such a good day today, and I didn't feel like being around my parents, at the risk of them ruining it."

He stops, and I watch his expression crumple. He rubs his hands up and down his face before dragging them through his hair. His arms flex at the movement, and as he reaches up to his head, the bottom of his shirt lifts slightly to reveal the muscled V pointing south. I quickly move my eyes, trying to hide the blush that rises on my cheeks, and I look for his eyes. Eyes that are squeezed closed.

"Noah, you're worrying me, is everything okay? Did something happe—"

"No, no... well... yes, but I just... I don't know..." He releases a sigh. My brain goes straight for the worst possible situation.

"Oh, my god. Did something happen to Matt? Are Mia and Ava okay? Where are they?" I move to reach for my phone, and Noah reaches for my wrists, taking steps to close the space between us.

"No, no, no no, I promise, everyone is okay. It's not... no, everyone is fine, I am just..." He releases my wrists, and the heat of his hands linger as he sits at the end of the bed opposite of where I am standing. The look of pain across his face is so tangible I want to do something to make it go away. *God, what is it?*

I walk towards him and plant a hand on each cheek and raise his head to look up at me.

"Noah, please talk to me, is everything okay?" I whisper to him.

"I... Addison..." he whispers as his hands, dangling between his legs, move to the back of my calves, grazing so lightly they feel like feathers. I inch forward at the touch, now standing between his parted knees, my stomach almost completely against his chest. *What am I doing?*

"I think... I think I really ...like you... Addison."

Oh.my.god.

He looks at me with vulnerable sad eyes, my stomach does a colossal swoop as my heart nearly skips out of my chest. I hold my breath at his confession, unsure if he is aware of what he has just said, and I try to scan his eyes again for traces of alcohol. *Maybe he is drunk.*

"The thought of you being hurt... or someone hurting you... it just... I don't know what these feelings are, I've never... and this scares me. I—" He squeezes his eyes shut before he leans his head against my stomach, looking down at our feet, releasing a sigh and continues, his words barely a whisper "—I have so much riding on this deal, I can't screw this up. I can't be distracted and I don't *do* relationships." The grip on my claves grows firmer, the words make my heart sink while also giving me butterflies. If I wasn't already confused, I certainly am now. What the hell happened tonight?

"Noah, I don't understand what work thing are you talking about... screw what up? Wait, is this about Jake?"

His head snaps up. "What? No—"

"Then what... what is it? What distraction are you talking about?" His eyes dart to my lips before they slowly blink up to my eyes again.

He looks like there are a million words running through his brain, like he isn't sure which ones to use, how to speak what he needs to say. The pain in his face slowly fades, and a different look seems to take shape—determination, or maybe need. "You. You are my biggest distraction." The words aren't cruel. In fact, they feel laced with promise in the deep way his voice teases me.

Thoughts and questions evade me. I'm too distracted by the feel of his hands gripping my calves. My hands move from his cheeks to the side of his neck, and my head tilts slightly as my thumbs run along the sharp line of his jaw. My eyes slowly scan his face, not wanting to leave his chocolate eyes, but make their way to his mouth. His tongue dashes out quickly to wet his lips, and I instantly wonder what he tastes like.

I try to blink the lust away and snap back to reality, but his grip on my legs tightens before I can push away. His hands slowly trace their way up my legs, his calluses softly grazing a burning path behind my knees and up the back of my thighs, stopping short of my ass. I am speechless and lost in his eyes. "Noah," I say on a whisper, as his eyes darken. "You can't keep looking at me like that."

"Looking like what," he says, with a grin slowly taking shape across that beautiful face, knowing exactly what he is doing. I force my lungs to remember how to breathe and will my body to stop the warmth that is spreading between my legs.

"Wait, stop," I say quickly and out of breath. His hands drop immediately as he leans back on the bed to put distance between us.

"*Fuck,* Addy, I didn't mean to make you uncomfortable..." he scolds himself, and his face becomes the picture of pain once again as he brings his hands to his face. "*What the fuck is happening to me?*" he swears to himself under his breath, and I back away towards the wall opposite the bed.

"You don't need to be sorry. I am sorry. I shouldn't.... we can't..." I can't get the words out. *We can't do this, Noah.* What even is this? We barely know each other, and I am not even remotely cut out for a relationship. Handling a boyfriend's expectations? Hard pass. Also, there is no way he has feelings for me other than probably wanting to fuck me.

He looks up at me, and his eyes narrow in confusion.

"Addy... I didn't come here to... do... *that*, or anything." He gestures to the bed, his eyes implying enough.

"Oh..." Of course he didn't, but he didn't have to sound so... disgusted. His eyes snap back to me as he searches my face. His eyes tweak at the corners as his arrogant smile grows back.

"Don't mistake my words, Addison, I have most definitely thought about it. Almost impossible to go a day without doing so." His voice is low and rough and my body wins the battle over the growing warmth.

"Noah, I am a mess. Today was okay, but yesterday wasn't," I blurt out like word vomit, looking down at my feet and shuffle uncomfortably. "Tomorrow might be good... or it might not." How do you explain to someone the unbalanced nature of your brain chemistry? He stands and slowly closes the distance between us, leaving only inches as my back is pressed up against the wall.

"You don't have to give me an explanation, Addison, but you should know by now that your emotions don't scare me." My stomach sours at the choice of words. His eyes are burning a path across my face as his jaw clenches and his gaze turns hungry.

"What do you mean?"

He closes the final bit of space between us, the tips of my now tightening breasts lightly grazing his upper stomach as he leans a forearm on the wall above my head, my neck craning to meet his eyes. "I mean, whether it is a good day or a bad day. Even your *worst...*" he says on a grunt, "can't scare me off that easy." His face pulls into a satisfied grin as his eyes trail the length of my body, noting the pace at which my chest is rising and falling, the breathing that is a quiet pant, and my lips part on a sigh at the warmth of his body pressed firmly against mine.

"Tell me to leave, Addison. I don't want to make you uncomfortable, but I'm struggling to keep a hold on my control when it comes to you." My breath leaves my lungs. I don't want him to go, but I don't know if it's really a smart choice for him to stay. He takes my silence as his answer to stay, and I can't help but be glad for it.

Then he leans in close, his breath warm as his lips graze the skin of my ear gently. "Are we done pretending like there isn't something here?" The electricity from earlier today is back with an intensity. It burns across my skin, and I feel my face heat as the air around us thickens. I'm lost for words, surprised to find that the sexual tension I feel is reciprocated, but confused as to how—why?

I can feel his heartbeat, almost matching the rhythm of mine as he looks to my lips, his gaze hungry. "Addy..?"

"Hmm?" is all I can muster with everything happening to my body and brain right now.

"I am going to kiss you now." His voice is deep, but the words give me clarity.

"You said you don't do relationships?" I internally berate myself, like a kiss means anything remotely close to a relationship.

"I don't have answers for what this is between us, Addison, but you can't tell me that you don't feel this. That when I do this..." He continues to hold my eyes hostage as he brings a finger up and lightly drags it across my hip bone, light as a feather. The contact sends goosebumps across my skin, my heart races, and the need to have his hands all over me overwhelms me. I attempt to wet my dry mouth with a swallow and his eyes track my tongue as I wet my lips.

"...that you feel nothing. Tell me, shortcake, what do you feel when I touch you?"

His face pulls away slightly, his eyes searching mine, trying to decipher my thoughts. Hilarious effort when I can't even decipher them. I attempt breathing, focusing my thoughts, and talk myself into not overthinking this.

You're literally overthinking not overthinking, Addison.

I could do casual. I mean, look at him, I can *certainly* end my twelve-month sex hiatus, and it would hardly be a chore. Relationship is off the table, he said so himself. But could I really go there with Noah, this man-god before me, and keep my heart out of it?

Doubtful.

He is barely a breath away, but he doesn't close the final distance and I realize he is waiting for me. My answer. "Umm." Barely a breath. Words? What even are those? His grin grows, and he chuckles deeply before he speaks again.

"Addy, baby?"

"Yes?"

"Will you let me kiss you now?"

The answer this time requires no thought. I get half a nod out before his lips slam on to mine, the arm by his side coming up to rest on my lower back, pulling me to him, holding me up against him to deepen the kiss. The light touch of his tongue against my lip a gentle invitation, and I open for him. The kiss is deep, passionate, and desperate. He tastes like the chocolate of his eyes. The feel of him, his soft lips against mine, is euphoric. I don't know that I could ever stop wanting this. His tongue searching mine, kissing me with such hunger, a soft moan escapes me. He brings his other arm down and wraps the entirety of his arms around my waist, every part of his body pressed against mine. I can feel where my skin touches his as the electricity of his warmth soaks through my whole body.

Before I know it, my arms are around his neck, my hands tangling his hair with a moan escaping me as he deepens our kiss. "Fuck yes," he growls. "You taste even sweeter than I imagined."

My left leg inches its way up his calf as I, quite literally, try to climb him. He doesn't miss a beat as his hands are instantly at the back of my thighs, and in one quick thrust he throws me up, my legs hooking around his waist as he slams my back against the wall, pulling his lips from mine, kissing his way along my neck and across my collarbone.

"*Fuck.*" Noah's hoarse voice vibrates through my body as my hips roll against him. He releases a grunt, his hands tightening against my waist and pulling me down against him, as he kisses down my neck. "I have thought about this since I first saw you."

My breathing becomes labored as he continues his wet kisses over the skin of my neck, my collarbone, his hands searching and pulling at the neck of my top.

"The feel of your skin, the taste of your lips. Your claws curling my hair and pulling." His voice is rough as he describes the act my hands are engaged in at his scalp.

"*Noah.*" I am not sure if it is a moan or a whisper, but my body is calling for him. The need for more skin, more of him, is beating against my chest with urgency.

"Tell me, shortcake."

"You. More. *I need more.*" He pins me to the wall with his hips and his legs as he makes quick work of grappling the back of his shirt and pulling it off over his head, instantly discarding it. Not missing a second before his lips are on mine again.

"That Monday, when I walked you home. I wanted to kiss you."

He stops and stares at me. *God.* He did hear me talking to Riley. "I didn't want to freak you out. Hell, I didn't want to freak myself out, but fuck, I wanted to kiss you so bad. I wanted to do *more* than kiss you that night, Addy."

"What did you want to do to me?" I ask on a whisper, excitement and something else making my heart skip as I struggle to slow my breathing.

"How about I show you?" His eyes make their way back to my lips, our breaths intertwining. The heat emanating from his body is making me insane. I can't form a coherent thought, can't say anymore words. More. I just need *more.* Noah's lips are crushing against mine again, and I meet his kiss with the same force and vigor. I roll my hips again as I feel the hardness of him pressing right where I need him, and I release the kiss, biting down on his bottom lip and dragging it with me. He grunts in approval before he grabs my waist with enough pressure to bruise in an effort to still my undulating hips, and he leans his forehead against mine.

"This isn't going to last much longer if you keep that up, Ads. If I am going to show you what I wanted to do..." He kisses me again, slowly, deeper, "...I am going to need all night long," he says between pants. Having him unleashed is officially something I need. I slam my lips back on his, arching my back off the wall and pressing myself against him. Finding my confidence grounded in that cage of fury that builds the foundation of my soul.

"Save your restraint for round two. Unless you don't think you could back it up again?" My seductive tone is unrecognizable, as my words have their intended effect. His grip on my waist tightens as he moans into my mouth, and my hands grip into his hair, pulling gently.

"Is that a challenge?"

"Call it a test. Don't make promises you can't keep, Noah, telling me you'll keep me up all night. Here I am hoping I don't get a wink of sleep."

Who is this person and what did she do with Addison?

His chuckle is deep and dripping with sexual prowess. He moves his hands, gripping me just under my ass as he pulls me away from the wall, my legs still wrapped around his waist, and he walks us over to the bed with our lips locked.

"I knew that fury and that mouth would be trouble in bed." His devious smile should be *illegal.* I all but groan at the sexuality just oozing from him.

He lowers me slowly to the bed on my back, his hands caress my body through my clothes, his thumbs landing just under the swells of my breasts. My legs remain hooked behind his back, and I tighten them to bring him closer. He moves a hand from my ribs to beside my head to support his weight as he hovers over me. Eyes locked on mine, the desire I feel coursing through my veins reflected back at me. Eyes of the only person to ever truly listen to me, eyes that feel like they see exactly who I am, right to my very soul. Those damn chocolate eyes that make me want to throw caution to the wind and give him my entire being.

His free hand moves to the buttons of my pajama top, undoing the first one before he stops.

"Yes," I whisper. Because despite the colossal mistake this will be for the health of my heart, that is not the body part in control right now.

My brain? Left the building.

A soft smile grows on his lips as his hands move from button to button, his eyes exploring my face before he lowers his head, leaving kisses along the path of my stomach in the wake of my now undone buttons.

"While there are a number of things I wish to do to you, Addison.

I want to take my time exploring with you." My heart squeezes, and every sane warning call wants me to tell him no. Despite practically demanding a round two, I want to instead tell him no, *this is a one time thing, Noah, make it count.* I lose my words of warning as his touch lowers, a light dust of his tongue for every kiss he leaves against my stomach.

The ache between my legs grows to the point of pain the lower his kisses go, and it's all I can do to stop myself from grinding up his body. The deep chocolate of his eyes sear into me as he looks up from the kiss he leaves just above the waistband of my pajama shorts, the calluses of his free hand move to part my top so my breasts are exposed, and his eyes soak them in. He rises up to bring his lips flush with the stiff peak of my nipple, sucking and pulling it into his mouth, letting it go with a *pop*. My hands are instantly tangled in his hair, pulling, my back arching off the bed, now desperate for friction between my legs, and he releases a low and deep chuckle under his breath. "You going to lie again, shortcake, and tell me you don't feel this between us?" Noah's thumbs lightly graze the skin of my breast, pulling my other nipple into a pinch as his mouth restarts its trail of kisses down my stomach, to the strap of my shorts. He slowly inches my shorts down, leaving alternating kisses every inch down my thighs. It isn't until he discards my shorts on the floor behind him, sitting back on his heels as he stares hungrily between my legs, that I realize *I forgot to put on underwear!*

"Umm..." Self-consciousness slams into me, and I start to close my legs as his hands grip my thighs, his eyes burning into the center of me.

"You don't need to hide from me, Addison." The last bit falling on a whisper as he climbs back up my body to steal my mouth in a searing kiss. He pulls back again and the loss of his touch frustrates me. I couldn't care less if he wants to sit back and ogle me. Need, *I need him.*

His eyes meet mine again, *screw this, I'll take what I need*. I sit up on my knees and practically leap on to his lap, planting my knees on either side of his thighs, straddling him, instantly latching my lips to his as his arms catch me, wrapping firmly around my waist, a surprised groan leaves his mouth, and I feel him smile into our kiss. Our kiss is wet, desperate, and my hips roll against his jeans, his hands move, searching my back, making their way to my ass where he squeezes before he releases one hand and brings it between us. He teases my inner thighs, and I release a sigh as he gently slides one finger straight down my middle.

"*Fuck,*" he says into my mouth before pulling away to lean his forehead against mine. "You're this wet for me already, shortcake?"

"You plan on talking me to completion? Because if you don't do something soon, I'll come without you." The sexual deviant in me has lost all control, and the depth of Noah's smile smacks me right in the heart. *Fuck, he is pretty.*

I close my eyes, my head tilting back as he softly kisses down my neck. "Patience, my little devil. I want your screams to be heard in Hell."

My God.

His fingers circle my sensitive peak, my hips rolling without control as each breath becomes labored. "Beautiful. You are the most beautiful thing I have ever seen, Addison." His free hand slides up to the back of my neck, interlacing his fingers in my hair and pulling gently, bringing my eyes to his. "That fierce attitude and curvy ass have been stuck in my head since I first saw you. Now I want to never stop hearing your moans as I touch you, and hearing the sound of my name on your tongue as I make you come." His words completely undo me. He takes my mouth again in a possessive kiss as he pushes a finger into me. Adding a second finger, I think I might be on fire as he pumps into me at a slow and teasing pace, alternating between his thumb and palm to circle my bundle of nerves. My breathing gets shorter, my heart rate quickens, and my inner walls tighten, and Noah picks up the pace.

"*Noah,*" I breath on a moan.

"Yes, shortcake?"

"I need..."

"Tell me what you need." His eyes sear into mine with a desperate intensity. "Tell me, Addison, what does your tight little pussy want? Say the words."

"*I need to come,*" I release on a moan, and he pushes me to the bed, my back landing on the mattress as he lands on top of me, moving his body down so his head is between my legs.

"I want to see if you taste as sweet as your lips. I want to taste you as you come undone. Are you going to be a good girl and come on my tongue, shortcake?" *God,* who is this man? As a person who needs to be commended with praise constantly to avoid feeling like a failure, he all but makes me combust with his words.

I wrap my legs over his shoulders and intertwine my fingers in his curls, and his tongue devours me. My back arches off the bed as he brings his fingers back to my center, thrusting in with determination. His tongue sucks and teases my peak.

"*Yess, Noahh,*" I breathe as my back arches more, his teeth lightly graze my clit as he curls his fingers around to trace my sensitive spot, his tongue grows hungrier, my inner walls tighten, and my stomach muscles clench as the coil of my orgasm constricts, the tingles beginning in my toes and working their way up my spine.

"Come for me, Addison," he growls into me, and my release barrels through me at his command, Noah's name on my lips. He doesn't stop, his fingers slip out of me slowly, but his tongue laps up every drop before easing into slow kisses as my body rolls through each wave, kissing his way back up my body. He lies on top of me again, one hand beside my head, the other he brings to his mouth, his eyes never leaving mine, as he licks me from his fingers and whispers, "Divine."

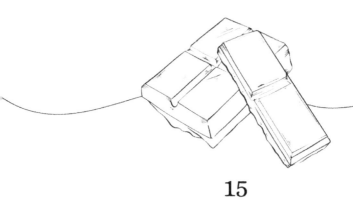

15

sappy words and insanity

Noah

I didn't come to Addy's room to seduce her into letting me touch her, not that I am complaining. I came here... to just tell her everything. The reason I'm here, the meeting with Matt before dinner, the conversation I overheard. Everything. I wasn't going to take this step with Addison until there were no secrets. No lies. Well, I don't know if it really is classified as a lie or rather an omission? I also don't know if that distinction really matters, or if I am just trying to make myself feel like less of an ass for keeping it from her. I practically pulled my hair from my skull on the walk over, trying to come up with ways to tell her everything. Each scenario I played out in my head ended up with her crying, distraught, upset, angry. After hearing her cry through the walls, the sound of her heart breaking, I just couldn't bear to witness that again.

All the things she would never turn to me to help her with—I mean, why would she? *I don't do relationships.* Tell that to the aching organ in my chest. Instead, she would let herself suffer alone. And then she opened the door in those tiny pajamas, with the softest legs I'd ever seen, and her scent knocked my brain around and I suddenly couldn't think straight.

She is now lying in my arms, in her bed, my chest still bare, her completely naked and sated tucked under my left arm. Her leg is hooked over my lower stomach and she draws idle circles on my chest as my hand rubs circles down her back. The whole thing feels perfect, like this is exactly where I should be, and it scares the fuck out of me. I have no idea what is happening, in my head, in my heart, or this *thing* between us. I don't know how to explain any of this, how to make sense of it. All I know is that this feels like something I want to do more than once, something that isn't just fun. Something that would have had Noah from twelve months ago running for the hills. One thing I know for certain is that I want Addison. I want all of her.

I feel her head tilt to look at me so I move mine to look at her. *Truly beautiful.* Something in my chest squeezes and my mind wanders for a moment.

When you know love, you can't live without it... it feels like slicing through flesh and nerve, leaving the endings open to the wind. Death is a kindness when your heart is taken away from you.

I shake the memory of my mother's haunting words, the words that are to blame for my no-love oath. Perhaps the mental warning is too late, because there is only one word I think and feel when I look at those furious green eyes.

Mine.

Addy seems to pick up on my accelerated heart rate as a smirk grows and her hand casually makes its way down the plane of my stomach. I grab her wrist before she dips below the belt.

"Addy, I didn't come here for this."

"Oh..." Her body tightens, a flush hitting her cheeks.

"Wait... no, I didn't mean it like that." She starts to roll away, but I tighten my grip on her as she lays to her back, and I sit up on an arm to lean over her, our mouths barely a breath away, and I give her the only words I can.

"I mean, I came here for you. To make sure you were okay... I had no... expectations. And please don't mistake my words, I very, very much enjoyed myself." I gesture to the growing tent in my pants as I recall the sound of her breathy pants as she came on my tongue with *my* name on hers. "But... I don't...." Why is communicating so fucking hard? "...know how to do... this."

"What do you mean, this?" she asks, and fuck if her expression isn't completely unreadable.

"I..." I don't know how to say anything. My stomach is in my throat, twisting and flipping. The part of me telling myself to keep my distance is at war with the part of me that wants to claim her as mine, tell her about the feelings coursing through my veins, that I'll wait for her to catch up, but I can't go another day without her. *Fuck.*

"It's fine, Noah. This doesn't have to be anything. Fun, right? We can have fun?"

Fun. *Fun.*

"Of course." I hope the pain of her words is hidden from my face.

Fun.

Well, fuck me sideways, Addy, the ache inside me feels anything but *fun.* My heart feels like it might stop beating. The thought of her being anyone else's, or that there are people in her life that hurt her, continuously, makes me murderous.

But I *can't* feel that way, right?

I look deeper into her eyes, hoping she can see the words I cannot say. I cough to clear the silence and pull myself away from her.

"Well, I should... ah, I should probably get going." Before I make a complete fool of myself.

"Wait, what? Where are you going?"

"Your whole family is here, Addy. We don't need them to know about any of our... *fun.*" I wish I did a better job of hiding the snark in my tone, but it's late. I'm exhausted, with a raging boner, and a head full of words I shouldn't say. I need to get out of here, clear my head, work out what the fuck is happening to me.

"Oh... are you sure... you don't want me to..." I look at her and see her gesture to my pants. Yes, Addison, I'd love nothing more than to fuck you into next Tuesday, to know how it feels to slide my cock between those pretty lips. But for some reason my man-brain has left the building, and I also want to hold you, kiss you, make *love* to you, and then tell you a bunch of sappy words that would have Caleb questioning my sanity.

I don't say any of that. I give her my most confident smile, lean back over, and place a soft kiss to her lips, and whisper, "See you soon, Addison."

I leave the room and head straight for my suitcase.

16

professor genius reporting for duty

Addison

"See you soon, Addison." Of course, Noah doesn't want to stay. He isn't going to want a bar of me when I practically threw myself at him. Shame and second-hand embarrassment flood me. After Noah left my room last night, I struggled to find sleep, meaning I woke up with a mad migraine.

Unlovable.

The stupid thought hangs in the black void of my mind. I didn't expect Noah to just fall in love with me. I thought at the very least we'd have some casual sex, you know, scratch the itch caused by *that thing* between us he kept talking about. But instead, I'm frustrated and annoyed that he left. What's worse is that he left because I'm a big dummy and doused our chemistry with the word *fun*. Fun?! Like I have any sense of the word when it comes to men. I have never been a casual person in my life, and here is a guy, solid dream boat with a mouth of dirty words and a body carved in heaven, that was cuddling me, and I said *fun*. Honestly.

I tell myself that I am not pining for him. No, not him, just... the touch of him. I don't even know if it is him specifically or just a man, in general. The touch, feeling wanted and desired. Because for a few minutes there, it really did feel amazing to have Noah whisper and moan about my body and how I felt against him. The buzz ended, as he obviously would rather be anywhere but naked next to me. Sure I said fun, but he didn't have to run for the hills like fun with me is the worst idea ever. *You're overthinking again.*

Maybe Rosie is right—and I will deny saying this if she asks—maybe I should download a dating app and get back out there.

I remember the promises I made myself after Jake, that I'd never let a man dictate my emotions or my heart again, not to get attached. Well, Noah just had to go and give me the most mind blowing orgasm of my life without even removing his pants. The image of his pretty mouth, that talented tongue and soft lips, is suddenly in my mind, and I have to shake myself. No more, Addison. You screwed the pooch on that one. That was it—he left. I shake any thoughts that are of the Greek sex god variety as I roll over on the bed, dragging my eyelids open, and blinking in the subtle daylight streaming in from the curtains.

I am unbothered.

Not a care in the world.

I'll go downstairs and pretend like it never happened. Let's see him try to avoid *that*.

Noah who?

Damaged goods.

Another word that slips the barricade I tried to put around all the hideous dark thoughts that take up a permanent residence within my mind. This one stings more. The words are my own and yet they are the result of another. My therapist has worked tirelessly trying to help me see myself as something else. It is harder to do in the wake of rejection.

Indifferent. I will be completely unaffected by him. I won't give him the satisfaction of my sadness. I will just simply give nothing, and I will be damaged goods no more.

I grab a cup of coffee from the kitchen and decide I will give myself some much needed exercise and fresh air to clear my head. Putting my mug down on the island bench, I sit at the breakfast nook to pull on my runners when I hear my name, ending my growing enthusiasm.

"Addison, where are you off to?" I cringe as I hear my father's voice approach from the stairs.

"Run," I say with a clipped tone, not turning to face him. He continues to stand to my left, I presume, waiting for more of an explanation.

"Ah. Nice day for it. Just want to say that it is important to make sure you put more feelers out for a real job when you get home. You don't need to be stuck in a bar forever." Literally can't make this shit up. *Give it a rest.* I laugh under my breath and shake my head at him before standing, meeting his gaze. "Perhaps I can give Geoff a call, get him to recon—"

"No. I don't need your help. I can take care of myself." He shifts uncomfortably, and I make to push past him toward the wilderness and fresh air beyond the front door.

He reaches for me, but like he sees me recoil on instinct, he drops his hand. "Addy. I am…" he squeezes his eyes closed and says the next bit through gritted teeth, "sorry."

HA!

Firstly, at his sorry excuse of an apology, but secondly, that a father is *struggling* to apologize to a daughter he belittles and ridicules constantly.

I turn to face him again, keeping the needed space between us. "…uh…okay. What is this apology for?" I raise an eyebrow at him and search his face, trying to connect with his eyes.

"Everything... I guess." He looks at his hands and shifts uncomfortably again. He isn't usually so shifty around me, he's usually more confident. It feels like... guilt? My stomach tightens. It feels like a gut reaction to him. After all these years, I can tell he's done something, and he feels guilty. And fuck if I couldn't care less what he has done now. I shove the feeling down and remove the question from my mouth.

"I know I don't always say the right things. I know I am not father of the year. I don't know when our relationship became so strained. I don't.... I don't understand how to fix this." He looks at me then, with sad eyes. Half of my heart breaks for him. The part hoping the dad I miss would come back to me, and I find myself wishing we could put everything behind us. Picturing the feeling of being a parent and staring into the eyes of a child who despises you, doesn't want anything to do with you. A child who you raised. A child who you taught to ride a bike and used to prank your other kids with. Because that is the dad I miss. The dad who used to laugh with me, used to take Riley and me to the DVD shop on a Friday as a treat. Before I can say anything, he continues. "Am I too late?"

"Too late for what, Dad?" My tone laced with the exhaustion I feel deep in my bones.

"To get back to where we used to be. I know I am not a good dad. But it doesn't mean I don't want to be. I want to... try more." I force my eyes to close to blink back the tears threatening to break through as I remind myself of all the horrible things he had said to me in the last five years. Damn him for making me feel this guilt, but the need to connect with him, to feel his acceptance, his pride. God, I wish I could make him proud of me. To love me unconditionally. He says all these things, but I wonder if he'd retract the apology if he knew I was considering never working in law after graduation. That I'm glad I was fired. I wonder how conditional this show of concern and remorse really is?

"Dad..." I release a pained sigh, "I—"

"Morning, Addy. Hey, Dad!" Ava's cheerful morning voice sounds from behind me, and I have never been so glad for an interruption. "Oh, sorry, I didn't mean to interrupt..." she visibly stiffens, recognizing the tension between us "...I'll just go—"

"No need. I was just leaving." Dad looks down and stalks for the stairs, my stomach sinking at his lack of fight to finish his apology. Ava turns to me, and I give her a pointed *don't ask* look, and she looks me over, replacing her look of concern with her trademark smile.

"Going somewhere?"

"Yes, actually. A run. Fresh air, wilderness."

"Ooooo, want company?"

"No." She winces at my short tone and I have instant regret. "I mean, no thanks. I just need to clear my head and... well, you know our morning personalities hate each other." I try, and fail, to add some humor to the last line.

"Ahh. No worries, babe. I hope you're okay." She rubs my shoulder, leveling me with a soft smile, then heads for the kitchen, and I leave for the hiking track.

The hiking track was quiet, the air fresh like every year. Spring is everywhere, the view clear, and the sun coats the distance like a warm blanket over the pretty green hills. At the top of the second highest track is a lookout over the lake and the mountains beyond; it is breathtaking. There is a bench seat right on the edge, and I park myself there for a few minutes. Or maybe hours. I've lost count at this point. My eyes closed, head leaning back on the seat as the sun warms my face, and the wind lightly kisses my skin. *Breathe.*

I try to ground myself, remembering the hard work I have done for myself.

You have people around you that love you. Rosie, Casey, Ava, Mia, Riley, Matt. Jessie, in his own way.

Remembering the mantras and the techniques that my last few therapy sessions taught me.

You are significant.

The last few weeks have been filled with such negative internal monologues it feels strange, yet refreshing, to try to replace them.

You are powerful. Loveable. Intelligent.

You. Are. Significant.

I remember now, my therapist telling me that every time I have one of those thoughts that are sent from that barricaded part of my mind, to throw one of my own back at it.

So much to live for. So much pain would be felt if I left.

So why is it so hard to believe it? I wish... it feels selfish to feel and think this way, but I wish I had someone in my corner who just *got it.* Who knows that a few quick tricks don't change my brain chemistry. Who knows that a hug, a walk, fresh air, and water don't suddenly make me feel like living is worth it. For everyone who is 'in my corner', I have to placate them. Dull down the severity of my *issues* so I don't scare them. So they don't feel guilt over my sadness, so they don't sit there for the next ten minutes giving me solutions that are just annoying. Or, god forbid, try to put me in a care facility like Mom tried.

Noah gets it.

I shrug off the thought. Noah doesn't get to take up space in this moment.

The need for a fresh start, to wipe the slate clean, is so tangible. How much easier would life be to enter a world where no one knew me? I could be whoever I wanted to be, and no one would be the wiser. No one would walk on eggshells, afraid to be the cause of an episode. No one would look at me with pitying eyes, wondering how long I'd last until I break. No one will make me feel good things and then just turn and leave, '*see you soon, Addison.*' I scoff at the memories and shake my head.

I will be that for me.

I can be my own person. Be in my own corner. I have to be—what other option do I have?

"Hey stranger, fancy seeing you out here."

"Aunt Dadi!" Mia yells and throws herself on my lap, Matt following and sitting on the seat beside me.

"Hello, munchkin." I grip on to Mia as she wraps her little body around me. Mia's hugs are always the best. Five-year-olds have the purest of hearts, and those hugs are packed full of love. I kiss the top of her head, and she relaxes into an embrace as we settle in. I turn to look at Matt. *Ugh,* I know that look. I roll my eyes at him.

"I didn't even say anything."

"You didn't have to," I grunt out. "Go on, then... say whatever it is. I am surprised your blonde handler isn't out here with you." Matt laughs under his breath.

"My manhood would be grateful if you could at least pretend that I run the show." His face is all humor, and damn if he doesn't make it hard to hide my smirk. "We're just worried about you, is all." He knocks my shoulder, but I keep my gaze on the view, twirling Mia's curls in my fingers as she plays with the zip on my jacket. "A lot of things were said. We just... wanted to see how you were. If you needed to talk." One day, everyone is going to forget about all this bullshit and realize how fucking strong I am. If it's the last thing I do. Holding Mia is about the only thing keeping my temper down at this point. The only thing stopping me from growling the words I really want to say, *I am not some fragile piece of glass with handle-with-care plastered on my forehead.*

"I'm fine," is all I grunt out. Matt assesses me, and I can see the look in his eyes. He is under orders to get more out of me, and it's setting my veins on fire.

"Matt, I am not a child. If you want to ask me a question, then just fu—dging ask me." I correct quickly, realizing there is an impressionable child in my arms. Matt doesn't waste time, about the only thing I appreciate about this conversation.

"Ava mentioned she interrupted a conversation between you and Henry, she said you looked upset after, and was worried because you'd been gone for so long. She and Riley went with Vicky and Lillian to the mall, so I figured I'd come find you and see if you want to hang. Take your mind off things."

"Dad tried to apologize."

"For yesterday?"

"Honestly? I have no idea. Felt like more, but I wouldn't be surprised if Mom just tore through him and made him come say something. They probably don't want Christmas to be awkward." I try to laugh it off, but Matt doesn't fall for my bullshit. "He asked if it was too late... I assume for my forgiveness? Maybe for us to be normal together? I have no idea."

"He's a dick. You just have to ignore him." Great advice. Thanks Professor Genius. Matt shrugs, happy with his wise words, but remains assessing. "Noah left." A statement, which I am not sure where he is going with. My cheeks heat instantly like I'm wearing *'he went downtown on me last night and it was awesome'* written on my face, as my stomach sinks. He left without even saying goodbye. It shouldn't hurt, but it does. I labeled it as fun and he just accepted that.

Not worth fighting for.

"Oh?"

"You guys seemed to have become chummy... anything I should know?"

"And why would you need to know anything?" I try to keep it light, but I don't think my tone has ever known how to be anything other than snarky. Matt giggles because, like all sunshine people, nothing bothers him.

"Just checking. I see how he looks at you. I was just hoping he wouldn't be dumb enough to make a move." I don't let the way his words hurt show. Of course, Matt doesn't want someone as damaged as me tying down his friends.

Damaged goods.

Was it me? Did I do something last night that freaked him out? Is it my body? I'm not delusional to think I'm a Victoria's Secret Model, but I run. I *try* to eat well enough, but it's hard when energy is involved in cooking. So I suppose by 'eat well', I really mean my diet consists of fruit from the free basket at the market and ramen noodles. Oh god, maybe it was me.

My positive work comes undone. The worst thing is Matt has no idea. He thinks he means well, and this is part of why I hate being here. Being so incredibly misunderstood, no one understands what it's like to be so in your own head. How words that feel and sound nonchalant dig the deepest holes. I squeeze Mia and ignore Matt's comments.

"Want to go for a swim, kiddo?"

"YES! Can I get my unicorn floatie?"

"Of course! I'll help you blow it up." I look at Matt and give him a soft smile. He watches his daughter with love all over his face, and it warms me slightly. Kids really do just make things seem brighter.

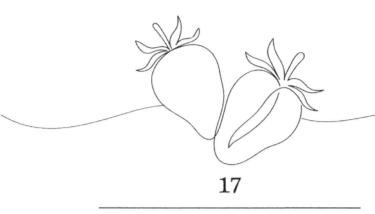

17

denial is a river in maplewood

Addison

The rest of the trip was a blur. Noah had apparently left the morning after he left my room. I didn't allow myself to feel anything by it, or at least pretended not to feel anything, or by the fact that he didn't say goodbye. Not even a text.

Dad and I barely made eye contact, and he didn't try to finish his conversation. I guess he didn't feel it was necessary. Mom had managed to seclude me for a few minutes the day after my soul searching hike to ask how I was doing. "Have you met anyone since Jake? It would be a pity if you let one bad egg ruin your outlook on love, dear." It takes every ounce of self-control to not tell Mom to focus on her own relationship before she tries to throw advice my way. Although, something tells me she is very much aware of the mess of her life and is doing everything in her power to remain sane about it.

Ava, Matt, Riley, Mia, and I mostly went on hikes, spent nights in town at the restaurant, and played games for the remainder of the trip. Riley told me about her plans, wanting to move into the city to be closer to us and JJ, to perhaps finally think about going to college and starting her life. "It would be nice to go to a bar and pick up a guy that wasn't in my preschool photos, you know?" I laughed at that, around the table playing cards with Ava and Matt. Mia sleeping soundly in her room. Vicky, George, Mom, and Dad outside by the campfire.

"Plenty of fresh meat in NYC Ri. You won't be able to get enough," Matt quips, and Ava and I both smack him in the arm.

"If you need a place to crash for a bit while you get on your feet, you can stay with us for a bit?" Ava offers.

"I might have to move to a cheaper apartment soon. Now that I am on a smaller paycheck, we can probably look for something together?" I give, as well, although secretly hoping she declines. I love my sister, I do, with every ounce of my being. I am really just not great at living with my siblings. Or anyone. Rosie and Casey seem to be the exception, and so far the only one.

"Thanks, it's okay, though. I have a friend in the city who will probably live with me, or I have been looking at campus housing, too, which could be fun."

"Campus housing is good, typically gender separated, though." Matt winks at Riley.

"Oooo okay, probably not so fun then," she levels with serious consideration.

"Playing by the rules never seemed like your style?" I quip back. Her devilish grin grows and a deep chuckle sounds from her throat.

"The wild side is more fun." Devil child. "So why did Noah leave?" Riley says to Matt while looking me dead in the eyes. I give her a pointed look. *Don't you dare.*

"Said he had a work emergency come up and needed to get back."

Ava looks at Matt. "Is this about—" Matt nods, and Ava doesn't finish, replacing her smile with a look of concern. "Hmm, he didn't say anything to me? He is also only two hours away and has cell reception.

Why didn't he just handle it from here?" Ava asks and Matt gives an unbothered shrug.

"Who cares? Who's turn is it?" I thought I said that without sounding bothered, but by the three sets of eyes burning into my soul, apparently I did not.

"Did something happen between you?" Ava questions.

Matt sits back in his chair, appearing relaxed, but I read his expression. He is curious, and considering our recent conversation, he is probably all too aware of whatever is going on with Noah and me.

"We aren't doing this. Nothing happened. Why would it? I barely know him, and he is Matt's friend. We just ran into each other a couple of times and he happened to join Matt on this vacation." Yeah, sounds like nothing happened, Addison. I cross my fingers and toes that they change the subject. They do not.

"Mmhmm. Unconvinced. The night you didn't come to dinner, he was looking over his shoulder every five seconds. Finally asked where you were, and when we gave him nothing, he was tense. I swear he went looking for you at one point, came back furious, and then excused himself without so much as a goodbye to the table," Riley fills me in.

"What time was that?"

"Mmm I don't know, maybe 9pm? I was practically asleep at the table waiting for everyone to stop socializing so I could leave."

So he left the restaurant at 9pm and at 11pm was knocking on my door looking disheveled and stressed? What on earth happened in those two hours?

Not your business. He left.

I shake my head. I don't care. Nope. Not my problem.

"I don't know. Can we drop this because I'd rather just keep playing the game." I nervously look at Matt, and he misses none of my body language. His stare is assessing and borderline lethal as he sits back in his chair, the picture of calm, sipping his beer. The girls give up their hunt for information, and the conversation continues as the game commences.

I manage to make it the rest of the trip without so much as a thought about Noa—he who shall not be named.

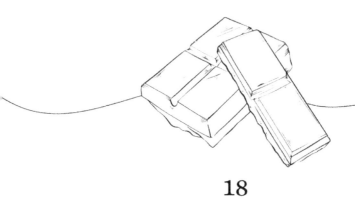

18

noah and addison, sitting in a tree

Noah

I end my phone call and throw my phone to my desk as I stalk for my window. The view only turns my already nauseated stomach into tighter knots, and I have to make like lightning to the bathroom down the hall from my office. As I run, ignoring the curious looks from my staff, my skin feels clammy, my heart is racing, and panic grips my chest, recalling the promises I made.

Mamá, everything is going to work out once the contract is settled. I'll have more equity to buy that building in Chicago we talked about. I'll hire more management staff, and then I'll be around for good. You'll be sick of me, I promise.

The contract is not settled. In fact, this new information makes me worried the contract will never settle, and not only will I get hell for breaking a promise to my mother, but I'll also have let my dad down, never making good on that promise, either.

Don't settle for mediocrity, son. Chase your dreams and leave a legacy worth being proud of.

I burst through the toilet stall and land on my knees just in time to retch up my entire lunch. *Him.* All of this—everything—at risk because of *him.* That dirty fucker. Lying, cheating motherfucker. Fucking hope I did the right thing. I did the right thing. *Right?*

Retching up breakfast, then last night's dessert, I wipe my mouth and breathe. She would have gotten home Saturday; it was now Monday morning, and I have heard nothing from her. Matt didn't mention anything about her over the phone or how she was, whether my leaving had upset her. Not that it matters, we aren't anything to each other. Honestly, I could have texted her, left a note or something, but my stomach is in knots and my head is in shambles. Between this deal circling the drain, my shame of disappointing my mom, and not living up to my dad's legacy, I all but feel like I'm a moment from crumbling beyond repair.

You left without saying goodbye.

I had to. I returned to my room, slept like shit for four hours, packed my bag, and hightailed it out of there. The need to go back to Addy, lay next to her, pull her into my arms and feel her warmth against me and tell her fucking everything, was agony trying to ignore. I retch again over the memory of what I had overheard, my call with Matt, and when I have nothing but stomach acid left, I stand and clean myself up at the basin. Looking at myself in the mirror and reminding myself to *get a fucking grip.*

"You did the right thing. Now is not the time for distractions. This moment is why you swore off relationships. Focus. You need to focus." Right? I look myself in the eyes and try to keep the pep talk going. "You don't get attached. Leaving was the right thing. Stop it before it gets worse." I don't even think I believe the words coming out of my mouth. Being closer to Addison is what would make this go away. The ache. She only wanted fun. I don't think I could do *fun* without getting attached to her because she's... *god.* I can't describe it. And the last thing I need right now is to get attached. It is nothing but a distraction, when this shitshow that just blew up at work is going to need all of my focus and attention. But, Addison has sunk her claws into every inch of me, my feelings for her are not as shakable as I had hoped. I can't fall for her, *I can't*.

☀

By the time I stalk back to my office, Caleb is waiting for me, throwing the toy basketball in the air as he lounges sideways in the armchair across my desk.

"What can I do for you, Mr. Smith?" I give him my best sarcastic smile.

"Are you pregnant?"

"Are you high?" I retort.

Caleb straightens on a laugh. "Well, there has to be some explanation for someone as cool, calm, and collected as you to be throwing up in the toilet?" Probably should fill him in. "The whole office could hear you. What is going on? And don't give me some bullshit lie, or I will call Ethan right now and he will give you the no-fuss serious guy chat." We both shudder at the same time.

Ethan, who is Lucas's older brother and went to college with Matt, Caleb, and I, is your typical non-nonsense finance guy. If he heard I was getting myself tangled up with emotions about a woman, he would say *grow up and tell the woman how you feel, or apologize and cut her out so you stop hurting her feelings. Put your big boy pants on, Karvelas, and stop fucking around.* But if he knew what had me so tied up I was struggling to keep food down, I'm sure he'd be a little more lost for words.

"I had some developments with Matt over the weekend about EcoX. It isn't good." His face goes white, and he slumps back in his chair. "Shut the door and I'll explain everything." I gesture to the open door behind him.

"Caleb, it's Monday night. Why did you order tequila shots? Are we not just here for one beer?" Ethan groans from the end of our table at Pucks. What is beginning to be a Monday night ritual of late, a beer with the guys at Pucks, watch some ball, and relish in the Monday blues.

"Trust me, if you knew the shit we were dealing with right now, you'd be slugging shots, too." Matt grunts as Caleb, Matt, and I throw back our shots. Ethan and Lucas give each other side eye, sipping their beer and refraining from finishing their shot.

"No work talk. I need a break. This shit is fucking with me." I run a hand down my face and stop any more conversation about EcoX. This is going to repeat on a loop in my head until it's solved. I just want a few hours of peace.

"Alright fine. What's up with you and Addison?" *Oh, for fuck's sake, didn't I just say peace?*

"Nothing is up with him and Addison. Right, Karvelas?" Matt levels me with a deadpan, sipping his beer.

"Right." I avoid eye contact, and Lucas snickers under his breath as I level him with a silencing stare. I have no idea what Addy has told him, if anything. I can't imagine it's much considering her first shift was yesterday. The thought of her already being close with Lucas, though, annoys me for reasons I am trying to ignore. But I plan to keep whatever those feelings are from Matt for as long as possible.

"Liar," Ethan provides his two cents, and his shit-eating grin establishes that he knows exactly what trouble he is stirring up.

"You were all torn up over her before you went away. Surely there is development there." Fucking Caleb.

"Seriously, Noah. C'mon man, I asked you to stay away." Matt's less angry, more resigned, almost like he knew this would happen.

"Look, she is an adult. As am I. I appreciate you wanting to look out for her, but I think you need to respect the decisions she chooses to make. Which I'm sure you'll be happy to know she shut me down." The guys, save for Matt, almost simultaneously spit their beers and laugh at my pathetic admission. Matt smiles and just shakes his head.

"You're going to need to provide details on that." Caleb states.

"At Maplewood... well, I kind of...well... we... well, *I*—"

"C'mon, say words, Noah, you're a big boy," Ethan chastises. I release a grunt, which was meant to be a sigh, dragging my hands down my face.

"She is under my skin. I don't know how or... *why*. I just can't stop thinking about her. She *certainly* doesn't like me the same way."

Fun.

"I think I blew it when I pretty much rejected her right after..." I cough awkwardly, glad I was able to stop myself before saying too much with Matt present.

"You dirty dog. You fucked De Luca's sister?" The size of Caleb's smile should be illegal, *Christ*. "No!" I direct mostly at Matt before he decides to land a punch to my jaw. "We didn't, we just had... a moment, I guess. A few moments. I don't know how she does it, but I just... ugh I fucking *feel* things, and I would like to stop. Feeling. Things." I hate myself as the words come out. I make myself look the guys in the eyes. Ethan is contemplative, Lucas is just enjoying my pain and total lack of game, Caleb's shit-eating grin reminds me why I never talk to him about serious shit, but Matt remains pensive, almost unreadable in his expression. Caleb is all but bursting at the seams from holding his laugh, his face almost purple. Before he finally relents and laughs in my face.

"Oh god, Karvelas, you have it *bad!*" He shakes his head a few times, his smile dying as I lean back in my chair and screw my eyes shut.

"Wait... isn't *finally* finding someone who doesn't bore you to death, and makes you actually feel things, a good thing? Isn't that, like, what people want?" Lucas chimes in, obviously confused by my pained look.

"Not what I want. Or at least it wasn't."

Ethan gives me a serious look. "Look, it's been a while since I have dated seriously, but we're thirty, or at least some of us." He looks to Lucas, who rolls his eyes. "Are you really going to just stay single forever?" Well, yeah, that was the plan... "And what about your very Greek family? When do you plan to tell them that you aren't giving them grandchildren because you prefer the bachelor life? If that were me, my Nonna would have a heart attack and then proceed to slap me around with a sandal." Lucas gestures the Sign-of-the-Cross, while Matt raises his beer in agreement. I think of breaking that news to my mother, and then I think of the novel-sized lecture I'd receive following that.

"Look, this conversation is pointless." Addison just wants fun. I have lost count of the number of ways I'd have *fun* with her, and none of them involve settling down, but I also don't know if she really knows what she is asking for. She doesn't strike me as a casual-sex kind of woman, and for some reason, I'm struggling to come to terms with her being like every other one-night stand.

"Okay, buddy, whatever you say." Caleb gives me an unconvinced smirk and heads for the bathroom as he sings on his way out. "*Noah and Addison sitting in a tree...*"

"Jokes aside, if you're actually serious about her, I won't stand in your way. If you make it work. I will still kick your fucking ass if you hurt her. If this is something you are just getting out of your system, you stay the fuck away, Noah. I'm serious." That he is. Matt looks a bit like he has blown a gasket with the redness of his face. *Jesus.* I nod at him and give him a thankful smirk. Glad he wouldn't stand in my way, but also anxious. I don't know what this is between us. I don't want anything to become between Matt and me, and I certainly don't want to cause issues between them. Then there is the shit with work that is really where all my energy and brain power should be spent. I just... Honestly, I haven't got a clue what I'm doing.

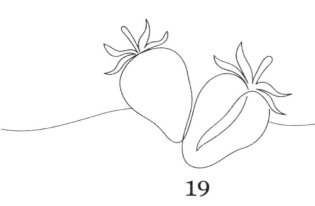

19

men, who needs them?

Addison

"The final revision lecture is on Wednesday at 3pm. If you want a chance to actually succeed in the final, I suggest you attend." The sound of my professor's condescension rakes down my spine as I exit the class and make a bee-line for the train, but perhaps this is the reason he has the highest attendance out of each class. So far, the intellectual law unit has been the smoothest. The final semester has been a bit more of a breeze than I had imagined, managing to squeeze my internship in while I was at Phoenix Legal last semester, IP is manageable, employment and tax law, those last two however, have been absolute killers. The Bar prep course is a fucking snooze—maybe because my heart isn't in it? These are just more anxiety inducing thoughts I am shelving for a time when my mental capacity has expanded, or I implode, whichever occurs first.

As I leave the train and walk down the street to my apartment, I applaud myself because I studied like crazy from the moment we got back from Maplewood. I had an excellent first shift on Sunday, and I managed to keep a certain tall-dark-handsome giant completely out of my thoughts. Well, almost completely.

I did have one or two moments in a daydream—remembering his lips, mouth, tongue. "Ugh, pull it together." Scoffing at myself as my thoughts wander there again on the way home.

See you soon, Addison.

The four stupidest words, and I still can't get the sound of his voice and the feel of his breath across my lips as he said them out of my head. I'm angry at myself, again, the usual feeling I get post Noah-induced thoughts.

"Woah," I grunt at being caught in my display of rage as I slam the apartment door closed behind me. I really need to stop being caught like this.

"I want to burn all the men," I say, looking out the window, blinking back the tears that are trying to escape as fury tries to find a way out from under my skin. The rage that picks something small, something inconsequential to latch on to, and fester until my skin thrums with a furious energy I can't expend. Casey and Rosie share a look.

"You've barely said anything since you got home. Have you heard from Noah since Maplewood? Maybe he doesn't know you're back?"

"I am sure he knows. I am sure he and Lucas have pow-wowed about me already. Sharing their judgments and side notes."

That probably isn't fair to Lucas; I barely know him. We've worked one shift together, and he has been a perfect gentleman. Slightly on the flirty side, but it's all been above board. After that one night with Noah, though, Lucas's flirty attempts didn't even make me blush. It was like my attraction gauge was completely broken and I felt nothing. Another thing that just pissed me off more.

"And what makes you think that Lucas is judging or giving notes?" Casey asks, knowing I don't have an answer. Noah's silence and the way he has ruined other men for me is just making me take my rage out on an innocent person who just happens to be of the same gender. I release a sigh of defeat.

"You know, he was the one who left *me* in that room. I see no effort being made on his end. And, anyway, we barely know each other. He gave me one mind-altering orgasm. That doesn't mean I owe him my heart." Not that I plan on giving anyone my heart. *You told him it was just fun.*

Casey nods and Rosie storms to her feet across the couch to give me a very intense high-five. "Damn fucking straight. Fuck that guy. Men, who needs them? Not us!" I look at Rosie and I decide she is right. The only thing men seem to be good for is one thing. And Noah was very, *very* good at it.

"Ooo, I like this look. Please tell me what you're thinking." Rosie cuddles up to my arm while Casey shakes her head, lowering her face to her palm.

"Oh, this can't be good," she says, huffing a laugh. I pull out my phone, and harnessing my fury and need to forget Noah, I log into the App Store. I flip the phone around and show them what I am now officially downloading.

"YES! Welcome to the SoulSwipe club. I can't wait to discuss our adult sleepovers together." Maybe the perfect thing I need to get Noah out of my system is to get under someone else. I was ready to try fun with Noah, maybe I can just try fun with other strangers. Rosie does it all the time. How hard could it be?

"Ugh, Rosie." Casey chuckles and gets up, walking towards the kitchen. "I am going to need a very big glass of wine for this."

"Hey, just because you've been out of the game for four years doesn't mean Addy can't join the fun." Rosie sighs.

"Yeah... about that..." Rosie and I share a look, then, snapping both of our heads and swiveling our bodies to lean on the back of the couch, we look to Casey who is standing in the kitchen.

"Umm... Connor and I broke up... this morning." Rosie and I audibly gasp at Casey's reveal, and surprisingly calm state. Four years she and Connor were together for.

"Oh god, Case, are you ok?" Rosie asks, and I bite back a similar question, knowing how much I hate to hear that sympathetic tone.

"Surprisingly okay. I was just honest with him. He doesn't prioritize me or our relationship. There was no intimacy, no loving looks, or exciting passion. We kind of just existed in this partnership. I mean, he hasn't stayed over in six months!"

"So, how did it happen?" Rosie asks quietly.

Case pours herself a glass of wine, staring into it as she huffs out a sigh. "How much time do you have?" she says sarcastically, but I can feel the pain in her words.

"All the time you need." I smile up at her as she makes her way back down to the couch.

"How about something stronger than wine?" Rosie asks gently. Casey and I laugh, but agree.

"You ready?" I sing-song out to Casey where I wait for her in the kitchen. I agreed to go to one of her classes, which she believes will help me to center myself, calming the anger that is overstimulated at the moment.

"Yep!" she calls from her room, and I lace up my runners. "Stop for a coffee after? I saw this new shop on the corner near the studio open and they have this weird Chocolate Matcha I want to try." She hums with an enthusiasm that reminds me why I hate morning people. I laugh softly at her, and when I stand to meet her at the door, I notice the slight redness to her eyes, the sadness she is so good at pretending she doesn't have.

"How are you doing, Case?" I try not to put too much pity in my tone. I know how much I hate to hear it. But I hate to see my friend hurting even more.

She shrugs and smiles softly at me. "I'm okay. Really, I think I will be better off. I need this space to grow. I didn't realize how much Connor was holding me back, how much energy it took to be there for him and look after him. I think I really just need someone who adds value to my life, rather than sucking up all the energy." It amazes me how self-aware she is, how strong and courageous she is. Without thinking, I wrap her in a tight hug that she returns. Letting go of the sadness with ease after pouring her heart out to Rosie and me last night.

She gave us the full rundown of the breakup. Connor, despite being the same age as us, was an actual child. He has so much growing up to do. Even if he didn't, Casey is years beyond him, anyway. I'm convinced she'll end up with an older guy. She'd have to if she wants to find someone on the same maturity level that she is at.

"You inspire me," I tell her. My tone is joking, but I mean it from the bottom of my heart. I aspire to be like Casey. She giggles softly as we leave the apartment.

"Just us today?" I ask, noting there is no one else but us in the studio.

"I thought it would be great for you to have a session alone. Show you the power of meditation for when you're at home, but also, because you're my best friend and I own this studio, so we can have alone sessions whenever we like." She laughs and we walk—well, she skips—through the main reception to the back studio. The studio might be owned by Casey and her older sister Grace, but it *screams* Casey in the design. It is all natural woods and greenery, modern design touches, with soft LED lighting. Walking in here feels like walking into some relaxing spa retreat in the middle of the rainforest. Not like we're on the Upper West Side of New York City.

As we enter the back studio, the lights are dimmed, the sound of Yoga music fills the air softly, and the scent from a lavender diffuser fills the room. Two mats are already rolled out, and Casey guides me to one. Facing the mirror, we sit down, side by side.

She walks me through a range of exercises that focus on controlling breath and focusing on the way the muscles move and stretch over our bones and under our skin. It is truly magical—the way her gentle voice and the control of my breath makes me get completely out of my head, even if it was for a few moments.

"So to cool down, we're going to sit in a cross-legged position, ideally, lifting your feet to rest on your thighs in *padmasana* if you can. But don't stress if your flexibility doesn't allow you to." She does it with ease, but I settle for just sitting cross-legged. "Resting your arms on your knees, palms face up, bring your thumb and pointer finger together and stretch out your other three fingers." I do as she tells me to, and I almost lose my composure, wanting to laugh as I look in the mirror. The position looks like the cliché yoga position to the point I didn't realize this was *actually* something they did. She notices my expression and she smiles as she explains. "*Gyan mudra.* Can help with blood flow to the brain, with focus and concentration. Also, it can help you to keep a stable and rational mind when practiced often enough. It is said to help alleviate symptoms of stress, tension, depression, and sleeplessness." She says it all softly, looking through me knowingly as she takes a deep breath and closes her eyes. I appreciate that she hasn't pinpointed all of those things within me. Hasn't outright said I am irrational, only allowing me to take this opportunity to learn a method of coping. If I wasn't trying so hard to stay within this moment with her, I think I could cry and wrap her in a hug. I whisper a quiet, *"thank you."* I see her soft smile before she chastises me.

"Close your eyes, breathe."

So I do. Letting go of all the things I am sure will be waiting for me the moment I leave this studio, but I let myself breathe and just exist here. Enjoying a rare moment of internal peace.

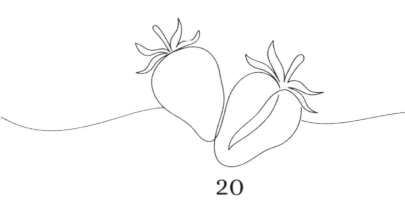

20

you are my problem

Addison

"I'll have the steak, rare, and put the sauce on the side. She'll have the salad."

Manners apparently aren't important anymore, and also, I'm having a salad? I was actually looking at the seafood linguini, but I guess that decision has been made for me.

Eric looked nice in his picture, seemed to be charming in his messages on SoulSwipe, but two minutes into this date, and I'm ready to bail. I was looking forward to dinner, so I had decided I would eat and flee. Now that he has ordered me a fucking salad, well, I don't know if I can wait for the food to come. Secretly, I can't wait to tell Rosie, 'I told you so.' I agreed to this date because of her, and I'm quickly regretting that decision. I didn't think casual sex would be so hard to do. A population of nearly 8.5 million in this city, and not a single bachelor who is decent?

"So, Addison, tell me about yourself." His smile is condescending, and I wish I could throw my glass of water on him.

"Oh, um... well, I'm in Law School, and I work—"

"Yes, I saw your profile, but tell me about *you*. You know, like what makes you special. Sell yourself to me." Gross.

His smirk picks up at the edges as he leans back casually in his chair sipping on his wine, and I fight the urge to physically cringe. This arrogant motherfucker. If only Rosie were here, I wouldn't need to say anything. She'd promptly apologize to me for making me agree to this atrocious date, then she'd flip a table on this guy.

"If she needs to give you selling points, then you don't deserve to be on this date." My back stiffens at the intrusion, but a warm buzzing coats my skin as that rich caramel voice approaches from behind me. I can't believe this, of all places.

"Okay, guy. You're interrupting my date." Eric doesn't even make eye contact with Noah. He just picks up and looks at the wine list.

"I know exactly what I'm doing. I think you're done here." Noah pulls the drink list from Eric's grip and slaps it on the table, which causes Eric to finally meet his eyeline. I see the gulp he swallows as he assesses the human giant towering over him. Probably working out his chances of winning should they need to test their masculinity and throw hands.

Noah stalks closer to the side of Eric's chair, his posture stiff and face pulled into a scowl, the kind I've never seen on him.

"Excuse me? Do you know who I am?" Eric Matherson, or the Sales Manager for Greyson Property, number one putter on the green, and a beast in the sack—according to his dating profile. "Anyone who puts that on their profile has BDE. You don't claim to be good that publicly unless you are," Rosie had explained, except I think she might be eating her words later. At least one of us would be eating. This is why you don't select dates based on looks and a guess as to whether they will measure up to the ghosts of orgasms past.

"A guy about to walk out of this restaurant."

"Noah, what are you doing?" I whisper-shout to the imposing Greek god standing beside our table. That spring scent, deliciously intertwined with his cologne, threatens to make me forget I'm mad at him and trying to move on from him right now. He's dressed casually, a simple sweater and pants that fit snugly against the muscles of his legs, that backwards cap ruining my ability to pretend he isn't attractive. The outfit is so at odds with the upper-class vibes of the restaurant, but patrons don't seem to mind. No, because the other women in this venue seem to be admiring him all the same.

"Saving you from a miserable night." He levels me with stern eyes, does a quick once over on my body, before turning away with a half-smile that could drop my panties in a flash. *God damn hormones.*

"Look, I don't know what your deal is, but you need to go. We were just getting to the good part." Beast-in-the-sack levels me with a wink that makes me lose my appetite, and unfortunately, I just can't do this anymore. Can't force this on myself, I just know the sex wouldn't be worth it.

"Actually, I think I should go. Early morning and all." I throw the napkin to the table and Eric stands. Noah moves to my side, not-so-subtly placing himself between me and Eric, satisfaction plastered to his face.

"Wipe that stupid look off your face. I was going to leave, anyway," I whisper for just Noah's ears, and his smile turns to a frown.

"Did you honestly think you'd find what you were looking for in this guy?" he taunts me, that deep voice making all kinds of promises he has no business making. He ditches me, goes radio silent after that little moment we had, and then, what? Is pissed I'm dating. Absolutely not.

"It certainly wasn't with you," I hiss at him as his anger visibly increases. "Besides, what I'm looking for is none of your business.

What are you even doing here?"

"Saving you. Like I just said." His words clipped and a little bit of fury makes its way up my spine.

"So you're following me now?"

"Sorry, am I interrupting here?" Eric clears his throat. I honestly completely forgot he was here. This is unsurprising, as Noah's presence apparently makes me lose my mind. See also: lapse of judgement in Maplewood.

"Actually, yes—"

"No, sorry. He was just leaving. So was I," I say, interrupting Noah's sentence.

"If anyone should be apologizing, it's him," Noah grumbles as he pulls my chair out enough for me to step away from the table. I make to grab my bag, but he does it for me, placing it on my shoulder. "I can't believe that this is where he brought you. A first date. Like this is worthy." I don't know if he realizes I can hear the words he is saying, his face is pulled into a scowl and he sends daggers across the table to Eric, who has now pushed his chair in and is looking at us with a mixture of confusion and disgust.

I'm not sure what Noah is so concerned about. The place was actually nice. Despite the over-inflated sense of self that Eric has, he picked a modest, if not elegant, Italian restaurant. Relatively reasonable prices and a sophisticated interior design that sets a mood, each table having enough space to have a sense of privacy. I make a mental note to come back here soon so I can actually enjoy it.

Eager to leave this testosterone pissing contest Noah and Eric seem to be stuck in, I turn and head straight for the exit. I make it to the pay counter and Noah is hot on my heels, calling my name, and I continue to ignore him. Before I have a chance to pull my purse from my bag, Noah hands over his card to the waitress.

"What do you think you're doing?"

"You already had to waste your time, I'm not going to let you waste your money on that piece of shit and a fucking salad you didn't even get to eat." His tone is judgy at the mention of the salad and my stupid hormonal brain wonders what first date Noah would have been like.

"You didn't answer me before. Why are you following me?" He nods and does a quick, polite smile to the waitress as she hands him a copy of the tab and takes his card to scan, before he locks his eyes back on mine. The energy between us is electric like always, an unexplainable intensity that seems to sit between us, like a bomb frozen in the last second, bound to explode at any moment.

"I didn't follow you," he all but growls. "I walked past the window and saw you in here with that douche." His face is set in a scowl and he gestures to Eric, who strolls on past us, doesn't even say goodbye or attempt to pay, but instead, openly flirts with the waitress near the entryway. Pig.

Swallowing the embarrassment that I apparently didn't warrant any farewells, or at least for him to fight to keep the date going. I jut my chin out to feign confidence and direct my fury at the appropriate person. "And what? You thought you had a right to crash? You do realize what I do and who I see is none of your business, right?" Not that this date was going anywhere, and I'm not overly upset about being interrupted. But what if this date happened to be with the one and he just ruined it? "Noah, you don't get to do this. You left *me* in that room, remember?" His frown deepens, the anger coming off him is like nothing I have ever seen on him before. Kind of a refreshing change, and if I wasn't so annoyed about my lack of sex tonight and this caveman act he was putting on, I might even laugh.

He pinches the bridge of his nose and heaves a sigh as the waitress hands him back his card. "I know... Addison." The words are practically a grunt, and he opens his eyes, the deep chocolate brown burn into me, like he is trying to communicate a million things he can't say. Things I can't read or decipher. Probably things I really don't want to address or get into, so I turn on a heel and leave, shaking my head at this stupid night.

Storming out of the restaurant and into the fresh spring air, the night calm and clear, and the street buzzing with activity as I begin a walk up the street while ordering an Uber.

"Addison, wait a second." Noah comes up beside me, his firm grip on my waist as he pushes me away from the road, making room for himself. I say nothing, rolling my eyes. Stupid caveman.

I try to keep my attention on my phone and ignore the way his proximity makes me feel like I'm on fire, steals the breath from my lungs, and has me aching in places that should absolutely not be aching.

"How's Bozzelli's?" Oh, we're pretending like he didn't just crash my date?

"Good, Lucas is a great boss. You wouldn't know he was only twenty-five." My words are clipped, and he is undeserving of my conversation, but this is just what happens when he is around. I lose the grip on the solid walls I have in place. What I give him about Lucas is only the truth, anyway. No harm keeping casual conversation about casual things.

Lucas does manage to keep everyone in line and everything running smoothly. Despite his modesty and lack of confidence in how well he is doing, he is killing it. I have helped out with a few behind the scenes things. He's run into a few supplier issues, and he leant on me for support. Probably a bad idea because now he throws more admin shit at me when I'm there for the earlier shifts. I'm not too bothered by it. It actually breaks the shift up a bit and keeps me busy. Keeps my mind busy.

Noah nods, looking ahead, and his hands stuffed in his pockets.

"What were you on your way to do when you walked past?"

"What?"

"You came in and crashed my date, Noah. I imagine you had other plans tonight?" I softly chuckle at his obvious frustration and the way he has no idea how to deal with his feelings. I'm not about to tell him any of that. Not my guy, not my problem.

The anger at him ruining my chances of getting laid decrease rapidly, especially considering it was probably more of a save than anything else.

"Oh, I was just on my way to meet the guys. I'll catch up with them another time." His voice is low, and he still looks like something is bothering him, not even meeting my eyes as he continues. "I don't understand why you were out with him."

"Because I'm a grownup, and I can see who I want to see." My tone taunts him, taking pleasure in his rare bout of frustration, and I think I might sense some jealousy there.

"But him, Addison? Surely you have more self-respect than that." Okay, we're done playing nice now.

I come to a stop in his path, surprising us both and forcing him to look at me. "That's enough. What is your problem?" I practically growl at him as I poke a finger into his chest. The contact sends shock waves through me, warmth spreading as I feel his heart beating rapidly.

His brows scrunched and body held tight with tension, his eyes search mine, for what, I have no idea. Before I can ask anything else, he heaves a sigh and grabs my hand that is poking a finger to his chest, as he shakes his head. He wraps his hand firmly around my wrist and pulls me slightly to him, mouth mere inches from mine.

"You. You are my problem." His voice is deep and gravelly and

practically oozing sexual promise as I feel the warmth from him vibrating around me. That always-there tension between us pulled taut,
and without my permission, my stomach flips. I lick my lips, desperately trying to ease my suddenly dry mouth as a few tense seconds pass
with him staring at my lips.

My phone beeps and a car pulls up beside us, severing the tension
like a slap to the face. My Uber. *Thank the heavens.* My chariot, here
to save me from more bad decisions.

I don't waste a second. I pull away from Noah and practically jump
into the car, closing the door. The driver wastes no time pulling away,
and I turn behind me to find Noah on the street, watching as I drive
away. I ignore the sinking feeling at the sudden loss of his warmth and
the way seeing him turns me into a hormonal sex-pest wanting to feel
his lips and his touch on me again.

That tingling lingers, and it makes me recall the way his lips felt
across my body, making me wish he had just made a move, whether I
was ready for it or not. Torn between wanting him near and wanting
him out of my system completely, I remember the way those eyes bore
into me, the feel of his breath on my lips as he had whispered his
goodbye at the lodge.

See you soon, Addison.

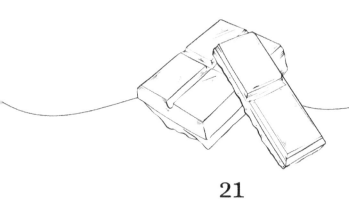

21

no longer interested? unlikely.

Noah

'What are you even doing here?'

Great question, Addison. Wish I knew the answer. I was on my way to Pucks and happened to walk past a mid-tier Italian restaurant and turned my head at the right time to see a pair of familiar green eyes and golden hair that had me double taking and backing up so fast I nearly tripped.

Through the window, she sat facing me without even seeing me. I couldn't see the guy she was sitting with, but I didn't need to. She looked about as comfortable as someone forced to sit in a pile of shit, and I knew he was going to be a straight-up fucking loser. No idea why or how, but I was suddenly in the restaurant and making a plan to save her. I have elected to ignore the fact that one thought about this sleaze running his hands on Addison, touching her in the ways I had, and hearing those same sounds, had all but turned me into a raging caveman. She was right—it was none of my business. What she didn't realize was that I, apparently, don't give a fuck.

Obviously, she wasn't nearly as affected by our time in Maplewood as I was, but I'm also surprised that I had her wrong. I picked her as a relationship woman, but she was definitely looking for a one-night stand. If the shitty pick in date wasn't a dead giveaway, her outfit sure as shit was. She tucked those perky tits into a tight black dress that left nothing to the imagination. Fuck-me heels and legs for days. One look, and the memory of being between those legs, was about to get me arrested for public indecency for the tent about to grow in my pants. One look at her sorry excuse of a date, I knew he wouldn't deliver, and the thought of him trying made me want to drive him down to Maplewood. Have him, Henry, and Jake meet each other at the bottom of the lake.

The buzzing from my phone pulls me from my violent thoughts about the other night as I had stood there on the street watching until Addy's car had disappeared. Eager to get this call over with, I click the green answer button. "Yeah?"

"Well, hello sunshine, lovely to speak to you, too."

"What do you want Ethan? I'm not in the mood." Unless the mood is murder, and the subject's name is Eric. Eric Matherson, the jerk from Greyson Property I'd seen his ridiculous billboards, and his website is absolute trash. Fuck, Addison gave *that guy* a chance. Between him and Jake, her douche-radar needed some work.

"You didn't show up at Pucks, and you've been uncharacteristically quiet. I'm just checking in." No, he is fishing. I know this because I'm in the office, and Caleb has also already tried this on twice today alone. Making small talk and hanging around more than usual. All the urgent work and stress about big deals meaning nothing in the wake of catching Addison on a date. *How many other fuckers is she taking to bed who don't even deserve to breathe the same air as her?*

"Fine, tired and busy. Do you need something?" He chuckles at my grumpy tone, and I roll my eyes at his ability to remain unbothered.

"Well, we're going to Lucas's tomorrow night, as in the bar. I was wondering if you would actually like to join us this time?" He didn't need to clarify that it was the bar. I'm sure the plan wasn't to head to Lucas's house, that he shares with two twenty-five-year-old children. I suppose Ethan hasn't quite gotten used to using the name of the bar, considering it is his last name, too.

I release a sigh and throw my head back against my office chair, thinking over my options. Staying in would mean lying around and pretending I'm not thinking about Addison. Having a quiet shower that would be inevitably interrupted by thoughts of Addison and lead to more frustration that all the '*self help*' hasn't been able to solve as of yet.

This is getting ridiculous; I barely know the woman.

Fed up with the fucking chokehold Addison has on me, I decide a night out at the club will be perfect. Pick up some stray and get Addison out of my system for good. "Yeah, count me in."

"Perfect, we'll see you there."

"Oh my god, you're so funny!" I really wasn't, but Hannah here is eating out of my hands, and if it means ending this sex-hiatus and getting a certain Strawberry Devil out of my mind, I'm in. I sip my beer and nod at her as she wraps her hands around my bicep, pulling herself closer to me.

I'm trying, I really am. Hannah is gorgeous. She has a short brunette bob shaped nicely around her sharp jawline, a stunning smile of white teeth, and curves that would look nice on top of me. But still my brain is just, *meh*.

"Lucas, can you come to the bar? We're having some issues with one of the patrons being a creep." Felix, one of Lucas's newest hires, comes over to our table and pulls Lucas away. He rolls his eyes and gestures that he'll be right back, and I catch the end of their conversation as they walk past me.

"We cut him off, but Addy can't get him to piss off." Fuck's sake.

Well, I'm not just going to sit here like a chump, am I? A woman is being harassed. Any normal man in their right mind would help out. It has nothing to do with *who* the woman is.

Nothing.

I follow behind Lucas, who surprisingly asks no questions, and I see Addison on this side of the bar clearing glasses and the harasser in question attempting to feel her up.

Burning, murderous rage floods my veins, and I do the best I can at containing it as we approach them. Before Lucas or I can do a thing, Addison spins on him after he finally lands a solid grope of her ass and places a firm slap across the guy's face. The blow sends him stumbling back, decreasing the level of rage and increasing how fucking hot she looks in those black jeans and crop top. "Fuck off, you creep!" she shouts at him.

Damn.

"We good here?" Lucas asks as he towers over Mr. cop-a-feel. Height is a common theme among the Bozzelli's, with Ethan being an inch or two above me. Lucas probably around the same, but our touchy friend here has a hell of an alcohol ego because he stands under Lucas's furious gaze like he could throw down and win. My money is on Lucas and those balled up fists.

Leaving the animals to their dick off, I turn to Addison. "Hey, are you okay?" My rage dissipates almost immediately when I look at her; the only person able to make me feel this at ease, forget every bit of stress from work, and every other person on the planet by simply existing in my presence. Also manages to make me lose any bit of focus, and any brain cell that remains evacuates completely when those eyes look at mine.

"Oh, God, you are literally everywhere." She picks up her tray and turns for the bar. "Noah, I'm working, go away." Not likely. Hannah, who?

"Just wanted to make sure you're okay. No need to get your panties in a twist, shortcake." I give her one of my lazy grins as she faces me, now standing behind the bar. That rage of hers working its usual damage to my self-control and making my desire for her grow rapidly.

So. Fucking. Hot.

Lucas has wrangled some security and managed to manhandle the perpetrator out of the bar, leaving me with Addison. I take a seat in her section and watch her as she busies herself.

"Why are you still here?" She levels me with a bored look as she polishes a glass, and I sip my beer with a shrug.

"Looks like you could do with a bodyguard. Maybe I'll perch here all night and make sure no one else tries something similar."

"You are such a caveman." Again, I shrug, but I don't miss the smirk she tries to hide.

She heads for the other end of the bar, not giving me a second glance, and like the spell she puts me under has followed in her direction, I somewhat come to my senses and scold myself for still hanging around.

Out of the system. Get her out of your system.

The feelings she stirs up inside me are ruining my focus and my sex life. I flick my head over my shoulder and see that Hannah has now moved on to Caleb. Great. Now Addison has ruined that, too. I pull out my phone and open SoulSwipe. Maybe I'll get lucky and find another match that can get this Addison bullshit out of my head.

"Jesus fucking Christ." Of course, the first profile in my search of 'closest singles' is the tiny demon that haunts my dreams. I drag a palm down my face and look over my shoulder to make sure she doesn't magically appear and see me as I click on her profile.

'*Law Student & Bar Tender–Just looking for some fun.*' Goddammit. This woman. She is practically advertising herself as a target. Does she not pay attention to crime statistics?

You don't even pay attention to crime statistics. But that is not important.

Addison finds herself back in my area of the bar, and I throw the phone in front of her and she stares at it. A pink blush reaches her cheeks as she pretends to be unbothered.

"And?"

"Fun?"

"I know the concept is apparently new to you, but sometimes people enjoy it."

"Fucking random strangers and putting yourself in danger?"

"No, you fucking idiot—*fun.*"

"And you think you'll find this with Eric?" She rolls her eyes and huffs a humorless laugh.

"You know, I offered you fun, and you left a Noah-sized hole in the wall from running so quick. Just because you couldn't handle it doesn't mean I can't."

"I never pegged you for a hit-it-and-quit-it type of girl."

"I'm a whatever-I-want-to-be type of girl. I don't need you or anyone else trying to boss me around."

"Oh, I think you like being bossed around." Her blush deepens, and I watch her tongue closely as she licks her lips. Those raging green eyes lock onto mine as she leans forward on the bar. The energy between us is enough to get me hard, let alone the passage between her breasts that sits in my eyeline as she leans closer.

"You'll never know." She looks at me through long dark lashes, her voice a tease as I grip my beer and restrain myself from grabbing that ponytail and tugging her lips to mine.

"Is that a challenge, shortcake?"

"No, it's a fact. Missed opportunity for you, and unfortunately, I'm no longer interested."

The way her breath comes in fast, and the way she has to lick and bite her bottom lip, tells me differently. I take stock of her features. An arrogant smile pulls across my face as I relish in this discovery. Oh yeah, she still feels this tension between us, too.

"We'll see about that." I wink at her and throw a tip on the bar as I head back for the table with the guys. After a few steps, I throw a grin at her over my shoulder, pleased to find her watching from where she stands behind the bar, head tilted. Definitely checking me out.

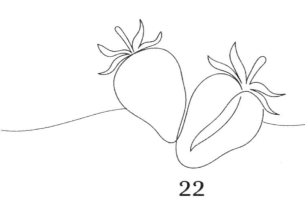

22

entering hoe era

Addison

Four hours. Four long and draining hours I have sat on this bed, nose buried in the *Copyright Act 1976* making me wish I could pour acid in my eyes because I think that might be less painful. The only positive right now is that from my position on the bed, lying on my stomach, resting my head on a pillow, and looking out the floor to ceiling window of my bedroom, I can see the sun setting over New York. Painting the sky in purples and blues, it sends a warm glow through my bedroom, bouncing off my clean white walls and white furniture. I try to keep my room minimal, plain white bedframe and side tables. There is a desk in the corner by the closet, but the bed is much comfier. And comfort is a necessity when my brain feels like it has completely dried and shriveled, leaving nothing but air in my head.

"You taking a break soon, Ads?" Casey says as she strolls through my open door and plops herself on my bed. I slap the text book and laptop closed and roll onto my back, stretching as I go.

"Yeah, I think that's exactly what I need."

"Perfect, dinner is up, anyway." She perks up and skips out to the kitchen, calling out to Rosie as she goes. Casey is our resident chef. She is constantly in the kitchen, if not baking up delicious and healthy treats, its gourmet meals that would rival any grandmother's secret recipe.

"I'll grab the wine!" Rosie calls back, to absolutely no one's surprise.

We settle at the dining table and Rosie pours us each a glass. "Oh my god, your chicken pesto pasta is my fave!" My stomach growls in appreciation and my mouth waters at the scent.

"How's that book going, Rosie? Have you finished the edits yet?" Casey asks as I shovel the most delicious food you'd ever taste into my mouth, refusing to come up for air.

"Amazing! We're almost finished with the first few chapters. I'm so psyched about this one and the MMC—oof. Girls. You want to heighten your standard for men? I'll give you an advanced copy and you can make notes because this one is elite." Casey and I chuckle and sip wine as Rosie tells us about the book she's editing. I hear my phone ping and I grab it from my pocket. Rolling my eyes, I swallow the groan that travels up my throat as I see who has messaged me. This guy will not leave me alone. Just let me get over you in peace. I can't enjoy any other date because tall-dark-and-handsome shows up—in person or in my brain—and they all seem to pale in comparison.

Noah: I have a proposition for you.

Me: Can't wait to hear it.

Relentless. Although, I'm not all that surprised. Typical for a guy to ditch, and then when he sees that I'm not chasing, thinks maybe now he wants a piece.

> **Noah:** It's the perfect way for us to rid ourselves of the obvious tension between us. You and me, just one night.

> **Me:** In your dreams, Karvelas.

Shaking my head, I put my phone back in my pocket and ignore the next ding and turn my attention back to the girls. I ignore the satisfaction of him chasing me. I am a hot-blooded woman, after all, and you'd have to be blind and a lesbian to not be attracted to Noah Karvelas and all his God-like sex appeal. I applaud myself for my restraint and strength in turning him down and just hope he doesn't ask again the next time he sees me. I'm not sure I'd be able to turn that down in person.

"What's that cheeky grin for?" Rosie says from across the table, and my cheeks heat when I realize I've been pushing my pasta around my plate in a daze, thinking about what it'd look like to not turn down Noah's offer.

I let loose a nervous laugh and sip my wine, buying some time for an excuse.

"Oh my god, it's Noah isn't it!?" Rosie's eyes light up.

"Why haven't you guys... you know, scaled the deal yet?" Casey asks from where she sits, her grin matching Rosie's, and she levels me with her waggly eyebrows.

"Because he wasn't interested, and I have enough dignity to not go asking again." Even though he has just essentially offered me a one night only Noah buffet, but I keep that to myself. I had given Rosie and Casey a highlight reel of the trip to Maplewood, including the night Noah had blown my mind and then bailed almost immediately. Rosie had just been confused that the man left without getting his own needs handled and wondered if maybe he had a 'problem'. Casey just laughed and said at least I was able to get my rocks off. Despite the fact he satisfied me better than any previous encounter I've had, I was still intrigued as to what I was missing. If he was that good with his tongue, imagine his other talents.

If I'm being honest, giving in to Noah makes me nervous. As much as I'm adamant I don't want to lock myself into something, that night in Maplewood was only a glimpse into what the electricity between us could do. I could only imagine the sex. What if he ruins me for all future partners and I end up never being able to have sex again?

"Maybe it's something you both need to get out of your systems." Funny, Noah had said the same thing.

"I have a feeling he'd only bury himself deeper," I mumble while shoving more pasta into my mouth.

"Is that so bad?" Casey asks gently.

"Yes, horrible, in fact. Let her enter her hoe era for a while. Enjoy yourself before you settle on a one-dick life. You need to sample the fruits of the city before you decide which one you'll settle for," Rosie says very matter-of-factly, and I nearly choke on my pasta trying to conceal my laugh and Casey does the same.

"Not what I was going for, but yes, it is bad. Noah isn't a relationship person, and as much I could try, I just can't do casual. With the way he gets me all tangled in emotional webs, I don't trust myself or my hormones to not get carried away." Casey nods in understanding and Rosie cheers' me across the table with her wineglass, and they change the topic as I discreetly pull my phone back out.

Noah: *Precisely. And it's becoming a problem because not only do memories of how sweet you taste interrupt my sleep, but they haunt me in my daydreams and I really need to get work done these next few weeks.*

Noah: *What'd you say, Shortcake? One night and we can get on with our lives.*

One night. Just one night and we can get it out of our systems.

Even through text, he is a delicious temptation I'm struggling to avoid.

No, I am strong. I can withstand the Noah effect and hold firm. I will continue on my SoulSwipe hunt. I'm certain there are other eligible men in the city that aren't losers and self-obsessed douche bags.

Me: *Take a hint, Karvelas.*

That should do it.

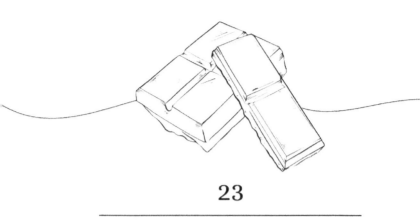

23

just another territorial five-year-old

Noah

Take a hint.

The way Addison can get my blood boiling in frustration and get me hard with desire is like a mental and emotional whiplash I still can't get a grip on. Just one night, if we could have one night, I could get her out of my system and stop fucking thinking about her.

I spent the next week figuring out my priorities and trying to get my head right enough to focus on the EcoX deal about to implode, while keeping the rest of my workload in check enough to hold down the fort until this deal with Matt goes through. Chicago was still the plan, and I really needed to get my ducks in a row so I could start looking at real estate and hiring more staff.

Since Dad died, I have spent every day reminding myself why the pain of losing love is not worth living with it. Since Addison, though...well, I was struggling to think of reasons not to pursue her. Maybe if I offered more than one night, she'd agree? Maybe she really was out there looking for a relationship and not a one-night stand and I had just misread her? After seeing her on that date with Eric and her turning down my offer, I still hadn't managed to shake the thoughts of her, the memory of her moans and the way she rains her fury from her eyes. The energy around her, the way she draws me in, I just can't get enough. Every time she is around, I just want to be there, too. And I can't work out how to make this stop.

Maybe I did want to try to do not-casual. Maybe that's what all this meant.

What I did know was that I wanted to see her again, explain that I had ditched Maplewood because I needed to clear my head, deal with some work stuff... maybe contemplate actually explaining it all to her... maybe counteroffer her an exclusive-casual thing? I'm sure I'll think of something on my feet. Hint not taken, I shoot my shot, yet again.

Me: Hey Shortcake, feel like getting a drink?

Nothing. Not even the little floating dots.

I lose my dignity and shoot her a text on the following day:

Me: You busy tonight?

Again, nothing.

Like I am surprised. Her ignoring me only makes me think about her more. Like a treat you're told you can't have, so you just begin to crave it. Her smile, her husky laugh, the way she bites her bottom lip when she is horny, it burns a memory in my brain. Taunting me, reminding me that I am a fucking idiot for leaving back at the lodge. Remembering the sounds she made, how she tasted, and when she moaned my name.

Staying true to our new routine, the guys caught up at Puck's again the following Monday, sitting in the Beer Garden enjoying the late April sun. Lucas was raving about Addison, the stupid kid wore his heart eyes for everyone to see, wouldn't take a genius to work out he was crushing hard on my Addison.

My Addison. Who have I become?

That catch up about did it. I only made it to Thursday before I decided we'd had enough of the space; I'd had more than enough time to pine and ponder. I wanted Addison. To hell with my previous promises and declarations of being single. If I need to sacrifice my bachelor-hood to get Addison, then I guess that's what I'm doing. Maybe the lack of sex had finally tipped me over the edge, sent me into a spiral of doom. Fuck it. I'll just figure that out later.

I don't know how much time passed between this decision and me turning up at her apartment door... but here I am. Knocking on her door like a madman.

I hear footsteps and encourage myself to handle this like a gentleman—cool, calm, and collected. When the door opens, it is not who I was expecting to find. A brunette with caramel skin and tight curls, almost as short as Addison. Rosie.

She opens the door, trails her eyes up my body, then leans against the door frame in relaxed arrogance. "Well, if it isn't the sex-god himself."

I give her my most relaxed smile, thoroughly satisfied about the stories being shared, and respond with my hands casually in my pockets. "Rosie, I'm looking for Addison?"

"She's out," she says, her grin pure mischief.

"Out where... exactly?"

"Work."

"She works at a bar. It is 10am, on a Thursday." I give her a deadpan look, not buying her excuse.

"So why aren't *you* working then, Noah?"

"Because I own my own company, *Rosie,* and I make the rules." She gives me an unconvinced nod, surveying me from head to toe.

"Sorry, today I am not lying. She went to the bar at about 9am, said something about helping Lucas with... his *thing*. She has had a lot of strange hours with him lately, now that I think about it." She taps her chin, but you can't bullshit a bullshitter. I see her game.

"You know, a lot of late nights, early mornings. Has her working *major* overtime. She comes home *soooo* exhausted. The work seems satisfying though. She's always happy and sleepy. I don't think I've ever seen her so relaxed. Well done to her, though, right? Lucas is super hot. I bet he is packing..." She uses her hands in front of her face, gesturing a guess at what I'm assuming is meant to be the size of Lucas's cock, given the wink she throws at me. I slam my hand against the door frame, needing to put my anger somewhere. I think my jaw is clenched so hard my teeth are cracked. I'll give it to her—Rosie is good. Great, in fact. She is so thoroughly under my skin I think she can see the green jealousy written on me.

Thoroughly satisfied with the possessive helix she has sent me down, she cracks a huge smile and throws her head back in a laugh.

"You boys are all the same. You'd think one day I'd get tired of playing you all like a fiddle, but you make it too easy."

I go to turn and head straight for the bar when Rosie continues.

"We are all heading out to Bozzelli's tonight. They are trying a new Thursday night, focusing on college students. Addy will be partying and not working. Actually, I think she might even have a SoulSwipe date tonight." There is that wink again. I knew about the college night because I run the socials for the technology inept child that Lucas is, but I had no idea the night was Addison's idea. Lucas conveniently left that part out.

I can see the gleam of satisfaction in Rosie's eyes, she knows exactly what she is doing, and I can't even be mad. I was the one who told her I didn't do relationships. I left without saying goodbye, and have teased a one-night offer, and here I am lusting and getting territorial over someone I have absolutely no right to. Well, that ends tonight. I'm sick of this shit.

Addison will be mine. I'm about done dancing around this shit. Worst case, we get one incredible night that potentially ruins all future women for me. Best case scenario, she wants to go for round two. That round two I promised her in Maplewood. I do like to keep my promises after all.

The bar is packed; the line is down the street.

I walk up to the door and find Lucas there. He notices me and waves me over.

"What're you doing here? Thought you'd still be in work-mode with it being a weekday and all?"

"Meeting some of the guys." *Lie.* "Addy working tonight?" Of course, I already know she isn't, why else would I be here?

"Nah, but she's inside with Rosie and Casey." I nod and go to enter when he stops me, eyes narrowed and a half smile pulled across his face. "Hey, are you guys seeing each other?" He is all boyish charm, his clear hazel eyes would deceive anyone into thinking he was a golden retriever, but I've seen this guy party, walking in on a few... questionable things during our years at college when he used to crash Ethan's parties. The king of making people see exactly what he wants them to see. My immediate reaction is to tell him yes, Addison and I are seeing each other, but I have no right to stake a claim on her after the way she has shut me down. I mean, really, if tonight goes the way I plan, I suppose I'm not really lying... right?

"Why?"

"I thought maybe I'd buy her a drink... is all." His self-assured grin grows across his face.

"Yeah, we're seeing each other." *You prick*.

Lucas seems unbothered by my answer, taking it completely in stride. "Oh, no worries, sorry man, didn't mean anything by it. She's a cool chick." He shrugs, and I can't work out why that reaction also bothers me. His attention is pulled by one of the security guards. He grabs the rope to let me through, skipping the line.

"Head on in, I have to sort out these drunk idiots." He gestures for me to enter, pointing to a verbal argument taking place between a guard and a patron. I nod to him and stalk in, immediately looking for my tiny blonde.

After walking through the main sports bar area, the corridor leads to a speak-easy styled bar and nightclub. The lights are dim, reds and purples across the bar, and booth seating with your typical club music playing through the DJ's speakers. Heading past the high tables, I instantly spot her in the center of the dance floor, the biggest smile on her face, swaying her hips, eyes closed, and head tilted to the ceiling. A relatively tall guy stands at her back, his hands placed on her hips suggestively, and it lights a match inside my chest, and words I have no business thinking start to rattle through my brain.

Mine.

The word that seems to be the label on the feeling that springs out of nowhere when I see Addy near anyone. Eric, that creep that was trying to feel her up. Like a switch finally flicked on, everything seems to snap into place.

Addison is mine.

My steps slow until I am on the edge of the dance floor, and I am completely entranced by her. Slimy dude aside, her smile so big, skin radiant, her gorgeous hair is down and curled around her face. I nearly die at the sight of her outfit. A silver dress, with shoestring straps, that loosely hugs her body, a deep v at the front that stops so short I am convinced everyone in the bar will have an eye full if she so much as scratches her knee. She does a twirl, now facing douche-date, as she wraps her arms around his neck.

Mine.

My heart is officially in my throat, the blood in my dick, as I notice the back of her dress... well, it doesn't exist. The back dips so low it rests just above her ass, strings of something sparkling barely holding the sides together, and I can see every muscle move under her soft pale skin as she dances. Douche-date's hands finding a trail down her spine and resting way too low for my liking.

That will do, buddy. Any lower and I'm going to have to break some fingers.

"Alright perv."

"*Jesus–Fuck.*" My soul leaves my body at the jump scare. I *was* staring at her like a perv, the sound of the music now slipping back into my mind as I look down and see Rosie smiling up at me with playful eyes. I shift nervously on my feet, hand reaching up to scrub the back of my neck, pretending I wasn't just caught ogling the fuck out of Addison and her douchy date. What a punchable face that guy has.

"Sorry, I... I wasn't..."

Rosie rolls her eyes. "Relax, Prince Charming, I know she is fucking gorgeous. Look at her." Oh, don't worry, I was.

"Are you going to go over and dance with her or what?"

"What about her handsy friend?" Didn't manage to hide my feelings from my words, but I don't care. All my control is going into not
committing assault on this prick.

"Oh, please, that guy isn't hitting anything outside of first base. Are
you seeing that polo shirt?" I am. The royal blue polo with the khakis
is a crime against fashion everywhere. This isn't the fucking country
club.

"So you're done torturing me, then? Got it all out of your system?"

"Plenty more where that came from. But I am doing this for her,
not you. She's into you, too, you big dumb idiot. This time, seal the
deal and then don't fucking leave. But so help me god if she sheds a
single tear over you..." she reaches up on to the tips of her toes and
leans in to whisper in my ear as I lower my head to her, "I will sever each
and every nerve of your member and feed it to you in front of a mirror
and make you witness the end of your ability to receive pleasure."

I swallow deeply.

Rosie scares the ever loving shit out of me. She pulls back with
a smile that would melt a grandmother and she winks. "Go get her,
tiger," she finishes as she slaps me on the ass.

I am still speechless, but I turn my attention back in the direction
of Addy, and she is now looking at me. Gone is her radiant smile, her
aura of joy, because that is a scowl, a look of death, pinning me in place.
The rage is almost tangible as it snakes off her skin, and she slowly
steps towards me, but I can't help but feel a sense of triumph. Rage
or not, in the 0.5 seconds that Addy's eyes have been locked on mine,
she all but forgets the existence of Country Club. Rosie gulps loudly,
whisper-shouting, '*good luck,*' before making a run for it.

"What on earth are you doing here?" Addison rage-shouts over the music, looking up at me through her dark lashes, her green eyes burning holes through me. Her date stands awkwardly behind her, shuffling on his feet. I manage to make direct eye contact with him, making sure my eyes say the things I know I can't voice. *Mine.*

I watch as he visibly shrinks, my eyes narrowing until he takes the hint. Not even thirty seconds, not a fight or a retort to be found, Country Club just gives up. "I'll, uhh, see you around." He nods and bails. *Pathetic.*

I trail my eyes back to my Strawberry Devil, the smirk of triumph spreading evenly across my face. "We need to talk." I look at Addy, those incredible green eyes.

She leans on a hip, her arms crossed over her chest, and *christ,* hitching her tits to almost falling from her dress. Her eyebrows knit together tightly and she leans forward. "You really can't take the hint, can you? Here to ruin another date, I suppose?" She stares into my soul, and I am speechless as she continues. "What is your deal? I said fun, and you practically ran for the hills. Now you just hover and act like a possessive caveman."

"I don't want fun, shortcake, and you're done with the date, whether you leave here with me or not."

"Where do you get off telling me who I can and can't date? What the hell do you want from me, Noah? What are you doing here?"

I take a step forward, crowding her space, and lean my head down to her ear so I am no longer shouting over the music. "I'm done with these games. I'm done fighting this *thing* between us. I want you... *all* of you. And I'm done sharing." I pull back to look at her face and not a thing has changed. The rage fire burns in her eyes and she pushes past me and storms off.

I run after her, catching her by the elbow and pulling her into a dark corner near the bar, quieter, away from the speakers and the rush of the dance floor. She practically squeals, and my heart finally snaps in two. I remove my hand from her skin and plead that my eyes can hold hers for as long as possible.

"Addy, I'm sorry for the way I have handled things, okay? I shouldn't have left at Maplewood, I shouldn't have acted like an idiot on your date, although, I stand firm on my decision—Eric was a class A fuck-tard. But you're right. I didn't know what was happening. In my head, in my life. I have... I have never—"

"Noah, save it. These are just words. They mean nothing. You're sorry your ego is hurt because I didn't chase you..." She takes a step forward, her face scrunched in a scowl, and she has never been sexier.

"You're sorry that I didn't come crawling. But you have no right to storm in here, scaring off yet another one of my dates, and saying all of this after everything. Because guess what? I won't chase you. I won't get on my knees and beg you to want me because I love myself enough to not need the acceptance of you or anyone." Her voice is so deep and low I feel like the wrath has taken over my body. That confidence and arrogance I knew was buried within her shows itself, and I have never been more attracted to this woman than I am now.

"So, these trust-fund country-club pricks are doing it for you then, Ads?" I try to tease, but really my jealousy just makes an embarrassing appearance and I try to save my dignity by giving her a playful smile.

"Oh, Noah, you're jealous? The one who can't work out what the fuck he wants enough to ask for it, the one too much of a *guy* to acknowledge he has feelings, is jealous?"

"Tell me, how many of those dates of yours..." I lean my body close, crowding her into the corner, "...have been able to make you scream their name as you came on their tongue?" I swear I hear her breath hitch, ignoring the jealous rage that grows, imagining Addison sharing any of that with someone other than me.

I pull back with satisfaction at the look of heat on her face. Except, to my utter surprise, she leans in and quips back. "About as many times as you have pulled your dick to the sound of me coming in your mouth."

A growl climbs my throat as I try to rein in my desire for this firecracker. I respond, closing the final gap between us so that her body is completely flush with mine. "Do you have any idea what you do to me?" I grunt out, our mouths inches from each other. She bats her lashes at me, but her stare is anything but innocent. She knows *exactly* what she is doing.

The look snaps all my self-control, and I firmly grab her lower back with my left hand, thrusting my right into her hair and pull her in to crash my lips into hers. I'm done with this game. I'm staking my claim if it's the last fucking thing I do—Addison is mine.

She instantly melts into my arms, lacing her fingers in my hair, deepening the kiss. Her tongue darts out, and I instantly open for her, pulling her tongue into my mouth, reveling in the strawberry vodka taste of her. She pushes me away, and I back up a few steps, but ache at the loss of her touch.

She huffs an incredulous laugh. "Have you ever gone a day without thinking with your dick, Noah? You are so predictable." My spine snaps straight, and the anger builds from deep within me. I am usually cool and calm, but this blonde has me discovering a plethora of feelings that turn me into a raging caveman. "Oh, shortcake, when you're around, my dick is the only organ making decisions." Her breathing comes in hard. A quick scan of her body tells me she is as turned on from that kiss as I am. At the risk of trying my luck again, I take a step closer. She steps back against the wall and damned if my chest doesn't expand at the quirk of her lips.

"I don't do relationships, and certainly not with *you,* Noah. I'm here with a date. You say you want me, well, you can't have me." Her words are sultry, but her scowl holds the rage of a thousand storms to match the raging feelings in my chest.

"We'll see about that. But Country Club already bailed. He knew you were mine with one look." She holds my eyes for a beat before leaning to the side to look around my shoulder briefly, confirming my words, noticing Rosie and Casey are also not in the near vicinity.

She recovers her look with one of confidence and considers me, looking me up and down. "Do you think you can handle fucking me without falling in love with me?" she taunts.

No. The answer almost slips from my lips, and I know I'm a goner for Addison. Like I told Matt, I didn't come this far by taking the easy road. I have every intention of making sure she knows I'm not leaving again. This time, I'm sticking around. Casual or not, right now I couldn't care less. Like I said, dick in control. No brain.

She tilts her head like she just asked me what my favorite color is. I take one final step, again caging her into the wall and pressing my body against hers so she can *feel* the effect she has on me.

"I think it's you that needs to guard her heart, sweetheart."

"Oh, don't worry, *Dolos*, I could never fall in love with you." The growing tension in the air fills my lungs. The string of desire between us pulls tighter than ever before; it feels like something is about to snap. She can lie to herself all she wants, but I see the way she bites her lip, the way her eyes are hooded and glazed with desire as she pants every time I'm near. It's okay, Addy, I can take your denial for as long as you need. You can't get rid of me that easily.

"We're leaving," I grunt into her ear, and I don't miss the goose-bumps on her skin as I pull away to look into her eyes. She looks into mine, and I see her chest rise and fall quickly, as breathless as I am, and she quickly nods.

As we exit, Lucas is still at the door, and his face lights up when he sees Addy. "Leaving already?" he asks playfully. I catch up and am now standing behind her.

"Mmhmm." She nods at him, clearly trying to avoid acknowledging who she is taking home. I look to Lucas. He seems to put it together, and the prick purses his lips, poking his tongue to his cheek as he suppresses a laugh. "Ahh... I see. Well, have *fun,* you two." He throws us a wink and hails a cab for us. I give him a nod, ushering Addy into the cab, and give the driver my address.

When the cab pulls up in front of my brownstone, I turn to give Addy my hand, helping her out, but she deliberately takes her time. The moment she is on the sidewalk, I give her a cheeky smile and bend at the waist.

"What are you do–NOAH!" I lift her up and throw her over my shoulder, grabbing cash from my pocket and handing it to the driver through the window who is now laughing at Addy over my shoulder. I turn and head for my front stairs, giving Addy a spank on the way.

"What are you doing?!" she shrieks.

"Getting you inside as quickly as I possibly can because I need you naked, and I need to be inside you. Now," I practically growl.

I open the front door, storm in, and head straight for the stairs, climbing with ease despite the feather weight of Addy over my shoulder. When we reach my room, I close the door, drop Addy to her feet, and slam her back against the door, as my lips slam on to hers. She releases a moan that I swallow immediately, her hands tangling in my hair as her legs attempt to climb my body. I grab the back of her thighs and heave her up, her legs wrapping around my waist, her center pressing against the hardness growing in my pants. The ease with which we move, the aggressive heat of our passion evenly matched, like we've spent years doing this. Like coming home, it settles within me, a knowing calm at odds with the unrestrained desire she brings out of me. She can throw her wildest, maddest chaos at me, I won't falter, and I'll be right here to help her back up when she is ready, however long it takes.

"This... doesn't... mean... anything," she says between pants. Our kiss is desperate and passionate, her moans turning my stomach to mush and my desire growing at an uncontrollable rate.

"Whatever you say, shortcake." I press my hips harder, holding her in place, as I pull the dress up over her head in one quick action, returning my lips to hers as though that is where they belong. She can tell herself all she wants that this means nothing—a one time thing. But the feel of her, the taste of her, the way she fits perfectly against my body. I'll be damned if this is the one and only time I get Addison.

Her body is hot and smooth, and I force myself to pull away from her to look at her. At the masterpiece of her body. My eyes graze over her as she pants, staring into my face.

"That's right. Commit this to memory because this is never happening again," she demands breathlessly.

She is wearing nothing but a bright pink g-string and... "*Fuck,*" I ground out at the sight of the tiny strawberries on the front of her g-string, completely ignoring her comment.

"These, for that polo wearing douchebag?" I grab the side of the string and pull it, causing it to snap against her skin as she gasps. "I wear underwear for *myself,* you oaf. But perhaps, I chose my favorites just in case my date was fortunate enough to tear my dress from me." She says the words with such deep teasing that my dick hardens at the same time as my furious jealousy I kept leashed snaps free. I grab the back of her head and slam my lips against hers, her hands at the hem of my shirt pulling. I pull away with enough time to yank off my shirt as she drags her fingernails down my back. I reach to kiss down her neck, across her collarbone, and back up to her jaw as my hands squeeze and flick her nipples. "Let me make one thing clear, Addison, from now on, the only man ever seeing this dick tease…" I pull on the string again, letting it snap to her skin, "is me. The only man you'll get to kiss you like this is me," I slam my lips to hers, my tongue searching, and I roll my hardness against her softness, "and the only man who gets you this wet. *Is. Me.*" I bring one hand between us, dipping under her panties to feel the truth of my words. She is soaked, and her head lulls back as her breath hitches at the firm graze of my fingers against her clit.

"I don't belong to you, Noah. I can fuck whoev—" she is cut off when I push in two fingers, reaching deep in her center, and she melts in my hands. "What were you saying, Addison?" She moans loudly as her eyes close. She shakes her head.

"Eyes on me, Little Demon."

Her eyes snap open and lock with mine, her mouth opened in a soft *O* as she struggles to get her breathing under control. "Tell me, who gets you this wet, Addison?"

"*You,*" she breathes.

"Whose tight little pussy is this, Addison?"

"Yours," she all but grunts, and I withdraw my fingers slowly and drag them lazily against her clit, teasing, eliciting more sounds that I commit to memory.

"If this is the one and only time I get to have you. I plan to ruin you for anyone else."

"I'd love to see you try." She moans. Oh, she is really trying to kill me. I reach my hands to each of her ass cheeks, rolling her hips as I grind against her.

"Noah…" She is a panting mess. "You. *Please.*"

"Please, *what?*" I growl.

"*Make me come.*" At her request, I lose all control. Fucking Addison and all her fury turns me completely mindless. It's like I become a thirteen-year-old boy again, seeing a pair of tits for the first time.

I wrap one arm around her waist, grabbing her to my body as the other grabs the back of her neck, pulling her into another searing kiss as I turn and walk us towards the bed, with her legs still tightly wrapped around me. When my knees hit the bed, I release her, throwing her to her back as I unbutton and unzip my pants with speed. Fuck self-control. If she thinks this is a one-night thing, then she has another thing coming.

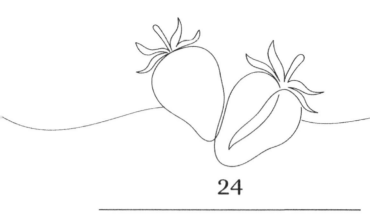

24

promises, promises

Addison

He stands over me, naked, the size of him now obvious, *very obvious*. I lose my breath as I realize I am going to have sex with Noah. I was determined to continue to ignore him until he went away, but he turned up to Bozzelli's dressed like sex, his black button down open slightly at the top, his jeans casual, and the mess of curls on top just begging for me to run my fingers through them.

I have forsaken my goal to remain in power over him, and here I am whimpering like a fool for him to fuck me, telling him he owns my pussy?! *What is wrong with you, Addison?*

He slowly crawls onto the bed; the way he looks at me is beyond possessive, and I hate how much it turns me on. Parting my legs as he travels up my body, leaving light kisses everywhere except where I need him. He gives me a deep chuckle at my inability to stop my groan of protest, and he lowers himself back between my legs. His lips lightly graze the sides of my wetness, teasing me, leaving hot breaths over my core, the need for friction taking over as my hips roll into his mouth.

"Ask nicely," he demands.

"Over my dead body."

"Ask. Nicely, Addison." He hovers, his warm breath against my apex, causing me to clench uncontrollably, needing him to touch me. I mentally slap myself as I give into his demand on a breathy moan.

"*Please,* Noah. I will die. *Just... ahh.*" His smile grows, and his tongue strokes the length of me, past my center, and to the peak between my thighs, teasing and flicking my clit until I am a writhing, moaning mess beneath him. He wraps his arms around the back of my thighs, throwing my legs over his shoulders as he places the whole of that magic mouth completely covering me and devouring me with a hunger that has stars appearing in my vision.

Just one time.

Just one time.

I grab for his hair, riding his face and moaning his name before he pulls away from me. The intensity that was building going flat at the empty space of where his mouth was.

"Not tonight, shortcake. When you come, I want it all over my cock. I want to feel you as you come undone around me." I practically combust and throw my legs around his waist, pulling him to me, wrapping my arms around his neck, and kissing him. Tasting me on his lips and his tongue, sending me wild with desire as I drag my center up his hard length, coating him in my wetness.

I tell myself this desire, this tightness in my chest, the stupid emotions, are all because of my hormones and the chocolate eyes of a Greek god, and nothing to do with my feelings for Noah. Nothing.

I want you. And I'm done sharing.

I don't even know where this is coming from. The weeks after he Irish-goodbye'd me at the lodge, he's done nothing but consistently tell me he just wanted to get me out of his system, giving me whiplash with his possessive act. I was done chasing men who didn't want me, and here is this hot as fuck guy sent from the heavens, now telling me he wants me, and I can't bring myself to believe him or trust any of it.

I don't do relationships.

Well, I don't do casual sex. Or at least I didn't. Until now. I mean, if you could see this man, I am sure you'd understand why I was considering giving it a red hot crack, and had all but fled my date.

I shove and lock away the thoughts that start to poke their way up. Making a choice Rosie would be proud of, I'm naked with Noah. Just stop thinking about it and fucking enjoy it.

Noah tastes like whisky and mint, his scent is always thick with spring, tonight it intertwines with the taste and smell of me.

My confidence skyrockets and words leave my mouth before I know what I am saying. "Can you feel how wet I am for you now, Noah?" I increase my moan on that last bit as his grip on my hips tightens. He pulls away, but not before grounding out a curse. Then he reaches across his nightstand for a condom. He stares into my eyes, the air around us sizzling with electricity so hot it feels like my skin is on fire. He brings the condom wrapper between his teeth and tears it. I bite down on my bottom lip as he removes the condom and unrolls it onto himself without leaving my eyes. *Danger. This is dangerous ground, Addison.* He lowers his body to me, his hardness teasing my entrance as he slowly drags it up and down, and I nearly erupt at the need for the pressure. "*Noah...*"

"Tell me, Addy."

"*Fuck me.*" It is barely a whisper as my breath leaves me, and he slowly thrusts inside me, not stopping until he is fully seated, releasing a rough, "*fuck,*" the whole way. He lies on top of me, his face in the crook of my neck, kissing and pulling at my skin with his teeth as I tightly wrap my legs around him and bring his ear to my mouth.

Sex has never made me like this before. Not with Jake, and not with anyone before. I never made it past second base with the guys I dated over the last few weeks, but the desire thrumming through my veins makes me completely unrecognizable. I want him unleashed, and I want it now. Taunting Noah, apparently now a hobby of mine, I whisper on a moan, "None of my dates fill me up like you do. They don't make me ache with need, not like you do." His final tether of self-control snaps. His arms tighten around me as he pulls back, sitting on his heels, bringing me with him in one swift display of strength, as I am pulled into his lap, straddling him. My hands are hooked behind his neck and his hands instinctively land on my hips. As I hover above him and raise my eyebrow in challenge, he guides himself in, smooth to start before he withdraws and slams home with a force that has me seeing stars.

"Such filthy things come out of that mouth of yours, shortcake," he grunts. His grip tightens and his eyes close as his head rolls back, his pace causing me to lose my breath. "One day, I'm going to fuck the filth right out of that pretty little mouth of yours."

His hips meet every thrust of mine with such force it has me gasping for air.

"Promises, promises." The words make their way out between moans I don't recognize as my own, the pleasure traveling my spine from the feel of Noah as he slides in and out in rapid succession, the curl of euphoria building and making me frantic with desire.

"The sounds you make, Addison, are going to make me insane." His rough words are my undoing as I move my legs to wrap around his waist and I grind onto him deeper. He rises onto his knees, his hands gripping my ass, his pace increasing. I'm suspended in the air as he drives into me, the pace building, the sound of our skin slapping against each other and the wetness between our labored breaths all I can hear.

"*Noah,*" I moan as my inner walls tighten.

"Yes, Ads, give it to me. *Come for me.*" His pace increases again, driving into me harder and faster, my breath turning into a scream as my walls tighten and the pressure from inside me builds until I explode with his name on my lips. Noah growls a low curse, dark spots fill my vision, and his pace remains as he slams his lips against mine, throwing us to the bed, with me on my back, his thrusts not faltering as we tumble. "I don't think I have ever felt anything as incredible as you coming on my cock." He grunts into my neck as he kisses down my skin and to my breasts. Pulling my nipple between his teeth as he thrusts into me again. He brings a hand between our bodies, massaging my clit, the sensation already building again, the orgasm traveling down my spine. "*Oh god... Noah!*" I scream his name as it crashes into me again, his length slamming into me, increasing for a beat as he comes with me.

Just once.

Bury the feelings.

Collapsing together on the bed, Noah on top of me, catching his breath as he remains inside of me, placing soft kisses to my neck before rising and kissing my lips. A different kiss to what we usually have. This one is tender but also... a *longing.* I gently pull away from the kiss, not ready to address any of those feelings or questions. His eyes snap open, confused, and search mine.

"Are you okay?" he whispers to me.

"*Mmhmm,*" I respond back. But really, no, I'm not okay. I just traveled through space and time when I thought this was meant to be revenge—a onetime, 'get-it-out-of-our-system', sex-capade. Instead, I think he stained himself on my soul. Marked me, ruined me. How was polo-douche ever going to live up to that?

I don't think I have *ever* experienced sex like this with anyone. This felt like a branding. Like he finally claimed me as his, and the scariest part of all, is that I liked it. I want him to do it again, claim me and never let me go. The thought of giving that much of me to someone again, though, scares the ever loving crap out of me. It's hard to hide the fear as it grips my chest. Just once, I'd like to have an orgasm that isn't riddled with all this fucking overthinking.

Every date since we got back from the lodge ended up being a game of comparison to Noah. Despite him crashing the date with Eric, and again tonight with—*oh God, I don't even remember his name*—he doesn't ever have to know that he never really needed to crash. None of them made me feel comfortable in my own mind, like Noah does. No one allowed me to feel safe in companionable silence like Noah. No one made me feel an even balance between desire, passion, and care, like Noah does.

No one looks at me and makes me feel quite as beautiful as Noah does. Like now.

His smile grows as he pulls out and takes care of the usual 'post-sex' gross stuff. I get up and head to the toilet, ensuring I, too, take care of the annoying post-sex activities. I make to grab my clothes and bail as soon as possible when Noah meets me by his bathroom door with one of his t-shirts in hand. Searing his chocolate eyes into me and I can't take another step.

"...uhhh, why are you looking at me like that?" I try to sound as unaffected as possible.

"You're so beautiful, Addy. I don't know how I have gone so long without knowing you." His statement is so raw, so serious and vulnerable, I have to swallow the emotion it raises inside me. I need to leave, need to get out, or I'm not going to be able to stop myself from falling for this man. Between those words and that sex... ughh.

"Noah..." I whisper.

"I love the way you say my name." His smile grows into something so sweet it snaps my heart in two. I shove past his hand holding the t-shirt and make to grab my things. "Noah... I can't... I mean, I don't think we..." I gesture between us, not sure how to tell him any of this as I fumble for my discarded clothes. *Christ, they are all over the place.*

"Addison, I care about you. In fact, I am pretty certain you're one of the only things I have had in my head since we came back from Maplewood." Not sure when he moved, but he is next to me now, grabbing on to my arm, one hand to my cheek, his thumb smearing something wet on my cheek—*oh God, I am crying again?* I shake my head and force a laugh. "We can't do this."

His face pulls into frustration, but his voice is gentle. "Give me one good reason why." He stands up straighter, bringing his other hand to my cheek.

Shaking my head, I tell him, "I am not doing this, Noah. We can't, and *you* can't." The last words are pointed, and I don't hide their venom with.

I am certain one bout of great sex, great for me, anyway, isn't going to change his mind about a serious relationship. It hasn't changed mine.

And, anyway, I am not about to have my heart ripped out by falling for someone emotionally unavailable.

"Emotionally unavailable?" *Fuck, did I say that out loud?* How badly did this sex ruin my brain?

"Yes, Noah. You say all these panty-melting things, and then you cover it with 'I don't do relationships' and saying you need to 'get me out of your system'. Confusing me with casual words while being possessive. You can't have both, your actions contradict your words."

"Addy, I told you at Bozzelli's what I wanted. To be clear, you're the one leaving *me* right now." He is confused and frustrated, but I just don't have the capacity for this right now.

"You have no idea what you want, Noah. Not sharing isn't just something that you can have. You're here now because what? Rosie dangled the fact I was 'seeing other people' in front of you, and you caught me on a couple of dates? You're acting like a territorial five-year-old that had his toys stolen. What happens when I do become yours and I am not seeing other people? Well, I am not sticking around to get my heart broken when you get bored." Fully dressed now, Noah not having moved a muscle, I grab my phone and order an Uber.

"Addy, wait, will you just wait a sec—"

"No, Noah. Thank you... for tonight. You're... well, I am sure you know what you are. Good night." I leave his room and head down the stairs. As I do, I take stock of the surprisingly nice interior design for a single guy in his late twenties. The details I missed because he threw me over his shoulder to haul me upstairs like a starved barbarian. *Damn, that was hot.*

His oak herringbone floorboards are accented by deep coloured walls of jade green and accents of brown. Surprisingly sleek and sophisticated. I definitely pictured beer pong tables and pinball machines. A pleasant surprise, I suppose, too bad I won't ever see it again.

Noah's approaching steps following me down the stairs snap me from my snooping, and I open the front door to the entryway alcove, my Uber only a minute away.

"At least let me drive you home. Or... just stay?"

"No, go back upstairs, allow your ego to settle from the knowledge you just did—*that,*" I say, pointing to the top of the staircase, unable to hide my smile. His gorgeous, disheveled face and exposed chest on display in the moonlight are like a sick kind of karma for leaving him like this. "But let me leave. Alone. We both know this won't work.

"Goodbye, Noah." I give him one last smile and leave the surprisingly sleek brownstone, entering the Uber out front.

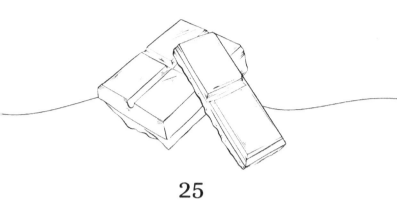

25

be a peach, and play along

Noah

"Noah, the meeting. Are you coming?"

I snap back from my daydreaming out of my window and realize I am sitting in my office staring out the window. Not lying in bed, on top of Addison, watching as the blush of arousal climbs her neck to her cheeks, and hearing her moans from those perfect plump lips.

We both know this won't work.

I, in fact, do *not* know that, Addison.

Your actions contradict your words.

Time to get fluent in the actions, then. She left my house after world-altering sex a week ago today. I sent her a string of texts, wanting to see her again, stating that I think this could work if she gave me a chance to show her. Singing a completely different tune to when I had messaged her before our night together. Obviously, she broke my brain. It is the only explanation of why it was like a chemical reaction when we were together and why she was now embedded even further, rather than being out of my system, like I had planned.

After she left, I asked if she would at least let me know when she was home. She didn't, and I had to ask Rosie instead, which of course led to Addison responding. '*Yes, I'm home, don't text my friends about me. That's... weird.*'

Pffft, weird. I was *concerned.* How's that for an action?

Well, I am not sticking around to get my heart broken when you get bored.

Fucking Jake is still ruining shit between me and Addison. She wants actions, I'll give her actions.

"Noah?"

"Right." I cough to clear my throat and my head of all things Addison. "Sorry, coming." I gesture to the door, as I stand and round my desk, for Caleb to lead the way. He halts a second or two, analyzing my eyes, trying to read what I am desperately trying to hide.

"Mmhmm. This meeting is important. I don't think I need to remind you what is riding on this going well?" His eyes narrow with scepticism, but he turns and heads for the boardroom. No, he doesn't need to remind me. EcoX and AIM are here to settle this issue of the contract being put on hold. They say they haven't finalized their investigation, but they have enough to clear us from any breach and are willing to at least come to the table to discuss moving forward. Despite mine and Matt's recent discovery, we've managed to remain tight-lipped enough to give the problem a chance to sort itself out without dragging us all down with it. I can only hope it gets sorted out once and for all, and soon. EcoX is understandably anxious, and any wrong move in this meeting could spook them. All my expert maneuvering would have been for nothing, and I can kiss this deal and my future goodbye. Caleb is right, I need to pull my head out of my ass.

The ever-present distraction still hovers in the front of my mind, despite me trying to wrangle my thoughts. Addison is probably prep-

ping for her exams next week. I wonder how she is. I'm glad she has
Rosie and Casey. They sound like they are a strong support system.
Not to mention Addison herself is incredibly intelligent and resource-
ful. She will be fine. Better than fine. I don't need to worry about her
in the slightest.

The thought lasts all of five seconds before I make a quick detour
to my assistant's desk on the way to the boardroom.

"Emery, could you please organize a basket to be delivered to this
address?" I say as I push a piece of paper across the desk while typing
on my phone with one hand. "I will text you the items."

"Yes, boss."

That will never not be weird. "Emery, it's just Noah." I give her a
reassuring smile, but she still looks pale, and I turn, catching up with
Caleb.

I slowly plot my way to win over Addy, bring her to the dark side of
not being able to focus on anything but on the way us together is like
sexual poetry, while I head into the meeting that is meant to make my
future. I pay as much attention as I can.

Overall, things went well, considering. They are still nervous, but I
managed to help progress the team on some of the marketing material
for the company as a whole, leaving out this mystery product for now,
giving us the green light to proceed with the proposal for a relaunch
of their website.

I spent the next two days burying myself in their work, trying
to drum up as many proposals and market approximations for their
future growth as possible, to encourage them to get a move on. It
wasn't until the cleaners were coming around that I realize it was dark
outside, and I was still hunched over my desk. I reach for my phone to
check what I've missed.

Shortcake: *Thank you for the gift. You didn't have to do that.*

Me: *Good luck with exams, shortcake.*

My heart squeezes as I read the text. Dying to ask more.

How are you?

Are you still dating losers?

When can I see you again?

I miss you.

I take back everything I said, I can do relationships. But only if it's with you.

She doesn't respond, and it is all I can do to not turn around and head straight for her apartment.

Actions.

I'm about as frustrated as they come. Between Addison ghosting me—I suppose karma for the way I bailed at the lodge—and all this bullshit with EcoX, I have a newfound energy that funnels through my veins. Unable to spend any more time in my office, and needing a break mentally to expel all the excess energy, I spent Saturday morning at the gym. The workout was especially intense, but I hit a new level trying to burn through the excess stress to exhaust myself enough to sleep.

Walking back to my house after the gym, my phone buzzes and see my sister's name pop up.

"Evie, is everything ok?"

"Why does something have to be wrong to call my big brother?" My heart pinches, and guilt settles in my stomach. "We don't hear from you. I was making sure you're still alive."

"Alive and well, Evelyn. I spoke to mom like a week ago. How are you doing? How are classes?" My sister is twenty-three, currently completing her degree at UChicago, following her dream of teaching the kids of America literature.

"Fine. Boring. Wish I was finishing soon. How's boss-man life in the big city? Any plans to come home and see your family soon?" I sense the usual tilt in her tone.

"What's happened?"

She releases a long-suffering sigh. "It's mom. She's fine, before you panic. She is just… well, she seems sad, reminiscing a lot, about the days with *baba* and when you were home. I think she misses you. Even though she pretends not to." Another pang of guilt spears me in the stomach; the desperation to get this deal over the line continues to grow as the need to be closer to mom and Evie continues to grip my chest.

"I will come home for a visit soon. I'm trying to sort things out here so that I can be home permanently, you know that. You know what it's like here. I have just been—"

"Busy. We know." And if that doesn't land the final sucker punch.

"I… I was planning a trip already. As a surprise," I lie.

"Mmhmm. I believe that." The sarcasm drips from her tone.

"No, really, I was. At the end of June it is the soonest I could get away. I have a few big client proposals at the beginning of the month, and I can't leave right now because I only just came back from time off."

"Time off? Where did you go?"

"Just to Maplewood with some friends."

"Okay… well, if you can come sooner, please. Otherwise, I am sure mom will be ecstatic to see you in June. I suppose me, too." The usual way between the two of us—pretend we have no feelings.

"I miss you, too, Evie."

"Ugh, whatever. Gross. Love you, bye." She rushes out the last part before the call disconnects.

I can't help but feel the guilt settle low in my belly. When was the last time I went out to see my family?

I immediately select a few dates on the calendar of my phone for the last week of June and send off a request for Emery to block it out and send out a notification of my leave dates. While I'm at it, I flick a message off to Rosie.

> **Me:** Think you could hook me up with Addy's exam schedule?

> **The scary one:** Depends. What creepy shit you pulling?

She wastes no time.

> **Me:** Just want to surprise Addison is all. Will you be a peach and just play along for once?

> **The scary one:** Not a chance. Men are dumb. Tell me your plan, let me fine tune it.

I roll my eyes, but I suppose there is no harm in having a best friend's opinion. I shoot off my idea to Rosie and continue organizing my trip home.

Trip home. The thought of going home to see my sister and my mother, who I love very much, still brings a nausea that unsettles me. Back to the house.

Christmas mornings.

Learning to drive.

Cooking as a family.

The house Dad died in. The house Mom grieved in.

The house holding memories of my mother's screams, her tears, and her pain. I had to go back there. And pretend everything was fine.

I could do this. I *had* to do this. For Evie, and for Mom.

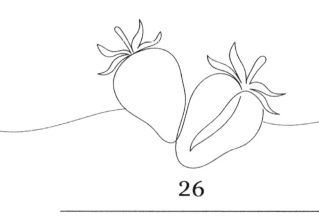

26

third time's a charm?

Addison

"To Addison!" Everyone cheers, and I throw the shot down my throat, feeling it burn the entire way.

Exams are done. My degree is *over*. I'M FREE.

I managed to nail my mock trial final and received *magna cum laude* for the graduating class, which has me riding a high like never before.

I did it. I actually did it. Sure, I could count my breakdowns and panic attacks over the exam week on two hands, but I still did it. Not only did I finish the degree, but I finished with *great distinction.* All the feelings have been plaguing me since I finished that final exam. Excitement, relief, dread. You typically sit the Bar in July, the time between now and then meant to be for preparation and knuckling down. Four hundred hours of pure hell for the longest final exam of your life. But... *I don't know.* I can't tell if it's me not thinking I'll succeed, or whether this is my heart telling me I don't want it, that I don't want to join that side of the corporate world, but I haven't made any efforts to begin the prep or commit myself to sitting the exam.

Then I'd need to start interviewing at the various law firms other law grads are clawing tooth and nail to get at, but the thought of sitting in a pencil skirt, my back ramrod straight, while I tell a wrinkly old man why I love his firm and why I will do anything for the opportunity to do grunt work, be shit on by the other partners, and be miserable until I am earning six figures, makes me want to bury myself in the ground for eternity and never come up for air.

But my friends don't need to know that part. They just need to know I am completely ecstatic to finally be out from under the study stress. At least until I make a decision about the Bar. Stress that was made slightly easier by my daily care packages from my very own secret admirer. Although, not so secret, every care package had either something endearing to do with strawberries or something that is triple-X inappropriate. Every day this week, I had something special to make the study less draining. From a fresh coffee and bagel on the doorstep in the morning, a little heart drawn on the cup with notes, *'let's bagel down and hit the books',* one package had a bundle of a couple of books from my favorite author, along with a voucher to my a local spa—that note said, *'self care is quite the page turner'.* My personal favorite was the red velvet cupcake with strawberries on top and an at home espresso martini kit, the note reading, *'A reminder of the taste I crave and an energy boost for when I finally get my hands on you.'* Despite his arrogance being presumptuous, that one sent flutters south and had my toes curling. He certainly is persistent, and I will lie if anyone asks, but a part of me is glad he hasn't given up. I wonder how long he'll keep going before he gets bored, whether he is doing this simply because I left him on his doorstep, or maybe he was serious about this, and maybe does miss me as much as he seems to.

But now, without the anxiety and stress about college, perhaps my moods will change for the better. Maybe I'll actually give Noah the chance he seems so desperate for. Maybe I will finally have a long stint of feeling good? I don't have an asshole boss anymore. In fact, I am strangely enjoying working for Lucas. Both the bar work and assisting in the business side. I haven't spoken to anyone in my family for a while, a few texts in our group chat with Riley and Ava, but otherwise, I have kept my distance. And we shouldn't be surprised neither of my parents have reached out. I quickly shove that feeling down and return my mind to my friends.

We are at Bozzelli's, and Casey, Rosie, Lucas, and the new Front of House Manager, Stella, are slamming shots. I never thought I'd find work friends who feel like *actual* friends, but Stella and Lucas have been amazing, and so easy to get along with. Lucas, despite his efforts in the beginning, is very much a platonic friend. Me finding him attractive left as quickly as it came, Noah all but ruined that. We have become close in the month and a bit we have been working together, and I truly value his friendship. He does have a good heart; I just don't think he lets anyone see it. He puts on his golden retriever act, but there is so much more depth to him.

Stella, she is a total badass. She takes zero shit and has mastered the role of being friends with her bartenders while ensuring they still fear her enough to work extremely hard. I mean, she sometimes still has me sweating from fear. She is older than me by a year, but we quickly hit it off. She reminds me of Rosie, but less extravagance, more of a silent murder-y vibe.

"We knew you could do it, Ads. We are so proud of you," Casey says as she rubs my arm.

"So, what's the plan? Do you know if you'll sit the Bar? Surely you aren't wasting your law degree on this place?" Rosie says with disgust in her tone. Lucas coughs under his breath, throwing a deadpan look at her face. "I mean no offense, Lucas." She waves him off as the rest of us stifle our laugh.

"Ads, you know I really do appreciate you. I know the work I have been giving you isn't... like typical stuff, but you have helped me so much. I am working out a position. Like a formal one. With a nice salary. I just have to talk to my acco—"

"Lucas, I don't plan on going anywhere, at least not for a while. I love it here, really! I don't know if I'll sit the Bar. I know I wanted to finish the degree to show myself I could." And prove to my parents, but again, we'll leave that bit out. "I just don't know if the legal life is really for me. I hated every one of my law firm jobs. Besides, how could I leave you and Stella?"

"Babe, please don't hang around for me. This is where my life amounts, but you are destined for great things. Get out while you can. Let's not think about the Bar exam right now, and instead think about the bar shots we have in front of us!" Stella, her warm mellifluous voice sweeps over me, and I smile deeply, feeling the warm and fuzzies from both the tequila and the friends surrounding me.

"Okay, why is everyone shitting on my bar? I will have you know we made New York Times top 50 bars in the city."

"They are just getting a rise out of you. Ignore them." I roll my eyes as Lucas straightens his spine.

"But seriously, I will give you something permanently, I promise. Just, please be patient with me. This whole being an adult running a business is new to me."

I give Lucas a pat on the back. "Alright next round is on me. What are we drinking?"

I head for the bar, taking no notice of any patrons as I try my best to memorize the drinks order—Midori sour, espresso martini, pint of draught, whisky neat. I am sure you can guess the whisky is for Stella; I really can't figure her out. My mind is so busy looping the order that I miss the group at the bar as I approach. Relaying the order to Felix, one of our bartenders, I get a tap on the shoulder. Turning to find Ethan, Lucas's older brother. "Oh, Ethan, hi! It's good to see you again!" I sound more enthusiastic than I planned. Ethan is older by five years, but he is cut straight out of a Men's Health magazine. Tall, broody, a neatly trimmed beard, and a no-nonsense expression that is sexy and intimidating all at once. We've met a couple of times. He works on Wall Street and helps Lucas out on the side.

"Addison, nice to see you," he says to me, but his gaze flicks behind me to the table I left. "What are you up to today?" His eyes dart between me, the drinks Felix is lining up on the bar, and my table again. *What the hell is he looking at?*

"I actually had my last exam today. I am officially done with law school! Me and some friends are celebrating." I almost don't know myself with the happiness and life bleeding from my tone. Ethan's eyes snatch back to my table again. *This guy must have some serious focus issues.*

He seems frozen in time before he shakes his head and looks at me again.

"Congratulations, that is amazing. Well, I won't hold you up, was nice to see you again." *Strange guy.*

"Oh, Lucas is over there drinking with us if you want to join?"

"Oh no, I won't interrupt, me and the guys are having a beer together so I better get back, I just came up to say hi and collect my turn of the shout." Felix places four pints on the bar. A knowing heaviness sinks low in my belly. I couldn't possibly know all of Ethan's friends. I know one of them is Matteo, from college. And I know Matteo's friends from college include Ethan and *Noah*. My heart races with anticipation at seeing him here, my sweat glands working overtime. I hadn't realized how much of a frenzy all those notes and gestures had worked me into, but the thought of seeing those chocolate brown eyes and arrogant smile has me nearly keeling over from lack of air in my lungs. It doesn't help that the last time I saw him in person, I was fleeing from mind blowing sex. Sex that ruined me so thoroughly I didn't even bother trying to date after that. Between my exam schedule and knowing no one could live up to *that,* there was no point trying.

My mind immediately runs over our last encounter, and I struggle to remember why it couldn't work between us. His lips and tongue on my neck, my lips, my breasts, his hands gripping me as he brought me to the edge—*pull yourself together, Addison.* I thought the clean break I gave us worked until he sent my stomach into a mass of butterflies, flipping and escaping with the care packages. Between the cute notes, the lavender-scented heat pack, a box of different teas meant to help with stress and anxiety, a bath pillow and salts, candles with hilarious labels, 'I'm a badass bitch' and 'born to argue' with a balancing scales icon. The raunchy messages, food and coffee, all of it, was adorable, stupid, and ridiculous, and my heart flooded with feelings I was trying so desperately ignore.

"Are you okay?" Ethan's question snaps me back to reality, and I shake my head.

"Ah, yeah. Sorry. Um, okay, well, enjoy your beer." I turn and hightail it back to the table, suddenly too nervous to face the Greek god himself.

"Addison." I skid to a halt so fast the drinks shake on the tray, and I only just manage to stop them from toppling over. I don't need to turn around to know the owner of that voice. The caramel richness of it rakes over my entire body and it comes alive. I turn slowly to see Ethan sipping his beer and darting his eyes knowingly between us.

Noah.

Even his name in my mind is a breathy sigh. I can't physically open my mouth to say anything in return. I did my best to leave him alone, spare him from the torment that would be dating me, and saving my heart from the inevitable heartbreak when he is bored of me. I knew—*know*—this couldn't work between us. It would hurt more to try, and find out I was right all along.

"How... how are you?" His voice is husky, and he clears his throat before leveling a look at Ethan.

"See you around." Ethan beelines for the front bar.

"I'm, ah, good. Actually, celebrating today." I don't even recognize my voice, and my heart lurches to my throat at the smile that spreads across his face.

"Exams? You're finished now, right?"

"Yeah, me and the girls and Lucas are celebrating." I gesture to our table, and when I look, I see them all staring, Rosie with her usual shit-eating grin and Casey wiggling her eyebrows. I turn back, and Noah's eyes haven't left mine.

"I am so happy for you, Ads. You must be relieved. Bar prep now, right?" He takes a subtle step closer to me.

"Mmm, I haven't decided if I'll sit it yet." It's one thing to say it to my friends, it's another to admit it to Noah, or anyone else. The sudden fear of judgment washes over me, and I feel my cheeks pink slightly.

He just shrugs, that smile of his never faltering, making butterflies take flight. "I'm sure you'll decide whatever is right for you."

I nod at him, appreciating the lack of judgment or suggestion, and all the reminders of the ways he has always done that flood my memory. The way he accepts me for everything I am without being scared off or judging me. I thought our night together would have gotten him out of my system and the space would have snuffed out the flame of energy that ignites between us, but his acceptance of me, quiet encouragement for me to just be unapologetically myself, makes me want to jump his bones so Goddamn badly. That familiar flame of desire awakens and burns across my skin furiously.

"Thank you," I whisper the words and try to tamper down the flames. Trying desperately to strap down my emotional boner for this man, trying to recalibrate my brain.

"What for?"

"The gifts. You didn't have to do that. I'll give it to you—you are persistent." I give him a soft smile, and my eyes trail is form. *Beautiful specimen, this one.*

He shrugs, but his cool confidence surrounds him as he leans casually on the bar. "Told you I wasn't going anywhere. I'm glad you liked them, though. I wanted to make sure you weren't too stressed, were giving yourself a break."

"The cupcakes were my favorite. Everyone knows the way to a girl's heart is with food."

"Is that where it got me, to your heart?" He winks at me, and my heart beats so fast I'm surprised I haven't passed out. I have no words to respond, and he must sense the increase in my heartrate as he continues with his salacious flirting. "The strawberry cupcakes were certainly mouth-watering. Gave it a taste test first, but I've had better." *Oh, man.* How does everything he says always sound like a dirty promise? I don't know how I manage, but I remain standing, no moaning to be heard as his smooth voice enters my ears like a dirty caress. See, this is why I was glad his original offer had been over text. How was I ever going to turn him down in person?

He steps forward slowly, and in an attempt, I try to move the conversation on, still trying to tie down that emotional boner, and now hormonal boner, thanking the heavens that God didn't give women a giveaway for when they are ready to go. "How have you been?" Not actually certain I can handle any words that come out of his mouth at this point.

"I've been better." His voice is rough and husky. I know this energy between us affects us both, and his lips just look so fucking kissable right now. I don't want to ask why he's been better. I know where this is going, and I can feel my resolve, my determination, slipping away at the seams. "Just the usual. Work, stress... lonely nights."

There it is. "Noah." My words are barely more than a breath as I take a step towards him. His eyes are whopping chocolate circles with a sadness to them that nail me straight in the stomach. "Don't. Don't say anything. It is better—"

"Is it, Addison? Is it really better? I can't stop thinking about you. You say we can't do this, but there hasn't been a chance for us to even try. I don't know when this happened, probably that day at the Play House, but... I want you. I know I want you, all of you. I don't want to share, but I will if I have to. I don't think I can handle not having you around. However that is."

He takes a step closer, the distance between us shrinking rapidly, stealing the breath from my lungs, my words stuck in my throat. *But what if it doesn't work? What if you break my heart?* I set the tray of drinks on the table next to me and mirror his steps. We are so close the toes of our shoes are almost touching. My head is tilted to take in his smooth brown eyes, his spring scent, and the lust written all over his face.

"Noah, I can't stop thinking about you either. But—"

"No buts. Please, Addy, give me a chance to prove to you that we work. Together, you and me. Tell me to turn around and leave. Tell me that you feel nothing for me and that this is in my head, that there is nothing here, and I will kiss your cheek and say goodbye. I don't want to be where I'm not wanted, shortcake. But if you'll have me, I want to prove to you that this is worth the risk."

I fight my emotions clawing to get out. Maybe it is the high from finishing college, maybe it is the great feeling I have about my exams, or the love I feel from my friends, both old and new, maybe it is even the fact my family has left me alone for the last month. Or maybe it's the declarations and emotions pouring out of this man before me that have my heart singing so loudly I hear nothing else. Whatever it is, in this moment, that voice in my head telling me no, that internal war between wanting to shield him from me and my heart from him. The voice that says I will bring pain to this person, that I don't deserve this, and that I am better off alone, has been snuffed out, and all I hear is, *yes*.

"Give us a chance," he whispers.

I search his eyes. Sure, he left me at Maplewood and kind of ghosted me. Then he gave me whiplash between keeping me at arm's length and saying he wanted me, crashing my dates like a territorial caveman. I guess I ghosted him after the night at Bozzelli's, so who am I to point fingers, right? Unlike me, he at least grew the courage to say what he wants, to act on this thing between us. I can see he was just as scared as I was at the feeling that magnifies every time we are near each other. Like Thursday night at the bar, the electricity between us was palpable, and right now, the air is thick, like cords of electricity between us.

"Okay." It is out before I even know what I am saying, the shock and light hitting his face so quickly my stomach dips.

"Okay? That was a lot easier than I thought it would be. I was ready to send more gifts... even kidnap you for a date." He huffs a laugh and takes another step forward, bringing our chests almost completely flush with each other.

"I guess you caught me on a good day."

"Thank God for that." And he doesn't hesitate, his hands are on my face and his lips are on mine.

The kiss is soft, testing, but I can feel him holding himself back. I lean into the kiss, my body melting into him, and one of his hands leaves my face to wrap around my lower back, pulling me to him. In the distance, I can hear the cheers, the *woop woop* from Rosie, and the whistle from Lucas. I break the kiss on a laugh at my friends being complete idiots, but I don't leave Noah's embrace. Both of us are catching our breath as Noah smiles down at me, the face of a man who could drop my panties in a public bar and I wouldn't question a thing.

"What was that for?"

"Needed to. My control is good, but it's not that good. It was that or throw you over my shoulder and head straight for the staff breakroom." His voice is deep and low, just for me.

"Oh," I breathe, the image of Noah treating me to another one of those world stopping orgasms I know his magic fingers and tongue could coax out of me makes my heart race as I bite down on my lip to smother a moan.

"Addison, you're going to have to stop looking at me like that, or I am re-visiting the whole shoulder, breakroom situation."

I shake my head and step gently out of his embrace. This is a lot right now.

"Umm, text me. We can hang out soon." I give him a smile and *twirl* around, pick up the tray of drinks from where I popped them down, and head for the table with my friends. I try, and fail, to not turn and look in Noah's direction, nearly tripping and falling when I see him still standing where I left him, his eyes trailing me with a dark look of hunger and a panty melting smile on his lips. *Ughhh.*

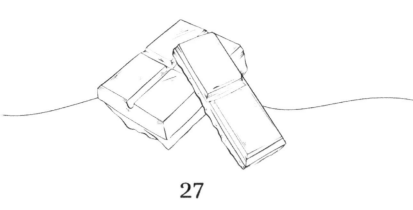

27

the elephant in the rage cage

Noah

I watched Addison walk back to her table of friends, telling myself not to stalk after her. I got lucky that she actually let me kiss her and give me another shot. This time, I wasn't going to let myself screw it up. I bury the sudden reminder of the recent developments with work. Matt and I have that under control, I tell myself it's nothing to worry about. Stuck between denial and being forced into secrecy gives me a bad taste about convincing Addy for another shot and not immediately coming clean. Not that I could without everything blowing up. Matt and I had a plan, and we needed to stick to it, for both our sakes. If we played this right, I could avoid losing the deal, my dream, and my dream girl all at once.

I refused to label this new thing with Addy in my head. If I say the d-word, I will psych myself out and sabotage this thing. All I know is I can't stop thinking about her, and the thought of anyone else making her laugh, seeing that smile, or hearing those breathless moans makes me borderline murderous. I tilt my head back to wrangle my brain and catch my breath before finally turning and heading for the bar where the rest of the guys are. Ethan immediately levels me with a knowing look while handing me my beer.

"So, how'd that go?" Ugh, the smug look on his face makes me roll my eyes. I am conscious of the fact that Matt is at the table, and I probably shouldn't gush too much.

"Fine. We'll catch up soon, I'm sure."

"Mmhmm." His eyes narrow at me, quickly dart to Matt, then land back on me.

"You slept with her."

Matt spits his beer out, almost choking on it. "You what?" His eyes are now searing his rage through me. "Noah, I specifically said—"

"Look, it wasn't like...*the others.*" God, even saying that made me cringe.

"Addison is different." How else do you say it? *She makes me lose my mind. I can't breathe without her next to me, but I also can't breathe when she is near? My heart feels like it might escape my body?* I try to put all these words into my eyes, hoping Matt understands without making me say it. I can barely say it to myself, let alone to the guys. And Caleb would never let me live it down.

"So after everything I said, you're going for it... you're that serious about her?"

"Yes. I told you. It's different this time. She is different."

"I fucking know she is different. She is my sister-in-law. I have known her for almost twenty years, and she has a lot on her plate. I swear to god, Karvelas, if you break her heart, I will hurt you."

A pool of guilt forms in my lower belly, but I shove it down. I have no intention of breaking her heart, doesn't mean I won't, but I will do my best to be what she deserves.

"You know, if she finds out now, she'll hate you," Matt says in a low voice meant for only me, except he has the subtlety of an elephant in a mall, and Ethan still manages to hear what he says.

"Finds what out?"

"Nothing," Caleb, Matt, and I respond in unison. Ethan gives us a confused look but drops the subject. Sensing the need for some privacy, Ethan puts his beer down and nods to the direction of the bathroom, leaving the three of us alone.

"You know she should find out from you more than she should hear it from me." I tell Matt.

"I'm on strict instructions from Ava to not mention a thing."

"Ava fucking knows? I thought this was a need to know basis, you know, considering the whole, '*If anyone finds out the deal is dead*' thing happening?" Caleb grumbles.

"I had to tell her. She's my fucking wife, and it involves her. She needed to know why we weren't seeing her family in the near future, or until this gets handled properly. I still haven't figured out how to address the very angry elephant in that room."

"You know, for an engineer, you're pretty stupid. That is not how that saying works... Wait, who is the elephant and what room?" Caleb asks.

"Fuck's sake, this isn't important right now. Addy won't hear anything from me. She will find out when everyone else does. She'll understand there isn't anything I can do. My hands are tied."

Matt shakes his head with a smile, like he knows something I don't, before he says quietly to himself more than to anyone else. "Oh, Karvelas, you have no idea who you're dealing with."

She won't hate me. She will understand, I'm sure of it.

Fuck, I hope she understands.

"Anyway," I make to move on, bringing Ethan back in as he returns, "I am more scared about JJ finding out about us, to be honest."

"He knows?" Matt looks completely shocked.

"JJ is her brother, right? How did you fucking his sister come into a conversation?" Caleb's amusement causes a wave of protectiveness to erupt at his words. Fucking wasn't quite what that felt like, and the word feels too impersonal for what we did.

"Easy, pal. Obviously, I didn't tell Jessie anything about... what happened was he said something to Addison, it upset her, and he might have caught me gawking a few times at the café, and his expression was... exposing."

Matt laughs. "Well, good luck with that. I am married to Ava, and Jessie still gives me grief. He takes protective brother to a new level." Well, I might just avoid him for a while, I think. "So how serious are you, then?"

"Boring! It doesn't need to be serious, Matt. Can't the man have fun?" Caleb scolds Matt before taking a huge swig of his beer.

"Sure, he can have fun. With anyone but Addison." This bubble wrap opinion he has of Addy is grating on my last nerve.

"What is your deal? Why do you treat her like she is a fragile piece of glass about to smash into pieces?" I tried, and failed, to leave the anger out of my tone. Ethan and Caleb share an awkward look as Matt levels me with an intense stare.

"Because, Karvelas, I was there when she did break into a million pieces—both times. And I am not sure she has completely put herself together again, and then you took interest, and I am worried about how quickly she will fall apart again." Matt throws his beer back, slams the glass on the table, and looks at Ethan and Caleb. "I'm going to get some air. See you guys later." Before he stalks off. Ethan and Caleb drag their eyes to me, looking a mix between shocked and pitying me.

"Fuck's sake." Not off to a great start.

"Rage Cage?" Addison's tone is judgy as she levels me with a plain stare.

"Don't knock it until you try it." I give her my lopsided grin, hoping I can tease her into agreeing.

"What kind of date *is* this?" And damn if my heart doesn't lurch at her agreeing this is a date. I take a step closer to her, looping my arm around her shoulders to drag her into my side.

"This is what a first date is meant to be. Not some half-assed restaurant filled with the wanna-be's of NYC." She rolls her eyes at me, but I continue. "This is where I came after my dad died to blow off steam. I come here every now and then, when the time calls for it. It is extremely cathartic."

"I'm sorry. About your dad." The emotion in her eyes is sincere, but doesn't hold any of the pity most people level me with. It's refreshing, and yet it makes me look to my feet. Clearing my throat, I shrug.

"I'm okay now. I miss him, and it still hurts like hell when I think about him, probably always will, but the anger isn't there so much anymore." I look back to her eyes, and I see all the questions, but as if she knows I could spare no more, she looks back at the entrance, bringing her arm to wrap around my waist.

"So you're all healed up and perfect because you threw some shit at walls?"

I chuckle and look back down at her, my tongue going dry at the smile spread out on her face. I can't even stop myself, I lean down and place a soft kiss to her lips. Needing to soak up all that joy and absorb it into my body.

"I can't believe I get to just kiss you when I want." She smacks my chest and chuckles as she leaves our embrace and heads for the front door.

"I don't think so, pretty-boy. You got lucky with that one. Better hold on to it, because it was your one and only for today." Her tone levels out on a sigh as she continues through the front door, it closing behind her. I shake my head and try to ignore the warmth rapidly filling my chest. *You're totally screwed, Karvelas.*

"Your cage number is 5, down the hall to the left. All the items on the table on the far wall are fair game, you can use either a bat or just throw the items and go nuts," the customer service lady says from behind the front desk as I pay for two entries. She gives us a pass to the room and we head down the hall.

"Using a bat?" I ask Addison, giving her a sidelong glance as she watches the chaos in the other rooms.

"Bat, for sure. But fair warning, we might end up in the emergency room." She chuckles softly.

We swipe the key and enter the room. It is a sterile white room filled with tables and typical breakable things. Plates, bowls, old CD players, radios, computers, TVs. The kind of crap no one uses, that you can break without hurting yourself. They have us in full body suits and protective goggles to help further avoid any additional damage to our bodies. I look at Addison and try to decipher her expression.

"What's going on in that head of yours?"

"I guess I am nervous. I don't really know where to start." She chuckles self-consciously, looking around and grabbing her waist like she is trying to hide. Like she doesn't have this incredible fury just begging for a release. To lead the way, I grab a handful of plates and throw them at the far wall. I turn to look at Addison, the exhilaration flooding my veins, and the mirth only grows as I see the look of excitement spread across her face. She reaches for a pile of plates, looks me in the eyes, almost questioning whether she should do this.

"Go on, shortcake. Give 'em hell."

She throws the plates against the wall with a grunt and then her body stills. She turns to look at me. "That was awesome," she says breathlessly and walks over to the wall with the smashing equipment to reach for a bat. Without a breath, she turns and slams it into a boom box laying on a table and it smashes into a few pieces. The stereo has barely anytime to recoup before she is bringing it down again, again, again before it is nothing but tiny pieces of metal. A deep guttural laugh comes from deep within her and it makes me laugh. Such a tiny person with such aggressive noises, noises that do all sorts of things to me.

She looks at me, panting, a slight sheen to her eyes and her cheeks rosy. The sight of her like this makes the blood rush south, my dick straining against my pants. *Fuck, she is hot.* Between the breathy sounds, the blush along her cheeks, and the exhilaration vibrating from her, I want to push her up against this wall and give her an even better release.

She closes her eyes and looks to the roof and lets out the most animalistic laugh I have ever heard. "Fuck!" she yells. I join her then. With a bat of my own, I turn and smack a few items, old TVs and computers. She grabs a few more plates and other breakable porcelain items, like old vases and salad bowls. After about two minutes of silent smashing, my movements slow, and that is when I hear it. Low, deep whispers that feel like a growl.

"Screw your opinions." *SMASH*

"All those times you made me feel broken." *CRASH*

"Every time you made me feel small, like I wasn't enough."

I turn slowly to watch her, her face no longer that smiling unabashed picture of joy, but now a picture of pain, her body thrumming with furious energy. I flinch as she tips a table of items that go smacking to the ground, and she lets out a pained groan. She brings the bat down on the remnants of the broken items, her face pulled into an angry scowl, her cheeks brightly flushed.

"*Addison.*" It is barely more than a breath as I watch the white-hot rage take over her mind, body, and soul. She becomes her rage, and, *damn,* if it isn't the most painfully beautiful thing I have ever seen. I can see the catharsis of her actions soaking through her. This is helping. I feel a sudden urge to hold her, ask her what she needs, and give her the entire world. I want to lift all her burdens and wear them for her. I feel the stabbing pain in my chest that she bears so much on her own, and I feel helpless that there is nothing I can do to help make it go away.

She lets out a scream that sounds a bit like it contained a sob, and that is when I move.

"Screw you. Screw your standards. Fuck you for blaming me, for making me feel less than. Fuck you!"

I grab her shoulders, "Addy... come here." I try to calm her, she jolts her body out of my arms, my heart in my throat and my brain in a panic. I try to reach for her, but she has her bat in her arms and is already across the room.

"I *am* enough. I *am* powerful. I *am* loveable. I am *not* damaged. Why..." A sob breaks from her throat as she brings the last smash down.

"Why can't people just love this side of me?" Her voice is soft. Outside the canyon breaking inside my chest, I can hear only her light sobs and her breath coming in fast.

Addison collapses to the floor, and I am instantly there. Dropping to my knees, ripping off both our goggles and bringing her to my chest. I wrap my arms around her tightly, unsure of what words to give her.

"Why…" *Sob, sniff.* "Am I really so hard to love? Why am I so broken? I just…" *Sob, sniff.* "I just want to be normal." My heart shatters, eviscerates into dust.

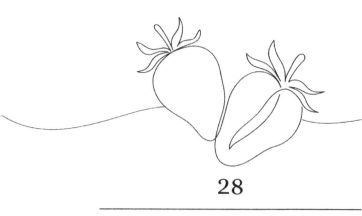

28

is rage-crying the new foreplay?

Addison

I crash to the floor, not feeling my knees as the bat leaves my fingers. Pain. I feel pain so deeply in my chest, that familiar burn of not being good enough. The outlet of the rage, causing it to grow, to break free and manifest into all the reasons it simmers under my skin. Jake's break up speech, my parents' constant bullying and belittling, my inner monologue and fear of failure, berating me. *Why can't I be normal? Why am I so broken? Can I not wake up and feel joy at being alive, grateful for what I do have?*

The sob that leaks from me is deep and filled with angst, and I feel the warm firmness and scent of spring wrap around me tightly as I finally let it all go. The tears are hot as they streak down my face. My stomach clenches from the pain and grief of letting it all go.

I just want to be enough. I just don't want to be in pain. To feel it anymore.

"Addy, you are more than enough. You are the furthest thing from broken." Noah's rich voice soaks into my body as he holds me firmly to his chest, rubbing soothing circles on my back, his other hand clutching my head to his chest in a firm grip.

"Addison, you... you are so, *so* incredibly strong. Your anger, your fury, is so powerful. You could rule the world with that gift." I lift my chin to look at him. Absolutely astonished at his words.

"Don't you see? I know I'm still getting to know you, but you have to know, your anger and your rage are not things that make you broken. They protect you, they keep you strong." I take a huge breath in, not handling the amount of vulnerability that is being emptied in this room, but not having the moisture in my mouth to swallow to be able to speak words. I search his eyes with mine. They are pained, deep wells of an emotion I can't name.

"Your ability to make it in life as far as you have, with the cards you've been dealt, is a testament to your strength, and I believe that strength comes straight from your anger. Your fury when it comes to sticking up for your friends, the reason you nailed every one of your classes, why you go above and beyond at Lucas's bar. The reason why, when we first met, you didn't turn around and apologize, but instead, nailed me with the fiercest scowl I have ever seen, to–*rightfully so*–make me accountable for my actions in ploughing you down." My lips part on a sigh at the raw emotion that seeps from his body as he speaks his words. His eyes darts to my lips, his tongue darting out to wet his before he latches back to my eyes and continues.

"You are the thing that helps fix that what is broken. You are not broken, Addison, so far from it." He releases a deep breath and drops his forehead to rest against mine before whispering. "You fixed me."

He raises his head slowly, vulnerability written all over him. My eyes then leave his and make it to his lips. His hand reaches up and swipes away the last of my tears, and he continues as I watch each word leave his mouth. My ears must be deceiving me. My brain doesn't register the words he says.

"Your fury is not your weakness. It is your greatest strength, Addy. I think this world would be so completely lost if it didn't have you." The pain nails my chest and I can't help the sob that leaves me. The spot his words land is so exposed and so personal; I have no idea how he knew what to say. All the other words said to me in the times I needed it pale in comparison. His words, his were everything I didn't know I needed.

Just like him.

The pain, the betrayal and the emptiness remain, but it ebbs, slowly receding into the background as my breath evens out. I pull back to see the sheen in his own eyes as they desperately search mine.

His hands come up to my face, and he pulls me in. I think at first for a kiss, but he just pulls me to his shoulder, bringing me completely in his lap until I am straddling him and resting my head on his shoulder, my arms wrapped around his neck in a death grip. His arms circle my waist and match my strength. I think I could die here, content, feeling warm and accepted, with the one person on this planet who *truly* understands me and my pain, or at least is willing to meet me in the middle of my chaos to help me find a way out.

"Plus, watching you let loose is hot as fuck." I pull back from him and find him smirking down at me, a smirk that makes my stomach flip, and a little laugh bubbles out of me. He chuckles softly before he pulls me back to him.

We stay like this for a few minutes while I cry and sob. His grip on my waist doesn't let up, his circles on my back never cease, until my crying slows and my breath with it. Until I am calm enough to speak without hiccuping, and I pull back to look him in the face.

"*Thank you.*" It is a breathy moan at this point, slobbery and with no sexuality to it.

"You have nothing to thank me for."

"I do. For... this. I am sorry if I ruined our date."

"Oh, shortcake, you didn't ruin anything. Thank *you*. For being vulnerable. For trusting me."

He flinches slightly at the last bit but recovers so quickly I let it go. I pull his face to mine gently and give him a soft kiss. But I can't help but wonder, how do you go back from this vulnerability? Was this too much too soon? Will he run? Will he leave again? How does someone *ever* want to go on a date again with someone who loses their shit so thoroughly?

"I understand if you don't... like, if you don't want to do this again. This is a lot, for anybody. And we barely know each other."

His smile is small, but it shines in his eyes as he releases a warm chuckle while brushing a piece of hair behind my ear.

"One of these days you're going to stop second guessing me. Stop expecting me to turn around and leave. Because Ads, I'm not going anywhere." His eyes never waver as he continues, "Like I said, can't scare me off that easily." He doesn't let me respond as he places a gentle kiss to my lips. His words sink deep into my veins, wrapping around my heart and injecting into my soul, begging me to let go, to trust him. I wrap my arms tighter around his neck, dropping my weight to grind into him as I deepen the kiss. I find myself hoping, praying, that trusting him is the right thing to do because he has buried himself so deeply into my heart and soul, to get him out will surely break me in two.

His hands become frantic on my back, searching, as he matches my desire. Our tongues break the seal of our lips, in a dance that feels practiced, like we have done this forever and it isn't until a moan escapes me that he swallows with a hungry desire and I break away in a pant.

"This is probably not the place... to get carried away." My eyes aren't even open, knowing I can't look at his gorgeous brown eyes without needing to rip my clothes off. He breathes heavily against my lips.

"Mmhmm, you're probably right. Should we go?" I open my eyes to look at him, the amusement clear on his face, and my heart skips a beat. I take a few breaths, and a laugh escapes me as I throw my head back.

"Who knew rage crying was a type of foreplay?"

"Addison, there isn't anything you could do that wouldn't turn me on." His eyes are still gorging on me hungrily, and I can practically hear the thoughts racing through his head. I attempt a swallow and a warmth floods south of my stomach as I try to wrangle my desire. He senses this and we both make the smart decision to stand. Still, without giving any space to the other. Like we need the proximity, the closeness.

"Let's get out of here." His voice is husky, and downright illegal.

"Yep." I all but trip on my way to the door, adrenaline and exhaustion replaced with a renewed enthusiasm to have round two of the last time we were alone together.

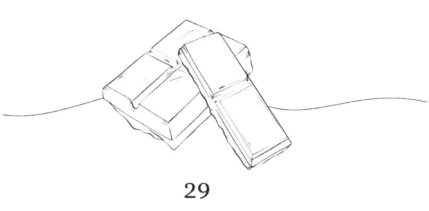

29

little demon, you've ruined me

Noah

Addy and I barely made it in the door of my brownstone before our clothes were torn from our bodies, leaving us in nothing but our underwear, if that's what you can call the tiny g-string she wears. *Fuck*, the need for her, to claim her fully, consumes me as her tongue dances with mine.

"*Noah.*" She practically moans my name, turning my self-control to dust. I reach for her legs, lifting her with ease as she wraps them around my waist. Our kiss is frantic, my fingers dig into her waist, pulling her down against the hardness of my cock that is begging to be released from my boxers, the talons on my little devil rake through my scalp as she pulls on my hair, turning me from man to beast.

"I almost wish you hadn't released so much at the Rage Cage, because I want it all. Will you give me all of your chaos, my little demon?" I taunt her, reveling in the husky laugh she releases. Her face turns, those fiery green eyes see right through my soul, and I feel her seductive rage wash over me.

"Oh, Romeo, there is plenty more where that came from. But I don't think you could handle all my darkness," she teases as she scrapes her teeth down my neck. *There she is.*

"Where have you been all my life?" My grip on her tightens as I walk–or rather, stumble–us towards the bed. I drop her and she bounces on the mattress, her breasts becoming a tantalizing display, and I remove my boxers immediately.

"I want to taste you," she breathes as she scrambles to her knees in front of me. I don't have time to calibrate what is happening, to tell her no, that right now I want it to be for her, to take her pain from before, before she grips my length, licking the tip, and moaning as she tastes me. The sight of her heaven, or hell, wherever it is, I never want to leave.

"*Fuck.* Addison." My head throws back as she takes me fully into her mouth, licking me from base to tip, hollowing her cheeks as she finishes on a pop.

"You said you wanted to fuck the filthy words right out of my mouth. Time to deliver on your promises." Her seductive taunt has me seeing stars, clenching my ass to not bust right on her tits. She looks up at me, her fierce green eyes through her long dark lashes, and a smile sent straight from the devil. Addison has unleashed something inside me I never knew was there, her fury and passion sending my heart into overdrive and my dick so hard it might just snap.

At her words, I reach down, wrapping her golden locks in my fingers for grip, and bend to whisper in her ear. "Take a breath, shortcake. You'll need it."

She opens, and I waste no time as I thrust in, right to the base, sheathing myself completely in her warm, wet mouth. I give her a few hard thrusts, her eyes watering before I slow and smile down at her, her lips pulling into a seductive smile. She might be on her knees, but it's clear she's the one in charge here. I am a goner for this woman. "*Fuck,*

Addy, you are the most beautiful thing I've ever seen." She moans lightly before grazing her teeth along my length, sending shivers up my back. "Those pretty lips. You take me so well, Addison." My release prickling at the base of my spine as it builds. I clench to hold back, not wanting to it to end this way.

"I want to taste you. I want you to come on my tongue, Noah," she all but moans, and it is my undoing. I grip her hair with both hands and thrust back into her waiting mouth, my pace relentless as she licks and sucks my length down her throat. The final kick as she reaches up and grips my balls, I come completely undone down her throat. I roar her name into the universe that appears in my vision, and I ease myself out of her. Her tongue licks her lips, her face thoroughly satisfied. I look down, soaking up the true masterpiece that is Addison Jenkins. "It feels like you've just stepped out of my dreams and turned my life completely inside out. Addy, you're everything I didn't know I needed." She squeals playfully as I all but throw her back to the bed and land on top of her. "You truly are exquisite," I say, admiring her, my hands finding their way to her sex. Finding her as ready for me as I always am for her.

"Who knew you could say such wonderful words with such a filthy mouth?" she taunts me back, and the images of her fucking my mouth as punishment sends a new wave of desire through me. *Another time.*

Still hard as a fucking rock, I grab a rubber from the side table and roll it on. Flipping Addison on to her stomach, she instinctively raises her hips, and I thrust home without a second thought. Grabbing on to those golden locks once more, I heft her up, her back against my chest, and reach a hand around to her bundle of nerves.

"Be a good girl and come for me, shortcake." A few quick thrusts, her tight wet pussy taking me expertly, with her claws imbedded in the sides of my neck, I feel her warmth clench around me as she cries my name, and I follow after her. Riding out our highs together and falling to the bed in a sweaty, panting mess. "Releasing chaos at my command. Such a good girl," I pant from beside her, admiring her sated and happy profile as she stares back at me, emotion twirling in her eyes, emotions I can't read. She slaps my chest playfully as I pull her against me.

"That's enough filthy words from you, Romeo. I'm going to need a break, I think... I think you ruined me." I pull her into my arms and she falls against me perfectly. Her head resting on my chest as I stroke my fingers down the smooth panes of her back. Her words, her body, *her*. All of it makes my chest heave with need and affection for this woman. So many new feelings course through me, but I bite back on my response.

Because she, too, has utterly ruined me.

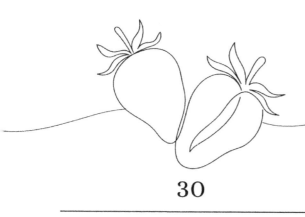

30

the return of james/jack

Addison

I roll over towards the side table, slapping my hand down, trying to grab my phone and check the time, but instead, I hit flesh, which properly jolts me awake.

"Ow." Noah's husky morning voice brings back all the toe-curling memories of last night, and I remember I stayed over. I didn't leave like last time, and neither did he. Instead, he was like a hot water bottle holding me, whispering sweet nothings, and saying the dirtiest things I've ever heard. Noah brings out this side of me I have never been proud of. A side that embraces my rage and all my mess, a part of me he has actually wanted unleashed. *'My Little Demon'*. Spirals of desire make their way down my spine at the memory of his new dirty nickname. Releasing this part of me has erupted a whole new pit of desire towards him. The way he wants to experience every part of me. I remember saying something like, *'fuck me,'* to Jake and he winced at how 'vulgar' I was.

Noah opens his eyes slowly. "What was that for?" His tone is coated in humor as he drags me towards his chest, wrapping those big arms around me, tucking me into his front and intertwining his legs with mine effortlessly.

"Sorry, I forgot I wasn't at home. I was trying to check the time."

"Have somewhere to be?" Oof, that sleepy voice is dangerous. I kiss his cheek and smooth his sleep-messed hair from his face, admiring him in all his beauty.

"Actually, no." I really don't. And there is nowhere I'd rather be than right here.

"Good, because I have plans for us this morning," he says, now waking up a bit more, his hands slowly exploring my still naked body.

"Is that so? What kind of plans do you have for us, Romeo?" I taunt as I play with the ends of his curls, looping my arms around his neck to pull us closer.

He hums seductively. "Plans of the sensual type, mostly." He chuckles softly and I copy as he maneuvers us so that I lay underneath him, both of us still completely naked. "Need to start the morning off with a bang, set the tone for the rest of the day. What do you say, Ads?"

"Mmmm, sounds delicious."

"That's my girl." The kiss he gives me steals my breath. How have I woken up without him before? In this moment, it feels like the best kind of wake up, and I want to make it my new reality. Oh boy, it feels too soon to think this way, but with the way his hands caress my body, the way his words soothe my mind, and the way he has so thoroughly invaded my heart, makes it impossible to ever want to leave.

My Girl.

After a morning straight out of a dirty romance novel, we eventually had to enter the real world. It was Monday morning after all, and Noah had to go to the office. I headed back to my apartment to make some plans before graduation, but also to do some research. I think I have all but decided that taking the bar exam isn't my plan, but I needed *a* plan. What was I going to do? I couldn't exactly coast, now that I am a new grad, and I want to make something of this life that makes *me* proud. To hell with what anyone else thinks of me. I also have no idea where this newfound confidence comes from. Perhaps Noah's constant adoration and compliments, but whatever the source, I'm harnessing it, and today is my bitch.

I twirl in through the front door, catching Casey on her way out. "Well, hello there, Miss Jenkins. Fancy seeing you here." Her tone is teasingly suggestive, as she knows exactly where I was, considering I left for a date with Noah, sending a 'don't wait up' text and never coming home. I giggle at her correct insinuation, unable to deny all the happiness floating in my soul and the memories of Noah and me together.

"Off to the studio?" I change the subject, but my answering smile is all the confirmation she needs.

"Yeah, Grace and I have a meeting with a realty agent. We're looking at a new location." This is news.

"You're moving the studio?"

"No, actually trying for a second location." The excitement in her voice is enough to know this is a big deal.

"Oh my God, that's amazing! I didn't realize you wanted to expand?"

"Neither did I. Grace mentioned it, she wants it to grow, she wants to start a family with Evan, and she wants to have the business in a position where she earns a comfortable living without needing to work in it, so we are going to try to grow it as much as possible. We have enough saved between the two of us, and the studio does well, so we are going to see how it goes." She levels me with a heart-stopping smile, the excitement emanating off her adding to my already warmed soul.

"Oh Case, I'm so happy and excited for you! Well, let me know how it goes. Is Rosie around?"

"No, she had an early start. She headed out an hour ago."

We say our goodbyes, and I have our beautiful apartment to myself. Lucas had increased my pay over the last few weeks of working, and I have managed to make up the difference in the rental payment, which is a relief. The thought of leaving this beautiful view made me sad.

After refreshing in the shower, my phone buzzes, lighting up with my mom's name, a call I choose to ignore, when it buzzes again with a message.

Romeo: *I can still taste you on my tongue.*

Flutters head south at his words, completely undoing my good work in the shower. If Addy from two months ago could see me now—smiling at my phone, my heart beating out of my chest, and the happiness I feel at the prospect of seeing Noah again after he finishes work—she wouldn't believe any of it. In fact, she would warn me to be vigilant because nothing is this good. Anything this good doesn't last, and I should protect myself. But Addy right now can't be bothered to listen or care. She just wants to see Noah's gorgeous smile and feel the warmth of his skin as he wraps me up, embracing all that I am and protecting me from myself.

Me: *Miss you too x*

I'm really not helping myself at this point. My toes curl, and I have to shake myself of the horny state Noah always gets me tied up in. I put the phone down and pull out my laptop, ready to make my future plans.

Noah

"Alright, I promised you one beer, but I'm off." I slap some bills on the table and salute the guys to leave Pucks and head straight for Addy's. I hadn't even wanted to come here tonight. I wanted to head straight to Addison and soak up every second with her, but the guys strong-armed me.

"Where do you think you're going?" Caleb questions, standing straighter.

"Addison's place."

Matt all but rolls his eyes.

"You're bailing because of a chick? What kind of friend are you?" Again, still unsure how Caleb manages to pull with an attitude like that. I shake my head at Caleb, but not hiding my smile.

"A friend with a girlfriend. I'll see you tomorrow." The other guys wave their goodbyes, and Caleb grunts his disapproval, but quickly moves on. No one notices my shock at how the word just rolled off my tongue. I hadn't even meant to say it.

Girlfriend.

I haven't actually called her that out loud before. Maybe it's presumptuous. We had one real date, and a night and morning of the best sex of my life. It's not that I'm worried about exclusivity, I know I'm not seeing anyone else, but I don't want to spring a label on her and scare the fuck out of her. It was hard enough to convince her to go on a date. Hard enough to convince myself to want something that wasn't just sex.

I shake off my descending thoughts as I make my way out of the elevator to her apartment when I hear that smooth voice I love. Except... it's not the same, it's... tense?

"I said leave me alone." That all but springs me into gear as I quicken my pace around the corner towards Addy's apartment. The pit of rage I've seen only a handful of times grips my chest at what I find.

"Problem here?"

She shoves Jake at the chest, who moves back from her at the sight of me. The prick had her caged in the corner.

"This is between us and doesn't concern you. You can leave, meathead." Oh, someone has a death wish.

"I think it's you who needs to leave." I fail to hide the growl in my throat. I give a quick glance to Addy and see the tears staining her pretty pink cheeks and my animal side rears his head. I step between them, Addison at my back, as I look down at this pathetic human being. "Time to go, buddy," I say low enough for him to understand the threat. His upper lip curls, and I find myself praying for him to throw the first punch. *Go on, Jake, give me a reason. Fuck around and find out.*

"I'm disappointed in you, Addy. You know better than to be hanging around with this wop." A booming laugh escapes my chest. *Wop, really?* That is the best this guy can come up with. If he wanted to insult me, he surely has something more creative than the most cliché racial slur on the planet. His words roll off my back, and I take a quick step forward as he falters and almost trips as he retreats.

"Catch you later, James."

"Its. Ja—"

"I don't care," I cut him off. He seethes, his face an adorable peach color. I take a step, making sure the wordless threat is communicated properly, my hands tightening into fists. He searches my eyes, and whatever he finds is enough for him to back down. He gives Addy one last look, or tries, but I step in his visual path before he leaves. I wait for the elevator door to chime closed before I turn around to Addison, wasting no time in closing the distance and pulling her into my arms. She wraps her hands firmly around my center and buries her head in my chest. Sniffing and obviously hiding her sobs. I pull back and place her cheeks in my hands and kiss her soft lips. "Hey, baby," I whisper against her, which somehow makes her cry more. "Hey Addy, my girl. Please don't cry. Let's go inside and you can talk to me." She nods and bends to pick up the takeaway food bag that I hadn't noticed before. "Hope you've got plenty. I'm starving." I try to lighten the mood, but it's a miss.

"You can have it all. I've lost my appetite," she responds emotion- lessly as we enter her apartment. Oh Jake, you're lucky you left. My fist suddenly feels like it needs a surface to hit.

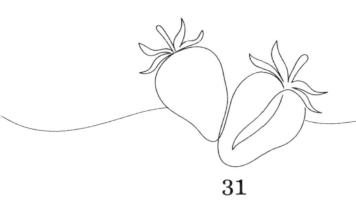

31

my nemesis, utter misery

Addison

Noah takes the bag of food from my hands as we enter the apartment, wrapping his fingers in mine and dragging me to the couch. He sets the bag on the coffee table before he sits and pulls me into his lap, sitting sideways so he can hold me, my head finding the comfortable location of his chest as he holds me close to him. The sound of his heart beating rapidly, the warmth of his skin, would be a dead giveaway to the wrath Jake elicited from him if it wasn't the typical display of testosterone the two of them displayed in the hallway. I hadn't had enough energy to tell him to stop. I'm disappointed in my feminism that I was glad for it. Glad to have Noah as my guard dog while I spiraled into all the dark places Jake sends me.

"You're wasting your life," he'd taunted me.

"Addy, you don't have to tell me anything. But I'd really like you to trust me enough to tell me if you're hurting." His voice is low, and I sense uncertainty.

"Jake ambushed me. I didn't know he was here. I was actually in the middle of writing you a text when I saw him at my front door."

My tone is flat but I don't raise my head to look at him, instead I give him my phone so he can read what I wrote.

> **Me:** Hope you've eaten, because I have plans and you're going to need the energy

Noah's body goes rigid under me and he all but growls, probably at Jake ruining what I'm sure he is picturing as a very fun night for him. He tosses the phone on the couch.

"What happened Addy? Did he hurt you?"

"Physically, no." And that's enough for him to shift, his heart ricocheting in his chest with his barely controlled rage. I decided to trust Noah, to let him into this part of me. Hiding from the spiraling thoughts, shoving down the signs of my anxiety, is just going to hurt me more. Noah has only ever accepted me, never giving me a reason to hide from him.

"He said my dad told him about Phoenix Legal. God knows why or where they managed to run into each other, or why Jake even cares. He reckons he was here to talk some sense into me. That I was wasting my life and throwing it away for a guy, never mind I was fired from the job before you and I even met. He told me that wasn't the Addison he loved and that he would help me get my life back together, saying he'd give *me* another chance." Noah growls, a deep rumble of disapproval, and I lean back to see his eyes burning holes into the wall opposite the couch, his face set in a fury that would rival mine. I grab his cheek and direct his eyes to mine, his face softening almost instantly as he leans into my touch.

"Hey, you don't need to worry. I obviously told him no and to leave. I told him he was wasting his time." He shakes his head slightly, a delicate smile gracing his face.

"I wasn't worried about you going back to that man-child, Addy. I'm furious that he came here at all. That he said anything to you and made you feel small." Tears well in my eyes, but I refuse to shed any more for Jake. I blink them back, and Noah reaches a hand up to brush a hair behind my ear. "There's more," he says, because he knows, because this man has the ability to read me like a fucking book.

I nod, but hold his eyes, hold on to the courage they give me. Knowing the reaction Noah is going to have. I take a deep breath and force myself to swallow, hopefully telling him with my eyes that I'm okay and he doesn't need to do anything to fix me. "He... after I said no, he came at me."

"I'm going to need to you clarify very quickly," he says, his words clear and his body heating.

"He crowded me. He tried to touch my waist, but I pushed his hands away. He..." I swallow again, squeezing my eyes shut because the hurt and rage in Noah's eyes make me anxious.

"Continue, Addison, please. My mind is probably suggesting things that are a hundred times worse than what happened, and I don't want to overreact, but I might throw you to the couch and go after him."

"He barricaded me into the corner and he just said a bunch of things to me."

You're a fucking whore. You jump from man to man.

Throwing your life away over some guy? I know a strip club where they take women like you.

Just another grad student who amounts to nothing. Your dad is right about everything he said.

"Addy," he prompts, wanting to know more, but I shake my head. I can't voice the taunts, can't voice the damage they are doing inside me. "Okay, okay, shortcake." He holds me tighter to his chest. My tears win the battle, and I cry. I let it out, the torment and the pain. The reminder of everything that floats around in my head. The drop back to reality from the high Noah had me floating on hurts like hell, like a slap to the face for being so stupid to think happiness like that lasts. Although having him here to hold me through the pain is a new comfort I haven't had before. After a few minutes, I hiccup through the end of my sobs, dozing in and out of my sadness, the darkness absorbing all my energy. I feel Noah shift as he stands and carries me to my room, placing me delicately on the sheets. He gets up to leave and I cling to his shirt. "Please don't leave," I whisper, hating myself for begging for his company.

"I'm not going anywhere. I'm just going to put the food in the fridge and get changed." He kisses my forehead and leaves the room, closing the door behind him, putting the room into darkness. My eyes snap open, trying to find the light, trying to ground myself, my heart rate picking up.

Wait, no. No, not now.

The robe on the back of my door comes into my vision as my eyes adjust, and it moves, the arms swaying, and the face of the demon forms as it smiles at me, focusing on me like I'm its next meal.

No, no, no, not now, not with Noah here. He can't see me like this.

The walls close in on me as my chest starts to tighten, my breathing erratic, and I can't control it, can't climb out of the darkness.

You whore.

I try to find a light, anything. It feels foreign in this room, feels like everything is moved like it isn't where it is meant to be. The room feels small but everything is far away.

Throwing your life away.

You're a waste.

A failure. You're worthless.

Not again. No!

It feels like I'm shouting, the blood rushing, like a ringing in my ears is all I can hear, and my eyes sting as the light floods the room from my door and I miscalculate the edge of the bed as I fall to the ground.

Humiliated, lost for breath, my heart beats so fast my chest hurts, and I claw at my neck to get air down.

"Addison! You're okay. You're okay." Noah lifts me and tries to plant me on my feet but I push off.

No, you can't see me like this.

I head for my bathroom and try to shut the door, but Noah is hot on my heels.

"Addy, you're scaring me. Talk to me." His tone is angry and pained, but I can't... I can't catch my breath and my cheeks sting with fresh tears.

"*Shower,*" is all I manage to get out before I collapse to the floor of the tiles, my body convulsing and panting. I bury my head in my knees as I rock back on the cold tiles.

Worthless.

Damaged.

A waste of space.

I can't, oh God, TURN IT OFF!

"Okay, baby, I got you," Noah whispers. The shower sounds like it's going, but I don't remember hearing it being turned on. Noah lifts me effortlessly and before I know it, the water is hitting my back. Sitting under the showerhead, my head buried in my knees as I cry in uncontrollable breaths, I feel a solid warmth behind me, rubbing circles on my back. "Shhh, I'm here, shortcake. I got you." His deep voice caresses my mind and my breaths ease up a bit, my body still shaking uncontrollably despite the hot water. I start to notice my surroundings, the rest of my senses coming back into the room. I sit in the shower, still in my clothes. Noah is seated behind me, his solid jean-clad legs on either side of me.

Noah. Like a sigh in my mind, the recognition of him here forces a huge breath of air into my lungs.

"That's it. Big breath. I've got you." He continues to rub circles on my back.

He is here. In the shower, behind me, fully clothed and getting drenched. "Noah." His name is a sob on my lips, and he sits forward, wrapping his arms around me, nuzzling my neck so his chest is fully pressed to my back. I feel the beating of his rapid heart between our saturated clothes.

"I'm right here, Addison. I'm right here." His warm breath coasts down my neck as he rocks us gently. "I'm not going anywhere."

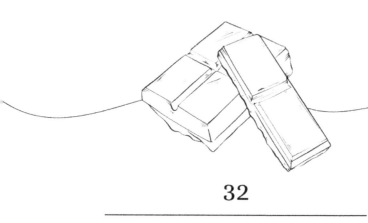

32

you put me back together

Noah

"Addison?" I call her name as I enter her apartment. I all but forced her into giving me a key after last week's attack, her panic causing me to lose my mind. The thought of her suffering when alone—I wanted to be able to help her without her needing to let me in or being aware enough to unlock the door. She didn't take much convincing.

"Out here." Her smooth voice sings from the living room, that sweet strawberry scent instantly wrapping itself around my heart as I take a big breath. Her apartment is elegant, making it very clear three women live here. But it's perfectly Addison, and in a way, that warms me. Mostly white furniture and soft accents of blue and pink throughout the house. A jaw-dropping view from the living room with floor to ceiling windows and a couch situated to look out at the view.

Home. Coming here and being in her presence. It feels like home. I walk through the kitchen and she comes into view. The picture of real beauty. Her soft smile in my direction, as she is bundled up on the couch, a coffee and a book in hand. I could stand here all day and just watch her, the way her smile creates the tiniest of dimples in her cheeks and makes the corners of her eyes crease. When she smiles fully, she smiles with her eyes, and every time, it's like the wind is knocked from my chest.

She had a long sleep–like ten hours–after her panic attack, and then she told me everything that Jake had said. I had calmed down enough to hold her through it and not make it about me and my rage. As she has told me before, I have no right to her rage, but *fuck,* if Jake doesn't make that hard to come to terms with.

She opened up to me more this week, too. I had asked, but didn't want to push. She gave it freely, and it's been a bit of a learning curve, understanding the way her mind works, how to support her. I don't want to wrap her in cotton wool, but it's hard seeing her in pain and having no idea how to help. So instead, she told me about her triggers, the need for routine–another reason I didn't want to be later than I told her I'd be. It was hard to hear that sometimes triggers are inescapable. Just having a bad sleep, being tired, having a bad run in with someone down the street, all things out of her control, and yet she is the one who deals with the consequences. Every day she gives me a bit more, teaches me a bit more, and my heart grows a bit more for her.

Addy is still my Addy, but I'm just awed by her. Her strength and her fight.

Rosie and Casey have been great. They give me secret updates when one of them is with her, and I manage to coax Lucas into information at the club, too, just to make sure she is happy, okay, and managing.

"Which book is that?" I ask as I stroll towards her and lean my forearms on the back of the couch behind her. She tilts her head back in a heart-stopping smile.

"That dirty book I was telling you about." She giggles, a bit of the little demon I love, making an appearance, and damn if it doesn't tent my pants instantly. I smile deeply and kiss her soft lips.

"Hey, shortcake," I whisper against her lips.

"*Yeia sou,* Romeo," she whispers back, stealing my breath and adding a twist to our usual greeting.

"Well, someone has been busy." I jump over the back of the couch and pull her into my arms, snatching the book out of her hands.

She shrugs self-consciously. "I wanted to impress you." A soft pink blush reaches her cheeks and my heart explodes in my chest, a million feelings I don't have time to label flooding through my veins. Reining in everything I want to say, I kiss the soft pinkness of each of her cheeks. "What else have you learnt?" I question, curiosity getting the best of me. This insane woman took the time to learn words in my native language, and I don't know why that does things to me, but I wish I had the power to eviscerate clothing with the snap of my fingers. She turns in my arms and leans forward, causing me to fall back onto the couch. That seductive temptress from before makes a rapid appearance, and her smile has my dick hardening in my pants. Now completely above me, her legs straddling my waist, she leans down to my ear and whispers, "*Se latrévo, Romeo.*" *My god.* I groan, reaching around to grab a handful and let her know just how impressed I am; the roll of her 'r' was perfect. Before I can ask, she continues, "*Yámise me.*"

"Learning all the important words I see." My voice is rough, and she bites her lip in response. I waste no time getting to my feet, throwing Addy over my shoulder and heading straight for her room, just doing as I'm told. She squeals playfully and laughs. "*Tha se káno na ourliáxeis kontó kéik,*" I taunt back and slap her ass.

We make it to the room and I slide her down the front of my body.

"What did you say back there?" she whispers, rising on her toes to loop her arms around my neck.

"Making you a promise." I kiss her pink cheeks again and grab the hem of her sweater and pull it from her. She grabs the hem of my shirt and does the same before I reach around and unclip her bra, our eyes never leaving each other. Despite our taunts and the chaotic sexual energy that burns between us, there is another energy between us, in this room, in this moment. Something deep and pulled tightly that has my heart racing. I'm suddenly nervous for an unknown reason, and like she feels the exact same way, I watch her swallow as she clenches her hands into fists before relaxing them again.

"Thank you." Her eyes are suddenly welling up and I reach for her, pull her close to me, her soft smile my only tell that she is okay.

"What on earth are you thanking me for now, Ads?"

"For showing up."

"Why would you think I wouldn't? I told you I was coming over, right?" I go to reach for my phone, and she grabs my wrist, pulling my eyes back to hers.

"No, I mean, showing up for me. For... not running away or judging me. For not treating me like I need to be fixed, like something broken and fragile. You make me feel like I'm living a high all the time, even when I drop into my lows. You've... *Noah.*" She drops a tear that I swipe with my thumb, but stay silent enough for her to continue. She takes a breath and her smile grows again. "You've put me back together, and you don't even know it." Another tear, but this time, I kiss it away, tasting her on my lips and tongue, and she releases a sigh.

"Don't give me credit for your hard work, Ads. You put yourself together, I watch you do it every day. I feel lucky enough to just be along for the ride. And right here, next to you, is where I'll be. Along for the ride, we'll weather the storm together." Her smile is like a warm sunrise, the promise of something special, easing you into its beauty as it rises. "You know, you're the one who fixed me."

"You said that at the Rage Cage, as well," she says softly, her eyes asking the question.

"You gave me hope, made me believe." In love, in a future with happiness. The oath I had made myself, to swear off love, to spend my days alone, was as much a protection for myself as it was a miserable part of my future I wasn't looking forward to. "Somehow, you made everything else seem like less. The only thing that matters is you. You made me want to be better, to open my heart, and to have hope. You gave me that, and I've never felt more whole than I do when I'm with you." That heart-stopping smile of hers is back, and it sets me on fire. She closes the final distance between us, sealing our lips in a kiss so deep and full of longing, so many emotions flooding my brain and my soul, I don't know how to catalogue them all at once. She breaks the kiss and my thoughts before they go too deep.

"What promise did you make before?" She bites down on her lip, those fierce green eyes firing back at me.

There she is.

I nibble her earlobe before whispering, "I'm going to make you scream, Addison." Her hand is at the top of my pants, pulling, and I chuckle deeply at her eagerness.

"You always say you keep your promises. Well, I'm holding you to this one." And that is challenge in her eyes. Eyes that are a raging forest of emeralds that I see my future in.

Eyes of my Addison.

My Addison, my *Love.*

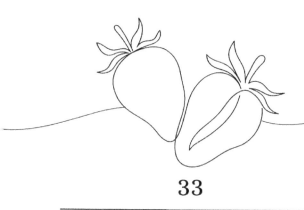

33

thank you karma gods

Addison

My hands are clammy as I wipe them on my robe, my graduation cap sitting uncomfortably on my head as I shift nervously on my seat, not ready to walk the stage with thousands of people staring at me.

"Now, we will begin the reading of our 2023 graduates' names," The presenter on the stage announces and butterflies take off in my stomach. I didn't have a chance to see Noah before he got here. Assuming he is here, I guess... he had to work, but said he would be here. I decided to leave it at that and not become one of those clingy girlfriends.

Girlfriend.

We still haven't established this yet, but in the couple of weeks we've started seeing each other properly, it feels like he knows every inch of me. Dating doesn't even feel like a big enough word for the size of the feelings I have for Noah.

Cheers erupt as the first of the names are called out. I never managed to make any college friends. A pit of embarrassment sours in my stomach at the thought. Everyone already seemed to have their cliques;

I had Rosie and Casey. I just wanted to go to class, study, and come home. I didn't really have the energy for all that socialization. But I'm here.

Graduating.

Magna Cum Laude.

Who would have thought? Certainly not me.

"Addison Rose Jenkins." The announcer calls my name, the clapping continues, and as I make it to the stage, I look out at the crowd. I try not to search, try not to let it be important, but telling my heart to not get excited isn't doing me much good because I'd give anything to be able to celebrate an achievement with people who care about me succeeding, rather than what it is I am succeeding at and by how much. When I make it to the guest speaker and the faculty, I shake each of their hands. I make it to the other end of the stage, and before I descend again, I look one last time, and right behind the friends and family gate where everyone is crowded, I see a tiny head of dark curls sitting atop the shoulders of a smiling Matt. Ava tucked to his side, beaming and clapping. Rosie and Casey on the other side of Matt clapping, the former cheering a '*whoop whoop*'. And behind Rosie is the tall, dark, and handsome Greek god sent from the heavens to guard my heart. My very own Romeo. I bite down on my lip to hide my excitement as I quickly wave. His face beams a smile in a whole new level of sexy, pride seeping from him, and my soul feels like it is slowly being completely repaired.

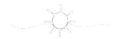

"We're so proud of you, Addy!" Casey and Rosie wrap me in a bear hug before withdrawing and giving Ava and Matt a turn.

"Killed it! Knew you could do it." Matt gives me a fist bump.

"Good job, Aunt Dadi! I LOVE you!" Mia shouts from Ava's arms, making everyone laugh together. I turn and see Noah, standing a distance away, giving everyone space to say their piece. Matt notices him over his shoulder and rolls his eyes before wrapping an arm around Ava's shoulders.

"Alright, we'll catch up with you later. Well done again, Ads, you deserve it." His smile is kind, and Ava just gives me the waggly eyebrows.

Casey squeezes my shoulder and winks before turning while Rosie slaps me on the ass and says, "Get 'em, tiger."

"Hey, *oraíos*." His sexy smile aims straight for my lady parts. His deep rich voice with a Greek accent he can sometimes just turn on, has me melting into a puddle on the spot.

"Hey there, Romeo," I say back as he saunters closer to me, stopping directly in front of me, his hands casually in the pockets of his suit pants. Using a delicate finger, he swipes a piece of hair behind my ear.

"I'm so incredibly proud of you, shortcake." I hum and lean into his touch, feeling full and warm that he is here, looking at me with those chocolate eyes that see right through me. "The afternoon is yours. What do you want to do with it?"

"You don't have to go back to the office?"

He shakes his head and my butterflies take off. "Took the rest of the afternoon off. I'm all yours." He leans down and places a kiss on each of my cheeks, soft, sweet kisses that are so at odds with the usual chaotic energy that follows us.

"Well, I'm glad I get you to myself." I lean in and wrap my arms around his torso, rising on my toes to take his lips in mine. He deepens the kiss and holds me around the shoulders, wrapping me firmly in that spring scent of his. "But I'm so tired. I didn't sleep much last night. I feel like I have been a nervous ball of anxiety, and I think I just need some downtime." His grin is devious, and it has my eyes narrowing in suspicion while my mind thinks of all the dirty things he could do to help me relax.

"I have the perfect idea." He kisses me quickly on the nose before turning us and directing us to the parking lot, his arm remaining around my shoulders, and I reach up to interlace my fingers with his.

"How come you always do that?"

"Do what?"

"Kiss each of my cheeks."

He laughs gently before planting another kiss on the top of my head. "Because, when you get that little blush to your cheeks you look so damn beautiful I can't control myself."

"Okay, can I come in yet?" Noah had me wait out in the living room while he "set up my surprise" in my bathroom.

"You know, patience is a virtue," he calls from the other side of the door.

"I have no need for virtues, Noah. I'm already perfect," I say in my best brat voice as he opens the door, a panty melting smirk plastered to his face.

"That you are, shortcake." He grabs my hand and drags me inside, the air in the room feeling thick, and the scent of lavender wraps around me, making me breathe deeply. The lights are off and there are candles everywhere, a chilled bottle of champagne and a little bowl of strawberries sit next to the bath. A bath that is full, with bubbles and rose petals. My heart lurches and my stomach sinks.

"Noah..."

I slip deeper into the bath, feeling the water inch up from my collarbone to my neck, to my chin, until I feel my lips go under... I wonder: is this the most peaceful way to go?

My last trip in the bath flood my memory and my heart races. This kind and beautiful man. This man who never thinks of himself and holds me on a pedestal. A pedestal I don't belong on because he has done this thing, this amazing, heart-exploding thing for me, and I'm five seconds from a panic attack.

"You... you don't like it?" He seems confused as he steps in front of me, his eyes searching me, grip firm on my shoulders. "Talk to me, Addy. What's happening right now?" He remains calm, but I see the panic in his eyes. He wants to help, and he has no idea how. I try to take a breath, squeezing my eyes closed, and try to make the words come out.

"The bath. The last time... I..." *thought about dying.* How do you explain this to someone? That the last time I was in a bath, I thought about ending everything. The thought of no longer being a burden or failing at everything I do, being washed away by the deep water.

"You what, Ads?" he whispers, the concern on his face morphing slowly into understanding.

"The last time I had a bath, Noah, I... I wanted... I couldn't..." *Words. Say words.* "I nearly didn't get out." The words are a strained whisper, shame and guilt slamming me as I close in on myself, the tears pouring from my eyes, and Noah squeezes me to his chest. He holds me for a few minutes, swaying us gently enough that it manages to calm my breathing. *Great, I'm essentially a newborn.*

"Do you trust me?" he says, pulling back, his eyes latching on to mine. I nod without hesitation and he reaches around to the zip of my dress. "Can I?" Again I nod, and he undoes my dress, letting it pool at my feet. He bends and slips my feet out of my heels. I lean my hands on his shoulders for balance, and he lazily drags his fingers up the side of my thighs, my hips, my waist, and then to my back as he rises. He unclips my bra with ease, letting it, too, fall, his eyes trailing my body. "God, you're so fucking beautiful, Addison. Every part of you." He removes my panties and then clasps my hand, keeping his eyes on me as he walks us towards the bath.

I hesitate as he gestures for me to step in.

"Do you trust me?" he asks again, although perhaps it was more of a statement. He leans down and gently kisses my lips. "I've got you."

He lifts my hand up, and I step into the bath. He goes to let my fingers go and I grip on to him. "Wait, please don't leave." The panic ceases me, and the last place I want to be right now is alone in the bath, romantic setting or not. All the lavender in the world couldn't make alone time in the bath worth it.

"It's okay. I'm not going anywhere." He drags over a stool and places it against the wall, and takes a seat at the opposite end to me and he waits for me to sit, his smile a calm and warm caress over my heart. "I'm going to sit right here while you enjoy your bath. It's your time to relax, Addy." I don't know what karma gods I satisfied, but I'd do anything to thank them right now.

He winks at me and grabs the champagne from the ice bucket. "Glass of wine, shortcake?"

I am so completely gone for this man.

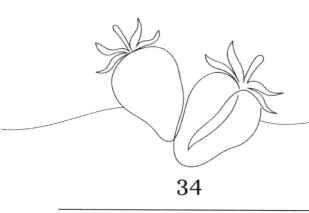

34

i do-you, too

Addison

"Come with me to Chicago next week."

My head snaps up so quickly I almost sprain it. "Wait... really?"

"Why would I be joking?" He chuckles at me as he twirls his fingers in my hair. My head rests on his chest as we lay naked in my bed. The last few weeks have been a euphoric bliss of Noah and I. After the night in the bath, Noah sat with me for an hour, adding extra hot water as I remembered why I loved them so much. Plying me with wine and strawberries, making comfortable conversation. He laughed with me, teased me, kissed me, and said all of those dirty words that have me melting in the palm of his hands. I have managed to keep the familiar dark and miserable part of my mind at bay since then, and it feels like I've been floating in a dream. A dream I hope no one wakes me from.

"You want me to meet your mom? Why?"

He chuckles at my expression, his eyes continue to caress my body, because that is how it feels when he looks at me. They burn soft teasing paths over every inch that they cover. I can never watch him do this without instantly needing to jump his bones. "Because, could be fun."

He shrugs, but there is more in his eyes than what he says. Words and feelings we seem to have skipped around of late. The words I feel and see in his gestures and hear in his sweet nothings, but words we haven't had the courage to say. I mean, we haven't even had the courage to label this thing between us. Also, too afraid to touch *those* feelings, I narrow my eyes skeptically.

"*Fun?*"

"Yeah, could show you where I grew up, where all the *cool* kids hung out. Where I had my first kiss, the first time I crashed my bike..." His tone trails off, eyes darting around before he drags them to mine, holding his heart right in their center.

"You know... the normal things a guy would show their... girl-friend." Uncertainty laces his words, vulnerability on full display across his face.

Girlfriend. My swallow is audible and my heart races. I want this—I do. *I do, right?* Yes, I do. Just the fact that it is here, in front of me, actually happening, and so far no bad repercussions, is making me think perhaps this is one of those times it's too good to be true, like landing a job at a big law firm before being let go, having a mind-blowing sexual awakening before I'm ghosted. Peak of a high right before a severe low. You know, *those* kinds of things.

"Okay, before you spiral on the worst-case scenarios, let me be clear." His words sting, and I flinch, but decide to hear him out. I move to sit up, bringing the sheets up to cover my naked body, and he almost looks disappointed.

"I know the things we said at the start still hover around us like plagues we can't shake, but I need you to know that I am serious. This isn't a fling. I don't do *this* ever and never have." He gestures between us, his eyes never leaving mine. He isn't wrong; these last few weeks have felt like anything but a fling. "I might not *do* relationships, Addy, but I sure as shit *do* you." I can't even stop myself—the laugh tumbles out and I slap a hand over my mouth. He levels me with a deadpan grin as he realizes what he said.

"Really?"

"*Do-you.*" A full-blown laugh sputters from my lips as I try to remember I am twenty-five and not five. "Sorry, sorry... continue." I cough to clear my throat and mind of childish thoughts. He smirks, shaking his head and rolling his eyes at me.

"What I *mean,* you child, is that if the definition of this is '*a serious relationship',* then I'm all in. Because I want it. I want all of it. With you. As much as I can have. And if you don't want labels, that's cool, too. I just want you for myself and I want to shout it from the rooftops."

Swooning.

His expression morphs from laughing at my childish jokes to something so deadly serious. His face and eyes are at odds with each other. The latter giving me his entire heart on a plater, the former is all stern strength and assurance. His declaration is a huge step, but *sigh.*

"Addison?" His voice is laced with nervous energy.

Landing my hands on either cheek and climbing onto his lap, straddling him as the blanket falls away, leaving nothing between our skin.

"I *do-you* too, Noah." His head shoots up, his relief and joy look like it is out of a golden retriever sales brochure, and it spears me right in the chest, my organ in there restricting intensely.

"I didn't... scare you?" He brings his arms around my lower back, and I let my arms fall behind his neck, playing with the ends of his hair.

"Please. I always knew you were obsessed with me." I give him a playful wink and that deep chuckle of his vibrates my chest, making me instantly ready for him.

"Oh, shortcake, you're an arrogant little thing, aren't you?" His smirk should be downright illegal as he pulls me closer to his chest and lowers me to the bed, his thickness instantly awake and already pressing at my entrance.

"I mean, I get it. I can't imagine *not* being obsessed with me." My words are barely more than strangled moans, aware of every inch of him that hums with warm desire, and he reaches a hand between us.

"Oh, baby, I think it might be you who is obsessed with me." The words are warm syrup over my skin as his fingers find out that if any part of me is obsessed with him, it's the place currently begging for him.

"*Noah.*"

"You moaning my name haunts me in my dreams, Addison."

"I need you."

"I know, Addy, I know." He places soft kisses to my cheeks, across my jawline, and my collarbone. He goes to pull away. "Wait."

"Relax, I'm just grabbing a rubber."

"But... what if you didn't?" His whole body stills.

"You're sure?"

"I take the pill, before you, there... well, there was no one for like twelve months. I was tested after Jake... for obvious reasons, and I'm clean." His body crowds me again, and it slows my heart to a comfortable pace as I babble with self-consciousness.

"I'm clean, too. Are you sure?" His tone and gaze are serious but drenched in affection.

"Yes, I'm sure. I want you. *Just* you."

His kiss is searing and affectionate, a caress of the soul, and I wrap my legs around him to deepen it. He teases me with his length before inching in slowly, allowing us to adjust. The feel of him is incredible. He continues to pepper me with kisses until he is fully seated and, thrusting slowly, he looks at me.

"Fucking Christ, Ads, you really were made to be mine."

Our bodies mold and move together, this time with less quick need and rushed desire, but more affection, care, something deeper that feels like it makes our souls intertwine.

Every thrust, every kiss, and every word is like a joining, like hitting a point of no return, and I *know* that this has to work between us. It just has to.

Because if it doesn't, I don't know if my heart will ever recover.

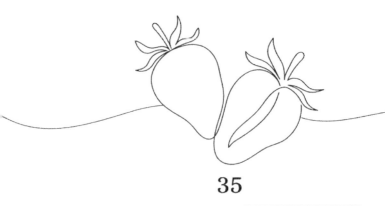

35

broken bits and all

Addison

"What if she hates me?"

"Why would she hate you?" Because I'm me. I shrug. I don't know how to respond, but I've never been so nervous about meeting another person before. Noah's mom. She is his sun, and he talks about her like she hung the damn thing in the sky. I just really want her to like me.

"Addy, baby, she will love you."

"How do you know?"

"Well, how could she not? Trust me, Ads. If I do, she will, too."

Ummm, what's that now?

I go rigid, my palms now clammy, and I feel the tension sitting between us instantly. Neither of us speaks. *Did he just say he loved me?*

She will love you.

If I do, she will, too.

What the fuck just happened?

I slowly turn my head to look at Noah. His expression is stark, like he has seen a ghost, pale and stunned as he stares out at the road from the driver's seat.

We flew into Chicago this morning, rented a car, and are now on our way to his mom's in Amberfield, a suburban area an hour outside the city. I've never been, but I did a nosey Google search and the area is gorgeous, somewhere you'd imagine raising family—safe, homely, and a sense of community. But all that is just noise right now because...

He just... he just said he loved me. *Love.*

Woah.

He quickly looks to me. His expression is so vulnerable, I want to reassure him. I know I feel it, too. I have felt it since the Rage Cage and have just denied it, telling myself not to get attached. His admission makes those feelings flood my system, and I want to shout it at him, scream it from the rooftops that I love him, too. I just... can't make the words come out.

"Noah..."

"It's fine. Anyway, I know you both will get along. Evie, too, she will lo—"

Oh God, he can't even say the damn word now.

"Noah, I—"

"Don't."

"Don't what?" My tone is accusatory. Excuse me, Mr. Greek. If I want to tell you I love you, I damn well will.

"Don't say it now. Just... I didn't mean..."

"Oh..."

"No, I *meant it.* I didn't mean to say it like that. I..." He grabs my hand and brings my fingers to his lips in a gentle kiss. He steals a glance at my face, and there is a small blush to his cheeks, lowering my hand to his lap as he holds it hostage. A small, bemused grin appears on his gorgeous face.

"Addy, I pictured this conversation going a much better way. No moving vehicles, a lot less clothes, and seeing those deep green eyes when you said it back." I feel my heart reach for him. I want him to tell me again, but with his body.

"Pull over."

"What?!" He looks at me, concern written all over his face. "Ads, I'm sorry. I didn't mean to freak you out. You don't have to say anything. I don't... I just I don't know when... Ads, wait—"

"Noah, you need to pull the car over because I need to kiss you, and I think if I can't touch you right now, I might combust." My words are breathless, the heat pooling lower and lower. His breathing is erratic as his head snaps to mine. Eyes searching my face, I pull my bottom lip in between my teeth, and his eyes snatch there for as long as they can before he focuses back on the road. Without any further words, he navigates us to a back road and pulls off the side, a healthy distance from the road. The engine is off, so I unclip both our belts and climb across the center to straddle his thighs.

"Shortcake."

"Romeo."

I slam my lips on his and spear my fingers through his hair, scraping at his scalp, and swallow the moan of pleasure he releases. His hands firmly hold my behind as I grind into him, desire eating away at my control and enhancing my confidence. God, I could take him right here in the car if we had nowhere to be.

I pull my face away, my hands framing his face as I search those big brown eyes.

"I am not used to trusting people's words so quickly. These weeks with you feel like a dream. When you say these things... my instinct is not to believe you. But I want to. I want to believe you so badly, Noah." Tears prick the back of my eyes as I pour my honesty into my words.

"Addison, I want you to hear me properly this time. I want you to know exactly what I am saying." His words are whispers, his grip on my hips tight, as he places a soft kiss to my lips and looks back to my eyes, a different expression. Certainty, tenderness, I can see his heart in them.

"I love you." Deep, rich whisky runs down my spine, and he moves a thumb to lightly brush a single tear from my eye. "Please don't cry, baby. I love you, all of you. Every inch of your skin, every corner of your mind, every smile, every laugh, every moan of pleasure, every time you're mad, every time you're happy, and every moment in between. I love you. In every moment you exist, and the moments where you live in my mind, I love you."

"Broken bits and all?" I say.

"You aren't broken. But for the sake of clarity: yes, shortcake. Broken bits and all," he promises.

A few more tears, a few more gentle thumb swipes, he wets his lips and I lose my words. This man, truly a God, sent from the heavens just for me.

Mine. He is all mine, and with every molecule on my skin, I am drawn to him. He doesn't just love me; he loves the parts of me I grew to hate, parts he is teaching me to love, and he's showing me how they too are beautiful in their own ways. That they make me who I am and that is the person he loves, scary bits and all.

"Noah..."

His breath catches, a soft smile to his lips as he searches my face, and the hope written all over him makes me feel like I am floating on Cloud 9 as I give him the words humming through my blood.

"I love you, too." He releases a small breath that sounds a bit like a laugh, or a sigh, I think—relief. He closes his eyes, and when they open, it's my turn to lightly dust my thumb above his cheekbone to swipe away a tear.

"My gentle giant, are you crying because I said I love you?" He pulls me down and places a firm kiss to my lips. Not desperate or sexual. A loving and tender kiss. It feels like the seal to a promise.

"That tear just slipped. I think this may be my happiest day so far." I kiss him again, but this time I need it, need him, to be closer. Connected. God, I want to peel these clothes off. He pulls back slightly, resting his forehead on mine as we pant and catch our breath.

"Say it again," he whispers to me.

"I love you," I respond without hesitation.

"Fuck. I really wish we had time before seeing Mom."

"Oh?"

I look up to his eyes, and they now burn a deep melted chocolate, hunger written all over his face, desire that matches my own, and I'm suddenly very aware of the tightening of his jeans.

"*Oh.*"

"Yes. Oh. You're going to need to climb back over there real soon or we aren't leaving this car until you're screaming those words again." His voice is deep, a sexual promise. I almost want to tempt him, make him prove his words. But the thought of rocking up to meet Noah's mom and sister for the first time, freshly fucked and blushing, is not quite the impression I want to make. I give him a devilish smile and kiss him softly on the lips as I climb back over. He holds my hands and helps me settle back in my seat.

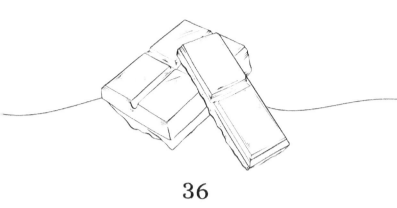

36

let me show you the stars

Noah

Nerves rack my body as we pull into the driveway. An unplanned detour, but, fuck, am I glad for it.

I love you, too.

She loves me. I swear my heart grew two sizes bigger. My chest sure feels like it has. It hurts enough. But a good pain, I think. Maybe this is what Mom meant when she talked about love with Dad. I never thought I would be here, in this moment, confessing my love for someone. But I also hadn't planned on falling so fucking hard for Addy. Being around her feels like a life force. The risk of her leaving me, while it would destroy me, it would have been worth it. Mom was right, if I knew this would end badly before I went into it, knowing what it feels like to have Addy, for her to be mine, I'd do it all again; consequences be damned. I send up a silent prayer that all this crap with Matt and EcoX goes away quietly. I'd rather avoid being a reason Addison gets her heart broken, and this secret is sure to do just that.

I want Mom and Evie to like Addison. I really, really want them to love her. It's not that I don't think they would, or that it would be a deal breaker, I just want Addison to know that there are more people out there that will think she is amazing, that the ridicule and pain she has been subjected to, that her distrust of people's intentions are not because of her. They are not a result of any flaws she perceives are built into her. This just needs to go well. It has to.

I love you, too.

I grab Addison's hand on the way to the front door, and it's clammy.

"Are you okay?" I say quietly as I lean over to her ear.

I let my concern for Addy distract the anxiety humming under my skin at seeing Mom and Evie. Hiding the guilt and grief that is ready to explode from the surface. Hoping they are okay, but also hoping they can forgive me for staying away so long.

"Umm... trying to be. I'm just nervous. I'm not good at meeting new people. New people who are important anyway." My heart tightens further.

"Guess you'll just have to compel them with those furious green eyes of yours, you know, like you did with me the first time we met." I stop just before the front door and lean down to give her a soft, chaste kiss, and she giggles against me. A megawatt smile spreads across her face and my heart skips a beat. I will never tire of seeing those smiles. They are my favorite thing in the world.

She bites her bottom lip. "You're really good at the whole distraction thing."

She smiles at me, and I give her a wink. "I have many more distraction tactics for later. Don't worry about that."

Almost a second later, the front door swings open with so much force I swear it almost left the hinges.

"*Aye, Málàka!*" Evie shouts the slur from the front door as she comes out to the front porch. My chest relaxing a little at the familiarity in her tone and from the way her eyes soften as she looks at me. Grateful that she is as happy to see me as I am her.

"Hey, trouble," I respond, but pull her into a hug. She relents, and it's how I know she missed me as much as I missed her. I give her a quick kiss on the head, the only apology I can make right now. She squeezes me extra hard for a moment, like she understands, before I turn to make introductions.

"Evie, this is Addison, Addy, Evie. Or I guess Evelyn."

"Ugh, call me Evie, or E. Evelyn was my γιαγιά. And a girl? My big brother brought a girl home? I honestly never thought I'd see the day. But I guess you'd have to actually come home for that." Evie wraps Addison in a hug and throws me a wink as I grimace. I guess I deserved that.

"Nice to meet you," Addison grunts out, having the air squeezed from her lungs in Evie's death grip.

"C'mon, let's go inside and meet the matriarch." I shuffle the girls in, Evie skips ahead and Addison whispers.

"Okay, I don't know like any Greek. I don't think I am going to be able to keep up."

"Oh, don't stress, we communicate almost 100% in English. Mom might say some things in Greek, but it'll mostly be English. Promise. Evie likes that she knows slurs in another language. She called me an idiot." Addison laughs quietly.

"My baby boy is home!" My mother comes around the corner, places her hands on my face, and pulls me in to kiss each cheek. "Hi, *Mamá.*" I lean into the embrace, and all the turmoil that has been settling in my stomach at returning home disappears. Her familiar scent of home-cooked meals and the rose garden out back fills me with contented nostalgia and my whole body just relaxes. Maybe I *should* have come home sooner. Maybe I really built this pressure on myself for no reason, or maybe its just simply that Addy is here, that she said she loved me, that I feel a little more whole regardless of the grief I hold.

Mom withdraws without a second look at me as she turns to greet Addy.

"And you finally brought me home a daughter-in-law." *Oh, Jesus fuck.*

Addison's spine snaps straight, and I pull my hand down my face. "*Mamá*... c'mon, don't do that right now," I grunt, and she turns to scowl at me, her Greek accent thick.

"I wait thirty years and still no grand babies. What you expect me to think? You bring home this..." and she turns her face back into a smile and grabs Addison by the cheeks and squeezes as she continues, "aye, a beautiful woman, and you think I can't see?" First of all, I am only twenty-nine. Secondly, yes, she is drop dead gorgeous, but she only just told me she loved me. I think weddings and babies are still a while off yet, not to mention, Addison is only twenty-five and has an entire life ahead of her. She pins me with a glare, motioning with her fingers from her eyes to mine. She kisses each of her cheeks and then pulls back and just goddamn stares at her. *This is just spectacular.*

"Addy, this is my mother, in case you hadn't worked that out... *Mamá*, Addison, my *girlfriend,* of like two months, so just... *irémise* ." I remind mom to take it easy, and I give Addy an apologetic look, although she looks confused at what I said. Didn't we establish the labels already? I shrug. We'll just talk about it later when we don't have an embarrassing audience. Mom finally lets go of Addison and does a chef's kiss with her fingers. She isn't wrong, Addison is beautiful on a normal day, but today her hair is down and curled around her face, a flowing summer dress that is a deep jade green that lightly dusts the top of her knees, leaving nothing to my imagination.

Despite my future being mapped out for me and my sister throwing out slurs, I don't think this introduction could have gone smoother. Everyone is met, happy, and making our way into the kitchen for food. The room in the house I spent most of my time in. Mom's cooking was always exquisite. Mostly traditional Greek food, but even her spaghetti was out of this world. I honestly don't know how she does it.

"Mrs. Karvelas, this is divine!" Addy practically moans on a fork full of lamb. That moan sending my thoughts to inappropriate places. *Would it be rude to excuse ourselves already?*

"Darling, just call me Iris. You are small, here eat more."

"*Mamá!*" Evie and I shout at the same time. Jesus Christ, I should have prepared my mother, not Addison.

"Ahh, it's fine... really." Addy gives mom her best confident smile, but I can see right through it—she is self conscious and uncomfortable.

"Noah, you don't feed her. She will blow away if you're not careful, and this one is special. You need to keep her." *And don't I know it.* Addy looks at me from across the table, her eyes pleading. I don't think she was ready for Momma Karvelas in all her glory. Christ, I wasn't even ready. I completely forgot what it was like to be home.

"Addison, tell me about your family," my mother grills. I send Addy an apologetic smile, hopefully encouraging her to just be herself.

"Umm... Well, I have an older brother Jessie, an older sister Ava, and my baby sister Riley. Except, well, she isn't a baby. She is twenty-one."

"And your parents?" I swallow roughly and try to keep my thoughts from showing in my body language.

"Um…" She swallows and pushes her food around with her fork.

"Henry owns an Investment Firm that's been in his family for several years. Lillian, Addy's mom, is a decorator." I got the rundown in Maplewood, plus I've been pestering Ava with questions about her parents, trying and failing to understand the dynamic better. I pray that no one can hear the anger that coats my words. Speaking of Addy's parents, or at least her dad, fills me with rage, and I'd like to leave the topic pronto.

"Why thank you, *Addison,*" my mother teases.

I roll my eyes at my mother and Addy thanks me silently with her eyes.

"You must be proud of your father. It sounds like he has done well for himself and the family." My mom sounds so proud and I hate it. Hate that this man gets credit for anything. If anyone should be celebrated, it's Addison, for turning out so goddamn perfect after what she has had to deal with.

"Addison just finished her Law Degree, actually received magna cum laude. And she is killing it at Bozzelli's. I told you about Lucas's bar, didn't it?" I take a swig of my beer as I redirect the conversation back to Mom. Ethan and Lucas were regular visitors here during the college days, with absentee parents themselves. They are like brothers, and my mom treats them as such. Mom gives me a quick, assessing glare. That woman misses nothing, but thankfully she takes the bait.

"Lucas, he is such a good boy. I knew he would do good things. They don't visit. When will they come home?" She feigns mad at this, but she means well.

"I'll bring them next time."

"So you like the bar Addison?"

"Yes, actually, Lucas is so amazing, super easy to work for. Definitely a change of pace from my previous workplaces, that's for sure. Plus, the other staff are great, so it makes it worth it." I elect to ignore the *so amazing* description Addy gave Lucas and decide to let her continue. If only so I can just hear her speak, watch those strawberry lips. I have other ideas for those plump lips. She told me she loved me and we barely had a second to soak in the moment. I had a plan, a really great, long, strenuous, and romantic plan. Those plans would need to wait.

We settle into comfortable conversation. Mom pulls out the photo albums in the most cliché thirty minutes of my life. Although, photo albums were the least of my worries. I was actually super adorable, didn't really suffer an awkward phase, so if anything, I was happy for the flex. Addison spends the whole time rolling her eyes and scoffing, "Of course you were fucking cute your entire life." I just shrug. What can I say? Just another pretty face.

I managed to steal Addy away upstairs a few hours before dinner. I had wanted to stay at a hotel, giving me lots of uninterrupted Addy time, but she had insisted we spend the time with Mom and E, which I'm glad for. I don't get much time to come home and see them, and this night has been great. I'm ready for it to get better. I give her a tour of my childhood bedroom, the shelf of trophies and collection of sporting photos, as the tour moves on to my favorite location—the bed.

"It's weird being in your childhood bedroom." She bites down on her lip and walks backwards towards the wall as I stalk towards her.

"How so?" I ask, although not really caring about the answer. I have one mission right now. Her back hits the wall and I crowd her space, leaning an arm on the wall above her, and I use a finger under her chin to tilt her head up at me.

"It's another side of you I feel like I don't know." She considers me questioningly, but I don't miss the hunger in her eyes as she looks me up and down.

"We have all the time in the world, shortcake. If you let me, I'll show you everything." I lean down and take her lips in a searing kiss, my tongue at the seam of her lips, and she opens to take me instantly. Our tongues dance slowly, intimately, as my hands find her waist and her fingers twirl and pull at the hair at the base of my neck. Something she does every time we kiss and I've grown to love this feeling, love the scrape of her nails on my scalp.

"My sweet Romeo," she says as she pulls away, panting from our kiss. "And what are you going to show me now?"

"The stars on the ceiling." I kiss down her neck, but she remains silent as I lower myself, peppering kisses along her body. Still clad in clothes, and unfortunately, my mom and sister are downstairs, so I can't waste time stripping off her clothes or risk them wondering what's going on. Now, my one mission is to thank Addy for loving me, for choosing to take a chance on us, ask for forgiveness for things she doesn't know, and to show her how much I love her.

"What stars?" she asks, panting as I kneel in front of her and trail my fingers teasingly up her legs then reaching under her dress. I run a finger along the seam between her wetness. "My needy shortcake. You'll understand what stars in a minute." I wink at her as I run my finger up her seam again, the soft cotton of her panties the only thing between us, and she throws her head back against the wall on a moan.

"We can't do this with your family downstairs," she pants and whispers but makes no move to stop me. My little demon loves the thrill.

"I guess you'll just have to be quiet." I slowly drag her panties down her legs, discarding them before I hook one knee over my shoulder, hiking her dress up to her hips, completely baring her softness to me. *Christ.*

"Can you be a good girl and be quiet for me, Addison?" I ask the question before running my tongue up her seam, tasting her sweetness, sending desire straight to my dick, unable to wait for her answer. She moans, biting her lip, but nods.

"Uh huh." Her finger intertwined in the curls and pulling me to her. My mouth meets her hungrily, my tongue lapping at her before sucking her bundle of nerves into my mouth, my teeth grazing lightly, which makes her wriggle in my palms.

"Fuck... *Noah.*" Her voice is strained as she tries to hold back her cries of pleasure. I continue the work on her clit as I slowly push in two fingers. Taunting and teasing her, sending her into a desperate frenzy, until she is all but riding my face. Using my free hand, I lift her other leg to my shoulder, my face and fingers buried inside her, and her back arching against the wall as she shakes with untamed desire.

"You're a distracting temptation in this dress, Addy. I've thought about burying my face under this dress since you put it on." I curl my fingers around, looking up at her face, the bite on her lips deep, the only thing keeping her moans of pleasure from giving us away. I pick up the pace of my fingers and use my tongue to lap her up, sucking on her clit as I feel her tighten around me, her body shaking. "Do you enjoy the power you hold over me, shortcake?"

"Make good on your promise, Romeo. Show me the stars," she whispers seductively as she pulls on my hair, making me need to clench so I don't embarrass myself in my pants.

"At your command, my little devil." I bury my face in her once more, my tongue on a mission, and teasing her, sucking and grating my teeth while my fingers work her sensitive spot so tight she arches almost fully off the wall.

"Oh my God! *Noah.*" Her voice is strained, and I reach a hand up to cover her mouth as I up my force one last notch. Her eyes squeeze shut as her mouth falls open against my hand, muffling her moans.

"That's it, baby, be a good girl and come on my tongue. Let me taste you." I suck her clit one final time, adding extra pressure with my fingers as I feel her walls tighten completely against me, clutching me inside her as her release barrels through her. With my hand covering her mouth, she manages only a grunt as she hits her peak, her hips bucking against my face as my tongue rides her through her waves, her softness squeezing at my fingers as they slow their pace.

I slowly put her legs back on the ground, licking her from my fingers, the sweetest taste straight from heaven, and I rise to meet her glazed and hungry eyes.

"How were the stars?" I whisper against her lips. Her breath barely caught.

"Spectacular," she pants. "You're going to have to give me a minute before we go back downstairs. Because now I just want to jump you. Give something else a ride," she says as she gropes my cock through my pants. My dick is now painfully restrained behind my pants. I let out a growl, cursing Addy for convincing me to sleep here and not at a hotel. My forehead presses against hers as I place my hands on the wall, each side of her head.

"*Fuck's sake.*"

She giggles at my restraint, another sound that does nothing to help the growing pain in my pants. I steal her panties from the ground and tuck them into my pocket.

"Noah, I need those."

"No you don't. Consider it punishment."

"And what am I being punished for?" Her smile is sent from the devil, taunting me.

"For rubbing my dick and making me picture you bouncing on my cock." She bites her lip again and this time I stop her, pull her lips into mine, and replace her teeth with mine, swallowing her little moan as she takes a step back.

"Okay. Yeah. You need to go in the bathroom or something and let me cool down," she whispers as I chuckle. I throw her a wink and leave her in the bedroom to pull herself together. My scent intertwined with hers, my heart full of her smiles making my chest feel like it's expanding.

I am so fucking gone for this woman.

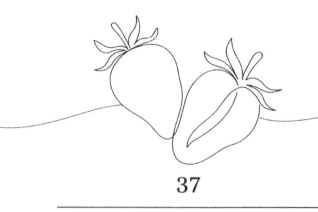

37

there are those stars again

Addison

"Hey, Noah?"

"Yeah, shortcake?" His morning voice is quickly becoming my favorite.

We lay wrapped up in the navy blue sheets of his childhood bed, my phone not stopping its incessant buzzing, as he pulls me into his arms, his big hands caressing my body, pushing my hair out of my face and his thumb brushing against my cheekbone. His eyes trail down me completely, nothing missing from his gaze, as though he is taking stock and committing all of me to his memory. So grateful that his mom and Evie had pre-existing plans these last two days. Something about the local library and the volunteering shifts Iris had, and Evie has been going to classes.

"Can you tell me about your parents? And... about your dad?" After these days here together, I realize I don't know much about him outside New York. He has spent so much time shouldering my burdens with me that I never ask him about his pain. The shame of that realization hit me this week as we spend it with his family, and I desperately want to know everything there is to know about him.

"What do you want to know?" Something like pain flashes through his eyes and he gives me a gentle smile. Telling me without words that it hurts, but he'd give me anything he could.

"Do you miss your dad?" It seems like a stupid question and his lopsided smile tells me it was and I instantly curse myself for asking. Before I can take it back, he answers.

"Every day."

"I'm sorry, you don't have to talk about him."

"No, I want to. I like to. It hurts sometimes, but it was long ago enough that talking about him also gives me some nostalgic joy." He continues to twirl my hair in his fingers and he readjusts so that he lays fully on his back, his other hand tucked under his head as he looks at the ceiling.

"You know, my mom used to have bad thoughts." He gives me a knowing look, and my face drops. I open my mouth to say something, *anything,* but snap it closed as he continues. "My dad... he died about eight years ago. But they were in real-love." He says it in a way that makes me jealous. That it is the kind of love out of reach for us. Like everyone else in the world has no idea what that is. "The kind they write movies and romance novels about. He'd get up every single morning to make her a cup of tea—yes, *tea,* not coffee. She was super into gardening and her flower beds were luscious as all heck, and yet he bought her a bunch of flowers every Sunday." His eyes go vacant as though he is back there, watching his parents. He slides back against the headboard, sitting up more and pulling me with him. "Every time he got her flowers, she would have this look on her face, like he was the first man to ever buy her something. She would make him his favorite desserts, and he would tell her there was nothing that made his heart sing like her cooking." He pauses and I wait for him, feeling his body shiver as he tries to compose himself, his hold on me growing tighter. "I think... I think when he died, a piece of her died, too. Of course, me and my sister were devastated, but I think the love my mom lost when she lost dad was like losing a physical part of her heart, like losing her soul." He runs a hand down my arm and shivers cross my body as I try to blink back tears. "The two-ish years after he died were the hardest. My sister had walked in on her with some pills and she had to be rushed to the hospital." *Oh god.* I tilt my head to look up at him and the battle against my tears is lost as I see the single tear falling down his cheek. He stares up at the ceiling as if he is back there, and I just... I need to take away his pain. I bring my hand to his check and pull his face to mine. He squeezes his eyes closed as I press a soft kiss to his lips. He lingers in the kiss, like a lifeline, his arm tightening to pull me against him. I release him and look at him, nodding to continue.

"I felt... I felt lost. I had my own grief, my little sister shut down on herself, too, and then there was mom. She didn't want to stay here with us. Hell, I guess I didn't either. But that feeling. Being helpless and having no idea how to help it sent me into a tailspin. Mom's medical bills ate up a lot of our spare funds. Dad did well for himself, but he wasn't saving for us when he died. He hadn't made a plan because no one expected it. I knew I needed to be the one to do it. So I left. I let my grief get to me, I avoided them because I thought every time I saw them and spoke to them it would just be a reminder of my responsibility, a reminder that Dad was gone and that Mom tried to leave, too. I didn't know staying away just hurt them more. I thought... I somehow thought it would just be better. Over the years, we still spoke, of course, and saw each other, but we just pretended like I didn't bail, and I think it put a distance between us. I'm still trying to repair that distance, but... I don't know how. I wanted to fix Mom, to fix Evie, and make sure that... well, that they didn't actually leave me, too."

My heart breaks into a thousand pieces for him. I know pressure, but I can't imagine being shouldered with so much and so quickly, having no idea how to process any of it. I can certainly understand wanting to escape.

I know he wants to help. His heart is huge, and I know how he hates when I'm in pain. How do I explain to him that his mom, me, we don't need fixing, that he doesn't have to worry about me leaving him, not like that. That this is who we are, and sometimes just being there, being consistent, has to be enough.

"I think she eventually realized that my sister was still here and still needed her. She started seeing a therapist regularly, still does every other week. She told me about her love with Dad, and… and I think it was the first time I truly understood how she thought death was easier than living without him, it was why I told myself I'd never love, never have someone need me like that, or never risk losing my heart like that, too."

"What changed?" He looks down at me, eyes nailing me with all the vulnerability he is trying to rope back in.

"I met you." My heart lurches, and I struggle to hold back my tears.

Holding his gaze, I urge him to continue. For all the pain he feels, I can tell talking about it is helping. "Tell me what she said about love," I whisper.

"She said the way he loved her was like standing on the edge of a cliff, the thrill of almost falling, but also like the weightlessness and the pressure of the deepest parts of the ocean. Feeling your skin burn, your heart beating in time with theirs, like your souls are joined by a piece of string. Losing him was like slicing through flesh, through every sensitive nerve, and leaving the endings open to the wind. The agony she felt went so deep it ached in every bone, in every muscle. Being in agonizing pain, while also being completely numb to everything around you."

"You Greeks really have a way with words." He swipes a thumb under my eye, his face softening into a small smile, and he huffs a small laugh.

"Addison?"

"Hmm?" I am so beyond words at this point.

"You don't have to tell me anything, about your experiences. But I want you to know I'll always listen. And when you feel like it's too much, I'll always be there to pull you out. I just want you to know you can always come back to me. You can't scare me away." Tears break through my self-control as I pull myself out of his arms, turning to straddle his lap, and his hands link behind my back. The position feels practiced, like I belong here.

"I... I don't know what triggered it. I have had this *imbalance* for as long as I can remember, but it kind of peaked not long after I graduated high school."

"When you traveled?" he questions, and I nod softly, not making eye contact. His fingers tip my chin, forcing me to meet his eyes. So much strength and encouragement pouring from him.

"It just sort of springs on me out of nowhere, the deep ache of being numb. The sense of defeat that tells me I just can't do *this* anymore, this life. That it isn't worth it." His eyes change to an urgency and the pressure on my back increases. "Sometimes it comes in waves with panic attacks. Sometimes it hits me in a silence that catches me so off guard it scares the crap out of me. Like that night you found Jake in the hallway." I tell him about my breakup with Jake, gory details and all, about the night after I was fired and giving him context, where the bath is concerned. I watch as he blinks back his rage and his tears, fighting for how to feel.

"*Addy.*" He reaches up and drags me to his chest, holding me as I nuzzle his neck.

"Don't even get me started on my rage."

His chuckle vibrates my chest. "I think I've seen enough of that to last me a lifetime." Humor coats his words.

He reaches a finger up and bops me on the nose as I sit up and I swat his hand away. "Ugh, what was that for?"

"Your scowl is adorable. You went from seductress to emotional, to shy, to angry in the space of about ten minutes, and I am just... awed by you. There are so many layers to you, and I love every single one of them." My expression softens as I roll my eyes and pretend not to be affected by his words.

I hold his eyes and his face changes, almost a smile, but it isn't condescending or arrogant, it's... *is he turned on right now?* My own smile grows and I narrow my eyes at him. "Why are you looking at me like that?" His face doesn't change as he responds.

"Like what?"

"Like you're ready to fuck me?" I give him a bigger smile, biting my bottom lip. The heat in his eyes already causing a pool in my lower belly. *How did we go from depression and crying to this?* He laughs and pulls me forward against him again, leaning his chin to the top of my head as I snuggle into his chest. "Oh, Addison... I don't think I'll ever *not* want to fuck you."

"But...?"

"But right now... I just want to hold you." He kisses the top of my head, and my heart grows two sizes as I take a deep breath and inhale the spring scent of him.

"For what it's worth, I think your rage is sexy as hell. I wouldn't change a thing." He releases a deep sigh as I feel his body relax, but not before he dips a finger under my chin, tilting my head as he lowers his, bringing his lips to gently brush mine. "I want you to know that this world needs you Addy. I need you." He doesn't give me a chance to respond as he presses his lips to mine in a gentle, lingering kiss. But I can't take it anymore, I lean into it further, teasing his lips with my tongue to deepen the kiss. His lips part without hesitation, and the taste of him sweeps through me, increasing my desire, his hands moving to grip my ass and grind me down. "*Addy.*"

"I know," I breathe into him, his desire now matching mine as our hands frantically search each other. The electricity between us sparks to life, the air thick with longing. Like a link, a string to my soul, that he just took for himself. He abruptly pulls back from the kiss and searches my eyes.

"I love you, Addison. Completely." My control snaps and I kiss him desperately, reaching down to remove my underwear. Noah helps and his boxers shortly follow. He wraps his hands around my waist, and before I know what is happening, he has flipped me under him, giving me whiplash from the pace at which our desire has jumped. He hovers above me, trailing kisses down my neck to my breasts, and he draws my sensitive nipples into his mouth. He kisses his way back up to find my lips, his fingers sliding through the slit of my sex, eliciting a wave of pleasure through my body. "Always ready for me." He slides a finger in slowly, so deliciously and painfully slow, as he continues his work on my neck, my legs wrapping around his hips.

"I need you, Noah. *Now.*"

"We have all day, Addy baby, I plan to take my time with you." He slides a second finger in, and I reach my hand to his length, hard against my stomach, and I stroke him slowly and firmly. His body jolts as he hisses a breath in my ear.

"Two can play that game, Romeo." He doesn't waste a second as he shuffles down my body, his tongue firmly sweeping up the middle of my entrance, landing on my clit as he suctions, his fingers still working their magic. My spine arches off the bed. "Ahh... *Noah.*"

"Let me be clear, shortcake. If your game is to tease and edge, there is one winner, and it'll be me." His smile is arrogant as he dives back in. His tongue works me into a frizzled taut state, my back arched so high off the bed, the sheets scrunched in my fists. "*Noahhh!*" The intensity builds, spots in my vision, or perhaps they are the same stars from last time. The tingles in my spine work their way lower as his fingers pick up their pace, not coming up for air. "Fuck, I—" He withdraws his fingers and moves his delicious mouth to the inside of my thigh, the loss of contact at where I need him jarring as I grunt and sit up on my elbows.

"Point proven, you win... oh, God..." I fall back and cover my face as my body continues to writhe below him, searching for the lost friction. *So close.*

"Ask nicely, Little Demon." If I wasn't about to have an earth shattering orgasm from this man, my stubbornness would tell him to go to hell.

"Noah, I need... *please* make me come."

His fingers begin their work again, their pace building as his mouth finds me, working me to my peak as his fingers slow and his lips trail back up my stomach. I open my eyes to find him staring at me. "Wha..." I try to swallow, the pleasure clouding my vision and my brain. I lose my train of thought as his fingers go deeper, curling around, hitting the spot, this thumb massaging my bundle of nerves, and it sends the sparks of pleasure over my body as the release builds instantly. His lips find mine, our tongues dancing desperately, and he pulls away just as the orgasm crashes into me. It goes, each wave lingering as his fingers slow and he kisses down my neck.

"You're so fucking pretty when you come." *Oh my.* He hovers above me, his hardness sliding at my entrance as he braces my head, brushing hair out of my face. "And you're exquisite when you moan my name." He slides home, his words rapidly rebuilding my spiral of desire. He wastes no time, when fully seated he picks up the pace, one hand gently grips my neck the other firmly at my waist for momentum as his movements quicken, rotating his hips just so, hitting the spot that sends me into a descent of euphoria.

"Noah, oh my god...."

He curses, his pace quickening, and I can't take it. The pleasure builds again. "You feel so good, Addy. You better come quick. I can't hold it much longer."

"Fuck." I almost scream as he slams into me. He brings his body down to mine, linking his hands under my arms and gripping my shoulders as his pace makes me lose my breath. "Noah, *yesss...* I love you!" I scream as the orgasm hits me again, harder than the last, black spots across my vision, and I grip his shoulders, nails digging as he continues his pace through each wave. He grunts and a few more jerks before he slams hard and falls against my chest.

"*Fuck.* Addison." He raises his head to meet my eyes, his face a perfectly sated softness, a vulnerability that makes my heart swell and my grip on him tighten. "I love you, too," he whispers as he places a lingering kiss on my lips. I moan into him and tighten my legs around his waist. Still inside me, he rotates his hips slightly.

"Oh my god."

"What?! Did that, oh, did I hurt you?" His expression is concerned.

"No..." I try to catch my breath as I caress his sharp jawline with my fingers. "You moved... I... *God.* Just don't move." A breathy moan leaves my lips, and his expression changes as I feel him almost completely harden again inside me.

"Ready for round two already, shortcake?"

"I don't think I'd ever not be ready. With that magic mouth of yours."

"You like the talents of my tongue, do you?" He uses said magic as he delicately kisses my neck.

"Not just its talents. Your words. I think... I think you could finish me with them alone. My own personal Romeo."

"I can be your Romeo. I can be whatever you want me to be, Addy. As long as I'm yours." Those deep chocolate eyes are full of love.

"You are." I kiss him gently.

"And you're mine, Addison." My legs tighten even further as I comb my fingers through his hair again.

"*Yes,*" I whisper as I pull him in for another deep kiss.

We become another tangle of limbs and breathy moans, before Noah has me writhing and coming undone under him, and above him again, and again.

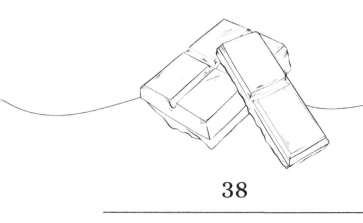

38

it's all very romeo

Noah

The sunlight streams in through the partially closed curtains as I squint my eyes open. My body relaxed, my eyes sore from the lack of sleep, as I roll into a stretch. Addison lays naked next to me, sprawled out on her stomach in a tangle amongst the sheets, her pale skin soft and smooth. I can't help myself. I roll closer, tucking an arm under her to drag her against me. Her back to my chest as I curl around her, she fits perfectly against me like this.

Mine.

I place gentle kisses across her shoulder, her quiet breaths deepening into a sigh, her lashes fluttering as she wakes up. She lets out a little sleepy moan, and it's the most adorable sound I've ever heard. Also, a huge turn on.

"Good morning, gorgeous," I say between the peppered kisses across her smooth skin.

"Morning." She stretches and turns to face me, her smile soft. She looks good this way. Cheeks lightly blushed from sleep and a content-ed smile across her face. So at odds with the version of Addy I first met, and damn if it doesn't tug on my heart strings knowing I put that smile on her face.

"Your phone has been going nuts for the last hour. I think you should check it." I kiss her lightly on the nose and move to leave the bed, her grip tightening around my waist.

"Nooo, can't we just stay here for a bit longer? I don't want the world to interrupt us right now." Laughing softly, I let her drag me back, because who am I kidding? I don't want to leave, anyway.

"You know something?"

"It's too early in the morning for cute words and sweet nothings, Romeo. Can you wait until I have some coffee so I can at least remember to tease you about them later?" The cheek on this woman. I land a solid smack to her bare ass and she squeals playfully into my arms.

"Fine, I'll keep all my sweet nothings to myself in the future."

"Wait no, no, no tell me. I want to hear."

"I don't think you appreciate my words. I think I'll keep them for myself." I turn my head, feigning offense, and she sits up to grip my jaw, pulling me to her.

Her eyes are bulging and sad, and she peppers my face with kisses. "Sorry, sorry, sorry. I'm just kidding. I love your words. Promise."

I pull her against me and chuckle. "That's what I thought."

"So...?" She tilts her head and looks at me seductively through her long lashes.

"So what...?"

"Will you tell me what sweet nothings you were going to say?" she asks me sweetly.

"I was going to say..." She bites her bottom lip as she smiles, her eyes growing wider and *damn* if the look of her this way doesn't send me into heart failure. "I could get used to waking up to you every morning. I don't think I've ever felt more myself than I do when I'm with you. I can't remember the last time I was this happy." A small tear slides down her cheek. "You really are an emotional woman, aren't you?"

"Ugh, says you!" She swats my hands and rubs her eyes as she smiles and shakes her head at me. "I've never known a guy to pretend to be so manly and tough, who then also comes out with the dirty pillow talk and swoony declarations. How many other beds did these words get you into?" She is joking, but it hits me that I've never shared moments like this with... well, anyone. I've had girlfriends, but Addison is different. I can't explain it, it's just more. Better.

"It's just you, shortcake. I think it was always meant to be you." I grip her jaw and pull her to me, my other arm reaching around to grab a handful of that delectable ass and press her into me, remembering we are both still very naked, and she melts.

After a few more tangles in the sheets, we decided it was best we actually made something of the day. Mom and E have been busy the last two days, so we've managed to soak up plenty of alone time, but today, we are meeting them in the city for some lunch. Mom and Evie plan to take Addy to the spa while I get some work done at home, perhaps scope some real estate.

I kiss her quickly as I move to head into the shower, and she reaches for her phone. "Ugh, fuck's sake," she grunts out from the room.

"What is it, potty mouth?"

"Oh, shut it. Ava messaged, said I need to go to Mom and Dad's. Some kind of '*family meeting*'." My stomach drops, time slows, my vision tunneled.

No, no, no. Surely not related, right? Matt would have warned me this was happening if he knew, if he found out? Okay, this might be happening. The last few blissful weeks with Addy flash through my head on a loop... *Addison*.

I slowly close the bathroom door to shake my head, leaning over the sink to sip water from the tap to clear my throat, last night's dinner threatening to make an appearance.

"Uhhh... what kind of meeting?" I shout back through the closed door.

"I don't know. Hopefully Mom and Dad are announcing a divorce." She laughs softly, and I hear her place her phone on the desk and pad her way over to me.

Pull it together right now, Noah.

She knocks on the bathroom door, and I turn on the shower immediately, needing to wash the clammy sweat from my body, and she slowly opens the door.

"Hey, feel like some company?" She throws me her fuck-me eyes, and it spears me straight in the heart. Oh, shortcake, if only you knew. Knew what a bastard I was, making promises. If she knew the truth, knew what a fucking liar I was, she wouldn't look at me like that anymore, that's for sure.

I should tell her everything right now? I thought when I kept this from her, it was the best idea. I had no idea what we would become, had no idea I'd fall in love with her. Mine and Matt's silence was the only thing holding everything together. I couldn't risk the information spreading further, and I certainly couldn't risk... I just know Addison won't be able to keep her cool. I hate how little faith it feels like I have in her, but I don't want her to struggle with control because of me. She'd need to explode, and I'd want to help her do it. But this... I can't have her exploding over this. I got so caught up in falling so fast and hard for this amazing woman, I completely forgot the giant-sized problem about to implode my life that is going to destroy Addison.

She is going to hate me for this.

I clear my throat and give her my best sex smile and hope she buys it. Trying to hold on to this last shred of happiness while I have it. Her eyes evaluate me skeptically, not buying my façade in the slightest. "Hey, are you okay, Romeo?"

"Romeo?" *Great deflection, Noah. She's only been calling you that for a month.*

"Yeah, you know, all the swoony words and sweet nothings. It's very Romeo." She winks at me and my heart reaches for her. I want to pull her to me and never let her go. Let nothing hurt her or touch her. Pause these moments. I finally got her to a point of trusting me, knowing everything I do about her trust issues, her judgement of people. She will never forgive me for this. "You didn't answer me?"

"Uhh, yeah. I'm good, just... tired." I give her a soft smile, kiss her on the cheek, and turn my back to her as I enter the shower. She says nothing, but I hear the bathroom door close quietly behind her as she leaves the bathroom. My heart sinks, and this feeling of everything falling away from me settles deep within me. Everything I worked for, everything I love, is about to come crashing down.

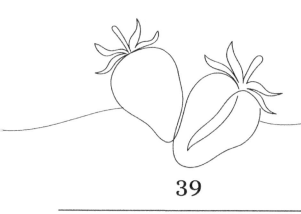

39

big-big love

Addison

Noah has been acting weird all morning. Since he left to go have a shower, I have no idea what changed. I went over our conversations with a fine-toothed comb and came up empty. Other than the fact he only kissed one of my cheeks. I didn't realize how much I adored those kisses until I realized I was waiting for the second when he turned his back on me.

Unless it was about last night, everything we talked about? But it just didn't make sense. All the sweet things he said to me after, he couldn't be affected by any of those things if he was able to say all that he said after.

I think it was always meant to be you.

Unless he had sex goggles on. I mean, I am no stranger to them. I was pretty much wearing them from the moment I met him, clouding my judgment until he finally wormed his way through my defenses against him. I've spent weeks looping my positive thoughts to drown out the panic, ignoring the sadness in the corner so I don't self-sabotage, and now I feel stupid. Noah helped lower my walls, between holding me through my panic attack and teaching me how to love baths again. It feels like he quite literally held my hand through all the chaos, bringing me out the other end. But did I hide from my own intuition? Is something up and I've just ignored it for so long?

You know what? No, it's fine. I won't be in my head about it. Everyone is entitled to their bad days. If anyone knows that, it's me. He is allowed to have his day, his feelings, and I will show him I'm not going anywhere. He says my emotions don't scare him, well, I will be that for him, too. I'm not going anywhere, Romeo.

"Do I really need to make the trip out? Can't you just give me the news now?"

"And what makes you think I have any idea what this family meeting is about?" Ava has always been such a terrible liar, also horrific at keeping secrets. I roll my eyes despite knowing she can't see me.

"Because you're insisting, and you literally said in your message, and I quote, *'you're going to want to hear this in person'.* How would you know I needed to hear it in person if you didn't already know what it is? Look, if it's a divorce, I couldn't care less. In fact, you know what, email me the details and I'll host a fucking celebration."

"Jesus, Addison. You could show a little sympathy. Why are you so blunt about the prospect of our parents getting a divorce? You know, just because you've given up on love doesn't mean everyone else has." She hangs up the phone, and I get slammed with instant guilt. Anger is there, too, rearing her ugly head. Anger at the situation, at Ava for not growing a vagina and telling me what it is, anger at myself for being such an asshole to my sister when all she does is love me. I haven't told anyone in my family about how serious Noah and I are yet. I don't know why. They already knew something was up given the whole graduation thing, but I guess I just wanted this little piece of joy for myself before it was tainted. Guilt always settles in my belly when

Noah asks about them, not having any idea they don't know about us. I'm sure they know, just maybe not the extent.

I let out a huge grunt as I flop myself face first on to his bed and muffle a louder groan, unable to shut off my head or give the growing anger an outlet. The bathroom door opens and the masculine scent of Noah envelops me, along with the minty soap and steam.

"Hey grumpy gills. Life just isn't that bad." I can hear his shit-eating grin in his tone as he fails to hold in his chuckle at my five-year-old tantrum. I sit up and face him, my face pulled into a familiar scowl I haven't felt in a while.

"Ava knows what's going on and she is refusing to tell me. This is why I have trust issues. Honestly, I'd rather just find out now than traveling to Virginia just to be told I'm right."

"Virginia? Wait, right about what? What is going on?" Noah drops his amused expression, and his towel, while pulling on a pair of boxers and a T and taking a seat next to me on the bed.

"Apparently, they need me to come home for this stupid family meeting."

"Now?"

I nod, and Noah pulls his lips into a tight sympathetic smile, and I can tell he is disappointed. Not in me, just in how this is ruining a nice week with his family. I lean in and give him a soft kiss on the lips.

"Don't worry about me. It doesn't look like I'm getting out of this. Ava isn't going to budge now that I bitched her out. I'll book a flight from here, see if I can get one in the evening so that we can still have the morning together." I pat his leg and make for the bathroom to give myself a shower when Noah grabs my elbow and pulls me to him.

"Wait, you're going?"

"Didn't you hear everything I just said?" I giggle, but it dies when I see the seriousness on Noah's face tying me in knots. The rage at my family comes back, and the guilt eats me alive.

"Okay, I'll come with you."

"Noah, I can't ask you to do that." My heart grows a few sizes, honestly the thought of having Noah there, supporting me and being in my corner, grounding me and keeping me from blowing my lid at my parents, sounds really fucking awesome, but he misses his mom, and his sister, even if he refuses to admit it. I can't let him leave with me. "You never get to spend time with your family. I'm not taking you away from them. I am sure Iris would murder me for stealing her *baby boy.*" That panty-melting gorgeous smile grows across his face. His deep chuckle alerts me to how quickly this man can pivot from worried, to cheeky, to loving, to the Greek sex-god I love. He pulls me closer to him.

"Please, let me come with you."

"It's just a family meeting, Noah. There won't be anything interesting, and I can promise you there is no reason for you to come." His face flashes with an expression that is gone too quickly for me to place before he continues to insist, changing tactics.

"If you keep saying no, I am just going to hold you here..." He nuzzles my neck and places soft teasing kisses along my neck. "Between the sheets. Making you moan my name, and... what was it you call me... *Romeo?* Oh yeah, I'll have you screaming it when I'm done. I'll keep you locked up in here, sated and compliant, until your sister has to come all the way to Chicago to pull you from my bed." *Where did this man come from?* "Please, Ads." His deep chocolate eyes meet mine, and the lust is replaced with sincerity and something that feels like pain. His big brown eyes melt my heart and crash through all my defenses, and I nod at him before he places a desperate kiss to my lips, pulling me tight to his body.

"Okay, you can get in there and shower now." He smacks my ass and I giggle as I watch him walk towards his suitcase, admiring his imposing form, all olive skin and muscle. *Yum.*

We managed to score a flight, landing us in VA around 6pm, so we head into town to collect Iris and E to spend the day in the city for lunch. The weather is perfect for an early afternoon stroll, sun shining and the late spring breeze flowing through my hair. The streets are busy as we make our way down casually to the cafe, Noah ahead with his mother's arm looped in his. He had decided not to do work today, made a quick phone call to Matt and Caleb and said he'd rather just spend the last day with his family before we left. He had assured me he was perfectly happy to leave and said I didn't need to feel guilty, that he wanted to be there for me. I believed him, but it didn't stop me from still feeling bad.

He and Iris are engaged in conversation. They look tense, but Iris beams with pride at her son. Evie struts next to me, her arm looped in mine. "So, what is it that you see in that *málaka?*" E says from next to me, very matter-of-factly, as I choke on my tongue.

"Just a charmer, I suppose," I say between giggles. I also don't really know how to answer that question. I can't exactly say he makes me feel whole. Like he picked up every broken piece of me and glued me back together with his megawatt smile, gorgeous deep brown eyes, whispered sweet nothings, and those should-be-illegal forearms that wrap me up and hide me away from everything horrible. Also a magic penis goes a long way. I'm sure his sister really doesn't want to hear about that.

Like he senses me staring between his shoulder blades, thinking about that goofy smile, he turns slightly to throw one at me over his shoulder, before he turns back to whisper something in his mother's ear.

"Ergh, yuck. The way you two look at each other is gross." She pretend-vomits and then smiles. "Truthfully, though, I am so glad he found you. I was worried for a while there." That gets my attention. I snap my eyes to hers, which focus on the path in front of us.

"What do you mean?"

"Well, he closed himself off after *baba* died. He stayed and helped, and I guess looked after us in some way or another. But my brother was gone." She shakes herself, giving me some assessing side eye. My heart breaks for her because I know what it's like to watch your brother's heart break and then to lose him. "Anyway, he just hasn't been himself. This week, yesterday and today... I feel like I can see my old brother again. That idiot who used to chase me around the house and hide my ice cream while telling every boy in school to steer clear or they'd lose their penis." Her wistful smile leaves a pang in my chest. An ache that Noah never really grieved his father and probably still hurts enough to be distant from his family. Avoiding the reminder and the pain. "Thank you," she says after a brief pause, finally making eye contact.

"For what?"

"For bringing him back to us. Not... like physically, because obviously he can just come by himself on a plane or whatever... I mean, like... mentally. I guess. I feel like that smile..." She points ahead at Noah, and I catch a glimpse of that gorgeous smile from the side as he and his mother talk ahead of us. "That's all because of you. I have no doubt about that." She unlinks our arms, slaps me on the ass before skipping forward and jumping on Noah's back. The whole scene leaves me stunned and also in awe. Evie loves her big brother and misses him so deeply. It has my mind wandering to my own big brother. The pain of missing him growing ever so slightly.

Iris now walks beside me as Noah and E chase ahead, Evie on his back messing up his hair as they laugh at each other. "You wouldn't know he is almost thirty with the way he acts," she tsks, her words contradicting that proud smile across her face as she watches her kids.

"You did a good job with those two. Great, in fact. You should be proud. Noah is a good man." She obviously doesn't get the privilege of seeing her son often. I feel like she deserves to know he is out there in the world being a nice person and looking after hearts, mine at least.

"Thank you. I did do pretty good, huh?" She smiles proudly. She links her arm in mine, and the guilt from earlier comes back with a vengeance. "You know Addison, that boy loves you. And I mean big-big love. Lifelong kind of love. I just want you to always remember that." I can't quite make out her expression, but she seems concerned about something. Maybe worried I'm going to break her son's heart. Despite the jealousy I feel over the way Noah has a mom that loves him this way, I can't help but be happy for him. I wish I had the pleasure of meeting his dad. I can only imagine the kind of man he was to have produced someone like Noah.

That guilt is just hovering with an intensity now. I've only just met Noah's family, and he is ditching time with them to come deal with my family drama. How will they ever come to like me if this is what they see of me on the first meet? I swallow my thoughts and words, unsure how to say any of it as we head into the restaurant.

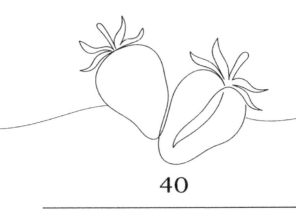

40

questionable behavior is on-brand

Addison

The Uber pulls us up to the front of the house and I look out the window to my childhood home. In its day, it was the best money could buy. Still is grand and exuberant, no expense spared, and upgrades through the years as required. The property is just under four acres, three stories of weatherboard and stone, wrap-around porch, four-car garage, surrounded by green privacy. My parent's way of saying, *'look how special we are—we have money!'* Most people would feel joy, nostalgia, or contentment coming home. I know Noah had felt happy finally being in his home again. I could tell by the way his shoulders had relaxed the moment his mother held him. Me? I'm still stuck in the seat of the Uber, staring at the front door of my house with nervous butterflies flying laps in my stomach as the initial telltale signs of a panic attack rear their head.

"Addy, you okay, shortcake?" Noah's voice is gentle. He has saddled up next to me, a warm palm on my lower back, his voice a warm melody in my ear. I shake my head to let him know that I am, in fact, not okay, because I think if I speak the words, those symptoms of panic

I am trying to bury will explode out of control.

In for 6, hold for 2, out for 8.

Useless.

Unlovable.

Nothing.

I squeeze my eyes shut and blink the sting in my eyes away as I try to slow my heart and steady my breath. *"Noah…"*

"Yeah, baby?"

"I… I can't—" I know what's waiting for me in there. Pain, drama, shouting, blame, guilt, rage. I can't go in there.

I can't. I don't want to do this, subject myself to that. I can't.

"We don't have to do anything you don't want to do. Say the word Addison. I will turn this Uber around in a second. We can go wherever you want to go." I turn my head to look into Noah's eyes and my breath is stolen from me. The sadness and the pain I feel in my chest is reflected back at me in his eyes. His sincere words are like an arrow to my heart, channeling a strength I had no idea was in me. No, I *can* do this. I control my own reactions. I can control whether I let their words get to me. Their thoughts and opinions. My rage doesn't control me, it is my strength.

Your anger, your fury is so powerful, you could rule the world with that gift… you are the thing that helps fix that what is broken. You are not broken, Addison. Noah's words come back to me, replacing all my doubts and worries, shoving them back down, encouraging me to believe in myself, be strong for myself, and love myself. Broken bits and all.

My expression changes from pain to determination, because I will get through this, and I will be fine and the world will not end.

Noah's smile grows as he places a soft kiss on my lips. "There she is," he whispers, and damn if it doesn't add a spring to my step.

Here I am. In all my furious glory.

Noah holds my hand clasped in his as we make our way to the front door. Before I can even knock–yes, knock, because this place has never felt like home–Riley rushes out the door and squeezes me in a hug. The air is thick with the promise of summer and Riley's skin on skin contact is making me clammy.

"Woah... uhh, Hi, Ri... What are you doing?" I try to sound playful, but I know this kind of hug. Hugging or any type of physical affection is unusual for Riley.

"I'm glad you're here." Her voice sounds somber, making my previous confidence falter slightly. Prickles of rage coat my skin, leaving goosebumps in their wake.

Everyone knows what's going on except you.

What, did they all just have their own little meeting to prepare for me to arrive? Am I really so volatile they couldn't have waited to tell me with the rest of the family? No, because the emotionally unstable get *handle with care* stickers and caution signs slapped to their heads.

Breathe.

Fury laces my throat as I try to breathe through my rapidly spiraling thoughts. Five seconds. I saw a family member for five seconds.

I swallow and return Riley's hug before she withdraws, noticing Noah. She gives him a soft smile before returning her expression to me. "Ads, this is a family meeting." She gives Noah side eye.

"Rude, Riley. He is a guest. He can come in, Jesus." I try to push past, but she lifts a hand to stop me. *What the fuck?*

"I'm serious. You don't want him here right now. This is just...

family stuff." My rage is hitting its limits, and before long, I'm not going to be able to keep it under the appropriate 'woosa' levels before it explodes. "Riley. Stop being a brat and move out of the way." Her eyes plead and she doesn't move.

"Addison, it's fine, really." Noah grabs my elbow to pull me toward him, and before I can protest, he slams a whopping kiss on my lips that catches me off guard. "I love you. You know that, right?" I nod quickly, but I'm confused by his words and his facial expression. I don't get to ask before he continues. "Text me when you're ready. I'll come back for you." His words are soft, but they hit me right in the chest, making me lose my breath.

It feels like a weird goodbye, his eyes communicating so many things I don't understand, but I lean in to kiss him again, whispering back, "I love you, too. I won't be long. Thank you." He winces, then nods and heads back to the Uber as I turn to Riley. Ignoring us and not caring that we just said I love you, but my family have no idea I'm even seriously dating someone.

"Okay. Now that that's sorted, will you let me in the fucking house, or is there some other bullshit you all need to put me through before someone tells me what in the fuck is so important?" Okay, yeah... so I blew past the 'woosa' level.

"Alright crazy, calm down." Ava's melodic voice sails out through the front door as she appears, her stupid words only making the rage grow. I really need to do a PSA for people who have never had to deal with an anger problem before; calling them crazy and telling them to calm down does not a relaxed situation make. In fact, you're essentially asking for a shit storm. How, in all the years she has known me, has she not worked this out? I shove past both her and Riley and storm my way into the living room. Mom is on the couch, crying, while dad paces the floor between the lounge and the kitchen. The mood feels very Armageddon. *What the fuck did I just walk in to?*

"Where are Matt and Mia?"

"Home." Ava's voice is pained as she struggles to make eye contact.

"And Jessie?"

"He's on his way." Ava's voice is soft and sad, and I feel guilt for being so brazen, but also furious that this is dragging out so long.

"For the love of god, someone tell me what is going on." I practically shout the words as I make my way to the couch to sit next to Mom, Dad giving me guilty eyes and bad vibes. The kind of vibes where my intuition tells me I'm going to punch him in the face because whatever the fuck this is, I'm almost certain this is his fault.

"Mom. Please, what is it?" She looks over at dad, resigned, and shame flooding her face.

"Your dad—"

"Lillian!" Dad growls from across the room.

I snap my eyes to him, ready to tell him to shut it, when Ava surprises me and scolds him, "Dad, enough."

Mom straightens her shoulders, a confidence boost from Ava's support.

"Your dad has been involved in some... questionable behavior... and... the money is just..." She shakes her head and tears spill down her cheeks. *Is it just me or is that sentence just not that sad?*

"What am I missing here? Because Henry behaving *questionably* doesn't seem to warrant that many tears." Mom looks at me accusingly, and I feel like asking her if perhaps this situation is just all a bit too much for her. See if she likes that backhanded sympathy.

Riley has had about enough and decides to be the mature woman of the group. "Our idiotic father was involved in insider trading and has embezzled funds over decades at his firm. The police have been tipped off, and there is apparently a warrant for his arrest. Our trust funds, my college fund, all our bank accounts, everything is frozen. The house will probably be taken and any other assets tied up with it... I don't know... I'm not a fucking lawyer, but there. The truth."

My whole world spins on an axis as I make my eyes travel across the room to my father. The man who spent his life berating me. If rage wasn't slowly taking over my mind and body, I'd probably laugh. I was right. It was his fault.

"And how did all of this come about? If there is a warrant... how long have you all known about this?" And lied to me and kept secrets from me.

"Ava found out first."

"Riley!" Ava silences her and then looks at me guiltily.

"Addy, before you flip out—"

"Flip out? Are you kidding me? You guys are harboring all this fucking information, and instead of treating me with respect, and like a normal fucking human, you coddle me, hide things from me, and lie to me, to what? Avoid an implosion. I'll give you all a hot fucking tip if you want to avoid pissing me off—stop fucking lying," I seethe at the people I am related to by blood, the people who don't feel like my family, not in this moment. The way they treat me, walk around me, lie to me, is making me angrier than the actual crime. Ava sighs and sits on the couch next to Mom.

"So?"

"Dad hacked into Matt's computer." The man who set standards for us involving integrity, honor, and never behaving less than the number in our trust fund? Am I hearing this properly? "He found information from AIM that was a part of a confidential deal with my work. It involved an environment company that went public about a year ago, and the product this information is related to is apparently going to increase their stock price, making them the market leaders.

Dad saw the information and leaked the tip for a payout." Ava's tone is bored as she relays the information. I look at the man accused. He sits slumped in his chair, pale to my probably cherry red cheeks, as his dirty laundry is aired. This man, being the same man who held impossibly high standards I was never going to reach, told me about what it meant to have a work ethic, to be high class, to be better than everyone else, to not be pathetic. To have honor and only achieve greatness because anything less would make you worthless. The man who told me dreams get you nowhere, and unless I got a real job and made real-adult choices, I would go nowhere in life. My heart beats rapidly as I try to control my breathing, my rage. All the times I was told I would amount to nothing, the times he shook his head at me, curled his lip and tsked at the disappointment I am. This liar and manipulator.

"Oh, and he was having an affair with his secretary," Riley chimes in with some finer detail.

41

you want rage? i'll give you rage

Addison

The edges of my vision tinge with red, hearing only the blood rushing in my ears as fury floods my veins and takes over my body. I feel nothing and everything at once as I launch off the couch.

"You motherfucker!" My fury explodes as I scream at Dad and storm towards him, hands in fists. I hear faint noises behind me. The blood drains from my dad's face as tears stream down his cheeks. He takes a few steps back as I gain on him before he is against the wall and I am in his face.

"You piece of shit coward! All these years you hold us up to un-reachable fucking standards, meanwhile you were down in the gutters lying, cheating, deceiving, and manipulating. FOR WHAT?! You lose the love and respect of your kids, of your wife, FOR WHAT?!" I slap the wall next to his head, needing to hit something as I scream the words.

"Ad—"

"You shut your fucking mouth! I don't want to hear a single word from your mouth, you dirty fucking liar." I lean in extra close, my eyes tracing over every pathetic inch of this monster's face as I make sure he hears me good. "I don't ever want to see or speak to you, ever again." I turn to storm my furious ass out of that godforsaken house when Henry grabs my arm to turn me to him.

"Addison, just wait a second, I am still your da—" His words are cut off as I throw a fist into his jaw, releasing his grip on my arm.

"You might be my father by blood, but you are not my dad." I scowl in his face and turn, making it only to the lounge when I see Ava and Riley, huddled on the couch, tears streaming down their cheeks, their faces frozen in fear. Jessie stands in the doorway, stunned, fighting between his inner rage and shock.

A sound breaks the stark silence. *Laughing?* Riley lifts her head to look at me, confusion and shock plastered all over her. It's me. I am laughing.

No one else seems to find this as hilarious as my brain does right now. Mom's face is covered as she cries, Ava looks a mix between shame and frustration at my laughing, while Riley still just looks confused. Furious energy hums all around Jessie, who is still in the doorway. Furious at what, I can't tell. Me, for laughing? At his father for being a piece of trash? At Ava, and whoever else, from keeping it a secret? Or did he already know, too? You know what? I don't even fucking care at this point.

I'm still laughing uncontrollably—perhaps this is my psychotic break. Laughing at the whole ridiculousness of this situation. My father, who is probably half the reason I have crippling depression and is 100% the reason for my rage, is just a pathetic, lying, cheating coward. *HA!* How fucked is that? Twenty five years of comparing my success, of listening to the words I'm not good enough, from someone who was never even on the same playing field because he was too busy living in the slums.

"Addy?" That smooth whisky voice I've come to love over the last month floats its way across the room, and I see Noah standing next to Jessie in the doorway–who is sizing up Noah with a mixture of confusion and anger.

"What the fuck are you doing here, Karvelas?" Jessie accuses.

"He's my boyfriend," I shout at Jessie. I wish it sounded more loving, but the rage simmering under my skin hasn't found its way out completely yet. *Maybe I could go back and smack Dad in the jaw again.*

Everyone looks between Noah and me with confusion, the ghost of a smile on Ava's face, and it settles my fury the tiniest bit to see that despite everything I think she might be happy for me. Noah shuffles awkwardly on his feet.

"What are you doing here? I thought you left?" I ask him. His eyes dart to Ava for a split second, so fast I almost miss it. When I turn my head to her, she shrugs and Noah nods.

"Okay, what was *that?*" My heart rate increases again and that intuition deep in my belly is screaming at me. *Wrong, something is wrong.*

"Addison..." Noah takes a step toward me, his steps are slow, his hands are defensive, and his voice is placating.

"Hear him out, Addy." Hear him out? *Hear him OUT?!*

"You knew?" I whisper, because I can't even believe the words are coming out of Ava's mouth. Hear him out, as in, not only did my entire family keep a whopping secret from me, but... Noah was in on this, too? Shame, embarrassment, and humiliation make my face heat, and my stomach turns, threatening to empty its contents in front of everyone.

He knew? I turn back to Ava, and she looks at me from lowered lids, sheepish and cowardly. It feels like the floor tilts slightly as I struggle to catch my breath, struggle to make this make sense. Like a spotlight highlights the spot where I stand and everyone I know and loved stands there, pointing at me, laughing at me. I'm the idiot who is toyed with and laughed at, the butt of everyone's joke.

"Please let me explain." His steps are quicker to get to me and I let him. Let him stand in front of me, so he can feel the wrath of betrayal seeping out of me, struggling for control. *He knew. He lied.* So easily he lied to me. Today. Yesterday? *I love you,* he said. What he meant was, *you can't trust me. God!* I feel so fucking stupid. How could I have been so *stupid*? Of course, there isn't a single person on this planet that has ever really accepted me for me. Not even Noah, despite his declarations of love, can truly accept me. Instead, they all walk on eggshells, labeling me this rageful monster, giving me no room for change or growth. No room to be better. Slap a damaged goods sticker on my forehead and leave on the bottom shelf of Good Will. I'm sure they'd treat me better there.

"When?"

"It was the trip to Maplewood." Before I can stop myself, my palm finds Noah's cheek in a stinging slap that I feel to the depth of my soul. He's known for three months. Told me he loved me when he could have told me this. Told me he doesn't break promises when he could have told me this. Told me he thought it was always meant to be me... but instead decided to hide this from me.

I love you.

I love you.

I love him, too. I can't... the pain... the... *I can't breathe.*

It takes the fresh air and hard soil hitting my knees to realize I am in the front yard, a blurring rage as I briefly recall turning and running outside. Tears stream down my cheeks as I soak in everything that happened. The night around me is dark, but the porch lights are enough to keep the panic demons from approaching, the warmth of the almost summer air is enough to keep the chill away, but not too much that it suffocates me as I struggle to catch my breath.

Dad lied.

Cheated, deceived, manipulated, belittled.

Noah lied.

Betrayed and deceived.

Ava knew this before I got to Virginia. She knew everything and made me come here for this. To be lied to and betrayed like this. Riley knew on the front porch. Mom tried to get away with a half-assed lie. God, she even lied to herself. A pit of sympathy forms low in my stomach. Low enough that I still don't care, but enough that it makes me hurt just a little bit for Mom. Despite the horrid pain she has caused me by not being there, not believing in me or supporting me fully in anything I've done, I know this comes from her own unhealed issues. And that she is married to a man like Dad. Well, I guess finding out all of this really is no easy task for her, either.

But was no one going to say anything about the affair if not for Riley? An affair? And he gave me shit about Jake being a piece of shit. I know that pain, the pain of finding out and the humiliation. That pit of sympathy grows a little bigger as I begin to understand the torment and pain Mom must be going through. Still, the hurt part of me wonders how she'll do handling this on her own. When everyone pitied me like I was damaged goods after the shitshow of Jake, almost implying a, '*how could you not see*', I wonder if perhaps Mom is eating her words. Ironic.

"Addy, baby." His words are pained, his panic obvious as he approaches me.

"Get away from me, Noah. You don't get to call me that."

"Please, let me explain."

"Explain what? That you spent the last three months lying to me?

Every day we spent together, every time you told me you loved me. You were lying. You knew all of this and you never told me."

"It's complicated."

"Give me a break. *Complicated.* Of everyone in my life, Noah, I never expected you to be someone who underestimated me. I thought I finally had someone who knew my strength, who *got it.* Someone who wouldn't walk on eggshells or treat me like I'm fragile. Instead, you just did what everyone else does. You lied and kept it from me, because what? You were worried I'd implode?" Noah lands on the ground. Kneeling in the front yard in front of me as I kneel there, my face turned up at the sky as I try to wrangle my rage. God knows I'll have regrets about how I handled this.

"Screw you." The whisper comes out between my cries. My heart feels like it's been ripped from my chest. My throat sore from the shouting. They want to see rage? I'll give them rage.

Fuck them.

Fuck Dad.

Fuck Ava.

Fuck Noah.

Fuck everyone for tiptoeing around me. Lying to me. Betraying me.

Fuck everyone for being less than decent humans and not being in my corner.

Casey and Rosie. My soul sisters. I just want to go home to my girls and hold them and cry and grieve this family that doesn't feel like mine. Grieve this life that doesn't feel like mine. I want to leave. I want to get out and escape. Get away.

"Get away from me, Noah." The words aren't more than a whisper as I get up and walk. I don't know where I plan to go, but I walk. Towards the road, out of the driveway, and in the direction of the main street. Perhaps I'll clear my head. Perhaps I'll catch a bus to the airport.

Maybe I'll even fly home and never speak to anyone else again.

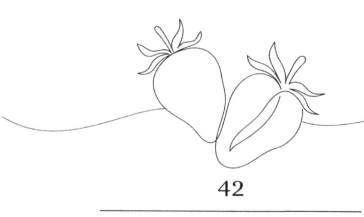

42

little rogue

Addison

I continue to walk these familiar streets of my childhood. I don't know for how long. Thirty minutes, maybe an hour. The roads are surrounded by trees and greenery, giving each house privacy and adding that little touch of class to the suburban area. The almost-summer night air fills my lungs and sticks to my skin like a dew. Or maybe that's just the sweat from the raging storm inside me. It's probably unsafe for me to be a woman walking alone along the road at night like this, but honestly, with the simmering fury inside me, I'd be more worried about the other guy.

Lie.

Cheat.

Betray.

The events of the night run on repeat in my head.

Prison.

My dad is going to prison for criminal offenses. Stealing people's money, cheating the system. Everything he used to lord over people, showing them why he was better than them, is just gone. Just like that.

He will lose his family and probably all or any friends he had. *Poetic justice.* The insane rage in me chimes in the background and a small smile plants itself on my face. It does kind of feel that way. Justice. For all the shit he put me through. For all the ways he made me feel less than and the ways he made me feel broken. For being the reason my brain works the way it does and for the money he wasted on medical expenses for my episodes. *Get it under control.* He growled at me in the hospital. I just finished having my stomach pumped and was being put on a psychiatric health care plan for an attempted suicide, but okay, Henry, sure, I'll just '*get it under control.*' See you in hell, you piece of shit.

Trapped in my thoughts, I miss the headlights from behind me and the sound of a truck pulling up next to me.

"Addison. Get in." I'd know that lovingly unpleasant voice from anywhere.

"JJ. Leave me alone."

"This is unsafe and ridiculous. I won't take you back to the house, but would you just get in?" I stop walking and stare at him and he stops the car. For the first time in two years, he looks at me properly. His intense eyes a confused mix of green and blue fighting between Mom and Dad's genes as he tries to fight all the things I know he wants to say. All the things I know he is punishing himself for because for all the bravado and strength he pretends to have, he and I, we are not that different. The same demons haunt us both, sent by the same devils. I heave a sigh and relent, dragging myself into the car without another word. After a couple of minutes, I break the silence.

"Where are you taking me?"

"We need a drink."

We drive for a couple more minutes before we make it to an Irish pub on the outside of town. An old style bar that has a few locals at the bar, one burly looking bartender, with a jukebox playing what I think might be Don't Stop Believin'. More irony for your Saturday Night.

We walk in, tense silence following us, not having spoken a word since JJ picked me up from my night time adventure walk.

"Two tequilas, thanks," JJ orders at the bar and the server places two tequila shots in front of us. Without a word, Jessie smacks them both back and orders another two and turns to me.

"I thought *we* were having a drink. Or should I order for myself?" I know he saved me from the side of the road, but I can't help the snark in my tone. I'm simply just not in the mood to pretend to care right now.

"Yours is coming. I needed it for this conversation." I scoff at him. He is absent for two years and now he needs liquid courage. Yeah, okay, Jessie. The bartender places another two shots on the bar and I down mine, leaving Jessie a third. "Go on, then. Say your piece. Tell me how I overreacted, how I'm an angry monster and they are still our parents and we should love them," I drone on, mocking Jessie's deep tone of voice.

"How long have you been with Noah?"

Wait, what?

My face must look as confused as my thoughts because he continues. "You didn't overreact—blood doesn't mean shit. If you hadn't of smacked Dad's jaw, I would have. Your anger is warranted, and sometimes love is wasted on the wrong people." He downs his shot and continues, drilling me with his sharp eyes that penetrate every defense I've ever developed, my old brother just behind them. I feel a quick sting of sympathy at his still sensitive wound. I wonder if he'll ever move on from Jenny. Despite the space between us these last few years, I do wish he would find love again, allow himself to be happy.

"Now, how long have you been with Noah? How serious are you?" His questions are more like statements. Venom laced behind every word. I swallow to wet my throat, confused that *this* is what he wants to talk about.

"Umm... over a month, I think?" I realize I'm not too sure. Noah had told his mom we were together for two months, but... that would put our start date at the night of Bozzelli's when he all but kidnapped me before I ghosted him. A quick pain in my chest at the realization that Noah thinks about the beginning of us from that moment, but I shove it away. The date I had been counting was more like the date to the Rage Cage than anything else... honestly at this point, who cares?

Noah has hurt me. His lies a betrayal. He's known since Maplewood and he never said anything. Noah's words and actions that night he found me in my room at the lodge come back to me. The state of his hair looking like he had spent time pulling at it, his face in pain. Telling me he didn't want to see me hurt, I thought he was talking about my stupidity with the zipline; I guess this is what he was actually talking about.

"So even after my warning about him, you still went after him." JJ and I settle into our usual sparring match; that seems to be the norm between us now. Both refusing eye contact and staring forward towards the bar.

"Not that it is any of your business, but he pursued me. We were friends first... I guess? We just had this *thing* between us. It's hard to explain." I throw my fingers up to the bar keep, indicating another two shots. Waiting for them, we both down our drinks before continuing.

"And anyway, you warned me about his behavior with women. You said nothing about his ability to lie and deceive in general. Up until tonight, I was getting ready to prove you wrong. Prove to you that all your asshole behavior and cruel words were a result of your residual rage against Jenny and nothing to do with Noah and me." JJ releases a sigh and hangs his head, elbows resting on the bar.

"None of this is coming out properly. Do you love him? Are you... *in love?*"

"Yes," I say without hesitation, surprising even myself. After tonight, I have no clue what is going on. Falling out of love isn't that easy. It's not like I can just decide that's it. But... he *lied* to me. So easily, about something so big.

"And after tonight?" JJ pushes, but his tone is more gentle. I shrug and land my head in my hands.

"I have no idea, Jessie. I thought... *God.* I thought that..." I can't say it. My eyes sting and the lump in my throat threatens to expose me. The adrenaline of my rage from earlier is fading, and I'm about to fall apart.

"Thought what, Addison?"

"That we were endgame."

"Addy—"

"No. Don't. You know... I really... I actually thought he was it. Like I didn't need to learn to be around another person again because he would be all that I needed. I bitched him out the first time we met, ignored him, and rejected him for weeks, and when I finally gave in and he took me on our first date, I had a complete meltdown. He even stuck around after I one-night-stood him."

Jessie grimaces and shakes his head. "I'm really scared to ask, but what the fuck is '*one-night-stood him*'?"

"Like we slept together, and I left without sleeping over. Rosie says I 'one-night-stood him' because I was essentially saying this is a one-night thing. But he was like a bad habit I couldn't shake. He was just there and was always sweet. He never judged my moods or my episodes. He just held me through them and was there to help me up afterwards. He... stayed. He didn't run or get scared. He didn't blame me or make me feel shame or guilt. Literally no one else in my life has ever accepted me that way. Not Mom or Dad. Not Ava, Riley, or even you. Casey and Rosie try, but even they don't. Noah. He was different. I thought he was it." He also had this unflinching ability to meet my rage, to tease it, tame it, and seduce it in a way no one has ever been able to do. Like he knew exactly how to provoke it enough to wake a fire and passion in me, giving me confidence and determination, never flailing or running. My very own snake charmer.

I still can't tell what hurts more, the lies my dad forced me to live with, the fact my entire family is terrified of me to the point of keeping secrets, or that Noah kept all of this to himself.

JJ stands from his stool and stands next to me, lifting my chin with his rough hands and swiping away tears with his thumbs. Tears I didn't feel falling amongst the aching numbness. Once again, a blubbering mess—over another boy, no less. He wraps me in a tight hug, and the tears break from a trickle to a downpour, as I fail to muffle the sobs that leave my throat traveling from the pit of hell within me. Leaching every bit of pain from my soul, and Jessie remains firm as he soaks it up, rubbing small circles on my back. Between the numbness and the heartbreak is a familiar awareness, the reminder of Jessie and who we used to be. It feels a little like I have my JJ back.

"Mind your business," Jessie growls at someone behind me, and I realize I am creating quite a scene. I pull out of his embrace and pull my shit together. If I wasn't so upset and angry, I'd almost be amused at how uncomfortable JJ looks with all this emotion on display. His usual gruff ruggedness is conflicting with his display of physical affection. His grip on my shoulders remains firm, his gaze assessing.

"I'm saying this for your benefit, not his. Because I think I might go back and break his jaw watching you cry over him. But you... *fuck's sake.*" Jessie's body is visibly tense, and he pulls away as he runs a hand down his face. "You should really hear him out. No point in me telling you anything. I think... I think you should just hear what he has to say, the reasons he kept it secret... it's just a bit fucking complicated."

"Fu—"

"Shut it, I'm not done." JJ holds his hand in front of my face, silencing me. The only person who could grumble enough to make me listen. "That wasn't a '*you can't handle it*' complicated. It's literally just fucking complicated. The details of the situation, I honestly don't even remember. I do know that you'd want to hear him out, though. Matt and Ava, too. But talk to Noah. If you really love him, if you actually think this is real and worth fighting for, then fucking fight for it. I wish someone would have told me that two years ago." Guilt nearly makes my knees buckle. I didn't tell him to fight for Jenny. I just told him good riddance. God, he really loved her, and it took me having my love crushed to see his pain for what it is. But forgiving and fighting were two things I had no energy for right now, and I really had no idea when or if I would again.

"I'm sorry for being so caught up in my own shit that I've been a horrible big brother. I wish I... I just wish I was there for you more. I wish I was someone you thought about coming to. I'm sorry for how I've acted and sorry that I screwed us up so royally that you no longer even try to come to me. I want it to be different. I want you to come to me. I want to be there for you. For all of you girls." My heart cracks open wider, another flood threatening an appearance in my eyes. I can't say words without causing another sobbing scene, so I give Jessie my honest smile. The warmth of his apology and his words flooding my veins, and I nod. His shoulders relax as he heaves a sigh of relief, pulling me into a breath-stealing embrace. Despite everything, I guess my one silver lining is the small path to repair JJ and I seem to be on. Maybe I should even thank Dad and Noah for ruining everything with their lies and deceit.

"I love you, Big Rascal." My childhood nickname brings a wave of charming nostalgia and the memories of JJ and I growing up. Us against the girls.

"I missed you, Little Rogue."

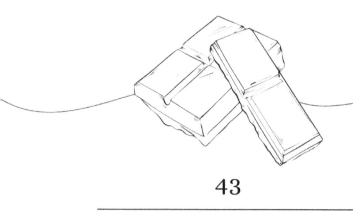

43

let's freak out safely

Noah

"Henry held up his end before everything came out on Saturday and EcoX has cleared AIM. The confession from Henry cleared me of any wrongdoing, and they are willing to work with us still. Have you heard from them about the contract?" Matt confirms from across the table. I shake my head, completely at a loss. I thought handling this issue personally and quietly would save Henry the humiliation, save a family from imploding, save Matt's job, save the deal that is meant to completely secure my future. Sure, Matt managed to keep his job. Henry's little side bet ended up being traced, uncovering decades worth of similar behavior, and next thing we knew, a warrant was issued and the family meeting from hell blew everything up in our faces. At least Henry had some form of dignity enough to let them all know in person rather than from the news.

Matt hadn't liked lying to Ava any more than I liked lying to Addy. In the end, it looks like I lose everything, anyway.

"Have you heard from Addison?"

His turn to shake his head. "Just give her space."

"Jessie said the same thing, but it's been a week. I can't just hang in the silence like this. I need to explain to her what happened. She needs to know about the contract, why I didn't say anything. I can't just move on with my life until I fix this." Matt doesn't offer any words, he just nods and pats me on the back.

"Hate to say I told you, but I did. She isn't going to forgive that easy, Karvelas. You're going to need to give her time. Rosie and Casey are on high alert. You just need to let her ride it out." Fuck this. Ride it out? Hell no. She is hurting, she is in pain. I'm not sitting on my fucking ass any longer.

Addison

"Addy, you in here?" Casey knocks softly on my door.

"No."

She chuckles at my lame attempt at telling her to go away, and I hear the bedroom door creak open. "You're going to have to do something other than sleep and work." Her tone is concerned and sympathetic and pitying, and I hate everything about it. Rage and sadness, mixed with shame, embarrassment, and resentment, fester and grow within me. Rage and sadness at how my family just continues to expect the worst of me and how Noah stole my heart clean out of my chest. Shamed and embarrassed that I'm apparently so volatile, no one trusts me with any information that might raise my blood pressure. Am I really so bad? Is there really this much wrong with me?

"I don't care what you think."

"What if I bribe you with espresso martinis?" Rosie says, joining Casey on this mission to bring me back to life.

"Make them all you want. I don't care." Words leave my mouth, but it doesn't feel like any thought goes into them. Like I'm on autopilot. I'm aware enough to know my autopilot is a bitch. I'm not aware enough to give a fuck, though.

"Ads, c'mon, why don't we go for a run? You love running."

"Why don't you both just get out and leave me alone? Stop pretending you understand how I feel. Stop trying to fix me. I just want to be alone." I wish I could feel guilt. Feel shame or regret. Maybe I do, maybe that's what this feeling is, but I'm just so riddled with it that I can no longer decipher the feelings from each other. Of course, my words and my rage don't deter them.

"Why don't I call Noah? Maybe he can fuck some sense into you." The mention of his name makes my stomach dip and my heart clench. Casey and Rosie got the full rundown of events. Unlike my family, they knew how crazy I was for Noah. They live here, after all, and were witness to my nonsensical high of ecstasy that I'd been living in. They've since become at-home nursemaids.

Like a knee-jerk reaction, tears well in my eyes, and I spin on Rosie and Casey. "Get out." My tone does nothing to hide my anger and my pain. They both sigh and leave without argument. I understand they mean well. I understand they are trying to help. What they don't understand is the control required to manage the fury that builds inside me takes up every last drop of energy that I have, and there is nothing left to give in any other aspect of life. I have enough to control my outbursts and enough to make it through the day.

That's all I can give.

The last week has been a cycle of the same thing. Panic, cry, sleep, work, rage, panic, cry, sleep, repeat. Panic about where I'm going, what I'm doing. Who am I if not the person I was told to be? I hate that I have achieved so much and yet it feels like it was for nothing. I was trying to make Dad proud of me. Trying to make sure he had a reason to rave about me and to love me. And now? His opinion means less than the lint on my towels. So what was the point? What was it all for?

I'm back to avoiding my baths. Without Noah plying me with strawberries and wine while holding my hand, it just doesn't have the same feel to it. The only break in my routine is when I have to dial Jessie's number to save me from myself. When I finally hit a point where it goes too far. When those spiraling dark and gooey thoughts come knocking, and try to swallow me whole. Jessie has been a rock. A nice quiet, only around when I call, rock, who has let me wallow, giving space and time. He only once asked, '*why haven't you called Noah yet?*' before I scolded him and he dropped the subject. The answer is because I can't. Because I know that I'll look into those eyes and want to forgive and forget, if only to just have my heart not hurt so damn much. I finally let myself care and trust and want someone, and I'm shown every reason why I never should have.

I feel him everywhere, too. In my bathroom, in my bed, on the couch. I see him at JJ's bookshop, and every time I try to tell myself that it will be a better day, some reminder of him springs to mind.

My little demon.

Shortcake.

It's always been you.

I love you completely.

All a lie.

Oh yeah. Angry doesn't even begin to describe the rage I feel. But it's reduced to a simmer. Like a white flame—all bark and no bite. Because bite requires energy and I'm all out of that.

"Addison?" Hearing my name from that same voice actually in the room jolts me from my thoughts.

"Noah, what are you doing here?" I sit up and see his form in the doorway of my bedroom. The smooth caramel of his voice is a complete contrast to how he looks. Wrecked. I mean, physically, he looks as delicious as always. Pants clinging to the muscles of his legs, his plain T shaping around his sculptured shoulders and that damn backwards cap. His eyes, though, red-rimmed and clouded in dark circles. He looks about as great as I feel, and as much as I should hate the feeling, I don't. It's nice to know he is as torn up as I am.

"I needed to see you, shortcake. I couldn't stay away any longer. I need to just... explain everything."

That boy loves you. And I mean big-big love. Life-long kind of love. I just want you to always remember that.

I think you should just hear what he has to say, the reasons he kept it secret.

The conversations that have been on a loop in my head this entire week. At war with one another. If Noah loved me so much, how could he have lied and pretended everything was fine so easily? Maybe Iris knew and was giving me some kind of warning about his heart still being mine despite his lies? But how do you lie to someone you love?

But then, after Jessie himself suggested I give Noah a chance to talk, it's hard to ignore the instinct telling me to just let him explain. I want to trust him. *God,* do I want to just believe everything he says. It would be easier to just forgive and love him and move on from this. But the pain, the reminder of the hurt and betrayal that I've now felt from everyone in my life, is a cute little reminder that I really am alone.

I nod my head slightly at Noah and he strolls across the room to sit on the bed, toeing off his shoes, climbing on and leaning his back against my light grey upholstered headboard, so he is next to me. He looks good here. Like he should have been here all week. The sight of him so close, the warm olive skin against my white sheets, and that scent of his clenches my heart tight, and I drop a tear.

"Oh, Addy." He reaches a hand and swipes the tear. I can see his heart fighting with his brain as he wants to linger, but withdraws his hand to rest back in his lap. "I'm so sorry I hurt you."

A wave of feelings I've been trying to bury hit me like a tsunami. The way he looks at me, the way I can feel his heart right there. It would be so easy to reach for him, to let the warmth of those chocolate eyes pull me back in and let him wrap me up. I want it so badly to feel him wrapped around me, but I can't. No, I need to be stronger. Need to bury it deeper.

"You wanted to talk. So tell me then, explain to me what warranted you lying to me. Telling me you loved me, but managing to keep such a secret from me at the same time."

"At Maplewood, the night you didn't come to dinner..." Oh, he is jumping straight into this. I readjust myself to cross my legs and face him as he leans back against the headboard, eyes never leaving mine. "I went to the bathroom, and on the way back, I caught the end of a phone call. I could only hear his words, but it was enough."

"What... what did you hear?"

"It wasn't until I heard the name of the company that I put it altogether. EcoX Tech is an Energy Company, relatively new but made it big in their first two years and are worth millions. They are the market leader in energy storage and smart grid tech. I only know this because they approached my company for the marketing of a new system they have engineered and are about to release. The security on this new item is so tight they couldn't give me the details for it, despite my confidentiality and NDA procedures. They wanted to build up the brand and find a way to get their existing material out to a wider audience before releasing the new product. Anyway, Matt's company was a part of the project and Matt was the lead engineer of it." *Dad hacked Matt's computer.* "I don't know how Henry managed to find out Matt was holding all the designs or whether he just caught wind of Matt working on something big, whatever the reason, he managed to gamble correctly, because he got it and found the whole folder." That disgusting piece of dirt. I almost feel bad for ignoring Ava and Matt this week. They've been betrayed too, Matt's privacy and integrity compromised.

"Word of the leak spread when there were whispers of a similar product from another company, the EcoX tech stock was taking a hit as this other company was growing. They got spooked. They put my contract on hold and said that my company and AIM were under investigation as the only two other companies who had been engaged to work with them. That was why I came to Maplewood—Matt and I needed to work out what happened."

Memories of the deal they celebrated, the work stress Noah had been under, flood back to me.

"I still don't understand why you couldn't have told me this. Why you and Matt had to keep the whole thing a secret. You told me all of that just now, and I still don't know about this fucking *product*. Why lie?"

"Matt worked out it was your dad. He might be stupid enough to make his password Mia2018 but he has security cameras in his office and the file had a login register. Matt filled me in after we got home, and I panicked. We made a deal with your dad."

My stomach sinks and my heart lurches in my throat, having no idea how to handle any of this information.

"Matt and I agreed to keep it from all of you if Henry agreed to tell AIM and EcoX what happened. Matt didn't want to lose his company.

I desperately needed to keep this contract to avoid losing everything I worked for. This contract would secure our future. I needed it so badly to work I hadn't thought about the repercussions. Addy, you have to believe me."

My blood hums with rage as I run over all the lies over the last few months. The information soaks into my brain, and I try to combat every instinct I have to allow it to control me.

"What about the phone call? What did you hear?"

"He... *Addison,*" he pleads. I know he doesn't want to be the one to tell me this. Well, too fucking bad.

"You love me?" His eyes widen and pain shoots through me at the look he gives me.

"With everything I am," he says without hesitation.

"Then tell me."

He takes a deep breath, and then his deep chocolate eyes hold mine. "After the crap about EcoX, he ended the call with a goodbye to whomever he was speaking to, and I quote, '*Isa, baby, don't worry. I'll always look after you. You and me forever. I love you, too, sugar.*'" Noah looks like he is going to be sick. I feel like I'm right behind him. The white fury turns red and floods my veins as I try to breathe through it. I have no idea how to expend any of it, but I need an outlet, need somewhere to put it. I stand from the bed, my heart racing, breath coming in fast as I pace the room. "Addison?" That dirty motherfucker, God! I could go for another round of smacking his jaw with my fist.

You'll never learn a work ethic, always entitled and wanting what you don't work for.

You leave a secure job at a law firm to sling shots like some hussy at a bar. No child of mine would work at such a venue.

If anyone here is entitled, it is fucking Henry. Fancy him belittling me, throwing me down a peg, when he shouldn't have even been on the ladder. That two-bit no-good lying, deceiving motherfucker. Or rather, *secretary-fucker.*

My rage makes my brain lose it. I can't understand why it's out of control, and by trying to control it, it just gets worse. I can't handle it coursing through my veins, can't deal with the way it makes my chest feel like it is about to explode. My fury mixes with my panic. Panic that has absolutely no business showing itself right now, but again, it doesn't discriminate. Before I know what's happening, I have my keys in my hand and I'm in the lobby of the apartment strolling towards the front doors, a Greek giant on my heels.

"Addison, you're freaking out, I get it. You can totally freak out. But can you tell me where we are going so I can at least make sure we freak out safely?" He seems out of breath, and I stop and turn on him, suddenly needing that solid grounding he was always able to give me.

"I need... *I need an outlet,*" I all but growl. He swallows, looking satisfyingly terrified, and he nods, pulling out his phone.

"I know just the place." That lazy sex-smirk appears on his gorgeous face and something like nostalgia or longing warms my chest briefly before the rage sinks its teeth back in.

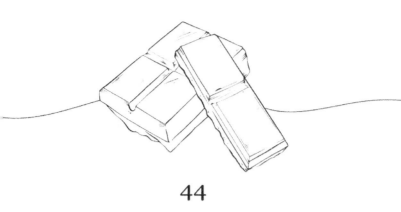

44

fun-sized firecracker

Noah

We arrived at Rage Cage, and Addison wasted no time getting settled in her destruction. I decided to stand to the side; better she have as many items to break as possible to give her fury an outlet. I wish I could help her, wish I knew how to take it away so she didn't feel this suffocating rage that takes over her. All I know to do is to just stand here, and I will. I will stay here, or at her apartment, or at her work. I will stay and stand or sit wherever she needs me, for however long that is, whether she wants me close or at a distance. I don't care how it is, but she will know that she has me, and that I am not going anywhere.

Her shouts and screams of rage mix with her tears, the ache and the pain of her expelling all that anger is like a nail to my chest. No words leave her mouth, just the sounds from deep within her soul that result from her pain. This time I don't try to coddle her, hold her, or calm her down. I let her be in it. Exist in it until she tells me she is ready. Honestly, if the source of her rage and pain wasn't so raw, her face and growls would almost be adorable. The deep scrunch of her eyebrows, the soft pink flush of her cheeks, and her plump lips pulled into a pout.

I send off a text to Rosie and Casey, thanking them for letting me in. Despite the warning look Rosie threw in my direction, I'm glad they gave me the time, whether I deserved it or not. I let them know that we aren't at the apartment but I have her, will take care of her, and I'll text them later. I also message JJ, who has been surprisingly communicative about Addison.

Me: I told her.

JJ: About fucking time. How'd she take it?

Me: We're at the Rage Cage.

JJ: Sounds about right.

Rosie's text comes back at the same time.

The scary one: The Rage Cage? That is very on-brand for our fun-sized firecracker.

The scary one: I haven't forgotten, Karvelas. 🔪

I gulp and shove my phone back into my pocket, bringing my attention back to Addison now that the crashing has stopped. She stands in the middle of the room, her back to me as her breaths come in fast. I still, unsure when or if to break the tense silence, when Addy moves first. Her hands release the bat and she falls to her knees. Her back shakes from her sobs and this all feels very *déjà vu*. I go to her, falling to the ground with her, and pull her to me, holding her tightly to my chest as she cries. The kind of cry that hurts, a cry that would break hearts, and I rub circles on her back to let her know she can cry as long as she needs.

"I'm so over this. Crying all the fucking time." Her words are low, remnants of her rage still there.

"There is nothing wrong with a healthy display of emotions, short-cake."

"There is healthy... and then there is me." I can't quite tell if that was an attempt to add humor, but to avoid any issues where my balls are removed from my body, I refrain from laughing and continue with my circles.

"You needed the outlet. This is just your body getting rid of all the bad shit and giving your rage a place to run rampant. Whether there are tears or not, this is healthy. This is what you need. It's okay to give yourself what you need, to hell with what anyone else says."

"I don't understand."

"What don't you understand?"

"You."

I pull away from her then, to see her eyes, and the anger in her emerald green eyes pierce my soul. *She is so fucking beautiful.* "What about me confuses you?"

She gestures to my body, her eyes searching mine. Pain, so much pain behind them my chest clenches. "Why... why are you still here? Why do you hang around? Why bother spending all this time trying to fix me or attend to me? Standing by while I melt down. Why waste your time and your energy on someone who is a raging psycho bitch? I don't understand what the fuck you get out of it. But I don't want to be someone's pity trophy. I don't want to worry about how all of this is going to affect you or how it impacts you. I don't want to hide or tame myself. I just want to be able to feel freely without anyone judging me or being scared of me. *Fuck.*" She works herself up into another state as she stands and starts to pace the room. Her words hurt, but I deserve them. "I know you said you made a deal, and that is why you couldn't tell me, but you still lied, and you did it with ease. Don't tell me it's not because part of you isn't scared of how volatile I am, because it's everyone else's excuse. Admit it—"

"That's enough, Addison." My voice is low but commanding, and I stand, towering over her. It's enough to get her to stop the accusations. It's about time I clear a lot of that up.

"I'm here and I'm not going anywhere. There is nothing to fix about you because you are not broken, nor are you a *raging psycho bitch.* What you are is a stunning, intelligent, and strong woman who has a furious fire in your soul that protects you. I don't hold you as a trophy. I hold you because I love you. With everything in me. You have my heart entirely and I never want it back. It's yours."

"But you lied. You *lied* so easily to me. Who's to say all of this isn't just some other lie for you to humiliate me with later?" Her meeting my commanding tone with her wrath does nothing to dissuade me. She sets a fire in me that makes me want to burn the world for making her feel so goddamn fucking small.

"I never did that with ease, Addison, and I never lied about loving you. I never lied about never leaving you. I can't begin to explain how much regret I have for hurting you and making you question your trust in me, but don't you dare brand me with that. You hold a lot of rage? Fine, I'll take you in every single way that you are, I want nothing else. I don't think you're volatile, Addison, and you've never once scared me off, but fuck it, you want to believe those things, then fine, believe them. I'll be right here to remind you every second of every day that I love you, anyway, because exactly how you are is perfect for me." My breaths are harsh now, her tears are seeping slowly down her cheeks, and that contagious rage is catching on as my anger thrums in my body. Vibrates through her lack of faith in my love for her, in the way people who were meant to love her have damaged her to the point where she no longer believes she is good. It causes me so much pain that she can't see herself the way I see her. So fiercely strong and so incredibly beautiful.

"I've never needed another person the way I need you, and I've never been given someone else's heart the way you gave me yours. I have never loved the way I love you. You're it for me, Addison. I want you, or I don't want anything at all."

I search her eyes, trying to work out if what I'm saying is making this worse or better. But really, I don't care, because it's all true. I lay it out, my heart and soul, hoping she'll take me, anyway. Broken bits and all.

Her anger has receded slightly, and I take that as response enough to continue. "I never want you to hide from me. I never want you to tame yourself or pretend to be someone you aren't. I want you to embrace everything and all that you are and feel safe to do it alongside me, knowing that when you need me to, I will be there to help you back up again. Not that I think you need my help. I think you're more than capable, but you aren't alone. That is why I'm here, that is why I'm around. You will never be alone. If it's the last thing I do, Addy, I will make sure that you never feel alone in this world."

She closes her eyes as she stands there sobbing, not letting me close the distance between us. Her fury dissipates to the background as she drops another tear. I move then and pull her closer to my chest. She attempts to swat me away, swallowing a grunt of anger at being wrapped up. Using my strength against her fight, the moment her body is wrapped in mine, she softens. And I hold her close to me as she silently cries.

I feel the tension leave her body as we stand there for a few minutes before she pulls back to look at me again. Her face soft and puffy, lips a kissable soft pink from her crying, but those damn green eyes threaten to undo me completely. She searches my face for something, so I try to give her more. More of my heart so she can trust the words and know I'm not going anywhere.

"Addy, baby, I have never been sure of love, never thought I wanted or needed it, but Addison, I can say with certainty I have never been more sure about anything in my life than I am about you. You're it, shortcake. I'm done. I need nothing else. Just you." She rises on her toes, planting a kiss on my lips that steals my breath. Her tongue teases my bottom lip, seeking entry, and I open for her to deepen the kiss. The flame of hope ignites in my chest, and I feel like I could shout and rejoice that Addy is mine, that she is still here. I add another vow, internally, to do everything possible to keep her close to me like this, forever.

"Noah, I... I don't want to be in pain anymore. I just... I want to forget everything. I want it to just go away," she whispers against my lips, her eyes closed.

"Okay, Ads. We can do whatever you want. I'm not going any-where. Let me help you, let me take it all away, please."

"No." The words cause my stomach to drop.

"No?" Panic ceases my chest, and the hope that built itself up inside me pops, or rather, explodes.

"I mean, I... I'm so sick of feeling broken, Noah. I just need some time. I need... I think I need to be okay with just me. Not rely on someone else to be the reason I'm happy." She pauses and heaves a huge breath, closing her eyes as she shakes her head. "I need to be able to wake up each day and know that I am strong enough to last the day because of me and who I am. Not because someone else is holding me up." *Fuck.* I feel her slipping through my fingers. "I'm tired, Noah. I'm just so fucking tired, and I just can't do this with you right now."

Words evade me, but I try. Try to salvage the clusterfuck I've made of this. Of us. "Addy, I won't... wait, I want to support you, and help you through pain caused by me. I don't mean to be—"

"Noah, it's okay. You weren't the first person who hurt me, and you certainly won't be the last." *Ouch.* "I need to heal myself and work on myself. I need to be better, and I can't rely on someone else to catch me if I fall. I need to be that for myself." She steps back and I am instantly there, too. My stomach drops and my heart increases. Is she... is this a break up? Is she leaving me?

"Wait, shortcake, please don't do this."

"It has to be done." *I love you.* It feels selfish to say it right now, so I bite it back. How she ever thought she was weak is beyond me. If anyone here is weak, it's me. Her strength is incredible, and I have to admire and respect her ability to look out for herself first. But fuck, it hurts. I don't know how I'm going to let her walk away.

"So... this is it? You're... you're not mine, anymore." A statement, a whisper. Too scared to voice it out loud. She shakes her head, a soft smile gracing her gorgeous face, set with determination as she steps closer and places a cupped hand to my cheek. I lean into the touch, committing her warmth to memory.

"I need to belong to myself before I can give you any part of me."

"I meant what I said Addison. I'm not going anywhere." And I won't. I will wait for her, and I will love her now and when she's ready, however long that takes. I turn and kiss her palm, then pull her into an embrace. Annoyingly keeping my hands at a respectable height on her back, a reminder that, for now, this is it. Until she is ready, this is what we are. She might need time, but I don't. I know she is it and I'll wait for her to catch up.

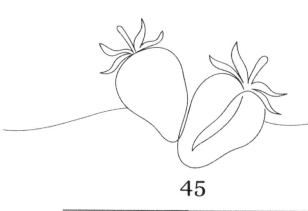

45

new boundaries, new beginnings

Addison

"Thanks for coming by." I nod at Ava as she holds the door to her home open for me. The dark sand-colored brick home is framed with perfectly groomed gardens on their acre block of land. Silverbrook Heights is a beautiful outer suburb of New York City, and Ava and Matt's house is the pinnacle of happy families. It is a gorgeous double story on a street lined with trees. In the winter, under a few layers of snow, it is like a Winter Wonderland. The entry way is a long hallway heading for the kitchen, with a staircase on the right. To the left as you enter, in the living room-turned-playroom, Mia's eyes are plastered to the TV, not having even noticed my arrival, and to the right is the study, which Matt is sitting in, studiously staring at a computer screen.

I'm unsure, really, what to say or where to start. It's only been a few weeks since I found out everything and put things with Noah on pause... or, I guess, broke up... at the Rage Cage. He's still tried to reach out, but I just haven't had the energy to see or speak to him. I just need... time. Time to heal and get myself better. Starting with Matt and Ava felt like the best way to go about that.

Matt gets up from his desk and throws out a fist bump. Despite the emotional tornado that ripped through our family, it's nice to know our relationship hasn't changed.

"I'm sorry I've been so mad at you guys. I know you didn't ask for any of this to happen, either." I look at them with sympathy, trying to tame the rage pit that churns inside me, that tries to tell me to hold on to my anger, to never let them see my weakness. That apologizing makes me look small and makes me lose my power. The emergency therapy appointment I had a few days ago has helped me try to reign in all those thoughts that threaten to ruin every positive relationship in my life.

Ava gestures to the sitting room just off the kitchen. Private enough that Mia can't hear our conversation, but close enough that they can keep an eye on her. "Ask us anything, we'll tell you. I'm sorry I made you come all the way out to Virginia to hear everything. I just didn't know how else for it to come out. I wanted to tell you as soon as I knew but... with Matt's work, we couldn't." Ava's eyes have a sheen to them, and I genuinely feel bad for being so closed off to her. She was stuck in a position between her husband and her family. The family that included a father who invaded their home privacy and exploited said husband's work secrets.

"It's okay. I get it." I think. I still hate that they walk around me. "I'm sorry, too," I direct mostly at Ava. "For always being so short with you. For pushing you away and always expecting the worst of you." She smiles softly and nods. "I wanted to come by to explain that I'm not mad at either of you. Noah told me everything that happened. Or, at least, I think it was everything. I think I need it to be everything because I don't know if I could take much more." That was supposed to be a joke, but it falls flat and the only person laughing at me, is me.

"Look, moving forward, can you guys just treat me like a normal person?"

"What do you mean? We do treat you normally, Addy." Ava looks genuinely confused, but from the way Matt pulls his lips into a tight smile, hiding a grimace, I know he knows what I mean.

"You don't. I know you were stuck in a hard place with the way everything went down, but even if Matt wasn't involved, you would have done the same thing. You act like I'm a bomb about to go off and you need to make sure you don't trip a wire. When really, you acting like that around me has more of a chance of setting me off than anything else."

"Addy, we just worry—"

"No. I don't want to hear those excuses anymore." I take a deep breath, desperate not to prove them right. Desperate to show them that I am a human being. I am not without my flaws, but I am still deserving of respect and to be treated like anyone else. "If you continue to treat me like I'm fragile, you give me no room to grow. You keep me stuck in this one place with this one label, never having room to change or be better. I don't want to be a hypocrite. I know I probably do this, too, with you and always expecting you to take everyone else's side but mine, or expecting you to call me crazy instead of understanding. If we keep treating each other like we belong in specific categories or slapping these labels on each other, then that is what we'll always be to each other. Give me breathing room, and I'll do the same. I'm not perfect, I'm going to have bad days, but stop expecting them. Let me show you that I can be better." Ava swipes a tear from under her eye and I do the same. Matt nods and leans back into the couch, a soft smile spreading across his face.

"I'm proud of you, Ads," he says softly, and I nod awkwardly, not used to this type of conversing with Matt. Before I can change the subject, he continues, "Noah was right about you." Quiet enough, I'm not sure I heard that right.

"What?"

"He said you were a lot stronger than we all gave you credit for. He was right."

"Are you sure you'll be okay?" Casey asks, rubbing my shoulder from the couch. She and Rosie are clearing out for a few hours while I have Mom and Riley over—the repair train in full force this week after my successful visit with Matt and Ava. After Matt's little bombshell about a hidden conversation with Noah, he clarified the details of everything that happened, solidifying everything Noah said as truth. That they'd made a deal with Dad for the sake of both their companies when it all inevitably came out in the wash, anyway. Matt had apologized and said he wished he could have handled things differently. It was pointless, things happened, and really it might even make the family better for it. Mom certainly dodged that long-term bullet.

"I'll be fine. It's not like they are bringing Dad with them." Well, that would be impossible considering he is officially in custody, awaiting his trial, impatiently, I'm sure.

Rosie nods and meets Casey at the door. "Just message us if you need, we're only going to JJ's," Casey says as they leave.

After about twenty minutes, Mom and Riley arrive, and I realize this is actually the first-time Mom has come over. "I love the sun you get through these windows!" Mom beams as she stands by the window. Riley gives me an awkward look and gestures to the bathroom, leaving me alone with Mom.

"Mom," I say softly from beside her. She lets go of a big breath.

"I'm sorry, Addison."

"What on earth for, Mom? You're the one going through all this shit with Dad."

"For being a bad mom." *Well, then.* I blink back the tears that prick behind my eyes, threatening to make this conversation way more emotional than I had been prepared for.

Be vulnerable, let them in, but be firm in your boundaries. You'll be surprised how much closer you become to them when you set boundaries. My therapist's words clang through me as I center my breath and place a hand on Mom's arm, getting her to finally look at me. Her tear-filled eyes hit me, and it hurts something deep within my chest.

"Mom, I love you." I whisper the words because if I say them too loud, I will implode and become a puddle of tears. Mom, on the other hand, does just that, and practically collapses in my arms. I stand there holding her. This woman, who looked at me like I was an injured bird my whole life, was here in my arms as I held her while she cried. I direct us to the couch and sit, and I let a few of my tears fall. "Mom, I'm going to need to say things, and I need you to let me finish without interrupting me." She pulls back and assesses me with nervous eyes, but nods and wipes under her eyes. "You are not a bad mom. Maybe for a few years, you haven't been there for me like I wanted or needed you to be. I think I have been really mad at you for not protecting me from Dad and the way he bullied us. But I forgive you, and I don't blame you. I think maybe you have... things you need to sort out, to heal. You were only acting through your own version of a trauma response, and I can see it now." She cries more and I have to look to the ceiling to center myself. Searching for my strength to keep going. To push past the sour taste of guilt left on my tongue as I speak each word.

Be firm in your boundaries.

"You need to give me room to grow—"

"I do give you room—"

"Mom. Let me finish. You don't. You worry for me, I understand that. You worry I might be unwell, not handling things and heading for a dark spiral. I know my history gives you probable cause for worrying. But I can't grow or change if you slap a fragile label on me and worry that something might be too much for me. I'm an adult, and although I'm your child, you need to let go enough to trust that I know what's best for me. And if I make a bad decision as I go, that's okay. That's *how* I'm going to learn and grow. We can't all be perfect. Please, just let me be exactly who I am and not make me feel like I can't or shouldn't." She nods and wipes a few more tears. Her interruption was enough to sober my emotions and that inner wrath powering me through my speech.

Your fury is not your weakness. It is your greatest strength.

Noah's words are a painful stab to my stomach. Not even three weeks and I miss him already. I can't... no room for those feelings right now.

"I don't..." Mom takes a breath, closes her eyes as she composes herself. "I don't know how to do that. I didn't know I was... well, I'm sorry. I will try." And that's all we can do. I smile at her and nod. "You know I love you, right?" she says as she sobs and that about does me in and the dam walls break, tears falling as I grab Mom. Holding each other for a minute.

At this point, I'm certain Riley is just hanging out in my room until the crying is done. Giving Mom and me the much-needed privacy.

"I know, Mom. I've always known. I was just too angry to admit it to myself." I hold her tight and she rubs my back a few times before we pull back. She cups my cheek, tugging a hair behind my ear, like she always did when I was a kid. "How have you been doing?" I ask.

"Well. Honestly, I don't know. I think I might still be in shock. Riley keeps me busy, distracting me. She is actually hilarious. Have you spent time with her recently? I don't know if she is making me laugh as a distraction or if she was always this funny, and I was too wrapped up in my own crap to pay her any attention."

"She's pretty funny." I nod and give Mom a little smile. Riley was full of surprises. I think with all of us moving out and Mom and Dad being a bit absent, she's had to entertain herself, possibly making her a little insane, but that's a conversation for another day.

"And... what about Dad?"

"I really don't want to think about that man for a good long while. Things with us have been crappy for a while. I'm glad for the excuse for the marriage to end, but it still hurts. It's important that you all understand... If twenty-year-old me knew what I know now, I'd still do it all again, just so I could have you kids. You're my whole heart, and I'd go through all the pain and torment again if it meant having you each exactly as you are. I regret nothing." Her words are strong and her face is set in certainty.

Goddammit.

Her declaration, the determination in her eyes, sets me off again, except this time, I hear sobs from the doorway. As I pull back and look over my shoulder, I see Riley standing there, arms wrapped around her stomach as she sobs.

"Riles. Come here." I wave her over and she all but runs and plants herself to my side, holding tight.

"I'm sorry I'm a crappy sister," I apologize to Riley. I really should have been there for her more, supported her more, instead we left her alone, through the years where she really could have done with some siblings.

"I forgive you," she says back to me between sobs that make Mom and I laugh.

"You're supposed to say that I wasn't a bad sister," I tease.

"No. You were." Guilt settles in my stomach at her words. "But it's okay. I still like you. Plus, I like this apartment. I want to come visit, so I need you to like me, too." I laugh as she pulls away and shakes off the hug, officially uncomfortable with the show of affection.

"I still like you, weirdo," I remind her.

"Okay, are we done with emotions? Can we go get some dinner?" Riley sobers us and we stand from the couch. Mom gives me a soft smile, nodding. I nod back. Like an acknowledgement.

The moment marking a change for the future. Boundaries in place, hearts on the path to healing, and all our futures looking just that little bit brighter.

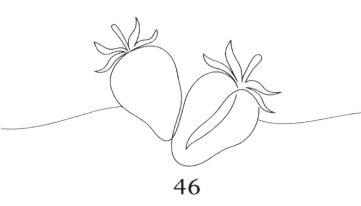

46

we're making smart choices this winter

Addison

Six months have passed, leaving summer and fall behind, winter now in full swing, my favorite time of the year because, Christmas! This year was like trekking new ground, unsure what the landscape looked like, but it ended up being a joyous event. We all gathered at Matt and Ava's place, and by all, I mean the Jenkins clan in full–minus Dad. He was found guilty on all counts and sentenced to twenty years, but JJ showed up with dessert and wine!

We laughed, ate, and gave gifts like the happy family we haven't been in a really long time. We didn't talk about any of the crap that went down earlier in the year; instead, we enjoyed the moments for what they were.

My birthday came and went. Rosie's first go at a start to finish edit for a title, which she calls her baby, was released and has topped charts everywhere. Casey and her sister opened a new studio on the Upper East Side, now giving them one studio to run each. So many things have changed. Everything with my family feels like a lifetime ago, but we've all been better. Riley comes out regularly, and we've gotten much closer, to the point she has now decided she would like to move to the city. Where she will live is currently undecided as she remains on a college hiatus, pending scholarship applications. Mom is enjoying a singles cruise while Dad enjoys his cell, and Ava and Matt are now awaiting the arrival of baby number two, due in May.

Lucas gave me an operations manager role and put me on permanent full-time employment, as I made the final decision not to sit for the Bar. The lawyering world wasn't for me. I love the random jobs popping up in the bar work and it keeps me on my toes. Between the late-night bar work and the general running of the business during the day, it feels a lot more satisfying. Now I have the choice of working from home, at JJ's, or from my office at Bozzelli's.

After the emergency appointment back in July, I retained my weekly therapy appointments. I've taken up boxing as a regular outlet to funnel my rage. My therapist's advice was to give myself an outlet, even when I don't feel it taking over, giving me more capacity to handle it when it does spike. Between the boxing and the running, it's been a lot more manageable. I brought Casey with me to a few classes, and now she is looking into a variation of the boxing and self-defense classes to incorporate into her new studio. Of course, Rosie had declared there was no need for her to attend, she has a strenuous outlet regularly enough as it is.

I've kept Noah at a distance. A physical distance, at least. He still plagues my thoughts every other hour, and the hollowness I feel in my chest hasn't reduced, no matter how hard I try. I haven't dated otherwise, wouldn't even think of it. I can't say the same for him, a part of me hoping he never does, no matter how selfish I know that is.

He texts me almost daily, he and JJ have also apparently become chummy, and it's annoying how much that makes my heart sing. JJ reckons Noah will keep messaging me every day until I '*stop breaking his balls and give in already.'* The first month, I held back from my replies, but his ability to break down every one of my walls and make my heart skip in my chest eventually broke me and now I respond. In denial probably, but I'm convincing myself that we're friends, if only because I'm pretending I want space, and that I don't lie awake at night wishing his hard warm body was curled around me, while his big hands explore and make me feel all the things, saying all those sweet nothings he is so good at saying.

It's not like I haven't seen him at all in six months. I first ran into him at JJ's–I'm sure it was staged on his part–about four months ago. It was surprisingly easy, despite fighting the urge to go to him and have him hold me. I almost, *almost,* dropped a tear, but his sex-smirk and deep chocolate eyes winded me, stirring all the old familiar feelings and sending bolts of energy south. But nothing was awkward. He gave me a kiss on each cheek, threw a heart stopping, *'Hey, beautiful,'* before winking and walking out. He followed up that same afternoon with a text telling me I still smell as sweet as strawberries and that he misses me. From there, I gave in bit by bit. He has come running with me a few times. I see him at the bar when he comes with the guys for a beer or when he is there for work with Lucas.

Despite how badly I miss him, us, I'm proud of myself for sticking by my decision. This time for myself has been good. I've spent a lot of time trying to learn awareness, learning about boundaries, and when I'm capped emotionally. The space I needed to work on myself, to learn about myself. I tell myself I won't be hurt if Noah moved on, but the truth is, it would still break me in two. All the self-love in the world couldn't stop that.

While I feel like I have learnt more about myself in six months of constant therapy and boundary setting than I have in the now twenty six years I've been alive, the string that ties my heart to Noah's has never been tighter. He remains the only person still making it past these boundaries, making me miss him endlessly while still being his usual charming, kind, and sexy self. I have days, or sometimes weeks, where I forget why I initiated this break in the first place.

Noah: How gorgeous is the sun today? Reminds me of your smile.

Noah: Summer storms are crazy. Did you see the lightning? Reminds me of your fury streak ;)

Noah: Damn... just turned myself on.

Noah: Hey, when was the last time you had Shortcake?

Noah: Not like... yourself... I mean the actual cake? I'll make you some. Mom gave me a good recipe.

He sends me basketball stats and gives me reviews on the espresso martinis at any new bars he tries. He sends me snaps of Caleb, Ethan, and Lucas with '*wish you were here*' notes. Everything he does reminds me of why I fell in love with him.

Noah: These smell like you and it made me smile <3

That was the most recent one, followed by a photo of a basket of strawberries at the local market. He managed to hold it open under his chin, the photo framing his goofy smile and deep brown eyes. That photo, after setting it as my phone wallpaper, I had stared at for about sixty minutes while I cried. What started as happy tears at his ridiculously happy face ended up being tears of longing to a point I was so confused by the decisions I'd made I needed an emergency therapy appointment.

"Hi Addy, how have you been this week?" Rhea, my therapist, says from the other side of Zoom. My laptop sits on my lap as I prop myself up on my bed, the blinds open as the early January winter sun tries to warm up the room, my tissues on the side table in preparation for some mental healing.

"Not bad, work has been busy, we just hired a new chef so had some tastings and new wine pairings for the restaurant." Rhea nods and smiles but presses on.

"And how are *you*, Addison?" Goddamnit.

"Ugh." I cover my face and throw my head back.

"Alright, I know that look. Tell me, let's unpack." She never lets me get away with anything.

"It's Noah." I told her about everything that went down between my family, Noah, Matt, Jessie, even updated her after I caught up with Mom and Riley. She knows everything. She had at the time congratulated me for how I handled it all. Despite what a colossal mess it felt like, she told me I was brave, how proud of me she was for acknowledging what I needed and being strong enough to go after it, no matter how much it hurt.

"Tell me more about that," she presses.

"I... I feel like I miss him. I just... I wish I could have him here. Have him hold me and say all those nice things again. Every time I think about him, my heart hurts a little. Like an ache." She nods at me but says nothing. "It feels like I'm failing myself if I give in and go back to him. I can't quite tell if this is just the normal part of breaking up with someone or if it's because I made a mistake." Breaking up doesn't feel like what we did. I really hate saying those words. "I thought I did this for a reason, giving us space, but now I can't remember why and I'm about to give in." Breaking up with Jake was solid ground. He fucked up–was a complete ass–and we ended things. Never speaking until I ran into him at Maplewood and again when he ambushed me. There were no leftover or residual feelings or confusing thoughts, no remaining friendship that made me ache. This break with Noah was so, so, so different. So much hurt still.

"But did you really have space?"

"Well, yeah…"

"How often have you seen him since the day you ended things?"

"Recently… I guess I see him every few days. He is really good to go running with… super motivational." Because he is sex on legs and he wears that backwards cap, and if we run in a gym because the winter air is too cold, he sometimes wears no shirt and… *yum.*

"Addy. Have you thought about *why* you haven't actually given each other space? Turning off the sex-tap is one thing, a healthy thing you did for yourself. But ask why you feel like you're 'giving in' to him–I don't like that phrase, but let's use it for the sake of this question." I think on her words and she lets me ponder. Despite all the mess that happened six months ago, Noah has still remained a solid force in my life. Constantly there, ready to stand by or swoop in and save me. Because despite everything, I love him with my whole soul. He said he gave me his heart, well, he still holds mine. But I am apprehensive about going back. I'm still scared of having my heart shattered by him again. What we went through was a glimpse of how fully I have fallen for him, and if anything were to happen, it would surely scar me more permanently than anything Jake put me through.

I want to trust him, and sure, he had a relatively good-ish reason for keeping the truth from me, but it doesn't mean it won't happen again.

The worst part was that I had no idea he was keeping such a secret from me. He was able to do it so easily, without me even picking up on an energy, or something being wrong. The only giveaway was the morning of the call, and that was only because he knew we were about to implode. Even then, he didn't give me a warning.

"I think I keep him close because I don't want him to give my heart back. But I still don't know what that means. I don't know how to understand this in my head, wanting to love him, but wanting to protect myself."

"You can't protect yourself from every evil out there, Addy. You might do more damage than good if you wrap yourself up too tightly from the lessons that are learned from pain." I wish therapists didn't make so much sense sometimes.

"So I should let him hurt me so I can learn a lesson? The only lesson that feels like is that I was right."

She chuckles softly, shaking her head at me, and I know. Know that I'm wrong and she is wise, and that she is about to school me. "Addison, everything that is bad that has happened is a lesson. It is what has built your subconscious protections. Of course, some of those lessons have led to bad protections that cause you pain and problems when they are engaged. But that is okay. We work on them, and you learn to manage them, to find better pathways for those responses. But sometimes we learn good lessons. Like when you chose to talk to JJ and hear him out and let go of all your anger towards him, you said you forgot how much you missed him. That lesson was what?"

I roll my eyes, but a small smile spreads across my face. I see where she is going, but I let her go there, anyway. I might need to hear it. "Sometimes letting go of the clutch to my anger and ego allows me to get closer to the people who care about me."

"Right, which in the future creates a response and won't automatically result in anger when something comes up. While that clutch to your anger has protected you, you are still in control, and when you recognize those signs, you can choose a path. The path you chose with JJ lead you to be closer to him. I know that you can't always choose. Sometimes, when we are too stressed or even too tired, our subconscious wins. That doesn't make you a failure, it makes you human."

"So, what does this mean with Noah? I don't know how to just forget everything."

"You're not meant to forget everything, Addison. You're meant to choose the path."

Choose the path.

I sit there mulling over everything and think about the path I'm on and the path that involves Noah. Those brown eyes and goofy half smile. His dark brown curls that sit in a mess on top of his head, or when they peek out of the bottom of his cap. The way his hands feel as they skim across the skin of my stomach. The way he says he loves me completely and then taunts me with his tongue. He held me, carried me, and wiped my tears. Sat with me, comforted me, and raged with me. Never leaving me alone and never making me feel small. He was always just there.

My path without Noah... I allow myself credit because I have worked hard on myself. I know I am strong enough to make it, to be alone and be happy-ish. Enough that I could have a nice life. I might even find another love at some point down the track, in the very, very distant future, if I somehow got over my Greek god. But... *I don't want to.*

My path with Noah might hold possible pain. It might hold more lies and deception. It might cause me heartbreak, and I might wish I would have moved on. But the possibility that we could be happy, that

I would wake up every morning with him, share my days with him, let him hold me through my dark days and save me from all my chaos. The warmth all of that brings me makes my heart sing and I suddenly have this need. God, I love that man so fucking much.

You're my whole heart, and I'd go through all the pain and torment again if it meant having you each exactly as you are. I regret nothing.

I remember mom saying this, and I wasn't sure I would make the same decisions she would, but it suddenly makes sense. Knowing all that I know, would I really choose to give up my love with Noah to avoid that pain?

As I look up at the screen again, Rhea has a knowing smile on her face, like she knew it the whole time, saw exactly where my mind went as she did what she usually does, letting me sit in my thoughts.

"So, who said giving in to your heart and to what your soul is trying to tell you meant failing? What if this is your subconscious' way of telling you that you're ready? Its way of thanking you for taking the time to work on your healing. Why are you really scared to give in?"

"Because what if he hurts me again?" I whisper, because despite everything, the heartache Noah is capable of inflicting is intense. He is so deeply imbedded within me.

"Mmm. And what if he doesn't?"

I roll my eyes. "You sound like Casey."

Rhea laughs. "Smart lady. But seriously, if you were to ask yourself honestly if you're staying away because it is adding quality to your life to be away from him or if you're staying away purely out of fear of the potential to be hurt again in the future, what do you think the answer would be?" I know what the answer is. I could tell myself all day long that life has been better without Noah, but it would be a lie. Sure, he is still *there* as a friend, but mornings are spent alone, nights are even worse. When something great happens at work, I still hesitate to message him because I feel like I shouldn't. I am the one who initiated our little hiatus, after all. I have been healthier, my connections with family and friends have been healthier, and my work/life balance has been steady, to the point that I am managing my mental health properly. All the space, distance, and Noah in the world couldn't heal my mental health completely. I am not without my dark thoughts or panic attacks; I am just better at my coping, healing, and management.

The only thing missing in my life now is him. No amount of therapy has replaced or repaired the Noah-sized hole in my chest. "You don't need to answer me. I can see it on your face. You don't have to do anything you're not ready for, but I think the path to healing has given you a greater capacity. You've been working so hard on yourself to be a healthier, happier version of yourself. Why not give back to yourself as well? Take something because you want it and because you can. You've talked at length about the kind of person Noah is and how he was with you. Despite his mistake and the hurt he put you through, it sounds like he does care for you. I don't think one mistake defines a person... do you?" No. Again, I don't need to think about the answer. I don't know if I even blame Noah for keeping it a secret anymore.

He made a sacrifice for his life, for his future, the same way I sacrificed having Noah's love for the good of my mental health. And look who stuck by me the entire time while I put all my puzzle pieces together.

"I think I need to go." My mind is made up and I can't sit still. I miss him *so* much. Rhea gives me a knowing smile.

"Our session has ended, anyway. I'll see you next week, gorgeous. Look after yourself and make good choices!" She gives me a beaming smile before the Zoom call ends. I leap from the bed and leave my room, finding Rosie and Casey in the kitchen.

"Hey, sunshine, where are you off to?" Rosie teases, but she knows.

She and Casey always know.

"Going to start making smarter choices." The smile on my face grows as determination sinks in and warmth spreads throughout my body as I sit at the table to lace up my running shoes.

"Oh?" Casey leans on the kitchen bench, some type of baking mixture in a bowl next to her as Rosie sits opposite her with... you guessed it... a glass of wine.

"There is a certain gentle giant I need to go see." I give the girls a wink and head for the door, wasting no time. I hear giggles and a celebratory high-five as I leave the apartment.

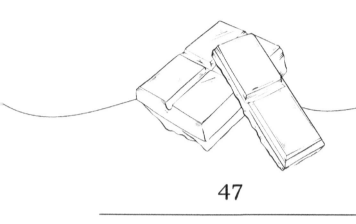

47

forever was meant for us

Noah

"That should be the pizza," I call out to Ethan, Lucas, and Stella on the way to the front door. Keeping myself busy these last six months with friends has been about the only thing keeping me from spiraling in Addison's absence. I see her every now and then, and her cute attempt at being platonic in her texts keeps the blood pumping through my veins as I wait her out. I can't quite tell if it's determination or denial, but I'm convinced she is softening to the idea of us again.

Work has now balanced out. EcoX's work has commenced since everything sorted itself out. I looked into Chicago locations for a new office, but I've put that on hold until some *details* get ironed out. By details, I mean my love life. I've tried not to hold my life back, making sure I'm just as happy, healthy, and successful when she is ready for us. I don't want to start from the start. I'm determined to pick up right where we left off. If she needs some healing time, that's cool. We have our whole lives.

Still doesn't help with the sting of loneliness, especially when nights roll around and I feel just a little bit colder. The updates from Stella and Lucas help, too, though. Knowing Addy likely still experiences her panic and bouts of rage viscerally, but has decided not to confide in me hurts. It makes me feel useless as a man, as someone who loves her. I'd be lying if I said it doesn't keep me up at night wondering how she is doing, but I get it.

Stella, Ethan, and Lucas are at my place, with Matt and Caleb on their way to watch the game and sink some beers before another week starts. Stella has been a new addition to our usual catch up of late. Coming to Pucks with us, she and Lucas have become good friends, and it sounds like she doesn't have a lot of those going around. Matt and Ethan didn't seem bothered by the added estrogen. Although, I would never say that around her. I'm certain Stella has a little black book and can make a person disappear in under twelve hours.

"Let me grab you some cash," Stella calls, following behind me as I open the front door.

"You're not paying for shi—"

"Hi." Fierce green eyes, sweet strawberries, and a show-stopping smile hit me and steal my breath from my lungs as I open my front door. Her hand is raised, about to knock on my door, eyes rounded and hopeful. *So fucking beautiful.* My memories of her never do her justice.

"Addison?" I say because I am not sure if I've finally had a psychotic break and am now imagining her here in front of me.

Before she can answer, Stella comes up beside me. "Here, don't be an idiot, take the $20. Oh, hey, Addison, I didn't know you were coming over tonight." Stella's face brightens as she sees Addy at the door, but Addy's face changes. Her eyes dart to me a questioning look, and *my god,* after everything that I've put her through, I'm not about to have her believe I'd go and sleep around, and with her friend of all people. I throw the door wide open so she can see Ethan and Lucas through the hallway at the table and I immediately clarify.

"Matt and Caleb are on their way. We're about to eat pizza and watch the game. Stella came with Lucas." I smile, somewhat awkwardly, but relax when Addy's smile grows a bit, her posture relaxing, and something like guilt flashes in her eyes as Stella reads the room and shifts awkwardly on her feet.

Before I can do anything else, Addison launches herself at me. Her head buries in my chest and arms wrap tightly around my middle. "I missed you," she whispers, and my chest squeezes so tightly I blink back tears as I return the tight embrace. I turn my head to Stella, telling her to get lost with my eyes. She holds her hands up defensively, biting her lower lip and mouths, '*okay,*' as she turns and heads back for the kitchen.

"You're... You're here?" Again, still not believing it.

"I don't want space anymore, Noah. I just want you. Will you have me back?" Still in shock, I can't seem to make words, not sure this is actually happening, and that she is saying what she is saying. Like she has to ask this?

I hook a finger under her chin to have my favorite green eyes back on mine. "I never gave you up, shortcake. Just gave you time. I missed you, too." Then I do what I've been dreaming about for the last six months, I plant my lips softly on hers, which she deepens instantly. It's like my senses awaken at the taste of her, her scent thoroughly engulfing my mind, body and soul, and I feel my heart pick up as it settles in. Addy is back.

I want you. After all this time, she has come back to me. I give myself a mental pat on the back at my restraint. Addy is back in my arms, and I'm being a perfect gentleman–ignoring the semi in my pants at her sparkling green eyes, pretty pink lips, and heart-stopping strawberry scent that consumes my lungs. At least I'm not ripping her clothes off... yet.

She pulls away slightly to spear me with eyes full of hope, the green forest of my future. "So you still want this? Broken bits, rage, and all?" she whispers self-consciously. The answer requires no thought as I give her my heart in a smile.

"You're so far from broken, Addy. And, shortcake, I've been falling for your fury since the day I met you." I seal the words with a kiss. Hooking her arms around my neck, she meets my need with hers, swiping her tongue with mine. *"Addy, baby,"* I whisper against her. My self-control from before is quickly slipping through my fingers.

"I love you. I'm sorry for taking so long. I'm glad I had time to sort myself out, but I'm done. I don't want to heal or grow alone anymore. I want you with me. I want to heal and grow together."

"Addison, you never have to apologize to me for anything. I'll always be with you. I love you." She bites her bottom lip and tries to hide that megawatt smile I haven't seen in a while, and it warms me from the inside. I return her smile. "You know, a heads up on this *90s rom-com-frat-house-meet-cute* would have been nice." She giggles softly at my choice of words, this whirlwind of Addison feeling like it's come full circle with her turning up like this. "I could have made everyone leave so we could have the house to ourselves. You know, make up for lost time."

"Oh?" The hunger and challenge reflect in her eyes. "I'm sure we can encourage them to leave early."

There she is. My Little Demon.

A chuckle travels up my throat as I claim her mouth again. This kiss hungrier, more desperate, needing to completely eradicate the space and time away from each other.

"I need you, Noah. I need you now." *Right back at you, shortcake.* Snap goes the leash on my control.

"Alright guys, I'll catch up with you later. Go watch the game at Pucks," I shout into the house, not leaving Addison's eyes. She smiles in return and bites down on her bottom lip. I pull her into me and replace her teeth with mine, drawing her mouth to mine as a moan slips past her lips. "Now!" I'm going to need to get her upstairs pronto, before I embarrass myself. It's been too long, and all those solitary showers did nothing to satiate my desire when it comes to her.

"Ugh, lame. I can't believe you're kicking us out for a girl," Lucas complains as he makes his way to the door, Ethan and Stella giggling together behind him. Ethan slaps Lucas on the shoulder, but looks in Stella's direction.

"Some men know how to prioritize." *Interesting.* Stella doesn't notice Ethan's attention, but Lucas does, eyeing between them, but ignoring it as they leave through the front door. I don't have the time, patience, or brain power to analyze that. I drag Addison against me through the threshold, slamming the door behind our friends as they leave without any more goodbyes.

"Where were we... oh, that's right." I bend and throw Addison over my shoulder to head upstairs. She squeals playfully and smacks my ass. "You're going to get it, Mr. Karvelas," she chastises teasingly.

"Oh, I sure hope I do." I pinch her ass as we enter my room, closing it off to the world, keeping Addison to myself and taking in every moment. Mine. She is finally all mine, she came back to me.

Addison

We lay in Noah's bed for hours. We made up tenderly, and then playfully, and then downright dirty, but now we lay here, catching our breath, allowing our heads to catch up to our hearts. Now, being here, in his arms, with his sweet nothings and warm round eyes, I can't believe I went this long without him, can't imagine him never being next to me. Like my brain senses the relief it is to finally have him back. No secrets or lies between us, someone who has never pitied me or judged me, someone who never made me feel guilt, or shame, or like I was too much. My walls come crashing down and the tears flow silently. I chastise myself for crying when I have nothing to be sad about. Well, nothing except what feels like lost time with Noah.

My eyes squeeze shut as I bury myself in Noah's chest. He holds me steady and continues to whisper his *I love you's,* one hand tangled in my hair, the other holding me tightly to his body. He leaves light kisses across my cheeks, between my sobs and my hiccups, not judging the disgusting mess I am as I cry uncontrollably into his chest.

After a few minutes, he pulls back slightly and uses a finger to lift my chin to look at him. "Oh, my girl." He closes his eyes and plants a soft, caressing kiss to my lips. The energy in the room changing, as our bodies pull closer at the contact. Six months without his touch and it feels like a lifetime. *God,* I almost forgot how good he kisses. He pulls away softly and his eyes open. "Why are you crying, Addy?" His tone has no accusation, just gentle curiosity.

"I'm embarrassed. I feel guilty for staying away for so long. I feel angry at myself for how much time we've missed out on. I just—"

"You don't have to feel guilty for anything. You did what you needed to do, and I was never going anywhere. You knew that."

"Can you promise me, Noah?"

"I'll make any promise you need me to."

"Don't hide from me. Let me in, all the way, trust me enough to give me the whole story, trust me to manage myself and to stay. Promise me that, and I promise I won't leave again." His face holds all the residual pain from the space and time between us, still holds what we couldn't wipe away from the brief time we've been back in each other's space. Holding what the apologies we made with our bodies couldn't wipe away.

"I promise." His smile is soft, and I know he means it. "And I'm the one who is sorry. For hurting you. For breaking your trust and your heart." Being open might be new territory for him, but I feel like there are going to be a lot of firsts where we are concerned. Certainly a whole lot of lasts.

"I want you to know that it's okay if you need space. I'm happy to give it to you. I'll give you whatever you need. You'll always be mine, no matter how much space is between us. If you ever need space again, you'll have it, and I'll still be yours." I don't know where this man came from, but it can't be earth. "And you *are* mine... right?" His smile is soft and hopeful, but there is worry in his eyes. I know the answer, without needing to think about it, because despite everything, I'd follow those chocolate brown eyes into the pits of hell if it meant never leaving his side again. And anyway, I've healed, or at least am on the constant path of. I've forgiven, and I am done denying my heart.

"I was never meant to be anything else." I whisper the words, but can't stand the distance and my lips are instantly on his. This time our kiss is desperate, making up for months without touching, exploring and loving each other, the energy spurs to life, and I manage to push Noah into the mattress, landing on top of him, straddling him, his hands searching my back, finding my hips and, despite the hours we've already spent apologizing and reacquainting each other through our bodies, he grinds me down into him, showing me exactly how much he missed me.

"God, I've missed you, shortcake." Noah wastes no time, flipping me, a gorgeous half smile that makes the brown of his eyes feel like melted chocolate as they look over my face from where he hovers above me. "You have no idea how many times I imagined us like this over the last six months and twenty three days." He lays between my legs, and I reach them up to wrap them around his waist, one hand supporting his weight above me, and the other lightly caressing my hips before traveling up to reach my breasts. "How many times I pictured that pretty smile when you come, the noises you make, and the way you sound moaning my name." *Oh, God.* His lips wrap around the peak of my tight breasts and suck, pulling a groan from my throat.

"Need you, Noah, *now.*" He moves to my other peak, his hand sliding back down my stomach to find how needy I really am. His touch, like coming home, closing the final gap our previous making up hadn't closed. Sliding his fingers through my slickness and thrusting them to the hilt.

"*Fuck.* I love how wet you get, just for me." He kisses his way back down my stomach before he settles between my thighs. Wasting no time, his tongue meets my center, following the path of his fingers as he laps me up. "As sweet as I remember," he all but growls.

"Noah!" My climax builds, his fingers on my skin, his mouth on my most sensitive part, the desire he draws out of me intoxicating.

"Don't you come until I say."

"Quick, Noah, I need... Oh, *God!*" His fingers find me and thrust in quick succession, curling around, bringing me closer. I tighten and clench around his fingers, my vision darkening as he kisses his way back up my torso, finding my lips and devouring me. He groans into me as he positions himself between my legs again, his tip nudging at my entrance.

"Noah, if you don't fuck me soon, I'll do it myself."

"Don't tempt me with a good time, shortcake. Play later." With that teasing smirk, he thrusts home, sheathing himself completely. "Fuck, so *tight*. You feel amazing, clenching around me."

"Fuck me like you hate me."

"No, I'll fuck you like I love you. Like I have spent the last six months pining for you, dreaming of you, and imagining all the ways I'd make you scream my name." He delivers on his promise. With my legs wrapped around his waist, he sits up on his knees, holding my hips off the mattress, his pace relentless as he shows me just how much he loves me.

"Noah. Oh my god, Noah. I'm going…"

"Yes, that's it, Ads, come for me. I want to feel you come all over my cock." Noah doesn't let up, and a hoarse scream leaves my throat as euphoria explodes around me, feeling each pulse of it as I clench around Noah. "*Fuck, fuck. Fuck! Addison!*" Noah follows as I feel him jerk inside me, relishing in the feel of him.

"I fucking love you," I whisper to him as he falls to my chest, panting and kissing my shoulder. "And I love fucking you," I finish. His chuckle rumbles against my chest.

"A poet, my Addison." He sits up slightly. "I fucking love you, shortcake." He kisses my lips tenderly, and I feel the warmth extend all the way to the tips of my toes.

He searches my eyes, his post-sex smile spreads across his face, and he leans down to nip the tip of my ear, his hot breath whispering, "*Forever.*"

And forever indeed.

We weren't meant for anything else.

THE END

EPILOGUE

five years later

Noah

5 years later

"I'll be flying in around 10am on Monday. I'll get a car and head straight for the office. How's the newbie?" I ask Caleb through the phone. Now the director of our New York office, since Addy and I made the final move to Chicago twelve months ago.

"Stella is a natural. She is going to do just fine. She'll shadow me for a couple weeks, so I'll hit the sales road for a bit, but otherwise she'll be on her own in no time." I nod at Caleb's reassurance. Hiring Stella had been a gamble. She had no sales experience, let alone marketing and design. But she was ready for a fresh start, to step out of her previous life and enter a new beginning. Ethan might have helped that decision and despite Lucas being mad at losing his bar manager, he was happy for her as a friend.

We end the call as I hear a knock on my office door. Spinning in my chair, I lock eyes with my golden-haired devil and feel my chest warm.

"Hi, shortcake." Standing, I round the desk and watch as her smile widens and she all but skips across to me. Looping her arms around my neck, I wrap my arms around her waist and lift her against me as I steal her pretty pink lips in a kiss. Over five years of her and I don't think I'll ever get enough.

Pulling away slightly, she whispers against my lips. "Hi, Romeo."

"What are you doing here today?" I ask her as I place her back on her feet and drag her fingers in my hand as I walk backwards. Leaning on my desk, I pull her between my legs, tucking an errant hair behind her ear and kissing those pretty pink cheeks of hers.

"I had some free time between classes, so I thought I'd bring you lunch." She lifts the sushi bag she holds in her hands, and I hear my stomach grumble in response. We sit and she hands me my usual rolls, pulling out a noodle bowl for herself. We dig in and I ask her about her day.

"Good! I actually have a particularly hard student that I think might take a bit to crack, but it'll be worth it in the end." Addy ended up going back to college not long after we got back together. Completing her teaching degree, doubling with a psych qualification. She finished just before we made the move to Chicago and works locally with a child trauma clinic, specializing in classes on dealing with anger, depression, and anxiety, helping kids understand their emotions and finding ways to channel them and explain them to people around them who don't know how to help.

My Addison is a hero, and every time I see her, I feel like I need to pinch myself that she is mine.

"I'm sure you'll get through to them. You always do." She scrunches her nose as she smiles at me, her tell that she heard the compliment and is trying to learn to accept it.

"How's your day? Oh! Have you heard from Caleb? How's Stella doing?"

"Good, just got off the phone with him, settling in well." I nod at her and she relaxes back into her chair.

"Good, I'm glad. I'm happy she is making steps to move forward. She deserves it." That she does. "Also, we have dinner with your mom tonight. Evie is bringing her new boyfriend, too, so play nice." I roll my eyes at her.

"I always play nice," I grunt, pushing my sushi around my plate and she giggles.

"You know you're a hypocrite. You chased me when both Jessie *and* Matt told you not to." I look up and wink at her.

"You were just too delicious, couldn't stay away."

"Well, maybe E's boy thinks she's delicious, too." *I'm going to throw up.*

"Ugh, really?" I physically shiver as Addison starts cackling, and I throw my sushi container to the desk and grab my little devil by the waist and pull her into my lap. Stealing her bowl of noodles, discarding it, and stealing the giggles from her mouth as I press my lips to hers.

A quick and passion-filled kiss before she pulls away, panting.

"What was that for?"

"Just because." I smile at her, the same surprise still hitting me every time I see her smile at me like that. She settles into my hold, her fingers twirling with the hair at the nape of my neck, and I reach to grab her left hand, bringing it to my lips and kissing her fingers.

"Still bizarre," she murmurs, staring at the diamond ring with a matching band on her ring finger.

"What's bizarre?" I ask.

"Being married." She scrunches her nose again but smiles up at me. A caveman-like warmth spreads through me at the memory of her walking up that aisle. Jessie clinging to her and firmly shaking my hand. Addison saying I-do and becoming Mrs. Karvelas.

"Mmm. I just like that I can now call you my wife," I hum back to her, reaching forward and placing a soft kiss to her neck. When I pull back, I see her assessment of my eyes and something like longing fills hers.

"Do you miss New York?" A pit of unease settles in me. We talked about this move for a long time. I proposed about four years ago, not being able to handle her being anything other than mine, and she said yes. To my displeasure, she made me wait another year and a half to become my wife, but throughout that time, we planned and plotted our future. I wanted to be close to Mom and E, but would stay in New York for her. She said Chicago felt like home and she'd love to move and start fresh, so we did. We had a small intimate ceremony in Central Park, went on our honeymoon, and decided we'd wait until her degrees were finished, then we'd move.

She shrugs and places a quick kiss to my lips. "I miss the people, Casey and Rosie, even though they are busy with their own lives and families now. I don't miss New York, Chicago is home. I wouldn't want to be anywhere else. Plus, I'm probably going to need your mom more than ever." I tilt my head in confusion and she gets up to clear the trash and grab her bag.

"Why do you need my mom?"

"Well, God knows Lillian isn't prepared to babysit on her own when I go back to work. I might take twelve months off, but I'm fully prepared to be a working mom." She spins on a heel and hits me with nervous eyes as she bites her bottom lip and suppresses a smile.

"You're pregnant?" A mix of joy, surprise, and fear grip my chest and steal my breath, and I feel like I can't move from this spot. She pulls a picture from her bag and hands it to me. An ultrasound image showing the little bean in her womb.

"You're pregnant," I whisper again. I mean, hell, it isn't like we hadn't talked about it. I want nothing more than Addison to have my babies. She is 31, I'm almost 35, no time like the present. But Addison had wanted to wait. She loves her job, loves working with kids and helping them. Wanted to open her own clinic. She wanted to help bring the boxing and trauma healing together. She had dreams and ideas, and a part of me is terrified that I'm ruining it.

"Are you... are you sure?"

She laughs and comes to wrap her arms around my neck, the pulling of the hair at my nape bringing me back to earth. "I think the ultrasound kind of confirms that, Noah."

"No, I mean... are you sure you want this?" That makes her throw her head back in a deeper laugh.

"Oh, Romeo. We aren't sixteen and strangers. We're married. We have steady jobs. We're happy and healthy." She kisses me softly as the information sets in.

I'm going to be a dad.

Me, I'll be someone's dad. I... *woah*.

"Hey... you okay?" She pulls her eyebrows deeper and assesses me, and it makes *me* start laughing.

"Are you kidding? This is the best day of my life," I whisper back to her and finally seal her lips with a kiss. An answer and a promise all at once. "I just want to make sure you're okay. I know how much working with those kids means to you. I don't want you to give up any part of yourself if you don't want to. I will love the little bean with every part of me, but I also love our lives perfectly as it is, shortcake." My little emotional firecracker drops a tear and kisses me softly again.

"Thank you," she whispers. "I don't plan on sacrificing any part of myself, but having something that is me and you, something more to love and grow with, makes my heart feel bigger. I love our life, but I want to fill it with more pieces of us and make it bigger and fuller. A family with you is a family I always dreamed of." She drops a few more tears and I kiss them away.

"So, why'd you go to the ultrasound without me?" I pinch her behind and she giggles, pulling on the hair at the base of neck in response.

"I wanted to be sure. I didn't want to get your hopes up because I know how much you've been secretly dying to have kids. I appreciate how easy you've been on me. How you haven't asked or haven't pressured me." She averts her eyes as she responds and I hook a finger under her chin to get those gorgeous green eyes back on mine.

"I always wanted a family with you, Addy. But I want you more. You never have to thank me for something like this. We're a team. We're together in everything, no matter what." I rest my forehead against hers and breathe in that same strawberry scent, and we stay silent for a while.

Every bit of pain, every change, and all the challenges we've faced feel like they were in preparation for this, for the next chapter of our lives. Addison sees Rhea, her therapist, on the regular. I found my own therapist in a local office around the corner from work and have been making progress on finally healing my grief, on missing Dad and the guilt I held onto for so long. Addy exists in her feelings so fiercely it inspired me, and I also knew I wanted to be healed, I wanted to give my kids every chance to be happy, healthy, and supported and hopefully not pass on any bullshit that we all seem to carry. Without knowing, it feels like we've been waiting for this moment, unplanned, but like a puzzle piece has just slipped into place.

The pages yet to be written and the paths not yet taken, but none of it feels scary. None of it feels like a challenge or like the impossible. Not when I have her by my side. Her strength and her fierceness.

"I'm really excited," I whisper, and she starts to giggle.

"Me too," she whispers back.

A little piece of me and a little piece of her. We've weathered storms and danced in the chaos together, but now in the quiet of my office, the sun filling it with warmth, holding my world in my arms I lose a breath, knowing that our story is far from over, and I've never been more ready to travel a path unknown and I know as long as I have my furious little demon by my side, all will be right in the world.

acknowledgements

T hank you everyone for reading my book! Being published is surreal to say the least, and when my reading and writing journey began in 2023, I never could have imagined it would lead here.

Whether 10 or 100 people read my worlds, I am forever grateful.

As is the way with these things, it certainly takes a village and I have a large list of people to thank and be grateful for. But there is one person in particular who I owe everything to because if not for her I would never have set myself on this terrifying but rewarding challenge.

Jeni! You are my OG book bestie. My number one fan and soul sister. Thank you for introducing me to SJM and helping me find my book obsession. Thank you for encouraging me to start a book Instagram, to put my ideas into a word document, for reading those first few chapters and encouraging me to write a whole damn book! For being my first ever reader of the full manuscript, providing feedback and input. I would be lost in this world without you.

To my friend Dino. My second reader, my Greek/male reference point. I am so sorry for causing you to choke on your cocktail as you entered the world of smut for the first time. Also, apologies for being your first smut read, but I appreciate your endless feedback and hilarious commentary, nonetheless. I may have ignored about seventy percent of your feedback when it came to the male POV, but this is simply because romance for women is written with purpose... we don't *actually* want to read about what happens in a man's mind, why do you think we read romance in the first place?

My love, Nick. Thank you for putting up with all my bookish-related crap. For the constant, "I care, if it's about *your* book." Always supporting me in whatever I do, even if I drive you nuts. But also, thank you for standing with me as I healed. As I learnt about my heart, my anger, my life. For standing by when it was hard, being my solid ground, my snake charmer, my calm space. Holding me when I needed, giving space when I needed, but always just being there. You've been a good sport about the "sex book" and whilst this book was a catharsis for many emotional and traumatic life events, I can confirm for family and friends – this is fiction. I am no demon, and Nick is not Greek...

Sharna, my girl, my law school bestie. Thank you for promising to read my book recommendations. Even if you don't actually read them. For giving me lots of bad-ass bestie inspiration and sharing your hilarious stories – anything for content. Your memes keep me alive and what would life be if we couldn't laugh at our shared trauma and law-school depression. One day I'm going to dedicate a bad-ass FMC, just for you.

My large and supportive bookish-community, with special thanks to Elleni, Kim, Ivy and Temeka. You ladies cheered me on and encouraged me without even having read the book, and even after. Jer'tarme, for helping me navigate the early days, including KDP and getting on Goodreads. Your assistance was amazing and I am so grateful for your guidance. To my Beta and ARC Readers for the feedback and encouragement, for making me feel like this dream of publishing and writing was actually possible. Without you all I don't know where I would be on this journey.

I would like to do another very special mention to my therapist,

Rachel. Maybe you inspired the brief appearance of Addison's therapist? But your role in my life has been formative and I can't imagine a time without having you there. Since I began my healing journey I have learnt so much about myself. Understanding boundaries, navigating relationships as I grew, changed and progressed, all because of how you have shown me to embrace all the quirks and elements that make me who I am. Teaching me to love those bits and pieces, for showing me I'm not broken.

This book was dedicated to all the angry girls out there because we deserve a voice. Rage isn't saved for the men who assert themselves. For people who have a reason. Anger that truly lives in you and vibrates through your skin and is not always controllable. When you live in a world that tells you to be gentle, delicate, feminine, quiet and to keep the peace, it's hard to tame that beast and to understand how to live through it. I just want you all to know you're not alone, and you are not broken. Perhaps this book was dedicated to my inner child, maybe it's for *yours* – the reader.

I hope you enjoyed this read and if you want more of the Central Sparks crew then you're in luck – book two is underway and we get to see everyone again. The story of Casey and JJ is coming! Stay tuned on Instagram & Facebook!

Printed in Great Britain
by Amazon